"Family secrets make for ripe hunting grounds for novelists. In this evocative book, those secrets hide mystery after mystery, like a set of Russian nesting dolls.... Baggott switches narrative perspective among the Wolf women as they struggle with their individual issues, and you'll grow to care for them all. No spoilers, but we'll say this: Baggott knows how and when to reveal answers for the ultimate emotional punch."

—Sara Vilkomerson, *Entertainment Weekly*

"Julianna Baggott's devoted readers have long known that she is a genius who can do whatever she wants. But with *The Seventh Book of Wonders* she has somehow outdone herself. This novel reminds me of the best work by the great Steven Millhauser: brainy, self-aware, tender, full of loss, but also full of grace and wonder. This is Julianna Baggott's best book, which is one way of saying it's one of the best books you'll read this year, or any other."

—Brock Clarke, author of the national bestseller *An Arsonist's Guide to Writers' Homes in New England*

"Baggott captures Tilton's oddness and charm with real affection. Hearing her internal voice, we can tell that she enjoys a rich imagination, seeded long ago by her famous grandmother.... As a novel about learning to love and forgive, *The Seventh Book of Wonders* offers some sweet moments of reconciliation."

—Ron Charles, *Washington Post*

"An intricate, tenderhearted novel."
—Dominique Browning, *New York Times Book Review*

"Some novels are a lot bigger inside than out. Case in point: *The Seventh Book of Wonders*.... It took Baggott eighteen years to write, and that's believable. This sprawling tale covers the entire twentieth century and multiple literary styles.... Readers will be reminded of the work of John Irving (especially *The Cider House Rules*) with touches of F. Scott Fitzgerald."
—Ben Steelman, *Wilmington StarNews*

"Dazzling and ambitious, Julianna Baggott's gorgeously written new novel explores the miracles born out of the desperation of three generations of women, all set against an astounding sweep of twentieth-century history.... This novel is so full of wonders that it leaves you haunted, amazed, and, like every great read, irrevocably changed."
—Caroline Leavitt, author of *Pictures of You*

"Julianna Baggott's very winning *The Seventh Book of Wonders* is only incidentally about a lost masterpiece, a marriage bound by string, and a lunatic literary family. Dig deeper and it's about mothers and daughters and the conflicts and compromises that amount to love."
—Joshua Ferris, author of *To Rise Again at a Decent Hour*

"*The Seventh Book of Wonders* tells the story of three generations of women as they navigate the world with all their neuroses showing. Novelist Harriet Wolf, her daughter, Eleanor, and her granddaughters, Ruth and Tilton, are distinct and developed narrators with defined quirks. Yet we can't help but love them for their vulnerabilities and the way they mirror the zeitgeist.... Baggott's matrilineal tale has much to recommend it: a love story, cross-dressing mobsters, and winsome details that ache with particularity.... The ultimate 'book of wonder,' Harriet's life story, demonstrates the resilience of unique spirits that go forth in the world, mothering themselves and rewriting the world to give it a measure of sanity."　　　　—Amy Pence, *The Rumpus*

"'All stories worth telling are love stories,' a character says in *The Seventh Book of Wonders*. This novel about a famous writer's lost manuscript, the complex legacy of family secrets, and—yes—a love story that unfolds across generations is inventive, playful, and deeply affecting."

—Christina Baker Kline, author of *Orphan Train*

"*The Seventh Book of Wonders* delivers a powerful sense of the meaning of motherhood and the bonds between sisters."

—Barbara Hoffert, *Library Journal*

"Moments of heartbreak balance moments of hilarity in Baggott's ambitious portrait of a family created from equal parts secrecy and love."　　　　—*Kirkus Reviews*

"Julianna Baggott's richly imagined new novel is filled with laughter and heartbreak, and—most wonderfully—with the bright, pained release of stories, which flutter from these pages like living birds."

—Elizabeth Graver, author of *The End of the Point*

Fiction

The Pure Trilogy: *Pure, Fuse, Burn*
Which Brings Me to You (with Steve Almond)
The Madam
The Miss America Family
Girl Talk
The Provence Cure for the Brokenhearted
(writing as Bridget Asher)
The Pretend Wife (writing as Bridget Asher)
My Husband's Sweethearts (writing as Bridget Asher)

Poetry

Compulsions of Silkworms and Bees
Lizzie Borden in Love
This Country of Mothers

For Younger Readers

The Ever Breath
The Prince of Fenway Park
The Amazing Compendium of Edward Magorium
(writing as N. E. Bode)
The Slippery Map (writing as N. E. Bode)
The Anybodies Trilogy (writing as N. E. Bode)

The Seventh Book of Wonders

a novel

JULIANNA BAGGOTT

BACK BAY BOOKS

Little, Brown and Company

New York Boston London

For the village:
Dave, Bill, Glenda, Nat, and Justin

———

Copyright © 2015 by Julianna Baggott

Hachette Book Group supports the right to free expression and the value of copyright. The purpose of copyright is to encourage writers and artists to produce the creative works that enrich our culture.

The scanning, uploading, and distribution of this book without permission is a theft of the author's intellectual property. If you would like permission to use material from the book (other than for review purposes), please contact permissions@hbgusa.com. Thank you for your support of the author's rights.

Back Bay Books / Little, Brown and Company
Hachette Book Group
1290 Avenue of the Americas, New York, NY 10104
littlebrown.com

Originally published in hardcover as *Harriet Wolf's Seventh Book of Wonders* by Little, Brown and Company, August 2015
First Back Bay trade paperback edition, August 2016

Back Bay Books is an imprint of Little, Brown and Company, a division of Hachette Book Group, Inc. The Back Bay Books name and logo are trademarks of Hachette Book Group, Inc.

The publisher is not responsible for websites (or their content) that are not owned by the publisher.

The Hachette Speakers Bureau provides a wide range of authors for speaking events. To find out more, go to hachettespeakersbureau.com or call (866) 376-6591.

ISBN 978-0-316-37510-8 (hc) / 978-0-316-37511-5 (pb)
LCCN 2014959606

10 9 8 7 6 5 4 3 2 1

RRD-C

Printed in the United States of America

"What happened to your mother then?" Daisy asked him.

"She aired her heart," Weldon said. "It turned and consumed her."

"And finally she was happy," Daisy said.

—From *Brutal Angels*
by Harriet Wolf

Harriet Wolf with the man presumed to be Eppitt Clapp
(date unknown).
Photograph courtesy of the Isley Wesler Estate

The Seventh Book of Wonders

Chapter One

THE BABY, TWICE BORN

Harriet

*T*his is how the story goes: I was born dead—or so my mother was told.

According to the physician, good old Dr. Brumus, I didn't cry. I wasn't capable of even this innate reflex. I was mute and sallow and already a bleeder, one red bead poised at each nostril. Imagine my exhausted mother—the saint, Irish and Catholic—her legs sagging wide beneath the bloody sheet like two pale, bony wings.

The year was 1900. The world was taking a new shape: the Paris Exposition's moving sidewalks, Freud's The Interpretation of Dreams, *and a tunnel being dug for the subway at Borough Hall, Manhattan. But in our house near the Chesapeake, not far from bustling Baltimore—with its canneries and foundries, its harbor of moaning steamboats, its tenements teeming with typhoid—there was little to do for either my mother or me, medically. Science had come only so far.*

But given that Dr. Brumus—winded, permanently over-whelmed—had delivered three stillborn babies from my mother already, it seemed, for the moment, he'd finally won something. He was always watchful, however, always squinting as if in bright sun, even at dusk, the hour I was born, mosquitoes whining past an ear. And Brumus knew, what with my bleeding nose and my pallid, lightly furred skin, that something wasn't right. He wrapped me in a blanket—though the summer hung wet and steaming outside. Like an aging football captain, he shuttled me down the stairs to the porch, where my father, the banker, was pacing. Dr. Brumus presented me to my father and gave the news: "It isn't fit." I wasn't a girl yet. I was still dangling before my father, midair, a lost pronoun, and it would take years before I would become a child in any real form in my father's eyes.

"No, it isn't fit," my father agreed, perhaps expecting as much, given the three lost before me.

"It may only live long enough for her to get attached," Dr. Brumus said, teary now.

"The baby's mother isn't fit either," my father said. "Mary has those dark moods. You've seen them. She couldn't withstand that kind of attachment and loss."

Dr. Brumus tried to hand me to my father, whose face was poised above mine, his nose fat and squat, a boxy fender, though he was youngish and handsome in his taut pink skin and glossy hair. He didn't like what he saw. "Take it with you," he said.

Dr. Brumus oversaw the Maryland School for Feeble Minded Children in Owings Mills, long before Baltimore started spilling into it with such ferocity. My father was betting that I wouldn't make it—but what if I did? Was he asking Dr. Brumus to be my father, or at least my warden? The two men had known each other since they were boys.

"Jackie," Dr. Brumus said, using the pet name normally reserved for times when he'd drunk a Scotch and soda and was looking slack and heavy-lidded. But that wasn't his mood now. His eyes raced. "I can't take the baby with me—"

"You said it's going to die. You said so!" And my father became a little boy, his face plump and sweaty.

"Where's the baby?" my mother called, her voice carrying from

the open bedroom window above, her Irish accent heavier because she was too tired to fight it. She could have been calling to them from reeds, a marsh with a fog rolling in.

My father shook his head. "No," he whispered to the doctor, fiercely.

And then my father marched upstairs, past the water stains on the wallpaper and into the bedroom. "No," he said to his wife in a lilting voice of his own. Was he going to sing to her? "Darling, no."

And so, for my mother, I was dead.

But still there was a baby. And this other baby with its dim pulse was bundled and taken away to start its other life at the Maryland School for Feeble Minded Children.

In just over a decade's time, this child would become a supposed Girl Genius, and, more important, she would find Eppitt in the laundry and love him too much. (You don't know Eppitt yet, dear ones, but you will.) And then this same child would make her way back here again—to this very porch, to her mother's bed.

Some of us are born dead, some never really born at all, and others are born fresh every day—as if they've had new eyes stitched on overnight—which is the best way to live.

I hope you will understand eventually why I've denied all of this for so long. Are you reading this, my Eleanor? My Ruthie? My dear Tilton? Are your eyes catching on these words, fastening one to the next, aware of my life collecting on the page? Are you here with me?

I still desire the veil of fiction, the means to monkey and fidget with the details so I can convince myself that I'm writing about another baby, another mother, another life. If not that, then I wish it were lovely. But what did I learn in writing out the lives of my characters Weldon and Daisy? You can't have love without knowing sorrow; you can't have miracles without desperation.

Here, then. My desperation.

Chapter Two

ONCE UPON A PLANE CRASH

Eleanor

My hospital room, which the nurses keep dimly lit like a child's bedroom at night, is only semiprivate. I share it with Opal Harper, who, although suffering some form of dementia, seems to understand that my mother was Harriet Wolf, winner of *this* literary award and *that* genius grant—the Guggenpulitzheimer, as I've come to call it all. One thing I know for certain: a child of literary genius doesn't care about "literary genius," believe you me. And yet it dogs me. My vascular doctor has talked about his mother's signed first edition. Two nurses have mentioned how interesting it must have been to be raised by a famous reclusive writer.

And now, for the fifth or sixth time, Opal Harper wants to discuss my mother's works, despite the fact that one side of her face is rigid with paralysis. Amid the gentle beeping of the machinery and the burbling of nurses in the hall, she says, "Have I told you how much I love Daisy Brooks and Weldon Fells?" The strange grip of her half-paralyzed jaw compromises her consonants.

"Yes," I say. "Many times."

"But have I told you that I was such a lonely child?" she says. "I was raised by an elderly auntie who loved cats and books. The books saved me. I don't care for cats." Here she goes on to recount

the childhood, which, I'll give her, was bleak. She was raised outside Tulsa. She had to stuff her bra. Her auntie didn't pick her nits
and so, for a solid year, her head was infested with lice.

But as she talks, I sit in my bed replaying the little speech I
have given the rabid Harriet Wolf fans over the years—die-hard
readers, reporters, graduate students, professors, and the oddly
wistful women of the Harriet Wolf Society—all of them rank
with desperation.

It goes something like this: "Don't you have *lives?* Don't you
have an issue with your *own* mother that needs working out?
Don't you have a terrible *marriage* to abandon? Don't you have
something, *anything,* to actually offer society at large? Go *do*
something!"

I modify this slightly for the neighborhood children who
come round while writing school reports, brazenly knocking on
our front door.

But Opal Harper is unwell. If she died after such a speech,
would I forgive myself?

She says, "Daisy and Weldon saved me! Daisy was so lonesome
too. So unloved and yet I loved her for it. I wanted to be her."

Sadly, I know what she means. It has occurred to me that
Daisy Brooks, my mother's heroine throughout her six novels,
wouldn't have let a man like my ex-husband, George, leave her.
No, she'd have thrown herself into a lake and expected George
to save her. And George would have saved Daisy Brooks, who'd
have been drunk, of course, drunk with the wind playing over
her wet, torn dress. They'd have fallen in love again while eating the flowers in the garden—the ones you can eat without
dying—and, yet again, while trying to lure the evening bats by
popping tennis balls up into the sky with their wooden rackets.
Daisy would have convinced George to move all of the living

room furniture out onto the back lawn, and there they would live, even in the rain and snow.

But those things only work in my mother's books. I don't like fictional stories. My mother ferreted through reality for parts to weld together to tell her untrue stories, which always struck me as careless and selfish.

Opal pulls back the curtain now, the metal hooks screeching along the rod, and I feel suddenly exposed, a frequent reaction since my heart attack, which unfortunately occurred in quasi-public. In fact, there was a crowd of neighbors on hand, staring on under the heat of the summer sun, as if they'd nothing better to do. And I was in a compromised position. Even my poor, dear Tilton saw it. She's twenty-three but she's still a child in many ways, what with her many conditions, and I fear the whole scene has scarred her! As a result of the incident, I crave privacy.

But I can't reach the curtain to pull it back into place and, too, I'm now a little mesmerized by Opal's face—her one stiffened cheek and its rosy shine of high blood pressure and a diabetic's puffiness. She might have been a very ugly child. It's hard to say.

"I started reading those books when I was twelve, which is too young," Opal explains, "but I knew they'd be with me forever. And then I read them again at forty, and my, my!"

I myself read my mother's books straight through during my fourteenth summer: *Tender Weeds, Let Go the Day, Brutal Angels, Klept of My Heart, Home for the Weary,* and *The Curator of Our Earthly Needs.* Some had been published by then but those that hadn't been were in manuscript form, boxed up in my mother's bedroom closet. I read them without her knowledge. My mother had sent out the first book in search of a publisher in 1947. All six were already finished by then. The storyline over the entire six novels is simple: Daisy and Weldon are young adventurers who fall in love with each other as children. They are separated by wars and disasters, by acts of God and calamities of the heart. When they finally reunite, they suffer. Book seven should have answered whether the entire series was a tragedy or a love story, whether humanity is basically good or doomed.

The series was unconventional, in fact unique, because my mother wrote it for an audience that could age as the characters did, as if Daisy and Weldon themselves were the intended readers of her books at every given age at which they were depicted. The genres also shift to best tell each portion. The first book is a children's story with fairy tales and talking animals, but halfway through the next book, when Daisy and Weldon are moving into adolescence, the story becomes darker, more surreal. When Daisy and Weldon are teens, they exist in the apocalyptic novel *Brutal Angels,* a dystopian tale of a doomed society of corrupt adults. It moves to realism in the next book, *Klept of My Heart,* when they're in their early twenties, but as they move into their thirties, time erodes and shifts; points of view meld. Modernism, or so I've been told. When Daisy and Weldon are middle-aged in *Home for the Weary* and advancing in years in *The Curator of Our Earthly Needs,* the magical childhood is as vivid as ever and the present is filled with absurdist twists. In fact, a writer shows up and the writer is named Harriet Wolf, of course! Harriet talks to Daisy and Weldon, sometimes asking them what they want from her. No one knew what to expect in the seventh book—not in content or genre. By the time they invented the term "postmodern," her books were already classics. The books were published over the course of only a decade, but, ideally, someone could read each one now as her life progressed through each stage; I believe that's how my mother meant for them to be read. Over the remaining years of her life, she was supposed to be completing the seventh and final book in the Wonder Series, as it was eventually called.

After I read the novels, I put them back into their boxes and never touched them again. I could appreciate that she had done something avant-garde, even if she had done it unwittingly, but the books themselves had too many characters willing to do anything for love, too much sadness and insanity. In one of the later books, Weldon is stuck outside a massive diving tank, his hand pressed to the glass while Daisy is trapped inside with a white horse swimming around her, and then her skirt unfurls slowly around her knees and becomes the glowing body of a jellyfish.

Plus, what did my mother know about life and love? She never even had a husband. She'd never even really been one to leave the house, for that matter, and she became a fairly devout shut-in during the winter of 1950, abandoning a tour for her second book, *Let Go the Day*, after a strange incident at a New York City book signing when she ran out into the snow and cried.

"What about the seventh book?" Opal asks, in an urgent whisper, her eyes glinting in the light of the machinery. "Do you really know where it is and just aren't saying?"

I'm thinking, *Why have I been forced to share my mother this way?* Still, to this day, someone will see me around town and make a little reference to one of my mother's books. "We're all just driving in circles!" they might say. Or "If you're living right, beauty overwhelms as much as grief." More than once, I have flipped them the ever-loving bird.

If my mother had published the seventh book when it was scheduled, the series would be complete and take up its allotted space of dusty shelving in libraries, but without it, the mystery puffed up. As famous as she was, my mother is more famous for what she didn't publish than for what she did. That irony chafes me since I believe she was quite capable of hatching this little plot just to prolong her reign. Even now, a dozen years after her death, I still have to share my mother with complete strangers!

"I don't know where the book is," I tell Opal.

"I see," Opal says, defeated, and I'm reminded of my burden to bear: I deflate people.

The truth is that Harriet wrote the seventh book a dozen times. After I returned home to the family homestead—the house where my mother was born in an upstairs bedroom—with my two daughters in tow, shrunken by the reality of my charred marriage, I supplied my mother with paper, fresh ink for her typewriter, and matches. If I refused her matches, she said, she'd eat the pages. She wrote daily and burned each page into a small pile of ash that she then brushed into the wastebasket beside her desk.

A reporter for the *New York Times* was writing an article about the hundreds of stand-in seventh books written in homage to Wolf by various people, in particular those in the Harriet Wolf Society. The reporter presumed that my mother would have delighted in the idea. After our short telephone exchange, he wrote, "Wolf's daughter, Eleanor Tarkington, who is known in scholarly literary circles as 'the gatekeeper,' has been historically cagey on her mother's alleged final tome. 'Who knows? Maybe it'll surface one day,' Tarkington said in a recent, rare interview."

I think of myself this way: *historically cagey.*

After my mother's death, the historical society asked to install a plaque by the front door of our home. I gave in, perhaps because my mother's death had weakened me—or maybe I was tired of deflating people. The plaque was bronze and handsome. In fact, it covered the aged drill marks from some previous plaque of sorts quite nicely. But before it could even form a green patina, I took it down. When members of the society came back years later to pay homage, I handed it to them in a box. Why announce my mother's house—the possible burial ground of the seventh book—to crazies?

This year, the year of the new millennium, the society invited me to a special gala at their annual conference, celebrating "One Hundred Years of Harriet Wolf." I despise the way they love my mother. Sometimes they nearly convince me that I've missed something magnetically lovable in her—something only visible from afar to strangers. A farsighted love.

But heaven knows I'm also thankful. My mother took me in with the girls after George abandoned us, and those books still produce royalty checks that keep us afloat—and I do surely squirrel money away.

"Bloomed," Opal whispers softly now. "'Doomed' and 'blessed' equals 'bloomed.' How does that line go?"

She's referring to a conversation in a canoe between Daisy and Weldon, a moment that so many people have considered the most important in my mother's books. "I haven't memorized the collected works of Harriet Wolf!" I say sharply. "I've had a life of my own to live!"

"Oh," Opal says, "I'm sorry. I didn't mean to—"

"No one ever *means* to!" I say, and then I shout, "Please close the curtain!"

And there's her face again, a half-pining, half-pinched expression. Then her thick arm reaches out and gives the curtain a sharp yank, and she's gone.

I close my eyes, feel the press of darkness—gravity pinning me tightly to the bed. The thrumming of machines is like small panting breaths. I can't help but think of Tilton, so easily breathless. Is she alone in the house? Or has she made her way next door to Mrs. Gottleib's? I do not trust Mrs. Gottleib, who promised years ago to help in times of need, but what choice do I have?

Tilton was a peaked little girl with fine white hair that wisped down over her ears. She is still a pale, wheezy-chested asthmatic who bruises easily and is prone to allergies, dizzy spells, shortsightedness, car sickness, and mysterious fevers. I prided myself on diagnosing her lactose intolerance before ever hearing the term. She's so sensitive to the sun. I kept her coated in lotion as a child so that all summer she seemed to shine like she'd been freshly lacquered. I protected her from her food allergies—nuts, strawberries. She's prone to hives. If she's stung by an insect—not even a bee, mind you—her skin bloats around the bite and is tender to the touch. The mosquitoes love her. In addition to the lotion, I had to add bug-repellent spray—which gave her skin the feel of a thin, brittle exoskeleton. It got so it was easier to keep her on screened-in porches when she needed airing.

And then there's her mind, a strange and distant world beyond anyone's grasp. She isn't interested in anything whole. The world is made of small parts of machinery—flowers, birds, toaster ovens.

Despite all of her weaknesses and needs—and, moreover, because of them—I love her mightily.

We all have our own weaknesses, needs, and tragedies, thank you very much, so Opal Harper can keep hers! I bear the stony tragedy of my childhood—the blank stare of fatherlessness. It wasn't called a tragedy because my mother refused to talk about my father, who had to have existed at some point. And so I could never claim the tragedy for what it was.

I vowed not to let that silence happen to my own daughters. When our tragedy struck, I seized it. I turned it into a bedtime story, our sole bedtime story, one I've told so many times over the years that it's taken on the feeling of something more marbled—its own monument. I told my daughters, "Human beings are shaped by tragedy and this one's ours."

And, just like that, the story lights my mind as if winding through a projector in a dark room. Without the words themselves to control the story, it begins to lose all sense of myth. I can feel it detaching, fluttering up wildly. Memory is nearly impossible to contain. There is the lit cigar, the plane engine steaming in the road, the suitcase handle on the ground. Even with the medications to lull my heart, my chest lurches, but my mind soldiers on.

I see myself as a young mother with large stiff brown hair and oversized glasses, sitting in the middle of the backseat, balancing on my knees the casserole dish, weighted with leftovers from a potluck dinner. The dinner was in Elkton, Maryland, one town away from where we lived in Newark, Delaware. The road connecting the two small towns was straight and flat. On one side of me, Tilton—baby Tilton—was strapped into a homemade car seat, a kind of crib with bars that I'd double-padded by hand. And Ruthie, a seven-year-old, was buckled on the other side of me, wearing George's old football helmet, with extra padding to make it fit in case of an accident, when she might strike her head against the door or window.

George, behind the wheel, sat alone in the front seat. He'd cracked the window, at my urging, and was blowing his cigar smoke into the cold rainy night air when Ruthie's voice rose up like a kettle whistle, inconsolable.

"It's that helmet," George shouted. He hated the helmet. He

felt that I smothered the children, in general. Was he jealous? When we were dating, had I doted on him too much? Maybe the shift after Ruthie's birth was too jarring. The cigar, just a nub now, was crammed into one corner of his mouth, so George shouted from the other corner. "I can't take that kid's noise!"

The chill draft was putting Tilton's frail respiratory system at risk. I fit my hand through the crib bars and pulled the blanket up to her small knob of a chin. "Ruthie isn't crying about the helmet," I said. "She's crying about the cigar smoke! It stunts the lungs of small children!" It was pollution, clearly, each smoker a factory. I tried to reason with Ruthie, shouting over her sharp-pitched cry, "What if we wrecked, Ruthie? And you cracked your head open on the window and died? You don't want that, do you?"

Ruthie quieted and then, always contrary, she nodded, the oversized helmet jostling on her head. "Yes!" she screamed. She would prefer to die. She glared at me—her eyes hooded by her thick bangs—and then arched in her seat and cried louder.

There was nothing I could do. She was a fretful soul, a born bully who, from birth, tried to make me her first victim. I had to watch her every time I said no, because she would run to the bathroom and pee on the pink mats next to the commode. She was George's child. The two of them would do me in—I could feel it. And what did I want? Only to protect my family from the world's dangers, to keep them out of the view of death's greedy watchful eye.

"Isn't that cigar smoked out yet?" I shouted.

George pinched it between his fingers and flicked it out the window. "There! Happy? Is someone in this car happy?"

Tilton was happy, I thought. Tilton was *always* happy with me. Her cry was only a little whimpery thing that was easily extinguished. I remember the soft tissue of her ears, so fine and thinly veined, how they perched like pink gargoyles on either side of her head, how they glowed when lit from behind, and the crusty spots on her scalp that I oiled up and picked off. Tilton, toothless, grinning—she loved me, unconditionally. I was unaccustomed to it. It wasn't that my mother didn't love me unconditionally. She did. But it was sometimes as if my mother was searching me for something—an unnameable trait—that I simply did not possess. My mother loved me *despite* something. I could never figure out what, exactly.

The evening had been defeating. I could smell the acrid tang of sour cream and onion soup mix from the spinach casserole on my lap. Why had everyone just picked at mine politely? Because they didn't like me. I was sure of it. Women punish one another this way—expressing disdain via casseroles. I've never quite gotten along in chummy groups like that. I wanted to exchange information on rashes, on poisonous household items, on the arsenic contents of apple seeds, for example. But they seemed to have no interest in such matters, were too interested in delighting in their children—as if it were a friendly game, a cute endeavor, something to put in a rosy frame and sigh over in their dotage. They all seemed to be constantly singing in their heads the same chorus to some cheery song. Even their complaints were laced with unwieldy joy. It was as if childhood were a sing-along, and I didn't know any of the words or even how the bouncy tune went. Really, I felt like I was always fighting the urge to grab the other mothers by their shoulders and shake them angrily, shouting, "Don't you know what's at stake here? There's nothing cute about this! It's life or death!"

And so the party was abysmal. While Ruthie dogged her father everywhere, I drifted to the patio, holding Tilton, saying that she needed some fresh air. I was sure that she was allergic

to smoke and nearly everyone smoked—a *roomful* of dirty fac-
tories. I didn't keep her outside long, though. She was as frail
physically as she would turn out to be mentally. I carried her
into the bathroom, where I peeked at her diaper and washed my
hands with dubious soaps cut into flower shapes, heavily perfumed. Tilton and I lurked around the food table and watched
people cough on the hors d'oeuvres. I sipped alcoholic drinks
because at least perhaps the alcohol worked as a purifier. Maybe
I was a bit tipsy. Maybe that was why I was letting myself fight
with George on the drive home. I usually tried not to.

He started fiddling with the radio stations, impatiently flip-
ping before I could even recognize a song. The rain was coming
down so hard now that it was drowning out Ruthie's fit. But
George hadn't upped the speed on the windshield wipers or
bothered to slow down. He cut off the radio angrily.

"Slow down, George! It's raining like mad! Can you see anything out of that windshield?" I was going to tell the story of a
recent car wreck I'd read about in the papers. But I didn't get the
chance.

A streak of lightning scissored across the sky and ended in
an explosion. For one blazing moment, the sky seemed to be
on fire. Even though I didn't see it happen—as George said he
did and recounted later—it was there in my memory: a plane
buzzing through dark clouds struck by an infinitely bright bolt.

"Shit! Goddamn it!" George shouted. He hit the brakes. The
tires caught a scrim of water, and the car seemed to be weight-
less, floating. I turned and somehow grabbed Ruthie by the
wrist while throwing myself onto Tilton's crib. The casserole
flipped off my knees.

A massive hunk of burning metal was falling toward us. An
enormous fiery engine, perhaps not so much falling as being

hurled at us. It landed with a deafening thud in the middle of the highway, and the road cratered around it.

The tires caught, mercifully, and the car skidded to a stop. How far were we from the crater's lip? Were we nose to nose with the engine? That's the way I recalled it. There was such detail— the heat, the engine's innards loosely exposed, the rain snapping at it, the steam lifting. It was like eyeing a beast—something that seemed alive—a heavily breathing bull.

I scrambled to get Tilton out of her crib. I unbuckled Ruthie and, while urging her out of the car, lifted Tilton to my chest. "Out, out!" I was shouting. "Before someone comes along and rams us!"

George opened his door and walked to the engine. His shirt was quickly splotched with rain. He turned slowly and looked across the cornfield at a small house surrounded by trees. The airplane's severed wing had landed on the house's garage.

An old man ran out of the house, wearing a raincoat over pajamas, and staggered around in his yard. He was wobbly, bowlegged, his arms spread wide, as if looking for someone to embrace.

George and I stepped onto the muddy cornfield. Although I had already wrapped Tilton in a blanket, I tucked her under my coat, a winter coat that beaded rain. Ruthie wriggled her hand loose from my grip and ran to her daddy, grabbing his arm.

It was quiet now. Oddly so. A white kite drifted down and settled in the upper reaches of a distant tree. A kite? It seemed like an odd moment for a kite.

The old man shouted to us, "Did you see it? Did you see it?"

But I looked down at Tilton's face—her wet mouth, her round eyes, the small soft cloud of her breath. The scene was slowly gathering meaning. This was a disaster. But we were alive. We were safe and alive.

And then I lifted my eyes. That's when I saw the handle of a suitcase—not attached to a suitcase at all. It sat there on the earth as if the suitcase were buried below it, as if it were the handle to a trap door. It seemed like it belonged in one of my mother's novels—a handle in the earth that would open a door to a different world for Weldon and Daisy to enter. It didn't have any logical meaning.

And then, not far from the suitcase handle, something shiny glinted. I leaned toward it and squinted—a jewel-studded buckle.

"Look, George," I said.

And he turned. "No, Eleanor," he said to me. His voice was gentle—a softness that I hadn't heard from him in a very long time.

It must have surprised Ruthie too. She said "Daddy?" as if suddenly she wasn't sure that it was him at all.

The buckle, I realized, was still attached to a woman's shoe. A modest high heel, black and shiny, it had at first blended into the mud, as had the dark-stockinged foot within the shoe, and the leg that ended abruptly just above the knee in bloody flesh with an exposed bone.

I pulled my hand to my chest and gripped Tilton tightly. Now, as I ran my eyes over the field, the scattered remains of other body parts were clear. Most startling was a hand, not five feet away, that seemed to be resting on the surface of a dark lake. I tore my gaze away and stared up into the tree—at the kite. It wasn't a kite at all. It was a man's dress shirt that had, most likely, popped from a suitcase in the cargo hold. The shirt sagged, wet and weighted with rain.

Ambulances, fire trucks, and police cars began to arrive. Reporters—rumpled and darty-eyed—showed up shortly thereafter. A young but jowly cop named Stevenson ushered me, along with Ruthie and Tilton, across the field into the old man's living room, which was opposite the side that had been flattened by the plane's wing. Another policeman, tougher and older, took George and the old man to his cop car for questioning. Stevenson asked me a few questions, and then joined the other men in the field. I sat on the plaid sofa. Tilton fell asleep on my shoulder, and Ruthie put her head in my lap and picked at the sofa's nubby fabric while she kicked the armrest.

The cornfield was flooded with the swirling lights of cop cars. Men trudged around, pointing, jotting notes. There were soldiers with torches. Unmistakable *torches!* I felt forgotten. Ruthie fell asleep too, and I was pinned by the children, unable to twist into a comfortable position—not that I would have been able to sleep. The old man had a large collection of decoy ducks, wood-carved and nicely painted. They sat on shelves, each casting an eye on the room.

Finally, a woman knocked on the front door and walked in. She was tall and stalwart, with a hefty chest.

"Red Cross," she said, as if that were her name, and she extended her hand.

I shook it while remaining as still as possible so as not to wake the children.

"You're doing okay?" the woman asked. She clearly wanted the answer to be affirmative, and so I nodded. "Well, the victims' families will be notified. They'll want to come and identify..." She didn't finish the phrase. We both understood. "And we'll be looking for volunteers to house them during that process. They'll be grieving and tired. It's been my experience that those who've been involved, well, they want to help."

Involved? It made it seem like this was my fault somehow. I wanted to clarify. "We were driving home from a potluck."

The Red Cross woman looked at me, momentarily confused, and then she glanced at the children as if noticing them for the first time. "What I'm saying," she went on, "is that sometimes it's part of your healing process too—being of use."

I wanted to explain that the image of the woman's foot inside the jewel-buckled high heel reared up in my mind every few moments and my goal was to erase it as soon as possible with the familiar—my toaster's yellow quilted cover, the salty belches of Tilton's humidifier, the nylon of my favorite nightgown. George and the kids and I, we were involved only in the sense that we hadn't been crushed to death by a plane engine. I was feeling an intense desire to insulate everyone.

"I'd be happy to do what I can to help," I told the woman. "But we don't have a big house, and we do have a growing family, so..."

The Red Cross woman nodded but still took down my name and address. I assumed this was for some kind of follow-up—maybe counseling for victims of a disaster. *The Tarkingtons were victims too,* I thought to myself. *Let's not forget that.*

But then the woman seemed to betray me. "Thank you," she said. "I think you'll see that this kind of generosity pays you back, threefold." She put her hand on her heart, a sweet gesture that didn't belong to her at all. I was sure she'd been taught to do it and had practiced it, but still didn't have it right.

I suddenly wanted to stand up and slap her. In fact, in my mind's eye, I did just that, so quickly and sharply that the woman spat blood. I have imagined the slap so clearly over the years that sometimes I can feel the rubbery contact of my hand with her flesh. But in reality I didn't move an inch—afraid of stirring the children. I only smiled tightly, thinking, *Stupid woman! I said no! No, no, no!*

My daughters grew up with this story. Was that wise, especially in Tilton's case? She'd interrupt the story only to clarify that she'd been the baby in the blanket.

"Yes," I'd say. "Yes, you were."

Ruthie, on the other hand, openly hated the story. She said she could still remember the stink of the helmet. By fifteen, she referred to it as "that *shitty* helmet," and I would suspend the story to correct her language. "Language, please!" I'd say, and Ruthie would snap back, "Oh, you want more of it? *Hell, damn, cocksucker.* Or would you like it in French or Spanish? *Merde!* Is that better?"

In the months before Ruthie left home, when she was sixteen, it became impossible to tell the story with her in the room. When I tried to press on through with something simple, like "They came with torches to search for bodies," Ruthie would interrupt. "Why didn't they come with flashlights? Flashlights were invented back then, right?"

"I don't know why. Was I in the Red Cross? Was I a soldier?"

It was around this time that I realized I might lose both of my daughters, that they would slip off into the wide world just as their father had. I explained that they were shaped by this tragedy and that they were fated to become poets to express this tragedy. Although I had no deep appreciation for literature, I knew well enough that poets, with so few options, often remain at home. "The world doesn't necessarily love poets," I said, "but mothers do."

Ruthie refused to write poems, on principle. "You can force someone to be an accountant," she said, "but not a poet."

After Ruthie left, Tilton longed for her sister and this was when her sensitivities bloomed into allergies, and then became chronic, ongoing conditions. It grew dangerous for her to be outside for long—she could go nowhere beyond the gate.

Although I had always made sure that Tilton socialized with a few handpicked playmates, they trudged into the house with too many germs. And how could I allow Tilton to be herded into stuffy classrooms where the kids traded childhood diseases like baseball cards? Besides, school had always been a struggle. The teachers didn't know how to reach Tilton in her miraculously fractured world anyway. Tilton needed to be home. I told myself I had no choice but to relent. My mother and Ruthie were gone, and so Tilton and I stayed home, together.

It was much quieter without Ruthie. I was struck by a strange sense of relief, though that relief brought its wallops of guilt; what mother would be relieved that her daughter ran away? She'd filled the house with a whirlwind of chaos—loud music, lewd images on record covers and cassettes. She insisted that they watch the nightly news—and what could be more violent and upsetting? "This is the real world," Ruthie would tell us. "We have to know these things if we're ever going to have normal lives!" But as soon as Ruthie left, I gave the television away to the local nursing home, and I had the newspaper delivered to Mrs. Gottleib next door so that its graphic images wouldn't find their way to each day's breakfast table. I knew that my bedtime story was too graphic. This hypocrisy wasn't lost on me. But Tilton had a right to her own history, to know her father.

As horrifying as the images of the crash were, I always worried more about telling the second half of the bedtime story, which was bloodless, but more violent—a rupture of family. George, the deserter. My own father might have been a deserter too. My mother never gave me the details. And then she died, and all I had left were her ridiculous fables of Weldon and Daisy. I wouldn't do that to my own kids. There were valuable lessons to be learned, and once Ruthie was gone I blamed myself for not having been more straightforward: this was a *cautionary* tale. Harriet Wolf was known for famously pooh-poohing stories laden with morals. "If I'd wanted to be a moralizer, I'd have done so," she once wrote. "As novelist, my job is to make things up. As reader, yours is to sort morals out for yourself." I, on the other hand, like my stories to have a point, thank you very much!

So I became my own Greek chorus. "You can never tell what form danger will take, Tilton. It can look so sad, so in need of sympathy—like a woman who's lost her husband in a plane crash—that you invite it into your own home."

When did Tilton truly understand that her father had an affair with the widow sent by the Red Cross to stay with us? When did she understand the word "affair"? Hard to say. She never questioned this part of the story—Marie Cultry and her love-lost air, her passionate, weeping impression collapsing around the house that chill December, how she seemed to carry heat wherever she went; Marie Cultry with her moist, exuberant wilting, her flushed, fevered cheeks, her wide-set eyes and quivering mouth; Marie Cultry, *the thief.*

After all grisly identifications were attended to and she was emotionally stable enough to travel, I watched George through an upstairs window cup Marie Cultry's elbow so she didn't slip on the icy driveway. He guided her gently to the passenger seat and shut the door. He unlocked the trunk and heaved the suitcase in, roughly. After he slammed the trunk lid, he looked up at me in the window. I knew how I looked: one hand on my hip, the other pulling back the curtain. It was midmorning. Tilton was napping. Ruthie was building blocks and kicking them down.

George waved, and I waved back to him.

Did he know that he wasn't coming back? Was he only 55

percent sure or was this the wave of a man without *any* doubts? Later, I took inventory of his things and realized that some of them—a few items of clothing, his toothbrush—had to have been hidden away in Marie Cultry's suitcase. This was plotted.

At the time, I was impatient for them to go. I urged George, mentally, willfully, to get into the car and deposit this woman far away. It hadn't crossed my mind that he wouldn't come home—not that day or the next; that he would become a check in the mail, sent monthly.

And now I am in a hospital bed, next to Opal Harper, and Ruthie is a grown woman out in the world and Tilton never really grew up at all. Years passed at freight-train speed.

It's possible that over the last few days someone's informed Ruthie that I'm in the hospital. A couple of months ago, Ruthie started calling Tilton almost daily—as if she could sense that something was coming—timing her calls for when she knew that I would most likely not be there. Over the years, Ruthie has only sent postcards, and there was a wedding invitation, on two occasions, that I declined. There was a birth announcement once as well. Hailey Ray. How old is that child now? In these calls, Ruthie has confessed to Tilton that she has the desire to know herself—an early midlife crisis? Something about a second marriage going down the drain?

Tilton reported that Ruthie almost has her PhD in something, that her husband is a professor, that they recently bought matching dogs.

"Good for her!" I told Tilton. "Good for *her!*" But I hoped that the flip side of this statement was apparent enough to Tilton. Good for *us!* That's what I meant. *Let her go and have her fun, her matching dogs. Who needs her?* Then I trained Tilton not to answer the phone when I was out.

I despise the idea that Ruthie find out about my weak heart.

I can see Ruthie and George the way they were the night of the crash. She's clinging to him in that field littered with the dead and the steaming engine on the road behind us. My memories have only gotten sharper as I've aged. Distant things are clear; it's the foreground that's growing blurry.

The bedtime story has always ended the same way: "The family was torn apart and it couldn't be put back together again. The end."

But now that Ruthie's started calling, I can't help but feel that my ending may be opening, like the seal of an envelope, moistened by steam. What if there's a force drawing us all back together again? I am sure that this has applied added pressure to my heart.

An alarm goes off at the nurses' station and the squeak of the nurses' shoes comes from the waxy floors in the hall, and when I open my eyes and glance at the door, their white uniforms scuttling by—all bustle and nerve—are like the kite all over again, the kite that was not a kite, like the rippling white shirts of Daisy and Weldon on a tippy canoe in the middle of a broad lake.

I don't want to think of my mother's characters or of these images from her books, but they come unbidden. Those famous lines that Opal Harper was searching for—they ring in my head.

Daisy said, "Love—it's how we're bloomed!"

And Weldon looked at her and said, "Bloomed?"

"Did I say 'bloomed'? I meant 'doomed' and 'blessed.'"

Chapter Three

AND THE HOUSE TRIES TO DEVOUR THE MOTHER

Tilton

My mother was stuck in the first-floor bay window, which was filled with hot, bright summery sun. The house tried to eat her. In the house's defense, my mother shoved her way into its mouth. It cannot be blamed.

If someone asks me, this is what I'll say, and Ruthie will want to know. She doesn't like our mother. When she talks about her, it seems like she's talking about some other mother altogether. Ruthie will know that something is wrong and she will call. She's supposed to be here with me, as she promised. We made a pact, now broken. It would be cruel to remind her of it. My mother says that I lack the genetic coding for cruelty. When Ruthie knew she was going to break her pact to never leave me, we made a new one. We stood in the attic, put our hands together again, and wound them in string as Wee-ette had taught me, until our hands turned red and puffy. Not a cocooning of our hands—no. We were creating a bond. Ruthie promised to return and save me. I was the one who pulled off the string, attached the small tape tab, and wrote "R. T. and T. T. 1986. Return & Save."

Return! This is what I want to say to Ruthie. But do I need saving? Does she?

As Mrs. Gottleib told me, my mother had a heart attack

while stuck in the house's mouth. I think someone could say that the front door is the mouth, but for me that's a dimple, and the bay windows are the wide grin. The windows upstairs are the eyes keeping watch over everything.

Did her heart attack her? Did she attack her heart?

Mrs. Gottleib said she didn't have time for silly questions.

I know the house has no mouths. But I'm in the house's head. I'm a thought.

I don't know much about human hearts, but I do know about bird hearts. For example, heartbeat-per-minute rates: the domesticated chicken, 245; the crow, 345; the house sparrow, 460; the ruby-throated hummingbird, 615 beats per minute!

Big, slow, unwinged humans? Only sixty to eighty beats per minute. I looked up the human heart just recently, in our set of encyclopedias that take up three full shelves in our wood-paneled living room.

Today I feel like a house sparrow: 460 beats per minute.

Meanwhile, I am injured. Highly injured. I tried to open the window so the house would spit my mother out or swallow her whole—either way, really, because I was in the house's head—and I gashed my thumb. There was blood.

Wee-ette was there because she's always with us even though she's dead. Wee-ette is my mother's mother. She died when I was ten, but I love her still. Wee-ette! This is what I sometimes whisper. Wee-ette! Like the call of a black-winged kite or a cardinal in the early morning. When I was little, I tried to say her name, Harriet, which is what my mother called her own mother. But in my child mouth, it came out Wee-ette. She had a desk and a buzzing, clacking typewriter. She let me play with scissors and glue. Wee-ette and I have secrets. We are bound. We have a like mind—that's what she always told me. Except Wee-ette's mind would know what to do now. And although she is with me, she doesn't speak.

I had been waiting for my mother to come home. I lock the doors and windows when she goes out. The winterized back porch is always locked, jammed with storage, things we don't want but can't get rid of. See, the world is vicious, dangerous, and full of suffering. Plus, I'm allergic to most everything out in it.

But also I keep the house locked because of the seventh book. If I'm left alone with the doors open, a Wolf fan could show up and ask me many questions that are none of their beeswax. One of them once pulled a wisp of my grandmother's hair straight from her head—ages ago, when she still ventured out. After Wee-ette died, there was a plaque on the house, but this made things worse. On one of the anniversaries of her death, a woman lit candles in our yard and knelt there until my mother told the police to take her away. Unopened boxes of fan mail fill the attic. Mice began to burrow so we burned the mail in the backyard one winter. My mother protects me from these people, but I glimpse them, begging at the door, calling on the phone, plus Mormons who ride bicycles and Jehovah's Witnesses who do not. I prefer to have the windows open, screens in place, so I can hear the birdcalls better. But I know the rules when my mother is out.

Why was my mother out? It's Mrs. Devlin's daughter's fault.

Toaster oven repairs can be dangerous. There can be problems with the electrical cord, main switch, thermal fuse, or solenoid. You may need to recalibrate the thermostat. I know these things because it's good for a person to have a job and be of use.

I also know about birds but I don't know how that makes me of use. I can't fix a bird's wing, for example. People think they could fly like a bird if they could strap big enough wings to their bodies. Wrong. Birds' bones are hollow and often can fill with air when the bird breathes. Birds don't have diaphragms because their entire bodies act as bellows. You'd have to change your entire skeletal and respiratory systems to fly, in addition to getting feathers and wings.

That morning, my mother told me Mrs. Devlin wanted me to fix a toaster oven and to write a poem for her daughter's wedding. This is another way that I'm of use—poetry. I know how to write poems for all occasions. I come from writers and should take advantage of the gift that God has given to me or it's rude to God.

I asked my mother if Mrs. Devlin had two daughters.

My mother said no. She was making me a glass of Tang and the spoon went clang, clang, clang, which rhymes with Tang, Tang, Tang.

I asked her if Mrs. Devlin's singular daughter was getting married again.

My mother said Mrs. Devlin's daughter is getting married again.

My mother left to get Mrs. Devlin's broken toaster oven, but she came home carrying a television down the street. I watched from the kitchen window. It was too heavy. She put it down and sat on top of it.

We would own birds if that were possible. You cannot own a bird, even one in a cage. Not really. But when Wee-ette was dying, she told us about a room filled with caged birds. She was delirious. Her eyes milky. Her eyelids violet. Her lips like a small crack in a vase. My mother bought five cockatiels for her. Then Wee-ette died, and my mother set the cockatiels free because I wanted them freed. Later, I read that caged birds set free die because they don't understand the wild. My mother says this is important to keep in mind. She says what you know is better than what you don't. She regrets setting free the birds.

Ruthie asks me how I can be trapped in this house with

nothing to see or do. She doesn't understand that there is so much to keep track of—the migratory birds, for example.

I have never broken a pact. Ruthie has never kept one.

But I remember when I was scared and climbed into her bed at night, and my blonde hair mixed with her dark hair like we were bound together by different kinds of silk strands.

Why did my mother bring me a television? It was too heavy! We used to have a car. It was struck by another car in a parking lot while my mother was pushing a grocery cart with both hands a mere twenty-five feet away. The car was old and therefore totaled. She could have been in that car. That was the end of cars.

My mother knocked on the door. She didn't have her keys. I don't know how to unlock the locks. My mother shouted at me through the closed kitchen window, telling me not to panic, but she was speaking in her panic voice—the kind you use when your daughter is crying while you're trying to get the birds out of a damn cage but they are idiot birds! Idiot birds! Damn idiot birds! They won't get out of the cages, and then, once forced out, they won't fly away! They stayed in the backyard for so long. Wee-ette was dead, but she stayed behind windows like I do now. She told me that we have matching souls, like mittens that are connected with a string and clips. I don't have to tell her things because she already knows!

My mother patted her pockets like she was trying to put out a fire on her person. She opened her pocketbook and her hand was a trowel, digging. No keys!

Tell me how to work the locks, I begged.

She shouted, No. No. No. You can't come out, Tilton! You're agoraphobic—on top of everything else!

I told her that in emergencies, like a fire, agoraphobics are supposed to go out through the bay window.

My mother jogged to the bay window. She isn't a jogger. Mrs. Frier and her husband, Joe Frier, of Frier, Wells, and Bender, are. The Eldermans' youngest son, a year older than I am, is a jogger.

I ran to the living room and to the other side of the bay window, trapped. I told my mother that I'm claustrophobic too sometimes.

My mother said, Yes! Sometimes. But I'm coming!

If you have claustrophobia and agoraphobia at the same time, it's not good, not at all. Ruthie says that I'm not either, but she doesn't know because she's not here. Sometimes I feel she's with me too. I feel a ghost of her, the way I feel the ghost of Wee-ette. They're here and then I look and they're gone. If I keep my eyes closed, they are both near.

My mother, her face red and glistening with sweat, tried to open the bay window. It was locked. She shouted, Tilton, open the lock!

The latch slipped, slicing my thumb. What was I supposed to do in case of injury?

Just hold on, Tilton! I'm coming!

There was a lot of blood rising from my thumb. I wiped it on my nightgown. There was blood on my gown.

My mother shoved the window up. It got stuck, though. She was too big to fit in. We stared at each other.

I said, I'll slip out.

No, no. Don't touch the windows. There could be lead paint.

We don't have lead paint. You fixed that a long time ago!

That's beside the point! I'm coming for you! I can suck in my stomach.

I doubted this was true. A sizable ring of fat pads her middle, which would help her buoyancy in a body of water. Can you really suck it in? I asked her.

Of course I can! I'm on Weight Watchers.

This was true. My mother attended meetings with Mrs. Frier and, for many years, has had a shiny scale on which to weigh her portions.

My mother heaved herself up and tried to wriggle her way in. A baby bird stuck in an egg would use its egg tooth. She held out her hands. I grabbed hold with my one unbloody hand and pulled. It didn't help.

My mother told me to call Mrs. Gottleib, and then said, No, don't. Then, Go ahead and call her.

I ran to the phone and dialed Mrs. Gottleib's number on the paper taped to the wall. I said, My mother's stuck in the window! Paralyzed! And I'm injured and bleeding—perhaps to death.

Mrs. Gottleib was annoyed with me because she loves *Jeopardy!* and the show was on.

My mother cried out, Wrap your thumb in a paper towel. Apply pressure!

Mrs. Gottleib said she'd call the fire department and the ambulance and that I'd better be shit sure this is an emergency.

I told her that I was shit sure and hung up. I pulled a dozen paper towels off the roll and bunched them around my thumb.

I ran back to my mother in the bay window. Her face was even more darkly rubied and puffed. Her upper arms, which are big and wobbly but taper to small hands, thin fingers, neatly trimmed nails, were shiny with sweat. Her hair was standing out wildly around her head—like a male bird trying to appear larger than he is, fearing attack. There would be an attack—of my mother's heart.

I told her that Mrs. Gottleib was calling the fire department and the ambulance.

My mother said, Jesus, Mary, and Joseph!

I applied pressure to my thumb and looked through the

window. A few neighbors had gathered. Mrs. Frier, Mrs. Gott-leib and children on bikes, and the cleaning lady who comes Tuesdays for the accountant and his girlfriend. We live in the old house on the block, here before the new construction, the nearby ball field, the buzzing chorus of lawn mowers every evening. I could hear the neighbors murmuring—like birds, throats and wings thrumming.

Mrs. Frier shouted, How can we help, Eleanor?

And others joined in. Do you need a shove?

No, we should pull her out!

There were sirens in the distance. Trilling.

How many people are out there? my mother asked. She couldn't see them as she was half ingested by the house.

I started counting.

Never mind, she said. Everything's changed, Tilton. Can't you feel it? We're doomed. There aren't even any more toaster ovens, Tilton!

But I pointed to the one on the card table that I'd fixed just the week before.

Listen to me. I can feel it. And my mother started to cry. Send them away, Tilton!

More people were showing up. The sirens were louder.

My mother's crying turned into laughter. She was laughing so hard that her body jiggled in the window. Vibrations. She said, I have to...

What is it?

I have to...

Yes?

Well, dear, I'm going to pee. This was what my mother said. I'm going to pee my pantsuit in front of our entire neighbor-hood! And...and...

And then she grabbed her shoulder. Her face went taut with fear.

I bent down and touched her moist face. I asked, And then what? What happens next? It felt like a story and she always knows the ending.

She said, Protect the house. Bar the door!

But the doors were already locked, which was how everything went wrong.

Firemen trudged across the lawn, like bears carrying axes.

And then I don't remember. And then I do. Walking the empty house, alone, because my mother was taken away.

My thumb has stopped bleeding and I'm sitting in the upstairs tub now, scrubbing the blood from my nightgown. I have the saltshaker. Salt helps with a stain. I use cold water. I wonder if Ruthie knows these things that I've learned from my mother.

The water goes down like when I bleed from below with my period—pink swirl.

Will tomorrow be like today? The Eldermans' youngest son lost his job and is back. You know what time of day it is when he opens his door—3 p.m. His legs swing like a metronome. The sheers glow bright these days. They don't ripple like in winter when the wind seeps through the window seams. The Eldermans' youngest son has his own beating heart and pumping lungs.

I've looked up the heart weight as a percentage of total body weight for your typical human: 0.42 percent. Our hearts are very small in comparison to our whole body. They take up one small corner. The ruby-throated hummingbird has a heart that takes up 2.37 percent of its whole.

I have two hearts.

I once ate the ancient heart of a mongrel king on display at a museum of antiquities when I was young—on purpose but also by accident. This isn't something I should talk about now. But I have two hearts, as a result. You don't have to understand it. Wee-ette understands, though.

What will be true tomorrow?

Mrs. Gottleib appears in the bathroom. Maybe she's been in the house the whole time since my mother was taken away in the ambulance. She asks me what I'm doing, but I don't answer.

Mrs. Gottleib tells me that my mother would want me to spend the night in Mrs. Gottleib's house. I raised seven kids in that house, she says.

I want to remind her that one of those kids is dead now. This is not good for her statistics. And her husband is dead. That house is a death trap, I want to say, and you know it!

I don't move.

Mrs. Gottleib's upper arms are covered in very loose skin with extremely fine wrinkles. Her skin is tanned and scaly, like the skin on the feet of certain birds, the kind of skin they share with reptiles.

Fine, she says. Fine. Maybe tomorrow I'll take you to see your mother in the hospital.

I tell her my mother wouldn't want me to leave the house, and she really really really doesn't want me to go to a hospital. That's where people die!

Mrs. Gottleib says, Let's hope that's not true in your mother's case.

I scrub my gown with my knuckles and salt.

You better prepare yourself, Mrs. Gottleib says. You might get the big call. Do you understand?

The big call will be someone telling me my mother is dead. Wee-ette died at home, asleep in her high bed. I sat Indian-style beside her. My mother put her head on her mother's chest. She heard the last beat, the last breath. And then my mother rubbed Wee-ette's arms and legs, which were splotched with age spots; her feet, which were pale as a new garden statue; and then her bony hands. My mother was trying to keep her warm and she was crying. She said that Wee-ette's body would turn to dust and ash just like the pages of the seventh book—Wee-ette's book.

Oh, but there are things that my mother herself doesn't know. This house is like the bones of bird wings, airy inside, used for breath and flight. There is no seventh book except that there is. Is it the one that Harriet Wolf fans want? Is it the one my mother would like to auction off so that we can have money forever?

Neither.

I don't know Harriet Wolf the writer. I've never read the Wonder Series books about Daisy and Weldon. My mother wanted to have one pure spot among us, someone who could see clearly the world without the clutter of lies. But I know what the seventh book contains because Wee-ette told me while I brushed her hair. And we have a pact—only to tell the location of the seventh book if the family is in crisis. I have the wound string of that pact too, hidden in a spot that Wee-ette thought would be good. Wee-ette knows hiding places. She's an expert at secrets.

Is this a crisis?

I ask Mrs. Gottleib if the firefighters broke down the door. I don't recall because I think I ran and hid.

Mrs. Gottleib says they opened the window and got my mother out. They were very professional. Then her voice goes bright as a happy jaybird: Looks like your mother finally broke down and got a TV. I brought it in for you.

It's supposed to be a toaster oven, I tell Mrs. Gottleib, and then I ask her if Mrs. Devlin's daughter is getting married again.

Patty Devlin? Mrs. Gottleib says. I never heard that. I'm good friends with her mother.

I tell Mrs. Gottleib to shut her piehole! Just like that. Just like my mother might.

And she does. She says she'll see me tomorrow and leaves.

I stopper the tub, take a bath in my nightgown. I can still feel in my hand my mother's sweet warm face, wet with tears and sweat. I'll go to the hospital and tell her that I took a bath in my nightgown and my thumb hurts and I need her.

My mother said, Everything's changed, Tilton. Can't you feel it? We're doomed.

If everything has changed, if all is different, then Ruthie is too. Even my father, George Tarkington, has changed. They don't yet know it, but they have.

Maybe things that weren't possible are. My mother must be thinking this too. Her brain is connected to my brain is connected to Wee-ette's brain is connected to Ruthie's and back again in every order. A forest of minds bound by birdcalls, like hummingbirds, beak-dipping, the dusted stamen of one thought to another's flower head. When one of us realizes something, loud and shrill, the others must hear an echo, even if they can't make out the words.

And my father too? Yes, maybe. Even though I don't remember him and wouldn't know him if he came to the door with or without a bicycle and asked my mother if she'd accepted Jesus as her personal lord and savior.

I won't tell Ruthie to prepare herself for the big call. Our mother isn't going to die, not in a hospital. She would never do that.

I turn off the faucet. My nightgown puffs with air and then it takes on water. It looks like a bird with damp wings. When I turn, it twists. When I stand, it clings.

Chapter Four

THE BLEEDER OF STUMP COTTAGE MEETS EPPITT CLAPP

Harriet

I was famous at the Maryland School for Feeble Minded Children—especially in the laundry. Nose bleeders tend to be famous in laundries, and I had been christened the Bleeder of Stump Cottage.

But how to explain it all? The truth this time, stark and true; it's like learning to write all over again.

If anyone is reading this, it's because Tilton and I made a pact and the time has come. If, say, the money from my books has run out or there is some family emergency that I didn't foresee, then Tilton has handed this over. If there is no need, if this family soldiers on, then she has let these pages turn to dust.

This might all be dust.

(But Tilton, my Tilton. You always understand me, even when I don't say a word. Pale golden skin and luminous hair—silken girl. You know me even though you haven't read a word of mine. Tilton, my girl, you are a piece of my own soul returned to me.)

But now the task at hand. How to make real the Maryland School for Feeble Minded Children itself? The galling notion of it might be so outdated that no one can believe it ever existed. You might think I'm being fictitious. Fair enough. I myself was once afraid that I'd made the school up—the ravings of my childish *brain, a severely imaginative thing. But to make sure it existed—in its massive horror, in its breathless details of stink and misery swabbed with bleach and hapless miracles (there would be many)—I went back one time. It was now called the Rosewood State Training School. This florid name change had happened while I was still there, but went unnoticed by those on the inside. I walked the gusty grounds, saw the children here and there, through windows and tottering by in rows amid the expansive buildings. This was in 1940, a few years after Leo Kanner (the psychologist who discovered autism, previously known as Kanner syndrome) exposed an illegal operation of selling the children—mostly the girls—into slavery, a ring that was overseen by, coincidentally, one Harry B. Wolf, esquire (no relation). But this was well before the* Baltimore Sun *dubbed the place "Maryland's Shame," before the series of investigations into abuse and neglect, and long before the U.S. Department of Justice stepped in and the older buildings were, mercifully, condemned. I imagine the enormous, pillared, mansion-sized homes, boarded up and sashed in asbestos warnings.*

As I held Eleanor, just a baby, while touring the grounds, the shame was still hidden away. I held her tightly to my chest, as if she could be ripped away from me, though there was barely a need to hold Eleanor. Some babies cling. Eleanor clamped. She still holds tightly to what's hers—especially Tilton. (Hello, Eleanor. If your eyes are on this page, I've written much of this for you. Long, long overdue. I owe you. I owe and owe.) I had to go there while Eleanor's brain was still a teacup-sized muscle, before she was old enough to remember the trip. I was determined to recite a rosier childhood, to erase her father too.

When Eleanor was little and looking for fairy tales, my childhood resurfaced—in distortion, yes, but there it was. That's how I wrote the first book, odd and otherworldly. I would like to say that

I made up all of the books, invented everything, even how darkness sometimes twists into light and heats up dust motes till they are a million flares, fragile chests of fire; that I had no heartache, but seemed to know just the same how to write love; that my brain is a little god churning out worlds. But really I'm more like the addled priest who wakes each morning and picks up his wicker basket to fill with every dirty thing he finds, and then spends his nights hunched over, polishing buttons and spoons. I looked around in my mind, I riffled through memory, so much freight, found what I found, and got out my own writerly tub of polish.

I handed these things over to the reader, all distortion, but maybe truer than if I'd had to face the truth. It was my brain, trying to string distorted pearls.

No, not pearls. Never pearls. Not something precious or cultivated.

My childhood is a necklace of fleshy beads, the warped faces of freaks.

During my visit back to the grounds, I asked a secretary if I could take a look through the records. I stole a photograph of children in front of the administration building, and when I held a magnifying glass to it, I found my own narrow, blurry face. "Blurry" is accurate. I was small and blurry at five. I couldn't be seen clearly for the person I was until Eppitt Clapp looked at me when I was thirteen—that moment with my bloody sheets bundled in my arms in the laundry.

My small nostrils were often clotted with tissue, and I was deeply pale. Even in summer I held on to a whiteness, a bluish tint beneath my eyes, a pale vein on either temple. I wasn't lit from within like Tilton. I worried my own inner light—held the bushel basket over it. Hands knotted together even with the laundry in my arms, I was in a state of constant prayer—a simple chorus of God, God,

God *much like a cowbell's* tok, tok, tok! *(There were cows in the surrounding fields, fenced.)*

We, the children at the Maryland School for Feeble Minded Children, were referred to as "inmates." A few of us were turbulent, others vacant. But families also dropped off their slight deformities. I will never forget: Arturo of the uneven limbs, Helen of the skittering walleye, and my own Eppitt, his sputtering lungs. He had no perceptible flaw except for a stammer and the way he collapsed two words into one—a tic more than a condition and far from a debilitating disease. Families feared contamination or stigma—or, in my case, pending death. (My death is still pending; pending death happens to be a life sentence. There's only one cure.)

In addition to the very sickly—epileptic and tubercular as well as the severely retarded, with swollen heads and tongues; these were my angels (oh, how they watched over us from the porch and doled blessings!)—there were other, mostly hale but blurred children like me who shuffled along, trying not to be seen. And there were categories: the idiot, the imbecile, the moron. I was a moron, which meant that there didn't necessarily appear to be much wrong with me, but because I had been dumped here, I was "a disturbing element," if examined properly, with the possibility of becoming "vicious and immoral." We morons needed to be "segregated very early in life" to be saved from "crime or a life of degradation." (In addition to the photograph, I took a copy of the biennial report of 1911, which I've kept all these years as it clarifies my own precious girlhood.)

At the time, I didn't know these words were used to describe us, but we all felt that we were despised for our burdensomeness and, once grown, to be feared. We were loathsome. We had no virtues, no promise or talent, no future.

But, sturdy enough, we were put to work.

Unlike Sheppard Pratt, a mental institution bent on being cura-
tive through a certain normalcy and cheeriness (light Swedish gym-
nastics, bowling, billiards, ornament making)—this was where I
would spend some time in my late teens—the Maryland School for
Feeble Minded Children seemed to believe that hard work was the
pathway to redemption, albeit not a cure. There would be no cur-
ing us—not even by God Himself, regardless of what Mrs. Funk,
the headmistress of our ward, whispered to us of God and Jesus
and Mary. (The name "Funk" is German, derived from the word
"spark.") The biennial report of 1911, put forward by the board
(overseen by its president, Herman Stump), clearly states, "No one,
except the very ignorant, believe that the feeble-minded can be cured
and returned to the community as normal citizens."

Boys worked the farm. The 1911 report tallied 20,069 pounds
of pork, 42 tons of wheat straw, 9,408 heads of cabbage. They
dug potatoes and hauled coal. They excavated new buildings and
a powerhouse. They laid pipe, broke stone, and helped with live-
stock, including 109 hogs, 20 cows (tok, tok, tok!), and one
bull.

We weren't taught to read or do simple mathematics. (I would
be allowed to later only by a twist of fate.) The girls sewed. In fact,
according to the report, from 1909 to 1911, we sewed $2,250
worth of articles, including 848 dresses, 393 petticoats, 954 draw-
ers, 222 men's shirts, 235 boys' shirtwaists, 496 bibs, 87 rubber
sheets, 34 rubber pillow slips, 123 ham bags, and two awnings
for the Duck Porch. I remember the Duck Porch awning specif-
ically, the heavy guttural chug of the machines trying to pump
through the coarse material. I worked both the foot-pump and
wheel-crank machines, nonelectric of course. Because the needles
would snap, we were forced to stitch by hand. If I was tired, I
had only to prick a finger. I'd be told not to bleed on the fabrics

and I'd be given a break. On a stool off to the side, I'd pump the blood to the fingertip instead of staunching it and I'd let my mind drift. I was a dreamy moron.

Shortly after I was freed from the Maryland School for Feeble Minded Children when I was fourteen, the girls began sewing kimonos. Reading these documents ages later, I caught myself thinking: Oh, I missed the kimonos! I would have liked that!

In addition to being seamstresses, the girls worked as cooks, waitresses, dishwashers, and maids. To this day, I make a taut and tidy bed. In fact, according to the 1911 biennial report, eight girls in the kitchen equaled four women, at \$12 per month for two years, saving \$1,152. And the sixty-three girls who cleaned the cottages equaled sixteen women, at \$10 per month for two years, saving \$3,840.

Sometimes the boys' heads were shorn because of lice. But the girls weren't. Perhaps the guards feared they wouldn't be able to tell us apart if all were shorn. Our heads were doused with oil. We picked nits with fine metal tines. If summer, we sat in the sun with our oiled heads—the skull made warm. If winter, our cold oily heads were still nitpicked outdoors. I was good at nitpicking: sharp eyes, nimble fingers. I knew to check well behind the ears, the crown.

Although the population was approximately 350 when I was there, it swelled to 3,500 at one point in the school's history. This simple fact makes my chest pound and my eyes sting with tears.

There were rules against babies being dropped off at the school, but I was an exception made by Brumus himself. I was raised in a series of cottages. That sounds lovely, doesn't it? But these weren't cottages at all, really. They were massive stone buildings with multiple chimneys, large windows, pillared porches—Thom Cottage, Pembroke, King, and Stump, plus a school building and the Custodial Building for Girls. The administration building had tall ionic pil-

lars of Southern-plantation graciousness, with a sitting parlor filled with lamps and rugs and sofas.

Puffed of cheeks, squinting, so rosy, Dr. Brumus dropped in to see patients—weekly. He stooped over the bloated faces on the sunporch, where the most sickly were aired. Their gowns, if wind-caught, arched like wings, though they were strapped to their cane chairs in case of seizure.

When Dr. Brumus was crossing from one building to another, he would sometimes look up to find me being shuffled from one building to another in a row of kids—we were always in rows. He gazed at me sadly.

Monthly, he called me into his office, patted my shoulder, and said, "Well, well. How are you, Harriet?" An obligation. My father, I assume, paid handsomely. He was probably one of the few who paid at all.

I don't know when Dr. Brumus told me I had a father named Jack Wolf and a mother named Mary who suffered from nerves. He must have done so before I could understand, as it was simply always something I knew. There was never a shock, only acceptance of factuality. I knew they loved me, but were unable to care for me—or even, truly, to look upon me, a moron. The mere glance would break their dear, kind hearts.

My father, good old Jackie, had been right after all; I wasn't fit. I suffered occasional mutism, especially in front of Dr. Brumus. I was a hysteric who often, under duress, would bleed from the nose. I didn't yet have a menstrual cycle, but this was a concern. Dr. Brumus had Mrs. Funk keep tabs. They didn't want me to start to bleed and simply fade away.

In his office, I could see sky from the window behind his large desk, and I would convince myself I was up there circling. This would calm me.

He told me my father was proud of my progress. He would some-times ask, "Do you think of him?"

I nodded, but I had confused my father with God. Like God, my father was a concept, a fatherly being who didn't actually appear.

Dr. Brumus noted things in my chart and sometimes he was in-spired to commentary: "Good, good, you're being responsive!"

I believed that God would look at everyone's chart on the final day and He would judge the living and the dead.

I got my first notions of God from Mrs. Funk's bedtime stories of how God had spared us: other ill children were locked away in basements and attics, the narrow cells of almshouses where maniacs were chained to walls, fed oats, refused sun, forced to bed down on straw, and abused by brutal keepers. She was trying to be kind, in her way.

"You're lucky," she told us while putting us to sleep in our rows of cots, stiff sheets, wool blankets that stunk of piss and feet. "You don't know your parents and so you will better understand the love of God, directly bestowed upon you." It was as if parents were mere interference. She sang "Onward, Christian Soldiers." I remember the verses even now, down to the very last, my favorite:

> Onward then, ye people, join our happy throng,
> Blend with ours your voices in the triumph song.
> Glory, laud, and honor unto Christ the King,
> This through countless ages men and angels sing.

Mrs. Funk was our singing angel. The high shine of her porcine cheeks! The faint warble of her voice! She loved us, I think, even if love was so foreign we didn't know how to love her back or one an-other or ourselves.

As expected, the boys were rough. But the girls of Stump Cottage punched one another too, when the staff was absent, and resorted to stealthy pinches when the staff was present. My arms were splotched purple.

It's impossible to be named Harriet Wolf and not be called a hairy wolf. I got it so often it became essential. A child trapped in a harsh childhood should be so lucky to have a nickname as vicious and strong as a hairy wolf. Worse things. When cornered, I growled.

The staff was overworked, harsh-tongued, even Mrs. Funk, and didn't spare the rod, but I won't detail the beatings or the vermin. There were always infestations. I feared things crawling into my mouth and my girl parts at night.

With fifty beds to a dormitory room, it was hard to sleep. The sickly wheezed, the traumatized screeched, and all of the patients were either sickly or traumatized or both. At their quietest, the halls echoed with labored breathing, coughing, gagging. One cry would lead to another and another and finally to a system of buzzers, wired throughout the building, to call the beleaguered staff.

The rise of panic from cries to buzzers to footsteps terrified me. My breath pinched in my throat; I feared that my nose would bleed—so much so that it usually did, and when I felt the first wet, warm tear of blood from my nostril, I was thankful. The pillow became damp as the red circle spread out around my head. If the lights flicked on, I was pulled from bed, my head yanked back, nose pinched tightly by a night warden—sometimes Mrs. Funk, sometimes another. I was marched to the bathroom to bleed over the rusted sink drain.

If undiscovered, I bled quietly, a surrender, the secret relief of it a pleasure. It must have been the same for children who pissed their rubber sheets—warm and predictable. Eventually, the bleeding stopped, and I slept in the wet comfort of my pillow. Maybe it recalled for me, in a deeply subconscious way, my first bloody *sheets—my mother's—where I was born or died, depending on when you heard the story.*

But one morning I was sitting on the edge of my cot tying my shoes when I looked up to find Mrs. Funk's face poised over mine—a lit bulb of a face, glowing with joy. I blinked into the light of that face.

She made the sign of the cross. "Oh, small Jesus!" she said. "Little Girl Jesus of the Dreaming Wounds!"

"What is it?" I said, trapped by Mrs. Funk's adoring gaze.

She had me stand up. "A wreath of blood. Look."

And there, on my pillow, was a halo dried stiff and brown like a crown of thorns above the smudged outline of my face.

"Little Girl Jesus!" she whispered again as the other children circled around. "Of the Dreaming Wounds!"

I wasn't even really human so how could I understand this thin sliver of divinity? (We are all human and divine.)

She whispered, "This is from God, Harriet Wolf. You are from God."

"I don't know if that's true," I said quietly, afraid to disagree with her.

She stripped the linens. "But a good Catholic needs no proof. Wash it away." She shoved the sheets at me and sent me to the laundry in the Custodial Building for Girls.

Once in the open air, I felt foggy and smaller than I'd ever felt—small as a pinprick in a piece of paper.

I was a small girl Jesus. I was from God. This was my conception.

And then I stepped into the laundry and, for the first time, I saw Eppitt Clapp, amid sheets and shirts, starches billowing like the dust of willows. He was pink and shining in the gusts of hot air, the stink of lye. He was alone amid the frail wicker and canvas laundry bas-

kets, the abandoned, rickety ironing boards, and he was cranking the wringer, a hefty machine that stood in the middle of the room like a large bony horse. His shirtsleeves were rolled up to the tough knot of his small biceps. It had been raining, so the sheets and small dresses, pants, and shirts hung from indoor lines. The air was damp and hot. His shirt was pasted to his back, and he was aglow. We were the only ones there.

I coughed loudly; he lifted his head. "What do you want?" he asked.

This was the first time I'd ever wanted anything, though I had no name for the feeling. He looked at me across the large fogged room and I was made real—incarnate. It was as if I was being seen for the first time; this was my birth and I was silent, as I had been for my mother. Eppitt walked over and took the bloody sheets. "Are you the one from Stump Cottage?"

I nodded.

"Why are you looking at me like that? Never seen a boy in the laundry?" His eyelids fluttered with the hesitations in his speech, as if the words were hung up for a moment and his lids could force them down and out of his mouth.

"I'm not looking at you," I said, looking at him.

"I got here not long ago and Doc Brumus put me here. Steam's good for me. I have wungs."

"Wings?" I asked, and I thought of him in flight.

"Wings?" He looked confused. "Did I say 'wings'?"

"You said 'wungs.'"

"I meant lungs, weak lungs." Then he muttered, "I get nervous and put words together."

"Oh. Wungs. Weak lungs. Are you nervous?"

He didn't answer. "You could work for us. You know that?"

"But I sew."

"*They're switching people around and we need help here. You could scrub these bloody sheets yourself.*" *He looked at me, his head cocked, his face sweet and damp.* "*The Bleeder of Stump Cottage. I like you.*"

"*Why?*" *I asked. No one had ever stated that they liked me.*

"*I don't usually like people, but when I do, it sticks.*"

And this was how the miracle worked. Now I was born. We scrubbed laundry together on washboards in large metal tubs, held by a cloud of steam.

Chapter Five

THE DIFFERENCES BETWEEN PIM AND POM

Ruth

Lying on my side in bed, I stare at the gauze curtains so brightly lit that it almost seems like there should be snow on the ground outside reflecting sun. I used to like winter when I was a kid. One time, Tilton and I built a small igloo in the backyard, though it didn't last. I was the kind of child always making houses, as if my own house didn't quite count. My husband, Ron, walks out of the bathroom and picks out a tie from a rack attached to the closet door.

"I was always making houses when I was little," I say aloud. "Igloos, forts out of sofa cushions, nests out of pillows. I once lived under the dining room table for two whole weeks. It had a white tablecloth with little yellow embroidered flowers that went all the way to the ground. It was my tent. I wonder why some kids do that."

"It doesn't take a psychotherapist to figure that one out," he says.

I think of Tilton—a sharp ache. Why now? Because I'm fairly sure that I'm losing Ron. New losses dig up past losses, as if one needs the other to remember how it's done. Before we married, Ron portrayed his ex-wife, Corinne, as high-strung, cloying, and humorless. But the last time I saw her, at their son

Justin's high-school graduation, she was dating a housepainter and made two bawdy jokes. How would Ron describe me one day? He could say, "She married me because she wanted a shot at normalcy. Can you believe how banal it was to live with her?" In a sense, it's true. Though I wouldn't meet Ron until my midtwenties, I ran away from home when I was sixteen because I wanted to make a new home, one where I would be deemed normal.

"Did you take the dogs out?" I ask.

"They've had their morning constitutionals, and yapped at the Doberman next door, in a perfunctory way. They're going through the motions, Pomeranian-wise."

"You're projecting." My husband is going through the motions these days, marriage-wise.

"Well, what's worse? Projecting or trying to fix a failing marriage by adopting twin Pompoms?"

Though it galls me to admit, he's right. I adopted the dogs, impulsively, a couple of months ago. I was introduced to them by a friend who rescues dogs, and at first I thought I was just overwhelmed by their cuteness, but as soon as I walked them into the house, I knew it was about our marriage. Ron and I have been married for only three years and together for five, a second marriage for both of us. It seems a little early to lose momentum. Already, I imagine the relationship as a beach, and I'm an old man wearing black socks and sandals, waving a metal detector over the sand, hoping for beeps so I can dig for a watch, anything that seems like it could have a heartbeat.

And then he adds, "It would be better for Justin if we stayed together. You know that."

Ron has two children from his first marriage: Colette, who's twenty-five, and Justin, who's twenty. Justin is a sweet kid, always sipping from water bottles to compensate for his dry mouth, the result of his antidepressants. He's been given a lot of labels over the years: light Asperger's, depression/anxiety, ADHD. He's tried a lot of therapies: occupational, behavioral, pharmaceutical…Sometimes I wonder what he and Tilton might have in common, though I doubt she's had any official diagnoses. Who's better off?

"It's hardly a matter of staying married for the sake of the kids," I say. I have a daughter too—Hailey. She lives with her dad in Tucson—her vehement choice when she turned nine, two years ago, after a year of living with me and Ron, who wasn't as interested in the realities of raising another child as he'd thought he'd be. Ron and I live outside Chicago, where he accepted an endowed chair at a liberal arts college not long after we met, and we have Hailey for winter holidays and two weeks in the summer after back-to-back camps. I'll see Hailey in two months, in early August. I shut my eyes. The bright sun is a dark blot on my vision. I haven't spoken to her in two weeks, even though she has her own cell phone now. I bought it for her so she could call me anytime. She uses it to call her friends. Hailey is my greatest joy and my greatest sorrow. It works that way sometimes. My grandmother, the famed Harriet Wolf, was the one who taught me this—not in person, not the way your average grandmother might impart wisdom to her granddaughter, but the way any of her readers might learn it: through her books. In *The Curator of Our Earthly Needs,* Daisy holds twin sparklers on a sloping lawn and thinks, "As if joy needs sorrow to understand itself. And sorrow, without joy, has no bearings." My response is a breath: *Hailey.*

As if sensing that my mood has shifted, Ron walks over and sits on the edge of the bed. In the bright sun, he looks old. He *is* old, I remind myself—nineteen years older than I am. But he's handsome, especially by academic standards. (I appreciate the low academic standards for beauty—by which I'm pretty, which is one of the reasons I like academe in general.) Ron is even a little rugged-looking, and he has young hair, which he tends to with expensive haircuts and products.

He brushes a stray wisp from my cheek, tucks it behind my ear. "Take away the expectations," he says, "and we could be happy."

For people on the verge of divorce, we talk about our marriage in unsettlingly calm tones. Ron wants to stay married—to keep the money intact. He was torn asunder by his first marriage. And by "take away the expectations" he means we should stay married but as housemates, maybe date each other and other people. The expectations are monogamy and fidelity. (He doesn't mention Melody Roth, the grad student he flirts with.) Due to residual sexual theories popular in the seventies—which stained Ron's indoctrination—he thinks that we're intellectual enough to separate sex from love. Or maybe he's trying to hold on to me any way he can. He claims to love me.

I roll onto my back and stare at the ceiling.

This isn't the first time he's made the suggestion. Another woman—one who knows herself better?—would slap him. But I've realized this: the reason we should get divorced—the apathy, the inertia—is the same reason we haven't. Can a casual marriage end in a casual divorce? Can human beings be that cavalier?

Perhaps some can, but not me. The divorce would be painful. Maybe I'd be happier, but I'd still have to mourn this loss. I've been through this before, and divorce can start as an idea but it becomes visceral. Ideas in this marriage, however, are cut off from emotions. Ideas are glittery conversational doodads to be collected and doled out as banter. In my current circle, banter has a bloated status. Emotions, on the other hand, are primitive.

"Hey, if we don't stay together, we'd have to decide custody of the Pompoms. It'll get messy." He's trying to lighten the mood.

"I think whoever can tell them apart should have to take them," I say flatly.

"Better yet," he says, "let's not get divorced at all!"

I try to pivot away from the dissolution of our marriage. "How is Justin doing? Have you talked to him recently?" The last I heard, he wanted to transfer colleges for the third time.

"He seems to think Towson has the best website. Students are consumers. I guess I'm just some product." I ignore the self-pity, and as the cue for me to reassure him expires, he fills the silence. "Are you coming to the wedding?"

Colette's wedding is only a week away, in New York City. Three days after it's over, the Harriet Wolf Society's convention meets in DC—the one-hundredth anniversary of my grand-mother's birth. Ron is one of the rare male board members of the society, a reviewer for academic papers on Wolf. I'm purely decorative.

"Would Colette want me there? Really?"

Colette, a lesbian in college and for a few years afterward, is now marrying a man named Phil. Full of righteous indignation, she'd hated me for marrying her father, for all the obvious, per-sonal reasons, but also because she had pegged my motive for doing it on my weakness within the strictures of a patriarchal so-ciety. Glaring at Ron and me at an upscale Thai restaurant, she said, "I don't know which of you is more fucking pathetic. Wait! Yes I do. You!" She pointed at me. "Your father abandoned you so you're marrying my daddy? That, my friend, is some fucked-up heterosexuality!" It was a moment I've never forgotten.

"Of course she wants you there," Ron says. "Anyway, she'd only misread your absence as an attempt to garner attention." This is so true. "What about the HWS convention? Are you going to leave me to wander it alone?"

The last and only time I've gone, Ron introduced me as Harriet's granddaughter. People drilled me with arcane questions about my grandmother's texts, complained about my mother's hostility to Wolf scholars, asked me to sign something commemorative, and openly pitied me—I was no Harriet Wolf, after all. What a shame! "I don't know," I say to Ron.

"You have no other obligations," he says, which is coded. He wanted me to take on summer teaching, and the subtext of his tone is that I'm spoiled. "Have you seen my cell?" he asks, and leaves the bedroom in search of his phone, which is in a perpetual cycle of being lost and then found and then lost again.

His scolding lingers, though. Ron used to make me feel adolescent in a good way. He knew so much more than I did when we met. He called me *mercurial;* I had to look it up. Now he reminds me of my tragic teen years, when I was so self-conscious that I didn't know what to do with my hands, how to stand, when to roll my eyes or laugh, or how loudly. My mother showed up for school functions wearing panty hose long after the other mothers had abandoned this formality. She didn't smile or chitchat. She held Tilton's hand even though Tilton was nine by this point. Worse, Tilton accepted it or perhaps barely noticed. It's hard for me to think of Tilton, especially after I was no longer there to protect her. Even the night I climbed out the window and ran off, I knew she could be locked away in that house with our mother forever. When I was studying psych as an undergrad, I diagnosed myself with survivor's guilt. I dropped the major, opting for ceramics, which I also then abandoned.

Because I didn't commit to psych long enough to figure out a conventional treatment plan, I came up with my own. I willed myself not to think deeply about the past. I've learned not to dwell on my failed roles—granddaughter and daughter, sister, wife, and mother. I don't know how to be a mother. I watched my mother be a mother to Tilton, but to me? Tilton and Hailey pain me the most. They're so linked I imagine that if I could save one of those relationships, I would save both.

To fail as a mother is to fail utterly, proof that I don't understand love in its most basic form, that I'm unworthy of the blind and unconditional love granted by simple biology. If I don't deserve this kind of love, what love could I possibly deserve? Hailey stated her choice to live with her dad in a letter written on strawberry-scented stationery. I keep it folded in my wallet. A good mother would have fought for her, but I know why she chose Jim. He teaches her Spanish by taping words to stuff in the house and paints rocks with her. I'm too much like my mother, awkward and clunky at love—too much or too little, like driving with one foot on the gas and one on the brakes, sometimes hitting both at the same time.

Ron loved me when I needed love. There's a lot to be said for that. He didn't judge me on my motherhood. And he gave me normalcy—better yet, high-ranking normalcy. I went from grad student to faculty wife. From student loan debt to stipends for summer travel. Plus, I could abandon my dissertation—not right away, but after a few years of my degree being ABD, it mercifully melted away. I'd never have to go on the job market dressed as a midlevel Russian bureaucrat or get rejected by academe or do all the shit I never wanted to in the first place. Is this antifeminist? Or just abject fear and desperation and laziness?

Colette was right. I married a daddy, which is some fucked-up heterosexuality.

But Dr. Ron Everly, PhD, did not marry an adolescent, not even just a grad student of his. It was worse. He fell in love with and married a relic from his area of expertise, twentieth-century modernism: a descendant of Harriet Wolf. But then the relic turned out to be just me.

I've heard Ron talk about my grandmother's rendering of adolescence—the loss of the magical for the darkly surreal, slipping into apocalyptic dystopia. "Once childhood is obliterated," I've heard him lecture, "the apocalypse is endured while the adult world imposes its corrupt rules of oppression." This lecture—sometimes given in an impromptu way at a social event surrounded by grad students, as if he's just coming up with it all at that very moment—eventually touches on my grandmother's treatment of middle age with absurdist postmodernism. But can he see how she would render us, if she'd had the chance? Wouldn't the two of us and our flimsy marriage be corrupt and postapocalyptic and absurdist and postmodern and therefore a form of undeniable realism? That's how I see it.

After Ron confessed six months ago to a serious flirtation with Melody Roth, it dawned on me that I needed family. They know you from the beginning—a version that's elemental. So I rekindled my relationship with Tilton, at least by phone, and we've talked several times now.

I pick up the receiver of the phone on the bedside table and dial my mother's home phone number, the same all these years later. It crosses my mind that once I hear Tilton's voice, I might hang up. I just started a dog-training class earlier this week. The teacher—a handsome man in his late thirties with doggy treats in his pockets and no wedding ring—said that you shouldn't chase the dog if you want it to come back. You've got to get the dog to chase you. This is also advice on men that I've never been able to follow. It wouldn't work on Ron. He's too stubborn. As a child, he once got in a breath-holding competition and held his breath until he passed out. He has a scar on his chin from the fall. It's hard to tell whether I really want Ron fully back in my life or simply want him to want me madly. I wouldn't have the heart to hang up on Tilton. But the line rings and rings. Eleanor's too cheap to spring for an answering machine.

Of course, I wouldn't mind being chased. I could have tried to get my father to chase me. A couple of months after I ran away from home, I ended up at a shelter and a counselor tracked him down. They called Eleanor too, but George had already agreed to take me in. I never spoke to my mother about it. What did she think of me back with my father after all those years?

But, in reality, my father didn't take me in. We only had lunch at a Steak 'n Shake. He was broad-shouldered, as brutish-looking as Eleanor had made him out to be in the bedtime story she shoved down my throat as a child, as if trying hard to raise victims. But he didn't chomp a cigar or yell and curse. He was a fast-talker, slightly marble-mouthed—nervous, tired, a little drunk? He still had a thick head of coarse hair, taut skin, a fresh tan.

He told me he had spoken too soon offering to take me in. His home life was tricky. "Things are delicate."

I'd hoped that my father had married the widow, Marie Cultry. I could blame his leaving us on true love, like Johnny Cash leaving his first wife to marry June Carter. But I was too afraid to ask. I didn't want to have to take the rejection personally. But I was so crushed that he didn't want to take me in that I told him I had a place to stay. By then I was dating Jim, who would become my first husband, Hailey's dad. Plan B was pushing Jim to let me move in, which was what happened. He was eighteen and a housepainter, working his way through college part-time.

My father asked if I was eating well, if I liked reading or movies or sports. He was probably trying to ferret out if I was doing drugs. (I was doing some drugs.) Eventually, he laid out his plan. "Why don't you let me get you an apartment? You get your GED, take community college classes. I'll foot the bill."

I took down my father's address and phone number. When I needed tuition a few years later, I called and he delivered, true to his word. But we had no relationship. I didn't invite him to graduation and didn't tell him about grad school. That would have felt like milking it.

The ringing is endless. I hang up.

One of the dogs trots in. I can't tell which one. Who gets custody of the dogs if neither of us can tell them apart? The dog stares at me, head cocked, reminding me of hosting foreign exchange students who were sometimes frustrated by an insurmountable language barrier.

Ron walks through the room then, into the bathroom, where he starts moussing his hair. "Found my cell!" he says. "It almost took a spin in the washer."

A rare memory of my father pops into my mind. "My dad got us a Lab from the pound. It ate its own poops after they'd been left in the yard to harden." He fed the dog fat rinds from the table, which Eleanor took as a comment on her cooking. The dog would be flatulent for the rest of the night.

"Eating your own poop—that's the height of vanity, if you ask me," he says, which is hard to take from a man who is moussing his hair. Ron's hair shifts unnaturally in wind, as if it's a single unit.

I hit redial and hope that Tilton picks up. She has a birdlike voice. She's a chirper. Not surprising, as she's spent more time listening to birds in the garden than to actual human beings—aside from our mother. Still no answer. I hang up again.

"Who do you keep calling?" Ron asks from the bathroom.

"Tilty." My Tilt-a-Whirl! How many times did I say those words as a kid?

"Just leave a goddamn message," he says. He's always been slightly jealous of Tilton even though he's never met her. He wanted to visit the house—home of Harriet Wolf—and pouted when I refused to reach out beyond the wedding invitation. I've admitted to myself that perhaps I've started calling Tilton, as my marriage is crumbling, out of a desire to reunite with my family, but the prospect scares me as much as it draws me in. I want to flirt with it, perhaps—the way one might flirt with, say, Melody Roth, if one were, say, on her PhD committee. "Why do people hate leaving messages nowadays?" Ron says.

"Eleanor Tarkington is stuck in 1974," I say. "There's no answering machine. I wonder if the phone is the color of avocado and has one of those ringlet cords."

"I'm making a pot of coffee before I leave. Do you want a cup?" He doesn't usually make the coffee. He struggles to negotiate the heaping-spoonful-to-cup-of-water ratio. His smile says, "I'm trying! Look at me trying!" He still thinks he might get his way—an open marriage that includes dating Melody Roth. I'd get his benefits, his pension, house privileges? It's very retro of him, vaguely prostitution.

But I do want coffee. "Yes, I'll take a cup."

As he jogs downstairs, I call home again, and this time Tilton answers. "Ruthie? Is this you?"

"Why haven't you been answering? Are you okay?"

"Yes."

"Are you sure?"

"Sure I'm sure." With this phrase, I'm reminded of how stunted Tilton is. At what age do you stop saying "Sure I'm sure"? "I didn't answer because I was watching TV. I watched TV all night."

"You did *what?*" Eleanor Tarkington despises television. When I was a teenager, she blamed television for my insubordination as well as the general collapse of society.

"I watched large women in bras and underwear wearing huge wide wings walk down this flat ramp over and over. And a man poured blue liquid into a pad. This morning there were people on couches, drinking coffee, trying on wigs. They had guests and a studio audience."

"Eleanor let you watch TV?"

"It's okay. I won't get the big call. The house tried to eat her. Then she had a heart attack. There was an ambulance. She peed her pantsuit. I touched her face. I took a bath in my nightgown, which had blood on it."

"Slow down! Wait," I say. The Pomeranians have started yapping downstairs. I can't be sure I've heard Tilton correctly. "Did Eleanor have a heart attack?"

"Yes," Tilton says. "Mrs. Gottleib is taking me to the hospital to see her."

"To see Eleanor because of her heart attack?"

"Yes."

"Eleanor is in the hospital." I can't imagine my mother with a head cold, much less in a hospital. Nor could I make sense of the rest of it. My mother was eaten by a house? What on earth did that mean? "Why was there blood on your nightgown?"

"I hurt my thumb trying to open a window."

"Is it okay?"

"It hurts."

"Mom wants you going to see her in a hospital?" This would expose Tilton to germs.

"I'm sure she doesn't. But Mrs. Gottleib is taking me there anyway. I want to see her. I'm both agoraphobic and claustrophobic so maybe they'll cancel each other out."

"You're not either of those things. How many times do I have to say it? You're fine, Tilton. You're *better* than fine. I mean, my God, you've been through a trauma and you're okay!" I am no good at crises myself. It's one of the reasons I let my ex get custody of Hailey. I was afraid something might go wrong on my watch. "Was it a mild heart attack?" I ask in a soothing voice.

"Do they come in mild?"

"Have you talked to a doctor? Will there be surgery?"

"Maybe Mrs. Gottleib talked to the doctor." Then Tilton's voice shifts a little deeper. "Have we come to an impasse?" It's Eleanor's voice.

"Don't say things like that," I say.

"Like what?"

"Eleanor things in an Eleanor voice!"

"But have we?"

"I'm sure Eleanor's made an emergency plan. A what-to-do in case of X, Y, and Z."

"She keeps that kind of thing in her head. But don't worry. She won't die," Tilton says. "Not in a hospital."

"Of course," I say, trying to be positive. "That's right."

"I have to get ready to go," Tilton says.

"It's going to be okay. You know that."

"I know!" she says brightly. "Because you're coming home!"

"I am?"

"You are!" she says, and then she hangs up.

My first thought is illogical: *Someone should call my father. He should know.* Of course it's none of his business. I do know how to reach him, though. Six months earlier, I found myself at the university library, doing a quick search for my father in their computer lab. It revealed that he didn't get far. His real estate practice is in Oxford, Pennsylvania. Within seconds, I had an office number, a fax number, and a home number.

I haven't called. I know what it's like to be the one who left.

My mother forced Tilton and me to make a pact as kids. "Never look for your father," she said. "It will only stroke his ego. He doesn't deserve us!" Our family was big on pacts. I remember the feeling of string winding around my hand pressed to my mother's and Tilton's, the too-tight weave, and afterward the red indentations from the string. I rub my hand as if the string is still there.

Ron reappears with a mug of coffee for me, but I don't reach for it.

"What's wrong?" he asks.

"Eleanor's had a heart attack. She's in the hospital. Tilton keeps saying she's not going to die, which makes me think she's going to die."

He sets the mug down on the bedside table. "Are you going to see her?" he asks.

"I don't know." I think of Tilton—a child in my mind's eye, blonde hair, round cheeks, a little bow of mouth. She's in her nightgown, now bloody. "I abandoned her, you know," I say.

"I'm sure your mother never saw it that way. She's very independent."

"No," I say. "Tilton!"

"Oh."

"Did I ever tell you that in middle school she cut my hair once when I was sleeping? My mother never even yelled at her about it."

"Maybe this is the time for all three of you to set things right," he says. "You should go. It'll put you on the East Coast, in driving distance to Colette's wedding and the HWS convention."

But his concern, I know, is false. He wants me to inch closer to my family merely so he can inch closer to Harriet Wolf. "Colette doesn't want me at her wedding," I finally say.

"Look, if you don't come, people will wonder why. I don't want to tell people at my daughter's wedding that you're divorcing me. It's bad form."

What if I did go home and reunite with Tilton and even Eleanor? Wouldn't they want to meet Hailey? Wouldn't Hailey want to meet them? And if Hailey met Eleanor and Tilton, wouldn't she have more sympathy for me?

"Come to the wedding. Just show up." Ron pauses a moment and then whispers, "Pretend you like me." It's what Weldon says to Daisy when the photographer has them sit for their wedding photograph.

"I do like you." And it's true. I'm not quite sure why, but the feeling persists—even when I hate him.

"I like you too," he says, and then he adds, "Wow, so the gatekeeper's really in the hospital."

The gatekeeper—I hate the term although I've employed it myself and used to dole out memories of Harriet and Eleanor to Ron and other members of the Harriet Wolf Society. When I ran out, I made some up. I've never told Ron that my grandmother burned the pages of the seventh book every day after she wrote them. In fact, I hinted that she shipped them to another writer—the identity of whom I said I could never quite figure out. Perhaps a lover? Perhaps a *female* lover, I intimated once, just to make it more interesting. The real confession is that I loved my grandmother's books—not in a scholarly way, but in a heartfelt way that I'd be embarrassed to talk to Ron about. "Don't call her the gatekeeper. She's my mother right now, okay?"

"But your mother could well have kept it locked up all this time. If someone unearths the final installment, I tell you, it'll be big news. The publishing event of the year, if not the decade! The feminists alone—they've *canonized* her for being a single mother. It'll be a feeding frenzy."

I'm trying to imagine my mother in a hospital. "The idea of Eleanor dying is surreal," I say. "She's always been so, I don't know, *vivante!*"

He starts pacing. "Maybe this is what our marriage needed. This—helping you through this—would give me purpose," he says, as if I give a shit about *his* purpose. And then he realizes this or reads my disgust enough to amend. "It could bring us together." He stands there, hands on his hips, waiting.

"Are you kidding?"

"What would happen if you needed someone? Really *needed* someone? And what if that person was *me?*"

"I'm going without you. I needed somewhere to go, and now I have it."

Chapter Six

THE READER'S BRAZEN HEART

Harriet

I'm not naive. If Tilton pulls these pages from their hiding place, they will likely move out into the world. Will Tilton read them herself? It doesn't matter, Tilton. We know each other as constants, deeper than any details. Ruthie will read these pages, if given the chance. She may be a grown woman with her own vexations, but she won't outgrow her curiosity, that beautiful suspicious gaze, and her deep need to be understood. No one can know someone else, I want to tell her. We can't even know ourselves. (Are you here, Ruthie?) She's taken George's absence the hardest. It's burrowed deep down and dwells.

Eleanor is so willful, she may choose not to read this. Hello, Eleanor, if you're here. For so long I didn't speak of your father. To know the truth now may be useless. I was too heartbroken to explain my own loss. I opted for fictions. I'm sorry. I wasn't capable of anything else. And I know that my choices took a toll on you. When George first came along, you grabbed hold of him like someone spurned. Did I spurn you? As for your father, you should know that you were no more spurned by your father than I was by my mother. You need to understand that. I hope I can make it clear. With your George long gone, I watch you push on. You're doing it more admirably than I ever could and with greater strength than I ever had.

Still, I can't write the truth through the lens of your perception. I held up some other version of myself for so long, thinking I was *doing you a favor. Forgive me if it's hard to change that now. I'll have to pretend you're not here.*

As for my readers, I'll pretend you're not here too. I know that you really want Daisy and Weldon. The books changed on you as they went, but Weldon and Daisy were constant—wanting, wanting, wanting. A love story. I didn't know it until the end. All stories worth telling are love stories.

I haven't forgotten you, my readers. You were young when you read my first book; I got in early and created a wild terrarium. Remember the family of sparrows, how Daisy and Weldon helped them burrow to the underground? Daisy's mother, a woman made of moths? How you wanted the monkey king to save you—yes, you—from your quarreling drunken parents? You wrote me letters about those parents, the cruel teachers, your sick pills. (The sickly often have the best imaginations.) One of you had a brain dysfunction. In a fit, you'd bitten off most of your tongue, but you wrote to me about the talking tree, filled with tongues. Could I get you one?

The tree wasn't make-believe, I told you. But at some point you probably didn't believe me and ripped the letter up.

You became splintered versions of myself, ones I wanted to mend and paste together to re-create myself, as if I, the writer, were only an accumulation of pieces of you, as if you'd written me. Maybe this is impossible to understand.

And after the first book, the second, the third, I started to fear that the terrarium was aired, bleached by a proper education, more metal filing cabinet than terrarium. You grew up, so did I, and there was Weldon in his loafers and adman suit. He felt like a pet lion wearing a strap-on bowler, belted into the motorcycle sidecar at a boardwalk amusement. For Daisy, in a library, dizzy as motes in shifting sun. Insanity was realism. I offered sex and death—you dog-eared the racy passages and passed them around.

You grew up. Your lisps dried out until they were as shrewd as purse strings. You learned to knot neckties and jostle into nylons. I missed the children, but I loved you too. I imagined you as you studied my work in college while hypersexual, forever pining. You sent me diatribes on love, violence, war, and symbolism, and I didn't have the heart to tell you that I never wrote a symbol in my life. If you gaze at any text long enough, it disconnects from meaning, from inkiness, and becomes a symbol of something. Stare at your floor for half an hour and you'll be able to found a new religion. Your papers were all wrong except in what they revealed about your own gazing and subconscious, a beautiful thing.

Your young faces became weighted by budding jowls. You've gone from doughy to taut to doughy again. We grew old together. You are bankers with fattened knuckles, pallbearers, librarians—like Daisy was—dithering through the stacks as if overseeing your own ward of loons. Some of you are dead. By the time you read this, I will be too. We'll share that as well.

I went through a phase of reading the professors who dissected my books. I was a feminist, absurdist, magical realist, modernist, postmodernist. They gave me psychological, sociopolitical, religious, feminist contexts in terms of Foucault, Freud, and Jung, and diagnosed my anxiety of influence. What brains! What effort! And yet, in the end, it was like having a deaf psychoanalyst. Not that I wanted to talk—not then.

Sometimes I worry that the scholars spent much too much time on me. I imagine their children painting faces on their knees, portraits of pretend parents while the real ones toiled away.

Deep inside each of you—reader, scholar, critic—a molecule of the terrarium still exists. If you still exist, that is. Why else does the word "tiger lily" make you think of a flower with petals growling open to show rows of large teeth—as Daisy imagined it? Why sometimes are you struck by someone else's full humanity, their rich imagined inner life, a version of a true self that can't be expressed, and in that moment you feel your own inexpressible inner life?

Or how, in your dreams, you can conjure the entire ocean?

Each molecule of story is a universe—grotesque and stunning, all sunlit steam and engines laboring in the chests of trains and creatures with small pink hands and horns and, yes, a tree with tongues; it returned after all in book six just as childhood reappears in old age.

I write this in my old age—as agog as a lamppost.

I hope, my dear readers, that your hearts haven't stiffened, rind-tough, or gone dowdy with flab—poor neglected hearts, a tragic crime. May you keep yourselves trimmed—hair, nails, suit jackets—but untamed within. (Be curious.)

Maybe after I die, you will all have grown weary of me.

But one lonesome biographer might soldier on to tell a quiet, falsified, feminist life—my blissful childhood, my daughter born out of wedlock without apology, and my reclusive end. Pale biographer, I want to comb the snarls from your hair and send you out to put your face in the sun.

To go on, I must ignore you all—by God, you're a glorious distraction. I must especially ignore the beautiful faces of my own progeny. Know I love you, that this is a feeble attempt to show that love before it's too late.

LITTLE GIRL JESUS OF THE DREAMING WOUNDS, AND CAT

Mrs. Funk made an appointment with Dr. Brumus and told him there was God in me. Candid about her faith, she probably called me "Little Girl Jesus of the Dreaming Wounds" and described the bloody crown of thorns wreathing my pillowcase, the divine imprint of my face.

It wouldn't have impressed Brumus, who wasn't a religious man. But it must have stirred the old debate between him and my father. Someone saw some glimmer in me. Maybe my father should have handed me over to my mother after all, instead of this deceit. He sent his monthly checks but still had never laid eyes on me.

Brumus told Mrs. Funk he would look into the matter. I was called in and Brumus said the words I'll never forget: "There may be something to you, Harriet. Perhaps we can prove it." He was a detective now. If there was something, he would find it!

There was often a new secretary outside Dr. Brumus's office. This one was young and pudgy, with a crimped chin and dimples. Dr. Brumus charged her with teaching me to read. This wasn't normally done at the Maryland School for Feeble Minded Children—it was considered a waste or, worse, a cruelty. The school was designed to shush the criminal element in our souls, nothing else.

The new secretary taught me letters in Dr. Brumus's office when Brumus was out. More than once, Brumus interrupted these lessons and took the secretary to a small room next door with a cot where he rested if too weary to head home at night. While he was in there with the secretary, I heard the sound of an owl. I wondered if it was caged. Was it a pet or part of some medical testing that would one day help the feeble-minded? A child who hadn't had such a stunted life might have understood the more logical reality, but I was a child trying to piece together how the world worked; my assumptions were sometimes illogical. I listened closely. The calls started as soft cooing and then rose louder and faster until they were clear hoots. I worried about the owl. What tests made it hoot like that? Did the secretary and Brumus have to hold the owl down while it struggled? When they came back into the room, they were always quite flushed, as if from exertion.

I asked them about the owl, and the secretary said, "You have to start acknowledging the difference between real and imagined." Her eyes jiggled between Brumus and me.

Once, alone, I peeked into the empty room with its lonesome cot and humid warmth. No owl. No empty cage that had once held an owl.

When the secretary taught me the letter O, phonetically in all of its variations, I heard the owl in her own throat. She was the owl. What had made her call out like that? Was Brumus holding her down? Poor, poor owl. In my head, I named her the Owl.

Somehow I never put together the secretary's hooting with what began to happen between Eppitt and me beneath the Duck Porch. There was too much of a divide between my own life—as a moron—and the mysterious lives of normal adults who came and went of their own free will. Plus, though young Eppitt and I foraged mightily for each other, we never had sex.

Things started up between us a few weeks after we met. I was standing next to the Duck Porch, which I had assumed had something to do with ducks, and the sickly children stared out at the world as if they were looking at something far off on the horizon. Ducks, I imagined. And so, whenever I could, I'd stop by the Duck Porch and try to see what they saw. The porch sat on low wooden stilts, with a crawl space below.

One day I heard a "Psst, psst" from under the porch.

I got down on my hands and knees and looked underneath to find the face of Eppitt Clapp. It was one to grow into. His nose, his lips, and his eyes crowded his face, so there wasn't much face left. The slightest emotion caused a lot of action. His pouts made his face look rubbery. His "Excuse me?" looked like shock. His worry looked like a sudden affliction. None of this sounds beautiful, but it was. I loved the drama of his face.

He was lying on his stomach, propped on his elbows, holding up that face, which seemed heavy with its oversized parts. "I knew it was you because of your shockings."

Shoes and stockings. That's what he meant. He was nervous again. "What about them?" All of our shoes and stockings were identical.

"Your shoes are in-footed and your stockings sag at the knees. One's got a hole and there's blue skin under."

My sharp shinbones collected bruises. With Eppitt, I was seen—in great detail. "What are you doing under there?" I asked him.

"This is my house. I live here."

"You live in King's Cottage."

"Yeah, but here too. Come in before somebody sees you."

I looked around—Parson, a guard of King's Cottage, swatted the wide rump of Miss Wingrit, who taught weaving. Wingrit squealed and smiled, wagging a finger at him. Rules about boys and girls mixing were strict, but not for our keepers. They liked to gather and smoke, huddling away from us whenever they had the chance. We were their unwanted children.

I wasn't sure whether I should go under or not. There was God in me. Would God scurry under a Duck Porch? I didn't know the answer.

I scurried under.

We dug our elbows into the soft dirt. It was summer but the dirt was cool, holding on to some memory of winter. From this spot, we could see over the hills.

"It's not a real house," I said.

"I know it's not."

"Did you used to have a real house?"

"Sure."

I'd been born in one but I didn't remember it. "I've never visited a real house."

He looked at me out of the corner of his eyes, surprised, I think, because he was now better than I was. "I lived on Sparrows Point."

"Is it full of sparrows?" I asked.

"Nope. Just people in little houses and red dust because there's steel mills. Red dust on everything, even this bowl of hard candies that the neighbor woman used to set out, all stuck together."

Later I'd know Sparrows Point myself. Sitting on the industrial tip of Baltimore, bitterly cold in winter and oppressively hot in summer, it was a grid of lettered streets, a company town. Row upon row of tiny houses were dwarfed by thick electric wires, conveyors on long metal legs, hulking warehouses. Oily, greasy, smoky, the red dust—just as Eppitt remembered—coating gutters, fence posts, even your own skin. The natural humidity of what was once low-lying marshland combined with the billowing steam from the boiler chimneys made the dust damp and pasty. Steeped in fumes and exhaust, the Clapp house surely suffered the noises of Sparrows Point: the rattling gusto of the Red Rocket streetcar, which took extra hands in and out of downtown; the blast of tugboats hauling barges; the constant bleating of trains.

Eppitt told me how on his way to school—where the boys learned machinery, gears, and small motors, and the girls learned sewing and tucking hospital corners on beds—he walked past seven giant caged fans, connected to the mills. "I thought if they were set to full blast at the same time, they could make a tornado and blow the whole place away."

"You wanted that?"

"It's better here. Gillup tells stories at night. There's food. I have my own bed. And I can't be kicked out because I already got kicked out."

"But what about your family?" I asked. "You didn't want them blown away."

"Not my sister, Meg. But the rest? It would be okay. I love Meg, though."

Eppitt's parents had seven children, all pale and slack with fatigue, a slouching crew, phlegmy and phlegmatic, often fevered. He was the worst off of the bunch. In the family photograph—he had only one—they hunched together by a puny tree. Eppitt was the only one to fix his eyes on the camera, to puff his chest proudly, as out of place as a parakeet. They ignored him, except Meg, who was three years older. "Meg is the only one worth anything."

The last in a long line, he was named Eppitt, after an uncle, although the Clapps already had a cat by that name. They didn't choose to have cats. The cats simply slunk in, and Eppitt's mother, accustomed to feeding hungry mouths, would offer scraps and, eventually, a name.

She stayed in bed as long as she could after Eppitt's birth. The previous births had been mired in complications—breeches, noosed umbilical cords, excessive swelling and bleeding. Eppitt, on the other hand, had slipped out like a greased pig. Recovery was her only time to be treated gently. She took her due.

One time she barked from bed, "Eppitt needs milk."

"And my father," Eppitt told me, "all bent up from years of work, reached down to put fresh milk in the cat's bowl, but it was full so he shouted at her. And my mother said, 'No, no, the baby needs milk. Don't you hear it crying?' And so they started calling me Baby so they could tell me apart from the cat. It became a family joke, and they didn't even like jokes." He looked at me squarely and said, "Why couldn't they have just called the cat Cat?"

"No one calls you Baby here, though," I said.

"Nope."

"I like Cat. I can call you Cat."

And he leaned over and kissed my cheek.

"Why did you do that?" I said.

"Meow."

I started to scramble out from under the Duck Porch, but he grabbed my ankle. "You should live with me in my house." It was like this for Daisy and Weldon in the underground burrow they built for the talking sparrows. He wanted her to stay with him there forever.

"It's only got dirt floors," I said.

"And a cat named Cat. Meow."

"Eppitt Clapp," I said, but I didn't say it like I was scolding him or even like I was about to ask him something. I said it like I was thinking about how important those two words were in my mouth. Eppitt Clapp—those two words changed everything. "There's God in me," I said. "Mrs. Funk told me so."

"I could have told you that, Harriet. There's God in all of us."

The floorboards creaked overhead. The first sickly child was being wheeled back inside. I was half out from under the Duck Porch as the nurse pivoted the cane wheelchair and the kid restrained within it saw me. I couldn't tell if the child was a boy or a girl. The child had puffed red cheeks, mumps-like, and looked at me, and I stared back. And I saw God, just like that.

"Eppitt Clapp," I said again, barely a whisper.

And once more, from under the Duck Porch, he said, "Meow."

THE FIRST PACT OF HARRIET WOLF

Young love is a consumption. It drills into your bones, burrows into your brain. It lives in your breath and your blood—forever. Because it's the first love to arrive, the train car is empty and airy, and love swells to fill the entire space.

Eppitt and I worked doubly fast among the girls in the laundry, scrubbing stains with wire brushes, soaking the urine-drenched sheets in scalding tubs, pinning clothes in the sun. We didn't talk in front of the other girls—boisterous with kettle-whistle voices echoing against the high ceiling.

I loved Eppitt's decrepit lungs because they kept him in the laundry—freshly steamed lungs were better than lungs packed with quarry dust.

Under the Duck Porch, Eppitt and I built a home. "This is the kitchen. This is the dining room…" We listed tables, chairs, chests of drawers, curtains, and plates with blue-flowered edging. "One day, we'll find it for real," he promised. According to Eppitt, we had a destiny to catch up to. He would lie back, hands behind his head, in the bedroom under the Duck Porch, and I would put my head on his chest. "Our sheaven."

"Shared heaven," I'd translate aloud with my head on his chest.

He convinced me we would have this, and we would, in a way, years and years later, but not how we thought. Sheaven.

We took turns lying on each other, kissing—always fully dressed. We were touch-hungry, neglected, both of us, but me more so. I hadn't known a breast, a fist of hair, a warm neck, an ear to a chest, a heartbeat other than my own. My childhood was a starvation. I'd have died of it, if not for Eppitt. At first, my body felt needled, but once my skin came alive, I couldn't get enough.

Eppitt said, "Will you marry me?"

I said, "Yes, Cat. I will." Sometimes I called him Cat.

One day, amid the outdoor laundry lines, I pulled the white sheet to my head, a veil.

He pulled out a piece of string—industrial-strength thread stolen from the sewing room. As we stood, face to face, and pressed our left hands together, Eppitt loosely wound them with the string. He told me to put my right hand on my heart. He did the same.

"Are you my wife?" he asked.

"Yes," I said. "Are you my husband?"

"Yes."

"Then we're married?" I asked.

"We are," he said.

We kissed. The sheet shifted in the breeze. I held it tightly, but it tugged away in the wind anyway and flew up, revealing us. When we looked around, only the sick children wheeled to the Duck Porch, out for their daily airing, were near enough to see us. Angels who didn't speak, only gazed. Maybe their eyes grazed us—a blessing.

Eppitt gave me the small circle of string. "Keep it."

I told him I would. Later, I pasted a piece of paper around the string and wrote "E. C. and H. W. 1913. Marriage."

That's how all weddings should be.

Eleanor and George's wedding was formal. We were strapped into our fitted clothes. Suits were worn by all. Even Eleanor and her sole bridesmaid wore tailored jackets, skirts, and matching hats. The reception consisted of a few waltzes, cookies and punch, photo flashes, cigars, a few guests pelting them with rice. Hooray. It was doomed. Maybe Eleanor was unsuited for marriage. She likes short conversations; marriage is a long one. She held on to George's arm—not for love's sake, but like he was a buoy and she didn't want to die alone at sea.

I promised to try to write without imagining an audience, but maybe I've asked too much of myself (or too little). Eleanor, if you're reading this, I'm sorry to describe your wedding this way. And I'm sorry I let you go into that marriage and never said a word. Not that you'd have listened. I thought, What's worse than a bad marriage? Perhaps no marriage. *We learn through our failures. And I wanted you to have children, to have something that, when you clamped onto it, would clamp onto you in return. You have your girls, and they, too, have God in them.*

My pact with Eppitt, that slip of string—it was the start.

GIRL GENIUS

What did I understand of the world while at the Maryland School for Feeble Minded Children? Very little.

I went out once. When gum rot exposed a nerve that made me cry out, Nurse Oonagh took me to the dentist. She had a tooth that needed looking at as well—probably the only reason I was placated. Normally, I kept the marriage pact tucked inside the small box beneath my cot, but I slipped it in my pocket—to help me not die.

We went by wagon. The roads were pitted. I saw a hedgerow, and then a house, a fenced dog, chimney smoke, shutters, a carpet being beaten on a line, baby prams, a man carrying a ladder. We were carted through the streets of Baltimore, toward the harbor. Children with mothers and fathers—they still existed! They hadn't all been sent to asylums. They bobbed in open air!

Together, Nurse Oonagh and I had three molars pulled. Pain can be mistaken for comfort.

On the way home, her hands occasionally fluttered around her bulging cheeks. She prayed—a whine through her nose—but I cast my starving eyes out the window. With my mouth cotton-clotted, my head bundled shut—this was the way the world preferred me: mute, behind glass, passing through. I was sure of that.

Some visitors brought glimpses of the world outside too. Parents visited rarely, but they sometimes brought their other children with them. *These kids moved differently, as if their bodies were built of fibers foreign to me. Sometimes a child left at the Maryland School because of destitution was picked up after a change in fortune. I watched them go until the backs of their heads were just dots, and then gone.*

Eppitt's parents weren't coming for him. Angry bull-chested debt collectors had come round his house on Sparrows Point constantly to threaten his father. "Baltimorons," his father called them after they were gone, his hands shaking.

His parents had dropped Eppitt at the Maryland School for Feeble Minded Children on a Sunday shortly before I met him. They'd prayed on it. The Word was clear. His mother didn't cry.

"You'll come back for me?" he asked.

"Yes," his mother said. "You keep that in your heart."

When she turned her back, Eppitt's father looked at him and shook his head. They weren't coming back. Eppitt appreciated his father's honesty, and there was little to appreciate about the man.

Eppitt told me this in the empty laundry room one evening after everyone had emptied out of the Custodial Building for Girls. I sat on the floor, relieved for a moment that I didn't really know my parents. There was nothing untrue to keep in my heart.

"I'm sorry," I said to Eppitt.

"It's fine," he said. "We're family now. We'll get out of here and have babies and our own house."

But this wasn't necessarily possible. The year was 1913. We were morons, remember, harboring the criminal element. The boys were taken care of—a mysterious problem with the penis, a sedative, an operation in the laboratory. Our deformities, even the unseen ones in our soul, had to be kept in check. (Girls too, though I'd never had the operation, perhaps because my father had told Brumus not to, or perhaps because Brumus alone chose to spare me.)

Dr. Brumus was the man with the scalpel in the operating room, instructed by a board of volunteers who sometimes walked the grounds, whispering. But he must have believed in his civic duty.

I've since put it in historical perspective. You see, Brissaud and Griffiths were performing vasectomies on rabbits and dogs as early as 1884. Steinach experimented on senile rats. Vasectomies were used to treat bladder stones and TB, as well as for the proper benefits of "rejuvenation." Sigmund Freud and W. B. Yeats were said to have had vasectomies to rejuvenate themselves. In 1899, the year before my birth, Ochsner published a paper on performing vasectomies on habitual criminals. Eugenics was revved! In 1907, Indiana passed a bill "to prevent procreation of confirmed criminals, idiots, rapists and imbeciles," in other words, sterilization. Twenty-nine states joined in. When Eppitt arrived at the Maryland School for Feeble Minded Children, Sharp had already published a piece called "Vasectomy as a Means of Preventing Procreation in Defectives" and was urging sterilization in all state institutions. (We were surely defectives.)

Enter the Kaiser Wilhelm Institute of Anthropology, Human Heredity, and Eugenics. Before Hitler's chancellorship started, a Reich sterilization law was drafted. Those who weren't deemed fit to marry were tried in the hereditary health courts, where the enforcement of sterilization laws led to three hundred and twenty thousand people being sterilized from 1933 to 1945. Worse crimes happened in those dozen years, but there's a bit of history.

Eppitt knew. Held steady by a guard's elbow, boys limped bow-legged across the field to their cottages. Girls, at some point after their first period, disappeared for an afternoon, returning wobbly, pale. Brumus was nicknamed Dr. Snip-Snip. There were rumors that a few of the older male guards had volunteered for the proce-

*dure. Even Brumus himself was said to have had it done by another
doctor in town.*

*The girls knew what it meant: no pregnancy, no children. A
few said they wanted the operation—girls from big families, like
Eppitt's, who'd been left because they cost too much to feed. They'd
seen their mothers swell again and again, screaming bloody babies
into the world, and then staggering through the house, slack with
exhaustion. Or some tough girls wanted to be with boys and not
bother with babies. Some had trysts with not only the boys but also
the guards. Eppitt's favorite, Gillup, was said to be a rounder. Spry
and handsome, he had favorites, a pecking order. But even the girls
who claimed to want the operation were different after it, mute
when the snip-snip came up in conversation, their faces blank with
a watery glint to their eyes.*

*I wanted to have a baby one day. There was a secret nursery
at the Maryland School—children weren't supposed to be accepted
until age seven. But there were a few clandestine cribs; one of them
had been my own. Eppitt and I deserved babies. This became my
motivation for learning how to read—to get into Brumus's files and
mark that Eppitt was already sterile, operation done.*

*I had a facility for reading that startled the Owl. At one point,
she asked Brumus if her task of teaching me to read was a joke.
"Harriet can already read. She gets it as soon as I say it."*

*Brumus, in disbelief, pulled a book from his desk, opened it, and
pointed to a paragraph. "Read it!"*

*It was a bit about the heart. "I don't know all of these words," I
said, skimming it.*

"See there!" he said.

The Owl looked at me.

*"I'm sorry!" I said. "I don't know what a 'ventricle' is. I've never
seen this word 'aorta.' And if a 'valve' is weakened by disease, what*

can anyone do about it? It's a heart! Hearts work because of love, right? Mrs. Funk says they work because of God's love!" I sniffled and wiped my nose, and there was a bright swatch of blood. I was an anxious bleeder as Eppitt was an anxious word blender.

Shortly after this, Brumus administered an IQ test, at the time a new phenomenon. He sat me at his desk, timing the test himself. Ever since I had talked about the ventricles and weakened valves and the love of God, he'd treated me differently. Actually, he seemed terrified of me and often spoke in hushed tones, and asked me if I was thirsty. He even offered me coffee, which wasn't allowed. I thought it might be a trap, and I declined.

I wasn't nervous about the test. Why would a moron be nervous during an IQ test? I knew that my answers would be wrong. Brumus graded the test while I stood by the window and he started sniffling in the middle of his grading, as if choked up.

When he stood to get water, he said, "By Jesus. Not one error. Not one so far."

He told the Owl and news traveled. A small crowd gathered in his office and in the hall—the Owl, Mrs. Funk, three guards—for the rest of the grading.

When Brumus finished, he reared from the desk, pulled off his glasses, and rubbed the oily bridge of his nose. "Contact the newspaper," he said. "I have discovered a genius."

I didn't believe him, of course. But I decided that his mistakes in grading my test would convince my parents to retrieve me. I would be the back of a head in a carriage and then gone! Could a genius with God in her also get Eppitt out? Was it possible?

I caught Eppitt's eye from my row in the lunch line. Did he know? Had word spread? That afternoon the reporter arrived. He took my picture outside the administration building. "So, what are you going to do now?" he asked.

"I'm not a moron anymore," I said. "So I guess I'll just have to go home!"

After he left, Brumus pulled me aside. It was October and gusty. "I've talked to your father. He wants to visit. But I'm not sure how it will go."

"My father is coming here?"

"Don't expect the world to change in a day," he said.

"But my world did change in a day! I've changed."

"Still," Brumus said. "I just don't know."

"Well, I can't stay here," I said.

BLOOD ANGEL

The Owl showed me the article—"Girl Genius Discovered at School for Feeble Minded!" This was where I learned that I had a bleeding condition—not hemophilia exactly, but something related to a nervous condition. The journalist noted my "occasional mutism" and "hysterical outbursts," which, according to the article, had forced my parents, Dr. and Mrs. Wolf, to send me to the Maryland Asylum and Training School for the Feeble Minded—which at other places in the article was referred to more simply as the Maryland School for Feeble Minded Children or the Asylum—as if the name of the place didn't actually matter.

Two days later I was sitting in the entryway of the administrative building—the spot where parents came to dispose of children, and sometimes where they came to collect them. I wasn't being disposed of, so this meant, to me, that I was being collected. There were Oriental rugs, and the wind outside was so strong that it rattled the windows and even made the gauze curtains ripple. I thought of my veil and my young husband, Eppitt Clapp. There was no need to try to spare him the operation by going through Brumus's files. I would bring him with me—home. That *would* be our new family.

Dr. Brumus appeared with my father, who was wiry and elegantly dressed. He had a cane but no limp. I hated the cane immediately. I wanted to love my father but something about the useless cane made me want to beat him with it. I didn't understand my rage. I mistook it for nerves. I was a hysteric, after all.

My father held a box, wrapped in yellow paper, under one arm. He looked sharply around the room. I was sitting right there, but for some reason he didn't identify me as his child. Was he expecting a baby wheeled out in a pram? Finally, his eyes fell on me. I must have looked small, my shoulders curled inward. What should a genius say? I hoped I wouldn't suffer mutism. I tried not to bleed.

Dr. Brumus said to my father, "Fit as a fiddle! See?"

This might have been a bit of goading. My father stiffened at Brumus's effusiveness, then looked at me, maybe searching for glimpses of my mother or himself or his mother. Eventually he seemed content that I was the right kid. He nodded, and we sat down.

"Hello," I said. I hadn't been told to pack my belongings, but I had arranged them neatly on my cot.

"So, you're Harriet."

"Harriet Wolf," I said. This seemed to surprise him—Wolf. Did I have a right to it? "Nice to meet you."

Dr. Brumus was towering over us. My father looked out the window as if searching for a pigeon to shoot. Eppitt had told me that rich people shoot pigeons.

"I'll leave you two to talk," Brumus said. He nudged my father. "You've got a gift?"

"I do," my father said, but he didn't hand it over.

Brumus sighed and left.

Once Brumus was gone, my father seemed a little softer. "It's not much, but I hope you like it." He handed me the gift.

"Thank you," I said, holding it in my lap.

"Open it!" my father said.

My fingers were too nervous to tug correctly. I felt spastic. I had opened only a few gifts in my life—an orange, new shoelaces.

"Do you need help?" Maybe he suspected that I lacked fine motor skills.

"No, I'm fine."

"Just tear into it!" he said.

And so I did, but then immediately worried that I seemed vicious. I looked up to see if he seemed to think I was.

Instead he was impatient. "It's a book!" he announced.

"Thank you."

"Not just any book!" he said.

I opened the book to its middle. The pages were blank. "It's an empty book."

"For you to fill!" he said. "I've gotten you a subscription to a number of newspapers. You must know what's going on out there! You clip the things of interest, paste them in the book, and make notations."

"Out there?" I said.

"You don't really need a newspaper to fill you in on what's going on in here!" A joke. He laughed a little.

My heart, already charged, started to beat faster. "So this book and the newspapers are to help me know what goes on out there," I said, clarifying, "while I'm in here."

"And to organize those thoughts, yes," he said. "Dr. Brumus says you're very clever."

I looked out onto the wide lawn. I wanted to crawl under the Duck Porch. "I'm a genius," I corrected him.

"*Well, yes, but you're a girl,*" *he said. "I don't know how much I trust a test like that. Plus, if it's accurate, then it's kind of ironic. I mean, a girl genius. What will you specialize in? Hems? Tulle?*"

I closed my eyes and imagined living under the Duck Porch forever. "My mother will want to see me. How about her?"

"Oh, her nerves would never withstand it. But she is so proud of you! So proud!"

"But I'm a genius. I could help her. I could help her nerves. Ask Dr. Brumus!"

"No, no," my father told me. "This has worked out well enough. It's best for everyone." He jabbed the book with his index finger. "Look at the first page. I've started it for you!"

I opened the book, and there was a clipping—the smudgy small photograph of me in front of the administration building, holding the IQ test. The Owl hadn't shown me the photograph. She'd chopped it from the article she'd shown me, and now I knew why. I looked austere, too gangly and small for thirteen, practically stricken by the flash, with my eyes flared and my hands gripping the test page as the wind kicked up one side of my hair. Dr. Brumus looked like a barrel, and we seemed trapped between the building's columns. Beneath the picture, a subtitle: "Wolf, 13, is interested in ornithology." I didn't know what ornithology was or where the information had come from. When I saw that photograph, I wondered how Eppitt could love me. I was ugly. I was diseased. I had conditions. The test couldn't be trusted. I was only a girl. If I was a genius, it was a waste of genius.

Brumus showed up once my father had said his quick good-bye. My nose didn't bleed, but I still felt the light-headedness that sometimes came with it. I remember it being dusk, and the old doctor picking me up, cradling me to his chest—even though I was too old for it. He carried me to the cot in his office, and told me I could sleep there if I wanted. I didn't have to go back to Stump Cottage. I lay down. He put on his hat and said, "You'll stay here with us, Harriet. This is home, after all."

I stared at the wall, and he left.

Then I got up and went through the files and found Eppitt's. I checked a box on his main summary—sterilized, yes. Then I found my own report and took out the results of my IQ test. I ripped the page to bits and ate the paper, piece by piece. This was what a moron would do. I was a moron. It was too late to really tell me anything different. "Moron" was my first self-definition; it had burrowed in deep. In some elemental way, I will always be a moron. The pieces of paper almost melted, gummed lightly in my teeth, and went down easily.

Once I was done, I rested my head. I waited for the blood to fill my nose. But it didn't. Instead, I felt stickiness between my legs. I checked my underwear—there was a dark red stain.

I fell into a restless sleep, bleeding like a girl making a red angel in snow.

Chapter Seven

THE GATEKEEPER IS WEARY

Eleanor

The doctor is a rotund man who possesses the hardened fat of a taut belly and a broad, padded chest; my own fat is soft, but does that make his fat better than mine? *You're not a great model of heart-healthy living*, I want to tell him, *and shouldn't be one to judge.* Yet that is his job.

He tells me I'm lucky, smiling at me with his shiny face, his polished-looking skin. And I think for a second that he's talking about Opal Harper's release from the hospital. The new patient on the other side of the curtain is very quiet, perhaps a mute. But he goes on to tell me that my heart attack could have been much worse, that I'll have to change my ways with diet, exercise, and stress management. "You should take this as a warning."

I've lived my life obsessed with warnings and precautions. "I live a very careful life already," I reply. "I have to. My youngest child is fragile. I've never been a drinker or a smoker. I keep a quiet house."

"Well, you've taken good care of your daughter, but it's time to take good care of yourself." He smiles, falsely, and I'm suspicious of him.

I clutch the gaping V-neck of my hospital gown. "It's chilly in here. When can I go home?"

"A couple of days. We're very pleased with everything we're seeing."

"I want to get dressed and walk around," I tell him. "I can't lie here in a sickbed looking like an invalid. There's such a thing as the power of positive thinking. If you act sick, you'll only get sicker." I don't believe in the power of positive thinking, but I don't like looking weak. By God, I want to button something. I want to feel the grip of a snug zipper. I want to lace up my tennis shoes.

"That's the spirit!" he says. "We do want you on your feet some." He smiles at me once more, his chubby cheeks glowing like the face of Mrs. Gottleib's jolly plastic Santa with the bulb that lights up its head. "Any other questions?"

"No." I stare straight ahead until he's left the room.

I'll have to call Mrs. Gottleib and ask her to bring me a few sets of clothes. I hate the idea of her riffling through my closets and drawers. Not that I have anything to hide. At most she'd find a stray prayer card left over from the dozens I received upon my mother's death. It's just the idea that bothers me, a violation of my privacy.

Nevertheless, I call her using the phone next to my bed.

Mrs. Gottleib says hello in an angry tone as if she's incredibly busy. Heaven knows she's not.

I say, "Hello, this is Eleanor Tarkington." I want to maintain some formality. Mrs. Gottleib gets personal if you give her any leeway. Asking a favor might be all she needs to discuss bunions or her Albert, God rest his soul.

"Eleanor! Well, this is a good sign. They're letting you use the phone."

"Of course I can use the phone. I don't need permission."

"Well, not everyone makes a fast recovery. You know, my sister Greta—"

I have to cut her off because she has countless sisters—enough that they collectively cover *all* medical emergencies. "I'm calling to ask a small favor. I need you to bring me a few changes of clothes. I'd like to get dressed, for goodness' sake."

"Okay. Okay, then," Mrs. Gottleib says. "Let me get pen and paper."

"You know what a woman wears. You don't need to take notes."

"Okay. I'll bring you options."

"Don't overdo."

"Listen, Eleanor. How about I bring Tilton along? I'm sure she'll want to see you."

I breathe in so sharply that my chest bones spasm. I almost yell, but I stop myself and whisper, "Dear God, Judith! No." Calling Mrs. Gottleib by her first name exposes my urgency.

"What?" Mrs. Gottleib says. "You think she should just stay cooped up? What if you die in there, huh? She won't have gotten to say good-bye."

"I'm not dying. Don't be vulgar."

"People die, no matter whether they're needed on earth or not."

This is a reference to Mrs. Gottleib's dead husband, Albert, as well as an insinuation that I am keeping Tilton dependent on me so I can cheat death. "Absurd," I say. "I know people die. I'm just not dying now." I sigh. "I'm coming home in a few days."

"The doctor said so?"

"Yes, the doctor said so! There's no need to bring Tilton into this cesspool, you hear? You'd upset her delicate psyche in the process."

"Okay, okay, fine."

I offer a quick good-bye and hang up.

And now I'm woozy. I press the button for the charge nurse. Maybe I'm having a physical reaction to the idea of Tilton being taken from the house. Or it's the medications. By the time the nurse arrives, wearing her cartooned smock as if this were the *children's* ward, I wave her off. "False alarm," I say. "I'm fine." I'm not good with people. I know this. I have to make an effort here, however, because I want the hospital staff to give me quality care. I stopped going to restaurants because I wasn't charming enough for the waitstaff and feared they had spit in my food. Even if they hadn't, they'd probably coughed into it, and it wasn't ever prepared the way I wanted it no matter whose germs were tossed on it. I hear my mother's voice suddenly: "Say what they will, but you know your own mind, Eleanor! That you do." I didn't like the expression "Say what they will." Who were *they* and what were they saying, exactly?

As the nurse checks my vitals, I ponder how, if I'd been nicer on the morning of the heart attack, I might have avoided this entire incident. But I was in a foul mood. For one thing, I told Tilton that Mrs. Devlin's daughter wanted a poem for a wedding but I forgot that I'd already invented that assignment. Tilton seemed to catch on. Then, on my way to Goodwill to buy a toaster oven so that I could loosen its wires and give it to Tilton to fix for Mrs. Devlin as well—another invention—I'd picked up the newspaper at Mrs. Gottleib's. She'd cut out the advertisements and taken the sales inserts.

"How am I supposed to read this Swiss cheese?" I asked her, holding it up, holes and all.

"Have it delivered to your own damn house," she said.

"You know I can't do that! Tilton can't be exposed to the world's traumas."

"Tilton should get a sweetheart. Write a love poem of her own. Get out and live a little."

"You know she's allergic to the sun, to insect bites, bee stings—you name it. She's asthmatic, lactose intolerant, and perspires to the point of dehydration!" I folded the paper and shook my head. "I don't appreciate this, Mrs. Gottleib. I really don't. If you weren't the girl's godmother, I would end our friendship."

If you'd asked me then, I'd have said that these volleys of argumentation were good for both of our old hearts.

The morning continued to take a toll as I paced the household items aisle of Goodwill with growing agitation. There were no toaster ovens. This day was bound to come. There sat three old microwaves. I wouldn't have Tilton work on anything radioactive!

I marched to the front desk. Jessica and Petie, the two teenage clerks, were on duty. They're newish, but I'm a regular, and my reputation precedes me.

Jessica said, "Can I help you, Mrs. Tarkington?"

"There are no toaster ovens."

"You bought them all," Petie said, smirking.

"When do you expect more?" A rational question.

"When someone old dies and their relatives clean out their house," Jessica told me.

"I don't like that tone," I said.

Jessica rolled her eyes. I didn't like that either.

"There's an old TV that your daughter can fix," Petie said.

"I don't want her watching television. She's delicate!"

"She doesn't have to watch it," he said. "She can just fix it. That's what you do, right? Break things so she can fix them?"

I stood there, exasperated. I was a mother doing right by my child who suffers what they now call "special needs." This was one of my daughter's special needs! Did they not recognize the urgency? You would think that employees of the Goodwill, with their emphasis on helping those with special needs, would understand. "I thought you were supposed to be retarded to work at Goodwill. Isn't that the mission? Are you two retarded?" I couldn't help it. There, I'd said it. All I could do was stand by it.

Jessica looked startled and then like she might cry.

Petie crossed his arms on his chest. "Sometimes there aren't enough retarded people and they have to hire regular people," he said defensively.

"Which are you—retarded or regular?" I said.

"That's not really funny," Jessica said.

"I wasn't trying to be funny." I'm not afraid of the help at Goodwill. They can't spit on my food or be lax about my medications.

I picked out a television. Petie carried it, rabbit-ear antenna and all, to the register. Jessica rang it up. And then when I picked it up, I couldn't possibly admit that it was too heavy. I had to stagger out of the store, homeward.

There are two nurses now. One of them has a broad forehead.

"You're racing a little," the broad-foreheaded nurse says. "We'd like to see you even out."

"Do you know what it's like to be *forced* to calm down?" I say, more sharply than I mean to.

"Take the news as a get-out-of-stress-free card," the first nurse says. "You're no longer allowed to get worked up about things! You're off duty!"

I close my eyes and try to smile, but it must come across as a grimace because one of them says, "Are you in pain, Mrs. Tark-ington?"

"Yes," I say, though I can tell it's anguish, really, which is dis-tinct from pain.

"We can tweak your meds."

"No," I say, eyes still closed. "I'm fine, dear. I'm fine. Do you think I can get out of this place faster than a couple days?"

"If you even out, the doctor might let you go in two or so. No promises, though."

"Two days." Anything can happen to Tilton in two days!

"Don't suffer in silence. If you need something, let us know!" the broad-foreheaded nurse says. They walk off, wearing rubber clogs with air holes punched into them. What is the world com-ing to? As if a shoe were a bug jar with holes popped in the lid? Ruthie had a jar like that as a child. Lightning bugs. She fed them wet grass. They blinked in her darkened bedroom. Then they died—hard, crisp shells on the bottom of the jar. Ruthie cried. She was seven. I picked up the jar and dumped the dead bugs in the garden. I told Ruthie that the world would betray her if she trusted it too much. We all get abandoned at some point. You've got to be tough.

Why did I treat Ruthie this way? I would never have let Til-ton have a jar of bugs, for the very reason that they'd just die. I protected Tilton as best as I could, but I knew that Ruthie was going to leave me. I raised one daughter to hand over to the dangerous world, and the other to keep.

Ruthie, seven years old and bawling over dead bugs—it's so frighteningly vivid!

The truth about my mother is that, while she loved me, she wanted something from me. She wanted a love that was bigger than I could ever be. She eventually needed me too, as her reclusive nature took hold, and this became a working definition of love. If you're needed, you can trust that love will last.

George didn't need me. The love didn't last. Tilton, on the other hand, has always needed me. The love lasts. Early on, I decided that Ruthie wouldn't need me for long. Maybe I quit her before she could quit me.

If Ruthie knows I'm sick, she'll sense weakness. She'll come. To make amends? Or like so many others do: for the seventh book? She might have convinced herself that I lied about its destruction.

After my mother died, I tried to write it myself. I thought it would be easy money, not that I needed it. My sentences sounded propped up with toothpicks. I couldn't think of what might happen next. I tried to repeat the tree of tongues from the first book and return the characters to the sighing river. I remembered how Daisy and Weldon, in their later years, had a house and set out a bowl of hardened candies that got dusted in red pollen from the giant poppies when Daisy left the windows open. Petals from apple trees wafted in, covering the rug, and she vacuumed petals. I opened the windows, hoping that would help, but who thinks up stuff like that?

The problem was I didn't love Weldon Fells and Daisy Brooks. Even once my mother was done writing the books, the two of them still felt like siblings of mine—ones my mother loved more, doted on, adored, her true creations. Once, she whispered to me, "I'm scared to love you too much. If I do, will you just be snatched away?" I thought she was worried that I'd be kidnapped, but when George was snatched away from me, I understood. I knew long before it happened that Ruthie would be snatched away. That's what the world does. It snatches. But my mother's characters could never be snatched away. They were always in her control.

Tilton was the child Harriet had always wanted. There was one time that Harriet left the house after she'd been a recluse for decades. No longer a clipster, she still read newspapers compulsively. She'd seen a small advertisement in the *Baltimore Sun* for the Isley Wesler Museum of Antiquities. She wanted to take Tilton. She said, "I want to see it as I see it and I want to see it as she sees it."

"What about the way that I might see it?" I asked.

"You'll see it the way it wants to be seen," she said. "I want the under and the over."

I barely understood my mother when she spoke this way, and I almost forbade her to take Tilton, but how could I refuse a shut-in who finally wanted to go out? I looked up the museum in a directory in the library. It didn't seem to be much of a museum at all, just an old man's country house. In the end I regretted not forbidding Tilton from going because, through a very confused course of Tilton's logic, she ate one of the artifacts on display. The heart of a mongrel king. It was a pruned thing at the time—leathery and tough. Instead of being horrified, Harriet loved it that Tilton—only seven at the time—had done it. It threw the proprietor, Isley Wesler himself, into a conniption. Later, while I was administering castor oil, Harriet called the newspaper. Probably because she wanted a clipping of the incident—proof that it had happened.

When I grilled Tilton about the event, she said she'd confused eating the mongrel king's heart with her desire for a father. How?

One thing was clear. If George hadn't run off with Marie Cultry, Tilton wouldn't have been confused and wouldn't have eaten a mongrel king's heart. Further, if George hadn't run off, I wouldn't have returned to my childhood home with my crazy mother. If she'd had a mother and father in a sweet small town like Newark, Delaware—ivy growing on doorways, a quaint Main Street, and a hallowed college campus—Tilton might have been more normal. Ruthie wouldn't have run off either. Without George's awful example, Ruthie wouldn't have known how.

Or maybe it was the lightning. If it hadn't struck the plane that night and sent a hunk of burning engine to the road and hadn't killed Marie Cultry's brand-new husband, then George and I might have survived the aggression of daily living. We may have even sweetened on each other—returning to our courtship—once the kids were older.

But why revisit that suffering?

The phone rings. I forgot that there was a phone even though I spoke to Mrs. Gottlieb on it a short while ago. People shouldn't be able to reach you when you're in a hospital. It's like having a telephone in the bathroom. Indecent.

Somehow I know it's Ruthie calling. I know it the way I know the most basic things—a toothache, a thunderstorm.

"Mom, are you okay?" I hear when I answer. It *is* Ruthie. I shouldn't be surprised that I'm right, but I am.

"I'm fine." I haven't heard Ruthie's voice in so long that I'm also surprised that I recognize it. It's like someone's rung a bell and it matches the exact same sweet note that resides in my memory. But the sweetness is tinged with sadness. I want to muffle the damn bell.

"I talked to Tilton. I didn't get very good details. What has the doctor said?"

The doctor isn't to be trusted. "Minor," is what I tell Ruthie. "It's all minor."

"Really?" Ruthie says. Her voice doesn't seem older at all. Her face appears in my mind but it hasn't aged either. She's just a teenager, yelling at me, breaking me. "A minor heart attack is still a heart attack, which is major."

"I know why you're calling." Ruthie always has an ulterior motive. I remind myself that I can't trust her.

"I wanted to feel you out on coming to help with Tilton. I thought—"

"No. You want what we don't have."

Ruthie pauses, as if she's confused, but then says, "I gave up wanting something from you years ago. Group therapy."

"Group therapy," I huff. You'd never catch me talking about my feelings with a group of strangers. "You want what they all want. The seventh book of Harriet Wolf."

She goes quiet and suddenly I'm afraid she's going to hang up. I know that I have to be tough with her but I still want to hear her voice, just a few more notes. I'm about to apologize, but then she says, "I was in graduate school, English literature, at one point. Do you know what being Wee-ette's granddaughter afforded me? A shitty marriage."

For years, I took control of the story like a gatekeeper, as they put it in that news article. Why didn't I see how stupid that was, just as it was stupid of my mother to love her characters because she could control them, when she had a daughter who would have done anything for her—anything? I should have recognized that my Ruth was always going to do what she wanted to. That was her way. I hear her breathing, waiting. There's nothing I can do. She's coming. I can feel it. "Ruthie," I whisper.

"Yes?"

"Be gentle with Tilton." I close my eyes, so tired now.

"Of course I'll be gentle with Tilton."

"Unfortunately," I say, "she loves you deeply." I take the phone from my ear and plop it into its cradle.

The room is quiet except for the distant racket of televisions, blathering up and down the halls, canned cheering and laughter—like there's a party I haven't been invited to. And if I were invited? Say what they will about me, but I know my own mind. I'd refuse to go.

Chapter Eight

AIR

Tilton

Mrs. Gottleib's station wagon is full of air. It shifts around my body. It's like flying. It wouldn't surprise me if Mrs. Gottleib's station wagon somehow relies on air; the motor breathes the wind in through its grille, pours it through the engine, and the car itself grows lighter because it's so full. I'm afraid that it will tighten my own lungs like a bellows—the way a bird's body works as a bellows—and I will start to lift. This is why there are seat belts. Plus the fact that people die in car wrecks. It happens all the time.

Luckily, (a) my surgical mask cuts down the gusts of air that I swallow. The mask was in our emergency kit, in the event that I ever go outdoors. And (b) I'm in the backseat, the safest spot in the car. Mrs. Gottleib wanted me to sit in the front beside her, but studies refer to it as the death seat. She told me to say no more. So I didn't. And (c) I have a heavy bag on my lap that secures me to the vinyl seat. It's filled with medical necessities: sunscreen, which I've already applied; insect repellent; EpiPen; various medications; water bottle; gauze; peroxide; Band-Aids. I'm wearing my mother's wraparound cataract sunglasses. Mrs. Gottleib tells me that I look like Michael Jackson. Ruthie used to have his albums. Mrs. Gottleib's comment makes no sense to me.

I ask if there's a train station out here. I don't tell her that my father, George, left with Marie Cultry while taking her to a train station in winter.

She says, You want to ride a train?

No thank you!

Also, in Mrs. Gottleib's station wagon you can forget you're moving. It's like the world is moving past you. When you stop, the world stops. There's nothing between me and the birds. Nothing but air. Air that they could beat their wings through and ride. I see them. They see me.

There are many houses; each is a space to be filled. In each house there's a family, ones who leave and ones who stay. Sometimes there is a building and it's filled with apartments. In each apartment there's a family of people who leave and stay. In each house, there's also the Wee-ette. Not my Wee-ette, but theirs. My Wee-ette is now alone in our house. She doesn't like to be alone. I closed my eyes in her bedroom—empty now, a chamber that doesn't hold a heart and lungs—and I told Wee-ette that I'm going to see my mother in the hospital via Mrs. Gottleib's station wagon. I will be home soon.

She sighed like curtains rustling.

I am the keeper of all the pacts: Wee-ette's old ones; the two with my mother; the four between Ruthie and me; and the one between just Wee-ette and me, which made me the keeper of the pacts. I checked on them before I left. The screwdriver is tucked under Wee-ette's old typewriter. I used it to unscrew the heating vent on the far wall of Wee-ette's bedroom. It's been a while since I've checked. The vent's grate popped off, a little sticky. There were the sheet metal innards of the heating system. The house is old, the walls so thick there's a ledge—a perfect shelf for a little box—and then the ledge falls away as the duct goes straight down. See how there are spaces within bigger spaces! On the shelf was an egg container, only half-dozen-sized, made of cardboard. I pulled it out and opened the lid. Inside the two rows of egg pockets—more spaces within a bigger space—were the wound-up pieces of string. All of our pacts—ten total—each with its masking tape tab labeled with initials, date, and keywords. Six of them include me and Ruthie together, either with or without our mother. Return & Save is the most important. The others are about sharing Halloween candy and not telling our mother things about boys Ruthie had a crush on. The Halloween candy is gone. The boys that Ruthie had crushes on probably sell things for a living. But it would be good to have another pact between Ruthie and me. Just one more to set it all straight forever.

I didn't want to leave the pacts. I wanted to fit them in my pocket, for safekeeping. For me to safekeep them or them to safekeep me? I don't know. But I didn't disturb them. After giving each a little pet-pet, I closed the egg carton, put it back in the heating vent, screwed the grate back, and replaced the screwdriver under the typewriter.

Now I close my eyes because Mrs. Gottleib says that we're here in the hospital parking lot.

I tell her just a minute, just a second, okay okay okay?

The hospital is full of rooms where people come and go and come and go and each person who comes and goes is a cavity of heart and lungs and some of them stop working.

Mrs. Gottleib says no. It's my car, Tilton, and I'm kicking you out of it. I'm not going to baby you. You've had enough of that.

She opens the door. Mrs. Gottleib's station wagon has filled me up with its air. I'm light-headed. I tell her that I have breathed car air into my head.

What? I can't hear you through that stupid surgical mask!

I repeat myself loudly.

We're at a hospital, she says, so if that turns into something real, we're at the right place.

Do you think it could turn into something? I ask.

Each of Mrs. Gottleib's pupils is small, like the dot you'd put into an apparatus to look at an eclipse, which can blind you.

Tilton! Out of my car. Shake your can!

I'm scared of Mrs. Gottleib. I'll tell Wee-ette this when I get home. I'm scared of not only her eclipse-apparatus pupils but also her nose, a fleshy crocus bulb; her nostrils, which are large and stiff; her arms that wag when she's agitated; and her growling voice. I decide to shake my can. I slide across the backseat. I put my foot on the cement, which is not at all like that on our back patio. I stand up and the sun is different too.

Mrs. Gottleib slams the door so loudly I think the station wagon might fall to pieces. Come on, Tilton, she says. Let's move.

And so I move. And my breath is caught in the mask like breath in a cupped hand. Like a trapped whisper.

Doors auto-open. We step through. They auto-shut. When I was little there were doors like this at the grocery store that opened when you stepped onto a rectangular rubber mat. These doors don't need mats at all.

The halls are loud. Room after room. Bags hang from metal poles. Tubes. Nurses and doctors. Food on trays. Everything on wheels—like roller skates. Like if the world shifted, everything could roll away.

Mrs. Gottleib holds a grocery bag of my mother's clothes. She talks to a woman behind a desk. The woman says something I can't hear. We move down a hall. Doors open for us and close, with deep sighs, as if they are annoyed by us.

Your mother might be out of it, Mrs. Gottleib tells me. She might say weird things. The drugs can make you loopy. That's how it was with Albert.

Albert is Mr. Gottleib and dead. He died in a hospital, which is where people come to die.

Lord! That's what I say, just like Wee-ette always did when she was annoyed by callers, book talkers, and fan letter writers. Lord, Lord!

We come to my mother's room, 315. I want to tell Mrs. Gottleib that I'm like the American widgeon. A nervous duck, it's always the first to sense trouble and will throw itself into the air, flapping wildly, calling out in alarm. In this way, the American widgeon alerts all the less nervous ducks, who spend their time paddling around, dipping under, and letting their feathers bead. I feel danger inside my ribs.

When we walk inside, my mother is asleep. She's small and tinted a different color, ashy. The room smells like the nurse's station in elementary school, like someone is trying to cover up the smell of barf. Lord, Lord, Lord.

I step closer. Her face is pinched, her eyes closed. Her large head looks small. Her hands are pasty. Tubes are stuck into her and taped down. Her lips are slightly pulled back, revealing a pectinate smile. I touch her skin. It's chilled.

She's dead! I scream. She's dead, Mrs. Gottleib! She's dead!

Mrs. Gottleib grabs my flapping arms. She's not dead! Mrs. Gottleib screams back at me, but it's a hushed scream, which is awful.

Then my mother's eyes flip open like someone turning on a light, and she's not dead. Just like that. Dead, not dead!

Mrs. Gottleib says, Jesus, Tilton! You'll put the whole floor on code blue!

I said not to bring her here! my mother screams at Mrs. Gottleib. Look what you've done. Then my mother says to me, gently, Tilton.

An animal moans on the other side of the curtain in the very same room. Do they let animals in here? I screech.

Tilton, come here, my mother says.

I fall toward her like I am on wheels. I put my head on her chest just like she did before Wee-ette died. Her stomach is fatty but her chest is dainty. I press my ear to it and hear her lungs and heart. Somewhere in there, a soul. That's what Wee-ette called her body: her soul case. Nothing more, she told me. Just a ratty old soul case!

Are you okay? my mother asks.

I am.

Is your thumb okay?

It's okay.

Is Mrs. Gottleib taking care of you?

No.

Mrs. Gottleib isn't taking care of you? You aren't staying with her?

No.

Mrs. Gottleib rolls her eyes. Tilton is twenty-three years old. She doesn't need a sitter.

My mother rubs my arms as if I might have caught a cold while not staying with Mrs. Gottleib. Did you eat?

I had cereal and Tang.

Did you sleep?

I don't tell her I watched television. This would upset her, but I do confess that I took a bath in the bathtub, alone, but I leave out wearing my nightgown while doing it.

Are you sticking to your routine? she asks me.

I fixed Mrs. Devlin's television. I haven't written her daughter a poem for her wedding yet, though.

My mother pulls me close. There's a new ending, my mother tells me. She pets me like a cat—long strokes—an exaggeration of the little pet-pets that I gave the pacts in their carton pockets.

And then I think of the lightning hitting the plane, the hunk of engine hitting the road, dead parts of people, men with torches, and my father—George Tarkington—cupping Marie Cultry's elbow. A new ending?

A nurse in the doorway wants to know if everything is all right.

It's all fine, Mrs. Gottleib says. Just a little panic.

Don't trust Ruthie, my mother whispers to me. The seventh book.

I don't say anything when my mother mentions the seventh book. I made a pact with Wee-ette before her soul case broke. I keep my pacts.

Mrs. Gottleib says, Your mother is agitated, Tilton. She needs to rest.

My mother is highly agitated. Her eyelids flutter as she tries to close them.

Homing pigeons have a complex set of systems, I say. Magnetoception lets them see magnetic fields because of a certain nerve. They smell home, which is called olfactory navigation. They feel temperatures too, and they know the way the sunlight slants a certain way when they're getting close. Sometimes, they fly over roads and follow them home like people. Ruthie is going to find her way home and you will too.

And my mother says, My pigeon, my pigeon, my sweet pigeon.

I say, Come home, come home, come home.

Chapter Nine

EMPTY BOOK

Harriet

I *suppose, looking back, that Dr. Brumus may well have uncov-*
ered my forgery of Eppitt's file and been aware that my file was
missing an important page. But Eppitt was spared, and my file was
never re-created.

I had unrestricted access to Brumus's office after my father's sec-
ond abandonment—at least when Brumus was out, which he often
was. His guilt gnawed at him. I'd catch him looking at me with a
pity so deep it had to come from some loss in his own childhood. I
never knew much about that, but he seemed to carry his own grief
around. When he wearied of one secretary and was about to get an-
other, he looked especially old and deflated. His new secretaries were
a pump, filling him temporarily with air.

I spent most of my time in Brumus's office clipping items from
the newspapers that my father had subscribed to for me. Dr. Bru-
mus, meanwhile, lent me a pair of durable scissors from the sewing
room and a tub of office paste. His office was outfitted with a set of
encyclopedias and a host of medical books. I read everything on ner-
vous conditions—the kind my mother might have—and mutism,
hysteria, bleeding conditions. I concentrated on lungs for Eppitt's
sake, and on other ailments that might afflict the angels airing on
the porches.

I looked into how to prevent pregnancy by investigating prevention's opposite: fertility. Although I had never had sex with Eppitt, we did fool around in our spare moments under the Duck Porch, in the pump house, the empty barn stalls. I needed to know the boundaries. I wanted to have sex one day, but only for the express purpose of having children.

Mostly, however, I loved the newspapers—inky fingers, the tangy scent of paste. If the clippings I chose were your only historical source, you'd think of the world as endlessly odd and perilous. People were killed by random gusts of wind, cyclones of fire, church steeples, Far East fish eggs, and shattered wickets in croquet matches. Locusts fell from the sky and butterflies swarmed the Atlantic. I liked stories of gender confusion. Headlines read, "Violet, the Man in Skirts," "Princess in Pants," and "Lunatic's Career as Duchess." If I'd been a boy, my genius wouldn't have been wasted.

I was interested in what people left behind. Two hundred and forty-four thousand items had been abandoned on New York City transportation: 42,000 umbrellas, 22,000 pairs of gloves, 20,200 handbags, and 12,000 tin hats; gas masks and rifles; plus a dulcimer, a case of beetles, a three-legged chicken, a woman's leg—complete with laced boot and stocking—and, of course, babies. Babies were left in theaters, restaurants, bathroom stalls. Was I trying, with my interest in the left behind, to prove that I was lucky, like Mrs. Funk wanted us to believe?

When I think of my first book, I fall in love with my child self. The book became so full that it sprang open when laid flat—like something that wanted to fly. I told Eppitt about everything I learned, and together we fell more in love with the world out there, as my father had put it. I walked around in a bruised, aching, transcendent state of lovesickness and homesickness.

Even now I remember the story of the Electric Girl, a "highly strung" eighteen-year-old who sent metal tea trays sailing through the air when she walked into a room. That's how I felt when I saw Eppitt and thought of our escape. After clipping an article with the headline "Wolf Woman Shot," I whispered to Eppitt under the Duck Porch that she made me cry—not just because I was Harriet Wolf, good old Hairy Wolf, and felt a kinship. And not just because of her tragic death. But because the shooting in some way must have felt like a relief.

Eppitt understood me. He said, "The Wolf Woman was alone but you're not. We're a family." And when I told him about the locust infestations and butterfly swarms, I worried that we'd get lost and separated from each other, but he said, "I'd come and find you. I'd never give up."

We held each other tightly. It wouldn't last, but there would be another miracle. There are always more miracles.

THE OWL AND THE GOOD WHEEL

This miracle was an accidental gift from Brumus's libido—his cycle of deflation and repumping with new air. None of his secretaries lasted long.

I walked into the office one day, and the Owl was gone. Her chair empty, desk bare.

Days later, there was a new Owl and she needed a new name. When she was with Brumus in the small room with the cot, she was silent. So I called her the Good Wheel. She never squeaked. Her sharp, pensive face was cupped by dark hair. Previously a nurse in the sick wing, she'd been bitten by a child on the meat of her calf and she limped. Human bites can be dangerous, as I knew not only from medical texts but also from the many human bites at the Maryland

School. They festered if not tended. Dr. Brumus looked at the bite himself, probably touching her leg tenderly. This was during the interview process for the Owl's replacement. The Good Wheel got the job because she could prop her leg while doing secretarial work.

This wasn't an easy time for me. True, I had access to encyclopedias, newspapers, the world—and I got out of a lot of labor. But some of the girls of Stump Cottage hated me for having been declared a genius. Susannah Traub rubbed it in, asking, "Hain't your father come to pick you up yet?" She'd been left by a young couple from West Virginia at age eight, which is old enough to remember whether they loved you or not. She pinched my arms, spat in my water glass (she worked in the kitchen), and ratted to the guards that I had gone off with Eppitt. If the tattle made it to Brumus, we were never reprimanded.

She turned the other girls against me. Soon barely a female soul made eye contact with me. We grew to despise one another, but like sisters in some grotesque family. If I saw one of them now, we'd likely hug like two girls trying not to drown.

I missed the Owl terribly. I ran into her as she walked out, fitting a letter of recommendation from Brumus into her purse. She looked at me with pity and swollen pride, as all the nurses did by this point. They muttered, "That one there. A genius. But still here." The Owl pulled me to her bosom, which smelled of sweet talc, and started to cry. "One day, one day," she said. This meant that I would get out, surely. I might even have a normal life—just not yet. I hugged her so long that she had to pry me loose.

The Owl's exit, however, is what brought me my freedom, in a roundabout way.

It was the secretary's duty to notify local parents of the date when we'd celebrate all the birthdays that fell within that month. It was a catchall party, at which "Happy Birthday" was sung once and cacophonously, as each family shouted out its own child's name. I never had a parent present, and so during the clanging singsong of other children's names, Eppitt and I would whisper each other's, as appropriate.

Dear Harr-i-et.

Dear E-ppitt.

This parental notification had always been done by post, but the Owl's departure had been so abrupt that this task popped up unexpectedly for the Good Wheel, forcing her to call those with telephones in their homes rather than sending a letter.

It was July, a full nine months since my picture had been in the paper, which I'm now sure my father had hidden from my mother. The Good Wheel knew that I was allowed into Brumus's office when he was out and that I filled the room with the smell of paste. She didn't know that the only number she should contact for the Wolf family was Mr. Wolf's office number. When there was no answer, she slid her finger to the next number, for my parents' home phone. There was a scribbled note beside the number, indicating that it was to be used only in an extreme emergency, but she missed it. Perhaps her leg bite was throbbing.

I try to imagine the scene that follows from my mother's perspective.

My parents lived in the house I live in now, though it was more hidden by tall trees then and an overgrown hedge that blocked the front bay window. My mother, a near shut-in by this point, preferred the dark confines of her bedroom, as do I. She often mistook the house's creaks and radiator moans for intruders, thieves. She didn't know that her daughter had been stolen, and yet she had a fear of burglars. The house's front and back doors were double-bolted at all times, the windows latched.

The phone rarely rang. But one summer morning before my four-

teenth birthday, the phone sounded out. My mother didn't usually answer. But there it was, so close, so loud and jangling—insistent.

She lifted the receiver to make it stop. And then, a reactive instinct, she said, "Hello?"

The Good Wheel explained that she was phoning from the Maryland School for Feeble Minded Children to see if Mr. and Mrs. Wolf would be attending their daughter's birthday party, a small event that she'd be enjoying with the other children born that month.

"I have no children. Why would you say such a thing? Is this a trick?"

"No, ma'am, it isn't a trick. I work at the school and I have your number on the birthday list. It's printed plainly right here next to your daughter's name: Harriet Wolf, July 11."

Mary Wolf, my sweet mother, let the static fill the phone and then hung up. The phone's ring was now in her head, a frantic echo. She hadn't named me. Someone at the school had been given the duty. But the birth date was undeniably right.

She called her husband at work and he answered—he was back from lunch now. In fact, he'd missed the Good Wheel's call by mere minutes. "Who is Harriet Wolf?" my mother asked him.

My father coughed. "What? Who?"

"Do I have a living daughter at the Maryland School? Do I? Tell me."

He tried to divert her. "Why would you say that? What would possess you?"

She told him breathlessly about the phone, its ringing, how she had answered it and the voice on the other end of the line—what words were spoken.

"It must be a hoax," he said. "The way you're boarded up in that house, you're a target for such awful play."

But she persisted. "Tell me. You must tell me. I'll drive out there myself!"

"You don't drive!"

"I will get in a car and drive there! Tell me what I already know!"

Finally he admitted it. "Yes, darling," he said. "Yes, you do."

She said, "I could feel it!" I imagine that she felt it in her body—like the Electric Girl. A pulse buzzing throughout her chest, her limbs.

Mrs. Funk found me making my bed, tucking the blanket under the mattress with a straight hand. "Dear girl, they're coming for you!"

"Coming for me? Who?"

"Your parents, of course!"

"What do you mean?"

"They're coming now to take you home!"

"I don't understand. My father and my mother?" The idea of seeing my mother was a new thrill. I could barely speak but finally blurted, "Now?"

"They'll be here shortly. In an hour or so!"

It was a Tuesday afternoon. Eppitt would be waiting for me under the Duck Porch after dinner. What if I didn't show up? What if he heard that I was gone? Just like that! Without him!

"I have to tell someone," I said.

"Dr. Brumus knows," Mrs. Funk said. "He and your father are old friends." I knew that they were acquaintances, but old friends? It felt like a betrayal, a collusion.

"No," I said. "I have to find someone else." I walked toward the door. "Excuse me."

"Harriet!" Mrs. Funk said. "Where are you going? You have to pack your things."

I started running then, down the wide set of stairs, through the bare foyer, across the lawn. I knew that Mrs. Funk might be watching me from an upstairs window and I slipped around the far side of the administrative building. Once out of view, I slid along the wall to the edge of the Duck Porch and crawled underneath it.

Eppitt wasn't there. It wasn't our time to meet. Did I expect him to know, deep down, and show up? The ground was damp. It had been raining off and on for a few days.

I was desperately happy—they were coming to bring me home! I was terrified. This was the only place I'd ever known. And I was heartbroken because I'd be leaving Eppitt behind, wouldn't I? I tried to keep my crying quiet, but it was no use. The sobs contracted my ribs and forced loud barks from my throat. I picked up a handful of dirt and put it in my mouth. I tasted it, crunched the grit in my teeth, and bore down on it.

I saw a pair of suede lace-ups, hemmed pant cuffs, a fat hand in the dirt, and then Brumus's face. He squinted into the dark. He saw me there—tear-streaked, snotty, my mouth smeared with dirt. "Jesus, Harriet!" He reached out his hand. "Come on out."

I shook my head.

"Harriet, you've got to get washed up. Your parents are on their way."

I muttered, "Eppitt Clapp."

"What's that?"

I said it again.

"That boy from King's who does the washing?"

I nodded miserably.

"Harriet," he whispered. "I hope you haven't ruined yourself on his account!"

"I want to see him."

"Harriet," Dr. Brumus said. "You're going to live a completely

*different life. A beautiful one. The one you were always meant to
have. There's no place for a boy like Eppitt Clapp in that life. Be
reasonable."*

"I want to see him," I repeated.

"There's no time. Look at you!"

"A note," I said stubbornly, my cheeks still laced with dirt.

"You want to give him a note? He can't read, darling. You know
this." He was speaking to me very sweetly.

"Yes he can. I taught him."

Brumus looked at me doubtfully. "Fine. You can write him a
note. I'll see that Mrs. Funk delivers it."

And then Mrs. Funk's shoes appeared, square-toed, boxy with the
meat of her ankles puffed around the tight lacing.

Brumus shoved his hand at me again. I crawled out on my own.

"Be quick," Brumus said. And Mrs. Funk steered me back to my
cottage with a firm hand on my shoulder.

The cottage was empty. Under Mrs. Funk's watchful eye, I
washed my face in the rusty sink, packed my small bundle of things,
and wrote my note to Eppitt. I couldn't say that I loved him—Mrs.
Funk would surely read the note. And I couldn't call him my husband. That might get him in trouble. I wrote as little as I could. "I
will never be the Wolf Woman," I jotted. "Locusts are falling from
the sky or butterflies are swarming. Find me." I pulled my box out
from under my cot and found the little wound piece of string—our
marriage pact—and wrapped the note in the string. It had the
piece of paper I'd pasted to it: "E. C. and H. W. 1913. Marriage."
I hoped Mrs. Funk wouldn't brood over the word "marriage," and
I hoped he would understand. Keep your promise—that's what I
meant. Keep it.

I handed the note to Mrs. Funk. "Promise you'll give it to
him."

"I promise." She fit it in the wide pocket of her apron. "Little Girl Jesus of the Dreaming Wounds," she said. "I always knew, didn't I?"

She'd discovered me, really. I was hers, in a way. She was mine.

Soon I was standing on the lawn. Children watched from windows. A few had stumbled from the laundry and looked on between sheets. Others had stalled in rows being shuttled one place or another. The groundskeepers; the nurses, including Nurse Oonagh; the Good Wheel; the guards, including Mr. Gillup; and Mrs. Funk—they were all out on the lawn, in loose clumps. Brumus showed up and stood at my side. They were all relieved to be seeing me off. I shamed them because my presence had exposed that it's a cruel twist of fate, whether you're a genius or a moron, to end up where you do in life. My departure helped them believe that the world could work properly.

Where was Eppitt? I stood stiff like a soldier, but pivoted now and then to search for him. I didn't see him anywhere.

A black car chugged up the long drive. A woman stepped out, not waiting for my father to open the door for her.

My mother. She wore a long skirt, a white blouse. Her hair was pinned up, her face pale. She was beautiful, red-lipped. She walked to me with her hands reaching forward, as if trying to catch me before I fell. But I didn't fall. I stood my ground, and she hugged me. "My girl," she said, "my sweet girl!" Her Irish lilt surprised me, as did the whole of her. I was thinking, These are my mother's eyes. These are her hands. This is her mouth, her voice. Right there on the lawn in front of the administration building. *This recognition of the truth—she had loved me all along. It was like I was a bird, wheeling through air.*

My father shook my hand as if we'd never met, as if he'd never given me an empty book.

In my first scrapbook there is only one photograph that wasn't snipped from a newspaper. That photograph was taken by the former nurse, now the secretary, who'd made the error that gave me my freedom. The Good Wheel was an amateur photographer, as it turns out.

The photograph isn't high quality. She positioned the four of us—my parents, me, and Dr. Brumus—so that our backs were to the sun, our faces shadowed. In her nervousness, she jiggled the camera stand while the shutter was opening, just enough to blur us, and a finger, or a bit of hair or ribbon, blots all but our fuzzy, dark faces and our upper bodies, floating. My father had cocked his head, his chin raised. My mother squinted even though the sun was at her back. She was unaccustomed to so much light. I was wide-eyed. Brumus is the only one grinning broadly, his face about to burst with emotion—joy or more simply relief?

After the photograph, Dr. Brumus cupped my face in his hands and kissed my forehead, a benediction. "Go home," he whispered to me. "Thank God and go home."

I climbed in the backseat of the car and looked out the window, searching for Eppitt one more time. There, in a circular six-paned window at the top of King's Cottage, I found him, his face trapped behind the glass.

Eppitt raised a hand.

Would he read the note? Would he keep the pact? Find me.

He waved as if he were on a dock and I on a ship, being cast out to sea. And that's how it felt. This ship would take me back to my motherland.

Chapter Ten

HOME

Ruth

I start to walk to the side door of my grandmother's house, where I lived for the majority of my childhood. It's the door that opens to the kitchen, the door I always used, but too much time has passed. I'm a guest now. I turn halfway up the driveway and take the flagstone path to the front door instead.

It's late afternoon. I stand under the dormer. I see four holes drilled into the brick facade where there was once some kind of placard—a warning to solicitors posted by Eleanor, most likely. Hello, old lion's head knocker. I'm home.

I glance back at the dogs, staring at me from the airport rental car, a Mustang convertible, top down, an upgrade that I flirted for, which is completely unlike me. I felt weirdly single on the flight, maybe the result of the groping I'd gotten in security. I hadn't been felt up so awkwardly and without warning since an eighth-grade dance.

Then there were all those men set loose in the world, their neckties like leashes, as if they'd busted free from their own-ers—suburban power-walking wives. And I was set loose too, carrying two Pomeranians in matching doggy carriers bought earlier that day at PetSmart. The dogs made me feel foreign to myself. What kind of eccentric carries matching Pompoms onto a plane? But I was free from my stifled existence as faculty wife. No one talked to me about my husband's departmental politics or literary theory. I was anonymous, and still vaguely pretty.

The guy at the rental-car desk was a little younger, smiley, with one timid row of tattoos on his pink, nearly hairless forearm—heart, spade, club, diamond—as if he were a poker player. I smiled back and got upgraded all the way to a Mustang convertible. I'd never driven a convertible before. It feels like a ridiculous excess that I should be embarrassed by, but I love seeing it parked in my mother's driveway. I've always rebelled against her frugality, emotional and otherwise.

The Pomeranians are in the passenger seat, paws poised on the open window frame.

I lift the knocker and tap a few times, but no answer.

Up above is my old bedroom window, the one that I climbed out of at sixteen and onto the dormer roof over this very front door, before jumping to the ground, in the dark—me, with my short angry haircut, my eyeliner, Converse high-tops, and backpack. I ran across the lawn and down the street, under one streetlight and then the next, and I never came back.

In five years, Hailey will be sixteen. At winter break, she was almost as tall as I am. Would she ever think of slipping out in the night and running away?

I put my hand on the knob and turn it. To my surprise, it's unlocked. This would never happen under Eleanor's watchful eye—proof that Eleanor is actually in the hospital, a fact that I haven't fully accepted until now.

The front door opens to the living room, with one coat closet tucked under the stairs. I turn directly into the kitchen, the heart of things—oblong Tupperware containers in descending order on the counter, same linoleum smelling of lemons, the toaster oven and the toaster sleeping under its quilted cover, like a birdcage at night.

My grandmother was born here. I know the exact bedroom. It's where she lived out her final years, an agoraphobe. Maybe a pyro. Maybe a little addicted to Valium. Maybe still a genius, a closet writer who'd given up on her audience. They certainly never gave up on her.

For so long, Harriet Wolf was only a name that I dropped, if the company was educated enough. In my personal statement for graduate school applications, I noted that I had grown up with her and that my childhood "was steeped in living, breathing, literary lore." When I arrived at graduate school, I told only one person and let the story circulate. Soon enough, everyone knew. I realized that I'd been drawn to a degree in literature for this sole reason: to get my legacy in front of the right audience. I also thought that I'd have some talent for literature—if not as a writer (I'd tried in my early twenties) then as a critic. That turned out not to be the case.

In the daily life of my childhood, the fact that my grandmother was a writer of note rarely surfaced. There were inquiries, of course—literary events, keynotes, graduation speeches—but my mother shut them down. It came up predictably during parent-teacher conferences. My grades were lackluster across the board. But the English teachers would always comment that my ability with language *was in there somewhere!* What with the family history, how couldn't it be? It was their job to draw it out. I haven't progressed beyond the third chapter of my dissertation on Salinger, another famous shut-in—shut-ins were my territory, after all. The dissertation sits in a cramped box in a closet, which seems to be the perfect treatment of Salinger, to my mind.

But here, now, in the kitchen, I remember my grandmother. Her hair in two strange knot buns, hornish on her head. She terrified me. She was gaunt and brittle but with veins that bulged on her hands like on a weight lifter's. She had a small tongue that popped out to wet her lips, lizard-like. Eventually she cloistered herself on the second floor. Why did Tilton and Eleanor call her Wee-ette? I can't recall; it likely had something to do with her being so shrunken, so *wee*. I recall my mother shoving me toward the shut door of Wee-ette's bedroom, where her mother had given birth to her in some bloody fashion, and where, we all knew but never mentioned, the old woman would one day die. "Amuse her!" Eleanor demanded. The command to smile became one of my greatest pet peeves. Later, it was one of the first things Ron ever said to me: "Why so glum? Smile a little!" I stared blankly and said, "Earn it." Did the world owe me something? Did everyone have to earn my affection? Ron would say it was one of my uglier flaws.

I lift the green wall-hung phone—its ringlet cord still there—and have a momentary urge to call Ron and make him guess what phone I'm calling from. He wouldn't remember our conversation about this phone, of course. If I questioned him about it, he would call it one of my love tests, and he would fail it. "But you set me up to fail," he'd admonish me. "So you win! You're right!"

I'm not ready to talk to Ron anyway, test or no test. I think of my own father. At least he made a clean break of it. He was already a ghost by the time we moved back into this house. Before every divorce, there's a period of reckoning, and I'm in it. My previous divorce was about failure and loss. This one is shaping up to be about the future—loneliness?—and my ability to fend it off or not.

I marvel at the kitchen's pristine, museum-like qualities. If it weren't the real kitchen where I spent the latter half of my childhood, the Post-Abandonment Years, it would pass as an exact replica. Except for some mess—piled dirty dishes, cluttered counters, open cereal boxes. Tilton hasn't been tidying, but still, the care and determination it must have taken to keep it just so! How have the appliances survived? The magnets on the fridge are for plumbers who have to be dead by now.

I'm overwhelmed by the feeling that the house wants to tell me something. *Be present,* I think, having heard this on a self-help tape. But my path has looped back on itself. When you've been enveloped by the past, how do you accomplish presence? Eleanor and that goddamn bedtime story. I can hear my mother's voice in my head: "Once upon a time..."

The shady house looms around me. I remember again, keenly, being in Wee-ette's room, telling her about a way of doing math called chisenbop and the box of SRA cards to help with reading comprehension and how I'd made it all the way to the purple level, which was probably a lie and meant nothing to Wee-ette anyway. When I ran out of things to say, I stood there. The room smelled of death, old newspapers, typewriter ink, burnt paper. One time in particular, Wee-ette wanted to tell me something. She even leaned forward in a way that made me lean forward. I am leaning forward now, out into the stale lemony air of the kitchen.

"Ruthie," a voice says.

And I startle and turn.

It's Tilton.

But Tilton is not an exact replica. She takes my breath. She's grown-up, fuller now. Her hair, still pulled back in barrettes, is only chin length, thicker and stiffer. The coiled curls are gone.

Her face is still dainty. She's wearing pale-pink drawstring sweat-pants with the elastic cut out of the ankles and a plain T-shirt, both of them inside out. Seams have always chafed her, as well as elastic. This small detail brings tears to my eyes. I'm here for Tilton. I'm here to set her free. I left her behind, and now I have to right the wrong.

"Tilton," I say. "It's you!" And I mean that it's not Wee-ette and not the house itself speaking to me. It's Tilton, and this is a relief. I walk to her and touch her hair.

She looks at me and says, "And it's you!"

And for a moment I wonder, *Is it me? And if so, who's that?*

Chapter Eleven

THE WIDGEON

Tilton

Ruthie is here. She touches my hair. I open my arms and wrap her up in them. I say her name again and again. I close my eyes and sway. She's warm but not soft. She's thinner and shorter than I remember her. My cheek rests on a sharp collarbone. She doesn't smell like her Jean Naté after-bath splash, or the baby oil and iodine she used in summer. I imagine that Wee-ette sees us here. Ruthie is the migratory bird. This is the nest that lasted through the long winter. Years of winter.

To describe her, I would say: head and body rather elongated, small bulk; dorsal slightly hunched, as if she's not exactly sure of herself; teeth large, white, but unevenly serrated because she left before she got braces; eyes wide, blue; the tip of her nose compressed and slightly decurved; her hair generally close, rather compact around her face; fringe of bangs sweeping her arched eyebrows. She's still pretty.

I want to show Ruthie everything so she can remember. I think about us winding our clasped hands with kite string in the attic, and I know that she's keeping the pact she made the night she left—to come back and save me.

I don't need saving, I say to Ruthie now.

I know. You can save yourself, Tilton. I've always been the one to believe that.

I think about this, but don't know what it means. Has she only respected half of the pact?

She says that her dogs are in the car. Her voice is flatter than on the phone. She whispers like she doesn't want to wake someone sleeping not far off.

I tell her we don't have a car and our mother is still in the hospital. It's strange to call her *our* mother. She doesn't belong to us. We belong to her. I tell Ruthie what Mrs. Gottleib told me—that *our* mother might come home as early as tomorrow. Tomorrow!

Really? she says. Then she shows me the rental in the driveway.

The driveway is where everyone is last seen. The driveway of our old house is where George put Marie Cultry's suitcase in the trunk and helped her into the passenger seat. This driveway is where I last saw Ruthie. She turned around and looked for me in the window. She waved and I waved back. And then my mother called my name and I dipped away from the window. I knew that Ruthie was coming back. I just didn't know it would be so long. Welcome home, homing pigeon.

I pick up the hem of the kitchen curtains, which are lacy, and I see a lidless red car with two white dogs. I tell Ruthie I'm allergic to dogs.

Mom made that up, Ruthie says. She wanted Dad to get rid of that stupid Labrador.

Our mother wouldn't lie about allergies, I tell Ruthie. Allergies are serious, and I don't remember a Labrador.

You were little.

I remember a lot of things from when I was little. Mother says it's preternatural.

Fine, Ruthie says. She walks through the kitchen and peers into the living room. Brown shag, she says. It's an ancient artifact! It's like it was inspired by Burt Reynolds's chest pelt. Do you remember Eleanor going to Burt Reynolds movies? The ones where he drove a truck? *Smokey and the Bandit*?

Our mother doesn't like movies or TV, I remind Ruthie.

She used to like Burt Reynolds movies, Ruthie says, and she knocks on the wooden doorframe like she's here to test the house somehow.

We already had termites once, I tell her. Some of the wood beams went airy.

So what's up with the TV, then?

I tell Ruthie that I'm repairing the TV for Mrs. Devlin. I don't tell her that earlier there was a show about lawyers and murderers. My mother warned me about TVs. Hypnotic, she calls them.

I went to school with Mrs. Devlin's daughter, Ruthie tells me. She was a pothead who wore fringed moccasins. That TV must weigh a hundred pounds.

It almost killed her.

The TV almost killed Mrs. Devlin?

Our mother. This TV almost killed her.

Really?

I want Ruthie to be happy that she's back in the nest. There are many kinds of nests—scrapes, mounds, burrows, cavities, cups, saucers, plates, platforms, pendants, and spheres. It makes sense to be happy to return to the nest you first knew. But if you were, you wouldn't call it a chest pelt.

Ruthie may no longer feel like a native species here. Invasive species like the mute swan have a very negative effect on the ecosystem. Mute swans were brought over as decorations from

Europe and Asia in the 1870s. But some escaped in New Jersey and then New York and then all over. And they invaded the Chesapeake Bay. They eat the native species' food and take over their nesting grounds. They thrive because they don't face the natural ecological controls, such as predators and disease, which develop alongside a species in its native environment. Nature has checks and balances, but when species move from one place to another—not just in migratory patterns—it's all messed up.

Mute swans smelled foreign too, I bet, when they first arrived.

I look at Ruthie and I tell her that mute swans are not really mute. They grunt, snort, hiss, and whistle roughly. And their wings are noisy. You can hear them a mile away, throbbing in flight.

That's beautiful, Ruthie tells me. I forgot the way you come out with things like that.

I don't make them up.

I know. It's how you say them, though, and when you choose to say them.

I don't choose to say them. It's like the words are in the air and they choose me to say them.

Jesus, Ruthie says, and she smiles and shakes her hair.

The words could choose you, I tell her.

But they don't, Ruthie says. I should go get the dogs. She pinches her nose, which is what my mother does when she's crying. And I know that Ruthie isn't an invasive species.

I'll make Tang, I tell her.

Does anyone still drink that? Ruthie asks.

Astronauts. And us.

Ruthie and I walk back to the kitchen. She leaves through the side door.

I make the Tang—clang, clang, clang—as well as I can. I close my eyes and tell Wee-ette that I can feel the new ending too, but I don't know what it is. For now, we're in the middle.

When Ruthie comes back, she lets the dogs loose. Their floating dander makes my heart edgy. But I sip Tang and give Ruthie a tour of the rest of the house.

The dining room, which we don't use, has four chairs and a table with the leaves folded down. She asks where the long white tablecloth with yellow flowers is. She says, I lived under the dining room table with a tablecloth over it for a couple of weeks. You were too little to remember. I loved that tablecloth.

I tell her that it's probably folded and stuffed in the bottom of one of the corner hutches.

Then the downstairs bathroom. I got my period here, she says.

As we pass through the living room again, she says, This room could inspire a double homicide. A suicide pact. It's that grim.

But it's not, I tell her.

But it is, she says.

The dogs pad around after us, like they've imprinted on us. The stairs whine a little. The dogs pad, pad.

The upstairs bathroom. She says, I cried in here a lot.

My mother's bedroom, which was hers even back in my mother's childhood. Ruthie says, I remember that smell. What is that smell?

I don't smell any smell.

That's because you're used to it.

Then there's Wee-ette's bedroom—dark, the way she liked it. Ruthie walks to the curtains, which are thick and heavy, a red brocade so long that the hems rest on the floor. They're drawn tight. Wee-ette liked to keep the sun out, Ruthie says, and peeks out at the yard. She walks to Wee-ette's high bed, and then to Wee-ette's little writing desk and the typewriter. She touches the ribbon and says, It's dry.

I ask her if she expected it to be wet and she says she doesn't know.

I want to show Ruthie all of our pieces of wound string, our pacts, hidden in the heating vent. But she says, My husband writes about Harriet Wolf. My soon to be ex-husband, I think.

Ron, I say. He writes about Wee-ette? Why?

He's a scholar. She published during the era he covers.

I'm not sure what to say because my mother hates Wee-ette scholars. Ruthie married the enemy. I ask her if he's cruel. Is he a bad person or good?

She looks at me, startled. Honestly, she says, I don't know if he's good. Deep down. Then she gives a puff of air. Huh! It seems like you should know this about your husband. Is he good—yes or no? It's the most basic question in the world. Never dawned on me!

She walks out of the room quickly, like it's grown cold, her arms tucked to her chest.

Then there's Ruthie's old bedroom. I tell her it's the guest bedroom now.

Do you get many guests? she asks.

I tell her no. We don't ever. It's also the sewing room, I tell her. There's a sewing machine in the corner, a sewing box, and stacks of fabric. There's also a stack of *National Geographic*s and boxes. She touches the boxes, which are labeled: Tilton Grades 1–5, Tilton Grade 6, Tilton Homeschool Grades 7–12. Tilton College.

Ruthie asks me if Eleanor tried to homeschool me on the college level.

I tell her that I did very well. I say, You'd be surprised how high-achieving I am on the bubble test.

The SATs?

Yes.

Where do you go to take them?

I got a home version.

So this is my box, she says, looking at the box marked Ruthie—Random.

Do you want to open it? I ask.

Like I want to see the contents of my entire childhood confined to one lousy box.

You left us, I tell her.

But I existed before I left, didn't I?

Do you want to sleep here? I ask, gesturing toward the small bed. You're not a guest, though, I tell her. You're family. This is your room again.

Sure, Ruthie says, but it's a sad and demented house.

Don't say that!

She apologizes and we walk into my room, full of bird books and manuals on how to fix common household items. As in Wee-ette's room, a typewriter sits on a little desk. This is where I write poems for people's special occasions, I tell Ruthie. I sleep in a canopy bed. I keep a journal. I point to it on my pillow. I paint birds too, like Audubon, but not as good.

Ruthie reaches between two of my paintings on the wall and lays her hand flat against the wallpaper—bicentennial, with little soldiers with guns, and eagles and stars. I remember this wallpaper. It's burned into my head, she says. Maybe I'll stay at a hotel, she adds.

I sit on the bed, and then let myself fall to the floor, cross-legged. The white dogs think I have come here, to their level, so we can sniff each other. But I haven't. Don't, I say to Ruthie. I want you to stay here.

She walks to me and sits on the edge of the bed and slides to the floor just like I did. Tilton, she says, this whole trip is even heavier than I thought it would be.

I tell Ruthie she used to be taller.

No, she says, you used to be shorter. And then she tells me that the world out there has changed. There are ways to help people who are different. There are ways to help people with fears and conditions.

That's very good, I say.

I mean, there are conditions that some people have that aren't bad at all, and they can get help. Therapies.

Are you okay? I ask her. Are you one of these people?

No, she says. Not me. And she stares at me, sad in her eyes.

I want her to cheer up, so I tell her that I can feel the new ending.

The ending to what?

The bedtime story.

She says, Jesus, Lord. I hated that bedtime story. She doesn't still tell it?

Of course she still tells it! I say. It's our story! And then, for no reason I can name, the new ending appears in my head.

Tilty? she says. Probably she can tell that some change has come over me—the American widgeon sensing something that no one else senses yet.

We're going to be a family again, I tell her. All four of us. A mother, a father, and two children, as it should be. Plus a grand-mother ghost.

Her lips form an O. You really would want that? she asks. Eleanor and George Tarkington? They're strangers now. And I am too, I guess.

I rest my head on her shoulder. It's the new ending, I tell her. It doesn't matter if we want it or not.

She pats my hair and she tells me to hush. We can't know the future, she says.

I tell her that I can because I'm like a widgeon. And I pet one of the dogs on its fluffed head, just like Ruthie was patting me, and I tell her, I don't think I'm allergic to this kind of dog!

LORDY, LORDY

And then, right around dinnertime, Mrs. Gottleib arrives with a foil-wrapped spaghetti casserole. She talks to Ruthie, a little breathlessly, like Ruthie's a movie star. She asks her where Ruthie's been all these years. She says that Ruthie sure has traveled, sure has lived an exciting life, sure has learned a lot, and sure has pretty dogs. And she goes on telling about Albert's death, and I should feel sad all over again. But I don't. Albert had a bug up his tush, permanently, and, as my mother says, there are worse things than your husband leaving you, and that's called Albert Gottleib staying with you.

Mrs. Gottleib says my mother is being released tomorrow morning at eleven, and insists on bringing her home. That way, she says, you'll have time to get the house in order.

I see the mess now. The plastic milk jug has swelled a little from having sat out in the warm air. The cabinet doors yawn into the kitchen. The cereal bowls have piled up. The butter is a slick shiny blob in its dish.

Ruthie says, No, no, Mrs. Gottleib. You've done enough.

I don't mind! Mrs. Gottleib says. And there's absolutely no need for Tilton to walk into that hospital again. Then she whispers to Ruthie that I got wound up last time.

But finally Ruthie gets her to leave. When Mrs. Gottleib is gone, Ruthie brings out a bottle of wine from an oversized canvas bag. She asks me if I want some.

No thank you.

But you're over twenty-one, Tilton.

I say, Okay okay okay.

Ruthie has done so many things in her life, and I wouldn't mind being a little bit more like Ruthie and a little bit less like myself all the time. No offense to me.

Ruthie pours wine into two juice glasses. We sip. The wine is not sweet, but it takes up more space in my mouth than a normal drink. I swish it because it seems like it could clean a mouth. The dogs have plopped onto the linoleum.

How's Hailey? I ask. I've never told my mother, but I think of Hailey a lot. I think, What does she look like now? What does she love?

She's good, Ruthie says. I think. I see her in August. She lives with her dad, you know.

In Tucson, I say. I want to meet her.

One day, Ruthie says, but she says it like a wish, not a promise.

I have to get the television back to Mrs. Devlin. I fixed it for her.

Who gets TVs repaired anymore? Everyone just goes out and gets a new one.

A lot of people get things repaired, I tell her. Toaster ovens, hand beaters, mixers, and record players. I swirl my wine, take another sip, and it's not as good as cough syrup. I tell her, Eleanor brings them home. I fix them and get paid by my clients.

You ever see these clients?

I never see people, really. You know that, what with my weakened immune system.

Do you really think you have a weakened immune system? I mean, do you get sick a lot?

No, but it's because we take a lot of precautions.

Right, Ruthie says. Eleanor. She's staunch about precautions.

I tell Ruthie that we have to watch out for vultures, that they could come looking for the seventh book at any moment.

Ruthie sits at the kitchen table, leans forward with her wine cupped in her hands, and says, while squinting, Do you think she really did write it? Did she write it and burn it like Eleanor says?

Don't ever tell anyone that. You know not to. This is one of the pacts. It's a pact between me and Eleanor and you.

She shakes her head. I haven't told anyone, but only because I don't buy it, Ruthie says. I think she did write it, and I think it's in this house and it's worth millions.

It's important to keep our pacts, I tell Ruthie.

Like the one where Eleanor told us never to go looking for our father? I already broke it.

You know where he is? But you haven't gone to get him?

Ruthie shakes her head.

Why not?

The question isn't why not. It's why.

George! Lordy, Lordy, I say. Where does he live?

In Pennsylvania. Mushroom country. Just over the line—if he didn't move, that is. I could take you.

Ruthie grabs the bottle of wine and pours herself another glass. I sip my same one. She leans forward. Have you ever been in love? she asks.

I shake my head and shrug. I've loved people from a distance, I tell Ruthie. It's easier.

That's called a crush, Ruthie says. Do you have a crush on someone?

I deny it, but then there's warmth in my chest and my face feels sweaty. And I say that I kind of like the Eldermans' youngest son.

Across the street? Benny Elderman?

He lost his job.

Someone once hired him?

Stop it.

Sorry. I'm glad you kind of like Benny Elderman. I remember him being a little pretentious as a kid.

He wore fedoras.

He did! I remember that now. See, but Benny Elderman could pull off a fedora at nine years old. He had that mojo.

He jogs now.

That's great.

Have you been in love twice, once with each husband?

I don't know. I've either been in love a dozen times or never. I can't tell.

You're strange.

And so are you.

Chapter Twelve

OTA BENGA, THE ELECTRIC GIRL, THE WOLF WOMAN

Harriet

*N*o one is ever suspicious of a happy childhood—though everyone should be. But then, what writer would admit to one? My publisher got wind of a rumor once that mentioned some institutionalization. He actually wanted to use the information to bolster sales. An unstable writer holds some cachet. I apologized to him. "Sorry, but alas, my life has been quite dull." As for those fellow inmates and guards who could have uttered the truth, God bless them: they didn't. Once upon a time, privacy was valued. For goodness' sake, a disabled president of the United States could ask that the press not photograph him in a wheelchair or being transferred to his car or generally in a weakened state, and the press would oblige. Those were the days.

The sum portrait I rendered of my childhood was the four years I spent with my mother in this house—this very house!—extended. It's what I talked about with readers, as well as with Eleanor and the girls. Who can blame me? These were the years I wanted to remember.

Plus Eppitt. Always Eppitt.

But he couldn't exist in this portrait. It wasn't possible. For the purposes of a pristine youth, I fixed on my mother. When I think of her now, I know the feel of her skin, the arrangement of her small bright teeth, the smell of her hair. Our love for each other was condensed, therefore more richly palpable. We were each other's figments made real.

In the months after the discovery that my father had stolen me from her, alive after all—and a girl genius to boot—the power shifted. If my father mentioned something that he'd read in the morning paper—the Great War was broiling overseas—my mother could say, "That sounds a bit off. Are you sure you read that correctly, or is it possible you've made some mistake?"

My mother swelled with confidence. When she refused to allow me to go off to school—"She's had enough time away from us, don't you think?"—my father conceded immediately.

She broke from her hermit's existence and strolled with me on her arm around town. She pointed out hemlock, spruces, finches, and goldenrod. She allowed me to study whatever I wanted. I collected butterflies, toads, moles, various insects in boxes and glass jars with perforated lids. I examined them for hours on end.

In summers, the sunporch became a biologist's study. The walls were covered with corkboards for my notations. At the start of the winters, I moved everything to my bedroom.

She looked for opportunities to run into neighbors and acquaintances (she had no real friends), to introduce me as her daughter, Harriet. "She was sickly," she'd tell them. "We thought we'd lost her. But here she is! The Lord had mercy!"

I stood there, beaming. My mother, pink with sun, bloomed like a fat bud in a hothouse. She was so charged, so happy, so brimming, she gave off a radiant steam—it reminded me of the laundry. I'll always associate steam with love.

Over these teen years, when most girls turn away from their mothers, I fell in love with mine. She took me into Baltimore, where we went to the movies, watching Fatty Arbuckle and Lillian Gish.

On our birthdays, we lunched at the Swinging Lantern, a Chinese restaurant run by Mr. and Mrs. Ling. It had an indoor fishpond of bloated koi. We folded origami cranes, a new fad.

She took me to church, regularly. I'd been baptized at the Maryland School for Feeble Minded Children—we were morons, not heathens. But my mother made sure that I took First Holy Communion, wearing a veil with a headpiece of chilled flowers. I loved the incubated feeling of the confessional. I confessed rapturously to sins I'd never committed and prayed with my hands wrapped in rosary beads. I went through confirmation as well, choosing Saint Therese the Little Flower—as most girls did—for my namesake. Other girls loved her abject humility, scrubbing floors with tubercular fervor. I loved that she coughed blood into a hankie. I was still a bleeder too.

My mother told me about her own childhood in Dún Laoghaire, a port town outside Dublin. She talked about Killiney Hill, where you can see mountains, sea, and city. The Irish knew suffering, but she said it made their sense of joy keener. She loved me more for having lost me.

Although I was supremely happy, I was still lovesick. I missed Eppitt. I missed being my husband's Wolf Woman. While my father slept in my parents' bedroom alone, I slept beside my mother, pining sometimes for the steamy laundry, its washboards and wringers. I missed seeing Eppitt through the strung-up sheets and our time at home under the Duck Porch—Eppitt's body pressed to mine.

But Brumus's words stuck with me. "A boy like Eppitt Clapp"—there was no place for him in my new beautiful life. I was consumed by my mother's love. If I asked to have Eppitt here with us, would she say no? Would this cause a fissure between us? If she said yes, how could I love them both at the same time? Surely my heart would burst. I had my mother back. This had to be enough.

I was her infant and I loved it. She combed my hair, wrung warm sponges over my back, and peeled my pears. My greatest fear was losing her again.

My desire to keep love—to hold on to it—grew stronger and manifested itself in a desire to keep track of the world. My mother doubled my subscriptions, gave me ivory-handled scissors that narrowed to the long pointed beak of a bird, and bought me a tub of paste with a wire brush connected to its lid. I began a ritual of sniffing the paste before I started. The newsprint smelled good too and blackened my fingertips, tacky with the glue that hardened beneath my nails.

As time passed, some of my clippings stated the obvious: the Lusitania *sank in fifteen minutes; the Panama Canal was finished, although six thousand workers had died in the process; Ambrose Bierce went down to Chihuahua to see the Mexican Revolution and was never heard from again; Mary Richardson, the suffragette, slashed* The Rokeby Venus *in the National Gallery in London; Typhoid Mary was a new form of killer; someone invented the light switch.*

But I was most fascinated by Ota Benga, a Congolese pygmy who'd been on a hunting trip when his wife and two children were murdered by Belgium's Force Publique during its exploitation of rubber in the Congo. An American named Verner traded Ota for a pound of salt and a bolt of cloth and picked up an assortment of pygmies for exhibition at the Saint Louis World's Fair. Ota later lived at the Bronx Zoo, posing with the patrons, and then in the zoo's Monkey House as part of an evolution exhibit. Following public outcry over the injustice of a human zoo exhibit, Ota was released to the Howard Colored Orphan Asylum, even though he was in his twenties.

This terrified me—the idea that you could be sent back.

Eventually they sent him on to Lynchburg, Virginia, where they dressed him in ordinary clothes and capped his teeth, which had been filed to points in childhood. Anne Spencer—the poet who wrote in her poem about the diving-tank girl "Guilt pins a fig-leaf; Innocence is its own adorning"—taught him to read and write. Then, in 1916—when I was sixteen—Ota Benga stole a shotgun and killed himself.

Was I Ota Benga in my family's home, free to walk the grounds as a human exhibit, the Found Child? Was I doomed, as he was, to shoot myself in the heart?

By this point, the assassination of Archduke Ferdinand had marked the beginning of the Great War. One of the seven would-be assassins struck a bomb against a lamppost to set its timing mechanism, and the owner of the car transporting the archduke and his wife thought the clang was a flat tire. A count who was riding with them said, "Bravo. Now we'll have to stop." But then the driver saw the black object hurtling at him and stepped on the gas. It was an open car. As the archduke covered his face, the bomb bounced off his arm, off the folded-down car top, and rolled into the crowd. The bomber swallowed his cyanide pill and jumped into the river. Long outdated, the pill only made him throw up. And due to a lack of rain, the river was only a few inches deep anyway. The other gunmen dispersed. Princip, the young, tubercular assassin, walked across the Appel Quay to Moritz Schiller's delicatessen. The motorcade took a wrong turn and backed up five feet from Princip. He pulled a gun from his coat and fired.

When I talked to my mother about the assassinations (an obsession of mine), I wanted to discuss the ending. I feared that one was coming. "It could have been avoided," I said. "The whole thing. But they died—the archduke and his wife."

"I know," my mother said.

The archduke didn't usually let his wife ride in the car with him because she wasn't real royalty like he was. But it was their anniversary. He was shot in the throat, and she in the stomach.

Sometimes I imagined that my father was the archduke. Now, in my teen years, I could still barely look at him. I shrank when he walked into a room. He worked late and began to allow office hours on Saturdays and Sundays. He was no longer needed at home to tend to his ailing wife. But when he did appear, he still seemed to expect hoopla, as if he were in a parade. He'd tour around the house in a grand motorcade of his own defensive pride.

I wanted to shoot him.

Some nights I heard them argue. My father suggested marriage. "She's of age."

"She's a genius. She could go on to study."

"Do you really think she'd fit in?"

"She can stay here, then."

"One day, she'll have to go somewhere!" There was a sharp nasal ring to his voice. I had no desire to be someone's wife. I was Eppitt's wife. I didn't want to go to college, genius or not. I didn't want to leave my mother, and also, Eppitt would find me one day. For now, I'd stay by my mother's side.

My mother would counter, calmly, "Will she have to go somewhere one day? Is that a fact? Are you sure, darling? Perhaps we should leave these familial decisions up to me. I may be better suited to make them."

Despite a small cough that had been developing, my mother was a great force, as mighty as a steamship. She was an entire fleet.

My father was a weakened enemy—like Archduke Ferdinand, a cocky fop, an easy target in his tall hat and open-air motorcar. Lying in bed, I dreamed of shooting him outside Moritz Schiller's. I'd hold my hand out, gun-shaped, and my hands would shake—the *archduke was always too close to his wife. I'd put my pretend gun back into my pretend coat.*

As soon as I closed my eyes, my skull lit up like a bright globe. The theater in my brain ran the reel of all that I'd left. Part of me forever belonged at the Maryland School for Feeble Minded Children, not here. Eppitt, Funk, Brumus, the Owl, the Good Wheel, Gillup, Oonagh . . . This life that I was in now was undeserved, unearned. Others weren't so lucky. I escaped by dumb luck. Sometimes I ran while lying in bed, my legs scissoring away from the past, but when I was most anxious, I lay completely still. I didn't dare bleed into my pillow for four years, not a single drop.

"STERBE NICHT!"

I've set out to tell everything—without interruption of the fubbery from my absurd mind. Still, I don't want to revisit what happens next. I don't want to bear it to the surface. I've lived with this weighty stone all these years, and the burden is its own comfort.

Just now, I walked to the bedroom window and saw Tilton and Ruthie outside after a heavy rain, wearing slickers and rain boots. Ruthie had turned her bicycle upside down and was rotating the pedals like she was working a machine. Tilton was washing worms in a cup. Two clear plastic kiddie-sized umbrellas, abandoned in the yard, swayed like big airy teacups in the breeze.

Eleanor bustled out, a jacket over her head although it wasn't raining anymore. "Out of the rain!" she cried. "Do you want to catch your death?"

Ruthie said, "Maybe I do!"

And Tilton started crying. "We're helping worms!"

Eleanor shouted some more, hustling the girls into the house, protecting them from... what? Imaginary rain? Worms?

I'm guilty of worse, Eleanor. In the name of protecting you from the world's unwieldy workings, I protected you from the truth.

Here's one that I couldn't utter, even now: my mother's death.

When our newly hired nursemaid, Lila, told my father that my mother had gotten worse, he punched the lowboy, nicking it with his ring, and then called Dr. Brumus.

Eppitt had once shown me how to drop a bead of water into a nick in wood, cover it with a washcloth, and pass over it with an iron, borrowed from the girls' sewing room. The wood swelled to fill the dent. That's what I was doing when Brumus found me.

"Harriet," he said. "My God, I barely recognize you." He looked at me the way he'd once looked at the Owl and the Good Wheel. Despite a narrow frame, I now had breasts and hips. Lila had gone home. I didn't know where my father was. Suddenly it was just the two of us again—Brumus and me.

"I'm eighteen now," I said.

"I see that," he said.

I went back to ironing. The iron steamed the cool air. It was early autumn. "How's my mother?"

He explained Spanish flu but I already knew about the early deaths related to it, the suspected points of origin, the effects on the war efforts. Some schools had closed. Movie theaters were aired out between shows. Hotels had been transformed into hospitals to handle the overflow. Weddings and funerals had to be small, private affairs. A woman wanted a marching band to play at her husband's funeral; they had to play on the parlor lawn. A clairvoyant was arrested for holding a séance, a pool hall owner for having too many people at a card game. Bankers wore masks behind their grillwork. Department stores weren't allowed to hold sales that would create a storm of business.

Brumus touched my arm lightly—as lightly as he may have once fondled the Good Wheel's bitten leg. "She might make it. Some do."

"Can't you do anything?"

"I'm afraid not. It's a difficult death. There may be a lot of bleeding." *And then he pulled his arm back, remembering, perhaps, that he was speaking to the Bleeder of Stump Cottage.*

"Did you know that the Lings' niece died?" *I told him.* "She drowned. She was four years old." *My clipping read* "Girl Dies in Chinese Fishpond." *I meant that there's death all around us, always.*

"I hadn't heard."

"You should read the papers."

"Stay on the first floor to keep clear of the contagion," *he said.* "You could set up a cot on the sunporch."

I hated cots. I'd grown up on cots, rows of them.

"Have you been happy?" *he said.*

I nodded.

"And you will be again one day."

He said his good-byes, and I didn't move. I stood there listening to him hammer a quarantine placard to the front of the house.

I slept on a narrow cot with weak springs and a mattress that smelled of mildew. They didn't allow me upstairs. I stayed out of the nursemaid's way. Lila was stout and proper, loudly bustling in the kitchen. I read my newspapers, clipped, pasted, and tended my menagerie, which stayed downstairs. I stole thread, upholstery-strength, from my mother's sewing basket. A pact. We needed a pact.

One night, I sneaked into my mother's room, the thread in my pocket. She looked thin, her cheeks streaked red. I pressed a cold rag to her head and feet. I tried to tell her the story of the assassination, something familiar.

I whispered, "Sterbe nicht!" *—what Ferdinand had said to So-*

phie after they'd been shot. "Don't die!" But I didn't want to be Ferdinand. My father played that part. His snoring from the other bedroom sounded like a parade of motorcars. I told her, "I'm married. I have a husband I love. Eppitt Clapp. One day I'll see him again."

And then her eyelids opened. Her watery, jittery eyes bobbed over her cheeks.

I took the thread from my pocket. I pressed her hand against mine and bound them, loosely. But what was our pact? I wound and wound, and finally I put my mouth close to her ear. "Let's never separate again," I whispered. "Promise me that."

She smiled. "Mháthair," she said, speaking in Gaelic, mistaking me for her mother. "Mhamai." She closed her eyes and they flitted under her lids.

I slipped the string from our hands and went back to the porch. I taped the string and wrote on the tape, just as I had after my marriage to Eppitt. I wrote "H. W. and M. W. Never separate. October 1918."

After that I could do nothing but wait for my father to walk downstairs one morning and tell me she had passed.

Finally he did.

I asked him where she'd passed to, willfully, but he didn't say another word.

And then I couldn't control the swell of blood in my nose, the outpouring. I couldn't stop screaming at the sight of so much blood. I swung my body around the room. A high-pitched scream, a caterwaul from my mouth. My father grabbed me by the arms and shook me. He struck me and blood sprayed on the white porch walls, on my corkboards of butterflies, boxes, and jars. When he let go, I sank to the ground but kept screeching, rocking, and bleeding, until my father bundled me again and took me away.

SHEPPARD AND ENOCH PRATT HOSPITAL

In some ways, he took me home. I'd been raised in an institution. I was returned to one as an adult, like Ota Benga.

I was a blood-drenched young woman. My voice too raw to shriek, I could only mutter, "Ota Benga, Ota Benga…"

My father jogged to the main building. It was a cool night. My breath on the automobile's window. I watched him go. He was bloody too, like a madman himself, shirt untucked, jacket flapping.

I lay on the seat of the car. Ota Benga, Ota Benga… Time frittered. Time was nothing. Time was a bridegroom who had abandoned me, a lake to swallow me whole; all around me I could feel pulsing gills like seconds ticking away. I had my mother's pact in my skirt pocket. It was already broken. What good was it? I wanted the wound string of my marriage pact with Eppitt to keep me safe, but it was gone. Eppitt had it.

Did he ever think of me?

Through the window, I saw a nurse with a serene face. What did I look like to her? I'd stopped bleeding but my face was smeared with blood, now taut as dried mud. When my father opened the door, I sat there, unmoving.

"Harriet," he said, "behave now. Don't be a savage."

A savage. Ota Benga.

He pulled me from the car. I hated him. He was the assassin. My mother and I—we were the archduke and his wife.

I dropped to the ground and kicked his shins. I'd lost my shoes. He grabbed my thin wrists and tried to yank me to my feet. The nurse took over. She had a hold—tough and sure. She used her weight as power, locked my arms, pulled me to my feet. Oxlike and meaty, she held me to her ribs in a way that was both paralyzing and comforting. I wanted to be overtaken.

The nurse spoke gently. "Cribbage," she told me. "There will be cribbage."

The entranceway terrified me—its wide expanse. Its carpet and cane chairs.

She led me away from my father, down the hall. A doctor's office. She was saying "anthropometric measurements." And "The doctor on duty is very good." Were there evil ones? I was shown a room, a small bed. I put my fists to my eyes and pounded my face.

Straps—like those used on seizing children at the Maryland School. I was stretched flat, a wild, bloody animal strapped down. My skirt with the pact was taken. I stared at the ceiling, high and white, at its crown molding, and started to cry again, tears running into my hair.

Somewhere else they were questioning my father, learning that I was a moron, I suffered hysterical bleeding, outbursts, mutism.

My mother was dead. Eppitt was lost. I was alone, a Wolf Woman.

A nurse monitored my blood pressure. Her lips pursed as she counted my pulse. I tried to claw her, but the straps held me back.

There was hydrotherapy. Stripped down, they set me in front of four nozzles and opened them up. I fought the water but it beat me down. There was one high square window—dark. The white-tiled room echoed. I became small and wet and clean.

There was a lumbar puncture. The nurse said, "This is for your own well-being. There can be too much fluid, too much pressure." Another nurse assisted a doctor, giving me salvarsan. "Steady...Steady..." she said, lifting the tube.

Next, a wet sheet pack. "For relief," the nurse said, and she wrapped me like an Egyptian.

I wasn't a curiosity. I was a mummy. Ota Benga. Wolf Woman. I was dead.

Chapter Thirteen

VITALS

Eleanor

From my hospital bed, I see distant parking lot lights through the window on the far side of my room. Out there, people are living their lives. Tomorrow morning, I will be among them again, going home.

I sigh. It's a gusty sigh. A sigh meant to be overheard. The kind meant to elicit "What's wrong?" There was a time when I could sigh in such a way to get George's attention. But looking back, I can admit that it was a tiny blip.

After George left with Marie Cultry, he wanted to stay, as he put it, "in the mix." I wasn't good at *mixes*. I didn't want a life that was a *mix*. I wouldn't have known what to do with Marie Cultry, other girlfriends, wives, or George with new children, babies in bundles. If George wanted out, that was final.

After our divorce was settled and I had full custody, he got a new lawyer. I prepared for battle. But then, for reasons I'll never know, he gave up. He sent his monthly checks, folded in a plain white sheet of paper stuffed into an envelope, without comment. When Tilton turned eighteen, the checks stopped. That was that.

Except I did see George once. I swear. It was winter. He was coatless, wearing only a jogging suit and wrestling a For Sale sign from someone's frozen front yard. This was a few neighbor-hoods away, so at first I didn't believe that it could be George. Even though we'd never officially drawn up boundary lines, his presence constituted an infiltration. This happened a year af-ter Tilton turned eighteen, back when I still had the Impala. I stopped at a stop sign and watched him in the rearview mirror, my blinker clicking. He had a belly and a closely shorn head of dark hair. Was this George? Surely he had dyed his hair, a fussy vanity that I refused myself. Hair should age to match the face; otherwise it's disconcerting. People know, deep down, when a forgery's going on. And his jogging suit in contrast with his ro-tund belly seemed to expose deeper lies. He was agitated in a way that was undeniably George. If I'd had any doubts about his identity, that impatience cinched it. He'd been impatient in bed too. Idling at the stop sign, I found myself imagining—ever so briefly—the two of us in bed, the arrhythmic squeaking of bed-springs, the awkward tugging, so like George with his stubborn For Sale sign.

I was struck by the instinct to park, walk up to him, and tell him it was all an accident—that lightning hitting the plane—and a fluke that we were out on the roads that night. If not for it, we could have survived. I wouldn't suggest giving it another try. No, no, no. At my age? With my own utter lack of patience? Heaven knows that would have been a disaster. I sim-ply wanted him to confirm or deny.

I imagined myself standing there in my wool coat, arms crossed, saying, "Confirm or deny, George. Confirm or deny." He would know what it meant. If not for the accident, if not for Marie Cultry's husband being on *that* plane, our marriage would have survived. Confirm or deny, George!

When he looked up, breathless, the sign finally dislodged

from the frosty ground and secured under his arm, he seemed to notice the idling car. He squinted, his breath chugging into the cold air—again, the idea of sex, his breathlessness. I took the turn and drove away.

His presence palsied me for days. I wanted him to try to claim me. I wanted the opportunity, once and for all, to tell him it was over. But of course it was long over.

For the next few months, I kept an eye out for him, as if he had the ability to appear anywhere. Months passed, then years, and I stopped. In fact, I began to doubt that I'd ever seen him with that For Sale sign. The world was full of men like George, liars with dyed hair and fat bellies stuffed into jogging suits.

A nurse walks in, here to check my vitals again. She flips on the light and pulls the curtain, the same sound as George pulling his shirts across the bar in the closet, a loud *scritch* and then each shirt at a time—*scritch, scritch, scritch*—until he picked one. I remember, too, the sound of a curtain in a confessional. My mother took me to confession once—*scritch*. She disappeared into it and came out changed.

Why must one thing lead to another and another? My weakened constitution allows my mind to go reeling. Heart or mind? I'd like to ask my own body. Heart or mind? Pick one.

Confirm or deny. Just like that. Confirm or deny.

Chapter Fourteen

PACTS

Tilton

Ruthie sleeps in her old room. I am in my own bed. My stomach feels warm, and my head wants to bob. I can't sleep so I try writing a poem for Mrs. Devlin's daughter's wedding. Patty Devlin who maybe was a pothead and who's getting married again even though Mrs. Gottleib never heard the news. I've never been to a wedding. Ruthie invited us to both of hers. My mother and I hadn't known where Ruthie lived much less that she was dating someone seriously enough to marry him.

My mother RSVP'd, Sorry we cannot attend. Congratulations. Sincerely, Eleanor & Tilton.

When I asked my mother if I should write Ruthie a wedding poem, she said no. And that was that.

Wee-ette loved poems. She had entire poems in her head and sometimes she would just say them—straight out of her mouth. Weddings are about hearts, bells, rice, and doves. I think of my two hearts—the one in my chest and the one I ate: the heart of a mongrel king. Sometimes, I swear, I can feel it beating inside me.

Two hearts. I write that down. Twin hearts. I write a few things about nest-building, which I always do. When people get married, they nest. Swallow nests are particularly foul—made of regurgitation. I don't mention swallows. I write the poem and fold it up.

I stand in the middle of my room. I feel Wee-ette's presence. I ask her if she thinks Ruthie is good.

Wee-ette believes in good. Sometimes it's just forgotten.

I ask her if I should go get George.

She doesn't like George, but she agrees with Ruthie. It's my life.

I walk down the hall to Wee-ette's room. I love the click the doorknob makes. The door swings slowly wide. Wee-ette's room at night has more of her in it, as if the part of her more wholly her was more alive at night, so she's more here then. She's here-er.

I get the screwdriver from under her typewriter, and I unscrew the heating vent grate. It pops off. I pull out the egg carton and open it. All of our pacts—labeled with initials, dates, and keywords—are there. I touch the one most important to Wee-ette. The first one. E. C. and H. W. 1913. Marriage. The string is dark with dirt, thin in places where it's nearly worn out, and fully broken once and tied back together with a small hard knot. Then there is the pact between Eleanor, Ruthie, and me, after Wee-ette died—never to talk about the seventh book being burned. Its label reads E. T., R. T., and T. T. 1984. Silence. And then there are the pacts between Ruthie and me before she left. I touch the one labeled R. T. and T. T. 1986. Return & Save.

I feel dizzy and sad and happy. I am whirling inside because all of this is finally happening. Ruthie, at last, here. The new ending is coming! But how will we get our father? We've gone a long time not understanding fathers.

I hold on to the pact with Ruthie, put the carton back, and replace the vent, screwing it tight. I stand in Wee-ette's fullest presence. Wee-ette, I say, thank you for being a good example in life. And for all of your hiding places.

I close the door, listen for the click, and walk down the hall, into Ruthie's room. Her breathing is purred, her back curved. The dogs are curled up, one on either side of her. They both lift their heads and stare at me. Shhh. I set the wound string with its small label on her bedside table, right near Ruthie's sunglasses.

I go back to my room. I lie in my bed and stare at the canopy's gauze. I tell myself the bedtime story—the potluck, the cigar, the lightning, the steaming engine, the dead, the farmhouse, Marie Cultry weeping, George cupping her elbow. But before the ending, I stop. I say, To be continued.

I'm still whirly inside so I sing. Wee-ette used to sing a song for sleeping. It didn't have words. It was very oompah, oompah. She said it was a song she heard when she was young, an endless loop playing on an organ. She told me that the song made her dizzy, like she'd been driving around in circles. I sing the dizzy sleeping song, and think of the wind in Mrs. Gottleib's station wagon. What would the wind be like in Ruthie's convertible? I think of buying two fedoras—one for me and one for the Eldermans' son. I imagine getting a dog, full of dander.

I think of the loop of string on Ruthie's bedside table. It sits there like a little bird's nest.

Chapter Fifteen

HARRIET WOLF: MURDERESS

Harriet

*D*espite my greatest fears, this institution would prove the opposite of the Maryland School for Feeble Minded Children.
*Having shed the word "asylum" from its name, it was the Sheppard
and Enoch Pratt Hospital. There was light Swedish massage, billiards, bowling, a nine-hole golf course, tennis, concerts. The staff, it
was rumored, hired semiprofessional baseball players so they could
beat the other local teams—the YMCA, police, firemen.*

*The problem was that I was guilt-stricken. If I hadn't been re-
turned to my mother, would she have ever gone out? Do shut-ins
die of contagion? No, they don't. But because of me, my mother was
out in the world again and died. The Maryland School for Feeble
Minded Children had been right about me all along. I was "a disturbing element," "vicious and immoral." I was unable to be saved
from "crime or a life of degradation." I was certain that I was a
murderess, that I had killed my mother.*

I told no one.

*When I think of myself at eighteen at Sheppard Pratt, as it was
known, I think of us. I was raised as an us, after all, a they—the
feeble-minded, mere refuse, a societal problem to be dealt with.
Ours were lives of domesticated sheep. We were herded into rows.
We sang in unison if we sang at all. We were so unaccustomed to being singled out and addressed that we had to be reminded to speak*

when spoken to. We kept our eyes on the shirt in front of us. When guards said "you," we thought they meant "all of you." The individual you was so rare that there was no time for an I to take hold. I didn't have a self. Eppitt confirmed my existence, and I confirmed his, and we touched each other—lustful proof.

Likewise, for four years my mother and I existed because we both existed. When she was gone, I was stripped to something elemental and foreign to myself. I looked in mirrors and didn't recognize my own face—pale and slack, with a bloat to my eyes, which wanted to drift.

At Sheppard Pratt, we were all psychiatric patients, each of us suffering, but doing so together allowed us to shift our burdens a little, each taking some weight on our backs. Beautiful and deranged ghosts—we haunted not the place but our own bodies. I was mourning, of course. And for a while I allowed myself to shuffle along with the others, their current buoying me. I was part of them. The nurses, in long white gowns with white bibs and white nurse's hats, floated. The male attendants wore all white too. Down a long dark corridor they glowed.

I was put in Norris Cottage. Cottages, cottages, like my childhood returned. But Norris held only four patients and our attendants. Dr. Brush said that small numbers were good for us. My father, I assume, was paying a pretty penny for this—blood money. I didn't care. There was one woman whose family built her a house on the grounds, Poe Cottage; it was tidy, with a duckboard walkway that led to the front steps. I never saw her. I heard later that she lived there until her death—a full forty years. Norris Cottage was large, stone, ivied. The three other patients were quiet. One was a teacher, one a wife and mother of two who'd tried to kill herself with pills meant to treat gout, and one was just a few years older than I was. This last one didn't have a husband or work. I feared her most of all.

When my skirt was returned, the pact with my mother was still there in its pocket. I thought of hiding it in my bedside table, but it wasn't safe enough there. Instead, I fitted it between my mattress and the web of wiring under my bed.

We were observed each morning from seven to seven thirty. Then there was bathing, dressing, eating until eight thirty. Food arrived on beautiful china with a silver teapot, linen napkin, and tray covering, a bowl of sugar cubes, a pepper shaker, a tiny bowl of salt with a miniature spoon. I loved the miniature spoon and lightly salted all of my food, but ate little and only sipped the tea.

Then we were to write letters. I had no one, and so I wrote to Eppitt. I wrote the way the others wrote. Niceties. But I folded the letters like origami cranes, the way my mother had taught me, and, because Eppitt would have outgrown the Maryland School, I had no address for him, so I hid the origami cranes up my sleeves and tucked them into the underside of my mattress, along with the pact.

From ten o'clock to one, we played games on the lawns, and did calisthenics while holding poles. I skirted the edges of badminton, volleyball, putting. On rainy days, in the casino, I watched people bowl on the two-lane alley and shoot billiards. We were set to work, but not stitching Duck Porch awnings. Here we made ornaments, stools, taborets. I sat before a loom. I didn't actually do any of these things, but I didn't have to. I was part of a group and, together, we managed. I see the patients now—golf clubs tucked under their arms and bowling balls cradled to their chests, whispering to themselves, singing marching songs, tapping their own faces as if trying to remember something that will never return to them. Many of them prayed, a soft motion of the mouth. They picked at themselves. Some had scabs that wouldn't heal. They cried openly and then would laugh with a sharp staccato.

At one o'clock we ate again. Then more baths—tonic baths,

rain baths, and showers with forceful nozzles. We would be washed clean, if nothing else. The soul? No one knew how to fix it once broken, but its flimsy case could be managed.

We were walked back to Norris Cottage, where we rested. Then we were up. We walked the grounds. If people shifted to the solarium, I followed. Flowers bloomed there, even though it was turning cool. Exotic ferns, a tiled floor, a cane rocker, stained glass, all reminding me of the sunporch at home—the outdoors that could grow so green and steamy, and love, love, always the association. Eppitt in the laundry. My mother, a hothouse flower.

There were no newspapers; we needed a break from war and pestilence. I itched for the ink smeared on my fingers, the small scissors (my ivory-handled bird scissors had been left behind), and my tub of paste, the light-headedness of breathing it in deeply. But I walked the library stacks, my hand bumping along the rhythm of bindings. I liked the quiet dust of books.

We played cribbage and gin rummy, and fit together intricate puzzles. Dinner arrived at 6 p.m. We were observed again, clinically. Again, we were sent to the lawn for an hour, followed by fifteen minutes on the ward.

And then night.

Night was the hardest. We feared the dark. Grief—melancholia—tells the brain, Too much, enough of this world. The brain is ticking all day, keeping up with the noise and images of daily life, but once you close your eyes at night, the brain lights the skull and asserts itself without the interruption of vision and sound. It's stronger than you can imagine, the lit skull at work on its own. Its will is tougher and you're tired. You must bend to it.

And what did it show me?

I don't need to go over this—we all know loss. We know longing. I see Ruthie and Tilton filled with powerful longing. I've told you *this, Eleanor, and you've responded sharply, "I'll monitor their long-ing—thank you for the tip!" As if longing can be monitored.*

The truth is, I felt dead and lost, but I didn't stay dead. First of all, there was the world all around me. It's insistent. When the lit skull works at night ranting about loss, there's always day again. This fact is unrelenting. It's the true insanity of life.

My food glittered with salt like a fresh snow. My letters puffed my shirtsleeves and were pinched by the bottom springs of my mattress—my aviary of origami cranes. They were trapped beneath my bed, but breeding. I had much to say.

And there was existence. I ran my hands across the clipped grass of the putting green, wet with dew. The bowling ball—a solid weight—I heaved it from myself again and again, to feel lightness, the thunder roll, the popping pins. A bath reminds your body that it has skin. I opened books, the creak of them, the smell. I let my eyes settle on words. My mouth moved. Words lifted from ink and became a taste and then an object held in the brain. John Donne, Walt Whitman, Shakespeare, Keats, Shelley, Byron, Coleridge. My cheeks burned. The solarium breathed. The playing cards were slick; the puzzle pieces could be wedged into place, snug.

The Armistice was signed in November. We made banners, sang songs, ate tea cakes, and danced on the lawn. The archduke and his wife belonged to history now.

Slowly, I returned to this relentless world. And what did I find? Dr. Wolff. Two f's at the end of his name, no relation to me and my Wolfs, or to the various other Woolfs and wolves, for that matter.

His bow tie bobbed at his throat when he spoke, very gently. He had a ruddy complexion—a strong jaw, black hair, closely cropped. He had beautiful eyebrows, tilted with just the right amount of sympathy. His eyes were large and brown. He had full lips, a small nose. He was broad, and unlike Eppitt when I last saw him—behind the paned glass of King's Cottage—Dr. Wolff was a grown man. His chest was powerful. He breathed beneath his thin white dress shirt as if his lungs and heart were giant pumping machinery. And I watched his hands—strong hands. He was jovial, with a quick smile, but he was also shy. He was thirty-two.

I sat in a leather chair, fidgeted with a button at my wrist.

"So." He looked at the chart on his desk. "Harriet, how are you?"

I'm a murderess, *I wanted to say, but instead I whispered, "I'm fine."*

"We hope you're feeling better."

"I have a lingering malaise, maybe."

"Sometimes that can be a state of mind. What's on your mind these days?" He leaned forward, one elbow on his desk. He was hunched slightly. My mother had wanted me to have good posture. "Stand tall," she told me once at the Swinging Lantern. "You don't need to hide anymore."

"My father hasn't delivered anything for me, has he?" I wanted my ivory-handled scissors, paste, and books of clippings.

"Just your clothes, which, by looking at you, appear to have arrived. Tell me something about yourself."

"I like Chinese food," I told him.

"That's very nice," he said.

"There's a very good restaurant my mother and I went to on our birthdays."

"That's nice."

"Well, there was a tragedy there too. The Lings' niece drowned."

"In the restaurant?" Dr. Wolff said. "How did she drown in a restaurant?"

"The usual way. Under water," I explained. "There was a fish-pond."

"Is that what's on your mind?"

Now it was. The Ling girl's swirling hair, her limp body, the goldfish circling stupidly. "Death is part of life." The guards repeated this banality at the Maryland School for Feeble Minded Children whenever one of us died. Some arrived so sickly that they lived only a few short weeks.

"Well, you don't have to worry about death. You're young and healthy."

"The Ling girl was just four." Afraid that I might cry, I stared at the ceiling.

"Why do you think you're here?" Dr. Wolff asked.

"My mother died and I didn't take it well. I loved her." This caused a fit inside my chest. I didn't have the energy for fits anymore, but these versions—maybe aftershocks—still existed in miniature. They didn't last long, but they were internally violent.

"That kind of loss can be traumatic."

"She broke a pact too."

"And what was that?"

"For us to never separate again. But I don't want to talk about death."

"You've brought it up. Twice."

"Have I?"

"The girl dying in the fishpond and your mother. Are the two linked?"

"It's just that death can happen at any time. And then we would miss out on all of this."

"All of what, Harriet?"

For the first time in my life, I was supposed to explain what it was like to exist. "Well, you know, Dr. Wolff, of course."

"No, I don't," he said. "Not the way you do. Tell me."

I had the doctor's full attention, and was realizing that my way of existing was not necessarily everyone's way of existing, and moreover, perhaps each of us had our own existence. This was over-whelming. Imagine Daisy at the convent school, after her gaping sleeve has caught fire in the chapel, how she whirls, aflame, know-ing for the first time that she is locked inside herself.

"What, Harriet? What would we miss?"

"I don't know," I said. "This!" I waved my hand around the room, meaning Everything!

"List for me a few things that you would miss."

And this was maybe the first, infinitesimal moment when I started to become a writer. This is the writer's first job: to list what's worth listing. "Well, the world is beautiful and ugly too, and some-times it's even beautiful when it's ugly. Like the Ling girl—I can imagine her head surrounded by fat orange gliding fish. And there were these children I knew once, sickly, ill fit. They were stunted. They would never grow old. But they were aired on porches and sunned too. They were angels to me. They were warped. Some had twisted spines, uneven legs. Their faces were open—gaping—a face that's more like a window than a face. Do you know what I mean?"

He nodded. "Go on."

"And those are the ones you don't expect to find beautiful. Then there are the ones you do expect to find beautiful. And there they are—hands, mouth." I indicated his hands, his mouth.

He looked at me, and I stopped. "It's okay," he said. "Go on."

"It's just beauty, that's all, like the view from my window. People moving on the lawn, the way trees sway, the way…It's all beau-tiful." I couldn't stop speaking. "I kept things before I got here, clippings from newspapers. I want to keep it all. Proof."

"Of what?"

"Proof that lives are being lived." I whispered, "I have a life within myself, an inward life that can't be expressed. It's sad that it can't be expressed. Maybe one of the saddest things I can think

of right now. And you're saying that everyone has these lives, aren't
you?"

"Yes, I think we do. Ways of perceiving, a life experience that is
unique to that individual."

"I don't know how everybody walks around just like normal," I
said, "as if everything is not beautiful and hideous and dangerous.
I used to know laundry steam. I knew how it billowed. I was caged
then like I am now."

"We're here to help."

"I forgot to say that I like the putting green and the solarium
and the little salt spoons. I do," I said. "Thank you."

"Well, I'll pass along your gratitude."

"My mother wore powder that smelled like a field of flowers! She
would wring out a sponge and the water made its way down my
back."

Dr. Wolff was staring beyond me now. He took a quick breath
and sat back. He pressed tears from his eyes, rubbing them into
his sideburns. He jotted a note, something diligent and professional. I decided that Dr. Wolff had a very full inner life as inner
lives went. Maybe he was a fellow sufferer, pained by the glory in
the everyday, affected by simple, ugly, gorgeous, glowing details of
life.

He whispered, "Harriet, by God. I swear the right opera could
kill you."

"What was that?" I asked. I wanted to hear it again. I wanted
to see the soft workings of his lips saying my name.

But it was something he wasn't supposed to utter aloud. "Sorry,"
he said. "Let's go on."

I hid the fact that I was thriving. If I got too healthy, where would
I go? My mother was gone, and all I had was the click of billiard

balls, Coleridge's "Kubla Khan," the nurses' white skirts gliding on air—and Wolff himself.

Of course, there was deep madness at Sheppard Pratt—two escapes while I was there: one drowned in a nearby pond and the other swallowed bichloride of mercury tablets purchased at a drugstore. This madness only made it all the more clear that I wanted to live—and I did want to, fiercely.

I missed Eppitt—the weight of his body under the Duck Porch. I was losing faith that I'd ever see him again. He was eighteen too. Perhaps he'd enlisted or was drafted and was finally home again—but changed forever. Would they let him serve? Had he outgrown his wheeze? Did he die a soldier? Was he struck down by the Spanish flu, like my mother, and did he bleed to death? And if he did bleed out, did that make him think of me, the bleeder, in the end? Dead, alive, in love with someone else? Did he ever think of me?

My origami crane letters to him tucked into my mattress springs had nowhere to go.

In my sessions with Wolff, I sometimes went silent. I pretended to have tics. I tried on Eppitt's habit of compressing words. One time I said "doomy" instead of "dark" and "gloomy." I corrected myself, but then kept doing it purposefully. I picked at the waistband of my dress, and whenever I coughed, I stared at my hands.

I could tell Wolff anything. I explained the Owl and the Good Wheel and even my heated moments under the Duck Porch with Eppitt.

Dr. Wolff nodded serenely, a slow singular bob of his head. He smiled sometimes too, and he jotted.

Sometimes he would make a small comment, like "You must have loved your mother very much."

And this simple fact, said aloud, made my body feel like it was

suddenly filled with air and light. "Yes," I would say, suddenly crying. "Yes, I did."

In April of 1919, when I'd been at Sheppard Pratt for six months,
Dr. Wolff told me that it was time for me to go home.

"I don't have a home."

"We have people in the community prepared to take in our patients. Mrs. Oblatt runs a quiet boarding house. Some of the girls
work in the mills. She provides breakfast and dinner."

I tried to think of two words that I could smear together as Eppitt
would to express how I felt, but none came. I picked at my waistband,
coughed into my hands, then looked at my palms and, for the first
time, knew what I was looking for: blood, death. "I can't go."

"You need to be out in the world, Harriet."

"The world doesn't need me."

"It doesn't need any of us. We need it. I wish you didn't have to,
but you're ready. You're well, Harriet. You are."

"It's crazy what can pass for not crazy these days," I said.

He handed me a piece of paper with the address of Mrs. Oblatt's
boarding house. "Your father's been informed and has paid Mrs.
Oblatt for the first three months."

I folded the piece of paper, the way I folded all of Eppitt's unsent
letters—a long neck, a beak, wings.

Within days, I was standing in the lobby awaiting a taxi.

Dr. Wolff was there to see me go. "One day," he said, "a few years
from now, I want you to come back and see me. I want to know
about the wonderful life you've made."

But I shook my head. "I won't come back. I need the world," I
said.

"You," he said. "Harriet Wolf." He sighed. "The world might
just need you after all. I think you're destined for..."

"What?"

"Great things, Harriet. Truly great things."

Of course I didn't believe him.

The origami cranes I decided to leave behind so that at least some small part of me would remain. I imagined them pinched by the bedsprings, flightless and trembling.

MRS. OBLATT'S BOARDING HOUSE FOR WAYWARD WOMEN

Mrs. Oblatt was squat and powerful. She moved like a wrestler. And when she was still, she sat in an armchair and did needlepoint ferociously. The living room was so densely packed with needlepoint it was muffled. The rest of the house was loud, the women boisterous. Mrs. Oblatt ignored the noise. She was a childless widow, and during the long years that slipped by while I lived in her house, I watched her fade—hearing loss, light dementia, a palsy in her frenetic needlepoint.

She appreciated that I didn't complain. (When raised in an institution, you know better than to complain.) Occasionally there would be another boarder who, like me, was institutional in nature, posture, and bearing. We recognized each other. We wouldn't say our hellos to each other. A nod would do. We knew, without saying a word.

The shower pipes cried out, and my room smelled of pee in every corner. But much to my surprise, I started to prefer being on my own.

Most of the women worked in cotton mills, which were plentiful. But I found work shelving books. One afternoon I wandered into a library, which, like Sheppard Pratt, was a gift from businessman

Enoch Pratt. It had airy ceilings, monstrous stacks of books. It seemed as if God Himself were a clipster and this library his paste book. Holy. As broad and lit up as a cathedral! Unlike Mrs. Oblatt's house, which needed the muffling of needlepoint, the library was hushed. The dust motes idled. The workers behind the checkout desk opened the wings of the books, piled them on their spines, and stamped them, like they were tagging birds.

That first day I wandered in, I asked if they had an opening. A woman at the desk shuttled me to an office where I met the head librarian. He had angular shoulders, a droopy chin, and a flat pat of hair.

Though I had no formal education, I told him I was learned, and quoted poetry from the library at Sheppard Pratt—without mentioning the asylum, of course.

He told me that one of their shelvers had just perished. "Perished." I loved the word. It didn't sound like death at all. The Spanish flu was still going strong, but libraries were trying to keep their doors open to the public during limited hours despite the potential danger. "Are you sure you want the job?" he asked.

"I'm not afraid of dying," I told him. I had been born dead, after all, but was still here. "If you live long enough, you've already perished a little. Maybe life is a bit-by-bit death."

"Very poetic," he said, and I got the job.

I was alone during the days. I walked the stacks, ordered and reordered. My mind started alphabetizing all that I saw, even the women in Mrs. Oblatt's house: Bartlett, Dresden, Inger, Martin. I avoided them as much as possible. They trilled about blouses, hats, hairdos—all foreign to me. Sometimes I tried to listen but heard only high-pitched squeaks. The conversation always returned to men—piggish, foul with desire, cursed by their hulking stature, their coursing arousal, their unruly pricks—and yet these same *women groused endlessly that these sops had abandoned them. Those were the ones living at Mrs. Oblatt's for the most part, the abandoned ones.*

I avoided the bawdy talk. I took my meals in my room, alone.

Plus, I missed men: Eppitt Clapp, who I hoped wasn't a dead soldier; Dr. George Wolff; even old Dr. Brumus and the guards, like Mr. Gillup. I didn't miss my father, of course. But surprisingly, he sent letters. They were short and dry. Mainly, he wanted to have dinner together. He wanted to talk. He missed my mother. I looked like her, you know, and I decided that this was probably all he wanted, some link to her. At first, I responded only by asking for my books of clippings. These never arrived. And so, soon enough, I stopped responding at all.

The epidemic was fading. The hotel hospitals became hotels again. The bankers' masks disappeared, as did the placards on people's houses. Life returned. But my mother was still gone. Maybe Sheppard Pratt had been a distraction more than a cure. For all my thriving there, I now felt like someone robbed blind. Sometimes I felt limbless, headless. I looked out and the world changed scenery before my eyes, motorized and modernized; the world steamed on without me.

One day, overcome, I passed Mrs. Oblatt needle-pointing in a corner of the living room and walked out into the cold. Coatless, I went to a stationery shop and bought paste, scissors, and a new book of empty white pages. I started up my subscriptions again, as many as I could afford, newspapers and magazines that appeared, daily, weekly, monthly. I couldn't partake in the world's changes, but I could take note of them. "A waste!" Mrs. Oblatt called it. "Why would anyone want to read all of this nonsense?" Why? So the world could be reordered from nonsense to sense.

It was during this time that I read that Dr. Wolff had been shot.

Murdered, in fact. He was killed at Sheppard Pratt by another doctor, a man that I'd seen only a few times, Dr. Ishida. The Baltimore Sun *followed the case with its "Veil of Oriental Mystery," as they put it. Dr. Ishida felt that Dr. Wolff had called him a spy and a traitor, and there was also the intimation that the honor of a woman was involved in the matter. Ishida shot Dr. Wolff while at work, and Wolff's blood soaked into the carpet of the corridor as he gripped the leg of a cane chair. I dedicated one full book of clippings to the murder alone. The world hadn't needed Wolff, but I had. His death made me retreat into myself even more deeply. The greed of death, of loss—it was proving insatiable.*

In a frenzied way, I kept clippings of as many of the world's oddities as I could—Ripley's exhibit of shrunken heads from the upper Amazon, medieval chastity belts, a man at the Chicago World's Fair who could swallow and regurgitate live mice. In came insulin, Yankee Stadium, Eskimo Pies, airships! Out went the Barbary lion, the Amur tiger, the California grizzly—and so many humans. Genocides (Assyrians, Greeks), the Rosewood massacre, the Great Kanto Earthquake, death by giant hailstones.

What I mean to say is that years passed, slowly at first, but then they picked up speed. Seasons blurred by. It was humid and then suddenly the heat was wrung from the air and it was chilly and damp. Winters rushed into summer so fast that I would find myself shrugging off my winter coat, struck by the overbearing sun.

I was aware that this is one way a young woman becomes an old maid—afraid of her desire, afraid of her power. I lived amid my clippings. I hid my breasts and hips under baggy dresses and heavy coats. On the streets I clamped library books to my bosom and, chin to chest, muttered, "Excuse me, excuse me," dipping and bowing like a criminal.

I worked in the shelves, read books beside the brightly lit win-

dows. I looked up the works of Dr. Wolff, for example, as well as Dr. Brush, titles like "Hysterical Insanity," "Insanity and Arrested Development," "An Analysis of One Hundred Cases of Acute Melancholia." I felt hysterical sometimes—that my development was arrested, that my melancholia was acute. As I moved through the dusty motes, I even diagnosed my own bleeding. Poring over medical texts, I found a Finnish doctor by the name of Erik Adolf von Willebrand, who attended the University of Helsinki, and writings about his interest in the case of a five-year-old girl, a pernicious bleeder.

What to do about it? Nothing. I actually had an easy case, according to von Willebrand's research. My platelets' clumsy efforts at adherence once injured, my inability to heal—these were metaphors not lost on me.

I collected survivors of the Spanish flu—Lillian Gish, Walt Disney, FDR, Woodrow Wilson, Katherine Anne Porter, Mary Pickford, Edvard Munch, Georgia O'Keeffe. I still blamed myself for my mother's death. The names of survivors were proof that if I'd been smarter or somehow better, more deserving, she could have survived too.

I lingered in poetry. Where else would incurables linger?

You'd think I would have spent these years reading novels to become the novelist I one day would. In fact, I've never cared for novelists. They don't know how to be essential. They lack self-restraint. If you can't evoke emotion—twist-tie one soul to another—in the density of a poem, then you don't deserve to work in words. Novelists struck me as brutes, using words like nails, trying to hammer a story into place. Poets, on the other hand, let words use them. Poets are pure. They are like the jazz musician who doesn't take a bow, but instead holds his saxophone above his head so that it can take the praise. I was receiving my own education.

By this time I'd been at Mrs. Oblatt's for more than a decade.

I felt that I'd lived a long time. A life of breathing in. I needed to breathe out—to create—but I didn't know how. For now, life itself and each word I read were an inhale, building the pressure chamber within. I followed the court case of Giuseppe Zangara, who, after being sentenced to death for killing the mayor of Chicago while taking aim at Roosevelt, said, "You give me electric chair. I no afraid of that chair!" And when Zangara was strapped in, he shouted, "Pusha da butt. Pusha da butt," meaning throw the switch and kill me already. I understood his fearlessness, on one hand. I wasn't afraid of dying—my body barely existed—and if I had relegated myself to living this life mostly in my mind, at least for the first time it was my own life. Mine.

When former tenants visited Mrs. Oblatt's boarding house with children in tow, I imagined what I must have looked like. Over the baby's plumped face and pulsing skull, my own face—the ugly dollop of madness—bobbed and swung like a gaudy flower as I tried to smile and coo. I'd watch the baby's eyes—merry-go-sorry-go-terrified. And I wondered, What must I smell like to them? Fear and loss and ruin, like caked talcum when it takes on a foul stench? *My own womb was hot and bright and hollow as a Dutch oven. Deep down, I doubted that I would ever deserve to have a child. Raised a moron, my genius a waste, my insanity festering while I lived with my mother until it swelled so vividly that I had to be institutionalized, I thought of myself as lowly, a scourge, and there was no one now—not Funk or Brumus or Eppitt or my mother or Wolff—to disagree with me.*

It seemed to me that each portion of my life had been cordoned off from the others. I left Eppitt and never saw him again. He never found me as he'd promised he would. My mother died, and I was gone. I wouldn't ever return to Dr. Wolff, years from now, to tell him about my wonderful life.

I didn't know if I would ever wake up from this deathly sleep.

Chapter Sixteen

DOWN IN MY HEART. WHERE? DOWN IN MY HEART.

Ruth

When I open my eyes I feel a little groggy. I'm met by the dogs, gazing at me expectantly. Last night, I took a sleeping pill, which I usually reserve for the insomnia that follows cocktail parties, awards ceremonies, and departmental potlucks. I hate these events. I hate the faculty. Of course, I'd expected the cliché—raised on media images of haughty and vain professorial types, insufferable droning bores with underlying insecurities that led the males of the species, in particular, to prey on female students. I was surprised to find it to be so very sadly true. (In fact, I was prey. Now married to the predator.)

There are exceptions, of course. Researchers who've devoted their lives to cancer, suicide, environmental hazards, et cetera, tend to be steadier than those who work on things that have no foreseeable effect on human beings—painfully close readings of *Middlemarch* or Harriet Wolf, for example. Literature professors must constantly prove their worth to society. Bombast is a natural by-product. Those who work on things that could actually affect the world are steadier because they're too busy to be petty. Their appearances are spotty at parties, dinners, potlucks—like the rare species that some of them study and protect. They pick over the cheese plate, have a drink, and leave. It's a survival strategy—of the fittest.

Ron always wants to come late, making an entrance, and then stay to the bitter end. Past the bitter end, in fact—until long after the waitstaff commences glaring. I would love to let him attend the parties alone, but he drinks, and then flirts openly, and I have to admit I get jealous. Even if Ron and I do split up, I assume he'll always carry some sway over my heart. Sometimes, if goaded, he sings—and he's easily goaded. We've developed a signal for *You've gone too far.* I look at him and smooth my eyebrow with my index finger. Once he spots me doing it, his face goes soft and fleshy—momentary gratitude. It's not his intention to make an ass of himself, after all. The problem for me isn't that he does this stuff, but the deeper insecurity that it reveals—he needs the adulation, craves it.

Over the last few years, I've tried to discover which of the faculty were second- or third- generation academics, for whom this is the family business. They have insights into the breed. They know who'll last, who's secretly on the market, who's backstabbing whom and why. They don't make conversation so much as they quip. I've gotten good at reading quips for deeper meaning. Mainly, I want to learn what they've mastered: how to disengage, float above it, and take what amusement they can.

Still, when I get home from these events, I invariably return to the evening—doomed to relive each moment: the foreign-destination-dropping (a semester in London, a fellowship in Indonesia), the Foucault-inspired readings of pop culture, Jung applied to *Buffy the Vampire Slayer* and postcolonialism sicced on *The Simpsons,* 50 Cent disambiguated under their brilliant gazes, and their new areas of research like "Reclaiming the Female Anus through Postmodern Literature of the Late Nineteen Nineties." Oh, the punishing detail.

One word comes to me: *sin.*

I wasn't raised religiously. Eleanor was too cheap to hand over money to a collection plate and had no communal instincts. She sent me to Vacation Bible School one summer because it was free. I made a Shrinky Dinks of the Madonna and child and sat on carpet remnant squares singing, "I've got that joy, joy, joy, joy down in my heart. Where? Down in my heart. Where? Down in my heart," in English and then in Spanish— *"Dónde?"* It's a catchy tune. I find myself singing it sometimes. *"Dónde?"*

But even I knew that academe is a sin—brilliant minds with nowhere important to go. Nothing important to do. I read that crowded-together dogs become neurotic and aggressive, biting their own paws. These professors are crowded-together lapdogs with a seemingly endless supply of small angry turds—the ammo of their discontent. They waddle around (the men, at least) with their jiggling peckers, nosing each and every passing ass, the frantic hunt and aimless hump of unknown shins. The worst offenders among the predatory profs are those who obviously didn't get any action in high school. Ron included. Paybacks. The weakest gain some power and turn the tables on the unjust world of their youth.

I rub the dogs' heads and wonder what Ron would be like if I could go back in time and get him a high-school sweetheart. A cheerleader isn't necessary. Just a clarinetist—third chair. Someone to come up with a pet name for him, jerk him off in the parking lot reserved for seniors who make the honor roll. He'd have been a better person, maybe. Just a little.

This is what I was really getting my PhD in: Contemporary American Professorial Assholes. Didn't Eleanor get a PhD equivalent in Assholes through her marriage to George Tarkington? Maybe I'm second-generation, in my own way.

As the dogs start to whine for me to take them out, I remember my offer to Tilton from last night: that I would take her to meet George. Why did I do that? I was a little tipsy.

What if I take Tilton on a day trip to meet George and I find out that he is, in fact, a bona fide asshole? I'd have to give up on the hope I've always harbored that George Tarkington loves me, misses me, regrets his marriage to Eleanor but never his girls.

And Tilton? Would she break down?

I consider taking another sleeping pill and dozing the day away. I love how sure-handed the drug is. At first, nothing, but then a little tug on the brain. Starting at the top of the skull, it pulls down something thick, almost woolen, that settles over one lobe and then another. I sense the woolliness until I no longer sense it, and when I no longer sense it, I'm asleep. I sleep hard. Best of all, there are no dreams. No Freudian dilemma to start the day. Maybe a tingling limb, but even this feels good, a little kneading of the needling flesh and the reality of my life taking shape around me, gently.

This morning, there's faint light from the windows. I rub my right arm, which is lightly numbed from the elbow down. The Pomeranians are curled on either side of me. I pat them. I own dogs. I'm a dog owner.

I am in the home I once ran away from. Mrs. Gottleib is going to collect my mother at the hospital and bring her home. My mother doesn't want me here and yet here I am. I might be divorcing my husband, my *second*.

It's just after 10 a.m. I'm supposed to tidy before Mrs. Gottleib delivers my mother. But my mother should have invited me back, should have tidied the house in eager anticipation.

"Leave if you want, but don't expect me to welcome you back! I'm not going to slaughter a lamb for an ingrate!" A good mother would regret that, would call and say she's sorry. That apology never happened, and I'll be damned if I'll tidy for that woman.

Before me sits the row of boxes. Tilton's childhood, beloved, and my own box—small, crumpled. It feels like the calcified remains of my mother's love.

I think of Daisy Brooks, who would throw the box onto the lawn. She was beautiful and scandalous and doomed, or so it seemed. Tragically honest and jaded, she uttered the most breathtaking things. She loved Weldon Fells, the leading man—crazy, yes, but also magical.

Oddly enough, Wee-ette's novels weren't on display in this house when I lived here. Copies existed, surely, in boxes, closets, and attics. But I refused to look for them even when, in my teens, my curiosity kicked in. I refused to give my mother or Wee-ette the satisfaction of my attention—in any way. Instead I read the books in my high-school library, housed in the school's musty basement. I didn't want to risk the paper trail of checking them out. I sat in a back carrel during my free periods and read.

For a time during my junior year, I practiced Daisy's verbal tic of compressing words. I would say "bread," mixing "brain" and "head," and then feign embarrassment and correct myself.

Once, a boy who played sax in the marching band called me on it at a party. "I know that thing. It's Daisy Brooks's thing in the Wolf books." One of the sophomore English teachers put her first book on the summer reading list, and because it was only 185 pages, it was a popular choice.

I blushed and said, "I know. I'm the granddaughter of Harriet Wolf." Later that night, the boy kissed me. We were stoned and sitting on a balcony overlooking an aboveground pool.

This is what the family never talks about—Harriet Wolf's books are beautiful. They're famous for a reason. They're full of grace and wisdom and mystery, and when I read them in that carrel in the high-school library basement, I sometimes cried.

I will always remember the moment when Daisy and Weldon are in the canoe and she says, "Love—it's how we're bloomed!"

And Weldon looks at her and says, "Bloomed?"

"Did I say 'bloomed'?" Daisy says. "I meant 'doomed' and 'blessed.'"

I shut the book then. I lay my cheek on the cover and whispered, "My God." This was in me somehow. This blooming. This unspeakable blooming.

Maybe this is why I hate Ron. He talks about my grandmother's work with detachment. He's never once told me what it felt like to read about Weldon and Daisy for the first time. But I've never talked to him about it either; it would be a confession of weakness. For him, literature isn't meant to be felt, but dissected and given context. I wonder if Ron and I would have a different marriage altogether if we could share confessions like this. Perhaps. But only because that would make us different people.

I remember, with a sick knot of regret in my stomach, that I asked Tilton about the seventh book. I told her it would be worth a lot of money—in the millions. I don't really care about the money, though the money would be nice, wouldn't it? I said it to shake Tilton up, to make her realize she has something of value, possibly, to offer the world.

Here's the truth: I want the seventh book for myself. I want it badly. I haven't been able to fully and completely admit that until now. It's part of why I'm here—not just my dying mother, not just to save Tilton. A chunk of my soul is here to find the seventh book, but not for its auction value or its scholarly worth. Honestly, I want to know what happens, in the end, to Daisy and Weldon. I want the rest of the story.

Ron's instincts might be right after all. It could be here. The thought energizes me. I rise from the bed at last and kneel in front of one of Tilton's boxes. I rummage through the typical things: drawings, paper masks, spelling words, cross sections of the heart, long division, reports—on birds, mostly. As I work my way down the row, Tilton grows up—geometry; an essay on Irish history and Yeats; physics; evolution; a photography folder, all of the pictures taken in the house and yard, close-ups of Eleanor sleeping, the fine lines of her face, and lots of birds. The dogs sniff the boxes, sniff me, sniff each other.

Finally, my box is left. "Ruthie—Random." I crawl to it and lay my hands on the dusty cardboard, but I can't open it. My mother would never hide anything of importance in this box. It contains the measly remains of a childhood, remnants and artifacts of a child who wasn't liked, much less loved. I fear finding that I wasn't a daughter, but a stranger here.

A car pulls into the driveway. I walk to the window. It's Mrs. Gottleib's station wagon. I see my mother's shoulder, just her rigid austere shoulder, and hate even that.

I look at the row of disturbed boxes. There's nothing for me here. What was I expecting? I'm going to see my mother for the first time in fourteen years.

I check my cell phone. There are two voice messages from Ron.

In the first, he simply says, "Call if you want to talk." And in the next, he says, "Justin and I might visit Towson U. It's eighth tier, I know. We'll be nearby. We could stop in! Let me know. Talk to you later."

Ron and Justin at my mother's house? I call him back immediately. The phone rings and goes to voice mail. "Hey," I say, trying to sound calm. "Don't come. Please." I immediately worry that this will only make him think I've found a Wolf artifact, maybe the manuscript itself. He'll claim he missed the message and show up at the house. He'll blame his provider. So I add quickly, "She's dying." And then I wrap it up as if someone's calling me. "I've got to go. I'll call you later."

Ron hates death. When his step-grandfather died, the only grandfather he'd ever known, he refused to go to the ceremony: "They don't need a bunch of gawkers." When I sent a card to his mimi, he said, "I hope you didn't mention Pop's death!"

I said, "I think that's the point of a condolence card."

"I think it's better to be positive," he countered. "Life is for the living and all of that." Death. He'd avoid it at any cost.

Should I feel guilty for lying about my mother's impending death? One day she will die. I think it was Harriet's books that drove this home for me, and in an instant I remember the scene in which Weldon is picking out carpet samples on what seems like an ordinary day until he finds an old woman dying in one of the aisles. Her heart stutters, crimps, then gives out. Later, he imagines her soul like a boat whose engine has been suddenly cut, and how the little vessel would continue to glide across the pond, eventually spinning out into slow circles. He wants to return her body—the way he wanted to return the bodies of all the soldiers who died next to him in the trenches—to sway-backed grasslands. That night, as they're driving to a party, he asks Daisy, "Will you be my gravedigger?" And Daisy imagines

Weldon's buried body becoming one with the soil that enriches the poisonous wax-coated milkweed puff. She imagines herself rotting too, lying beside Weldon and holding her purse just as she's holding it in the car, and how one day a prairie dog might burrow into its fine leather hide—as if nesting in a stiffened womb.

The dogs' nails click on the hardwoods. I have to take them out. I get dressed quickly, head for the door, but then turn back, grabbing my pocketbook and sunglasses.

That's when I see it—the small looped string. I recognize it immediately. A pact. Its masking tape tag is written in my own clunky childhood scrawl: "R. T. and T. T. 1986. Return & Save." A pang of guilt hits me. I pick up the small loop, delicately, and think of my hand and my sister's pressed together, held by the string. I lift it to my nose and smell the perfume—my mother's. Tilton sprayed it on the string so that it would smell good forever.

It wasn't here when I fell asleep. I imagine the house itself delivering this gift, Wee-ette padding through the rooms at night. But Tilton. Surely it was Tilton. She's kept this small fragile thing all these years.

If it has been kept all these years—tenderly kept—what else is here? This house is filled with small spaces, pockets, holes. I think of the long white yellow-flowered tablecloth draped over the dining room table and how I lived there for a couple of weeks—a house within a house. This house could hold everything.

Chapter Seventeen

HEARTS AND NESTS

Tilton

I'm standing in the kitchen and thinking:

Coach Flynn. Conical nose, large nostrils, thick brow, heavy lower mandible, broad dorsal, inflated rib cage, heavy bulk, long arms, dense forearm fur, sparse head plumage.

When I was little, he taught the theater camp in the elementary school gymnasium. He smoked too much and chewed mints. And he wasn't at all dramatic except when he got angry for no reason.

This was near the end of my formal education. I was in fourth grade. Coach Flynn read an acting exercise aloud from a book: each of us had to swallow an imaginary pill that he shook from an imaginary bottle and act like we were shrinking.

The other children popped their pills and shrank to the floor. I stood there.

What is it, Tilton? Coach Flynn asked me. What's wrong?

I was embarrassed to tell him the truth. He'd been in a war of some kind. Over the course of the class, he would abandon the drama book and we would reenact shooting deaths in rice paddies. It was babyish not to be able to swallow a pill. And so I whispered, I can't swallow pills.

He said, Well, Jesus, Tilton, you can *pretend* you know how to swallow a *pretend* pill, can't you?

That ruined everything. We weren't acting. We were just pretending.

Do you have some in liquid form or chewable? I asked.

Fine! He pretended to open a medicine cabinet, pick up a bottle, and pour the medicine into a cap.

I asked him if he'd read the directions. I weigh sixty-two pounds, I said.

Just take it! he shouted at me.

Later, during the imaginary battles that Coach Flynn seemed to enjoy, he killed me more times than he killed the other kids.

But I learned that acting is pretending, sometimes, and you can pretend to be able to do things you normally can't. I never mastered this during the class—I refused to take up arms because guns are dangerous and I'm not allowed, which is why I was always a target—but in the kitchen, with my mother on her way home, I decide to become her. How else will the kitchen go back to the kitchen she wants? A dirty kitchen can't act like a clean kitchen. Kitchens can't even pretend. So I have to.

Wood creaks overhead. Ruthie is awake. I could ask her to help. But she doesn't remember where it all goes. I need to do this myself.

I take on my mother's quick wiping gestures. I whistle like her, angry and shrill, while scrubbing dishes with a small wire brush. I don't sweep. I jab the broom at things. My mother gets angry at the house and takes it out on the floors. I close cupboards with the flat of my palm, giving them each an extra little shove so the latches click. Sometimes I say Damn it! for no reason at all.

Then Mrs. Gottleib's car is in the driveway. Ruthie's shoes are on the stairs, the little dogs with her. I've run out of time!

I look out the kitchen window. The car door opens and Mrs. Gottleib's voice rings out. Lookee who I found!

For a moment I wonder if she has forgotten my mother and instead brought some mystery guest. But Mrs. Gottleib opens the kitchen door. My mother holds its frame with one hand and Mrs. Gottleib's protruding elbow with the other. My mother's plumage is flat. Lying with her head on her pillow squashed it.

I expect to feel a rush of love. Tumbling, tumbling inside of me. But I feel stiff and small. What I really want is for my mother to feel a rush of love for Ruthie—tumbling, tumbling. And I want Ruthie to have the same tumbling, tumbling for my mother.

Ruthie walks into the kitchen from the living room. The doggies pad around the linoleum.

Tilton's allergies! my mother says.

I've inhaled the dogs and I'm fine! I tell her.

I guess she's not really allergic to pet dander after all, Ruthie says.

They're probably that kind of dog that's been bred not to have dander, my mother says.

Poodles don't have dander, Mrs. Gottleib says. I read that somewhere.

These are Pomeranians and they have dander, Ruthie says. And Tilton isn't allergic.

I'm standing between them. This isn't going the way I want it to. Not at all. I look at my mother and then at Ruthie. If we were caged birds, we'd be pacing back and forth, claw-grip, claw-grip, claw-grip, along our swings.

My mother is walking fine, but still Mrs. Gottleib's got her elbow because Mrs. Gottleib always has to feel necessary.

Tilton, my mother says with a smile.

I'm so glad you're home, I say—but it contains the smallest sliver of a lie.

She hugs me and I return her hug, but she can tell that I'm holding something back. She senses my smallest slivers. I'm holding back airy convertibles, fedoras, and a danderful dog of my own, and wine.

She holds my shoulders. I was only gone three days, she says, but you look years older. How is that possible? Did you grow up while I was away?

I cleaned the kitchen and pretended to be you, the way Coach Flynn taught me acting is really just pretending, so I could get everything back just right.

Coach Flynn was a jackass, my mother says.

I'm still waiting for Ruthie and my mother to say that, wow, they haven't seen each other in fourteen years! Birds address each other with different kinds of calls. Some learn their calls from other birds in their species and some have their calls encoded in their DNA. Groups of birds in the same species can have different dialects. It's a fact. Professor Kroodsma proved it. He worked at the University of Massachusetts in Amherst and has a book on the subject with a companion CD.

I step aside so there's just air between Ruthie and my mother. They're face to face.

My mother says, I told Mrs. Gottleib I'll believe that Ruthie's home when I see it.

And here I am, Ruthie says.

And here you are.

Ruthie offers my mother a seat at the kitchen table.

I'm fine, my mother says.

You had a heart attack. You're not fine. Sit down.

My mother slaps her hand on the counter. Don't tell me what to do, she says.

It goes silent for a moment. Birds go silent like this before forest fires.

Saints preserve us, Mrs. Gottleib says. And she turns to go.

Bye, Mrs. Gottleib! I say cheerily because that's how I've learned to say it.

Good luck, she says. She shuts the door, and the curtains on the kitchen window fluff their skirts.

Ruthie walks to the fridge, pulls out the spaghetti casserole that Mrs. Gottleib gave us yesterday, rips off the foil, digs out an oversized spoon from the drawer, wedges it in like a shovel, and sets it on the table. It's lunchtime.

But you haven't even warmed it up, my mother says.

It's fine, Ruthie says. Are you hungry, Tilton?

You only have to eat if you're hungry, my mother says.

I don't want to pick sides. I'm not hungry but we should eat a meal together, like families do, so I help Ruthie set the table with forks and spoons and knives even though you only need a fork for spaghetti casserole.

And my mother says so. We don't need knives and spoons, do we? she asks.

But Ruthie doesn't answer.

Soon we are sitting at the kitchen table—my mother included.

I fixed the television for Mrs. Devlin, I say.

Good, my mother says.

I bet she's anxious to get that thing back, Ruthie says. You want me to drive it over?

That's okay, my mother says.

And I wrote the poem for her daughter's second wedding.

Nice, my mother says. I bet you she'll love it.

What's the poem about? Ruthie says.

Hearts and nests, I say.

Perfect, my mother says. I know that will strike the right chord.

Are you going to that wedding? Or did you RSVP with a little handwritten note? Ruthie asks.

We RSVP'd to Ruthie's weddings with a little handwritten note and I'm sure my mother understands this comment.

And mix with all of those people? my mother says. Are you kidding? Tilton's system would implode.

Or is she just a worry stone you've rubbed bare? Ruthie mutters.

What's that? my mother says. Speak up!

I wonder if I am just my mother's worry stone. Is that what Ruthie thinks of me?

Ruthie doesn't repeat herself. She looks at me and says, What exactly are your diagnoses, Tilton? Who's your doctor?

You don't need to get into it, my mother says to me. Medical conditions are your own private business. Last I checked this is still America!

Right. America, Ruthie says.

It's quiet.

Ruthie says, I think Coach Flynn defiled some of the girls in my class.

That's not true, my mother says.

I'm surprised you let Tilton take an acting class with him. Acting? I mean, Coach Flynn?

He was fine, my mother says. I knew him when I was young. He kept his nose clean.

He tried to shoot me a lot, I say.

Shoot you? my mother says.

It was part of our acting lessons. I had to die repeatedly in rice paddies.

He was post-traumatic, Ruthie says. A classic case.

Well, my mother says to Ruthie, you were already gone so I don't know what you could possibly have to say about the matter. My mother holds her head high and glances at Ruthie just to see if she's done some damage. She wants to do damage to Ruthie. We all know this—even Ruthie should know this. Ruthie is probably interested in doing some damage herself.

The whole thing was a really long time ago, I say.

And luckily Tilton came home, my mother adds. School wasn't for her in the end.

With home school you can work at your own pace, I say.

With the right intervention from a specialist, Ruthie says, people with various conditions can adapt very well to things like school and college and jobs and their own apartments and boyfriends and life.

My mother says, Is. That. So?

Trying to distract them, I say to Ruthie, Who did Coach Flynn defile? Did he defile you?

But this only further upsets my mother. Of course he didn't defile Ruthie! my mother says.

No, no, Ruthie says. My life of defiling and being defiled was all before me then.

Tilton has an active imagination, my mother says. She doesn't need acts of sexual perversion put into her mind. It's still lunch, for shit's sake.

Then you lead the conversation, Ruthie says, her voice mimicking calm.

I want to know whether or not the vultures have descended, my mother says.

Vultures? Ruthie says.

Vultures are people who want Wee-ette's seventh book, I explain.

They'll tear this house up looking for it, my mother says. If they know I'm sickly, they'll move in and prey on Tilton's kindness and gentleness.

Ruthie says, We didn't send out a press release updating the media on your condition, if that's what you mean.

That's not what I mean, my mother says.

Ruthie leans forward and says to my mother, Do you have any questions for me? It's been a while.

Tilton has filled me in, my mother says.

Really? On fourteen years?

My mother scoops some spaghetti casserole onto a fork and says, If you have something to add, feel free. Then she fits that bite into her mouth.

Ruthie cuts her spaghetti casserole with her knife as if to prove that a knife is necessary. How can I add anything, she says, if I don't know exactly what you know? Tell me. What's your daughter Ruth like?

She's still herself, my mother says, very quickly. Unchanged.

Ruthie's voice goes soft then, like the air in the room has changed. Am I unchanged? Fourteen years? Look at me, she says.

My mother shakes her head, an angry shake, and continues to eat.

Ruthie pushes her chair back, stands up, and says it again. Look at me.

My mother says, Really, Ruthie.

Just look at me.

My mother looks at Ruthie, and I can tell that my mother's eyes drink her in. She loves Ruthie. After Ruthie ran off, my mother languished. She didn't eat. She let her hair get oily. She didn't want clothes touching her skin. She lay in bed naked. When Wee-ette asked her how she was doing, my mother said she was sick. She said she felt bruised all over. The doctor found nothing wrong. She was never really the same again. I look at my mother looking at Ruthie, and I look at Ruthie, too thin with sloped shoulders, her small nose tip, her blue eyes—and I hope my mother cries. I want her to go weak and give in. It's what Ruthie wants too, and that's why my mother can't give in. My mother says nothing.

Nothing different at all? Ruthie says. She presses her paper towel to her lips and squeezes her eyes shut. You'd have to have known me, she says, really *known me* back then, to be able to tell if I've changed. Wouldn't you?

My mother is afraid of Ruthie. She pretends not to be but she always has been. It's too late for my mother to say anything. The moment has passed. Ruthie sits down and puts her paper towel back in her lap.

It's quiet. The fridge clicks on and hums.

Ruthie finally says, Thank you, Tilton, for the little gift you left me.

I nearly forgot the string, our pact. I wish she hadn't brought it up in front of my mother. You're welcome, I say. I smile big and then dip back into my food, meaning I want her to let it drop.

My mother cuts her eyes from me to Ruthie and back.

I wonder how many pacts like that we had as kids, Ruthie says.

Six, I say.

She looks at me like I've answered one of those kinds of questions that aren't supposed to have answers. She says, It's funny that you still have it here, in the house, after all this time. This house is what's unchanged.

I think you'd have to have known this house back then, my mother says, *really known it,* to be able to tell if it's changed or not. Right?

Wee-ette is here. She's with us. No one knows this house as she knows it, as I know it. A world is tucked in here. A universe. I feel a strange sense of calm because of Wee-ette.

I say, At night sometimes my body can expand so that I am the house.

I become its bony-kneed joists, dimpled plaster, clavicle attic beams, the vacuum's one stiffened lung—ancient, puffed too tightly—the bleached toilet bowl. I'm all of it, down to the umbilical spiral of the phone's cord, down to one shining sunlit dust mote.

I ask Ruthie if she remembers what she thought of this house when we were kids. You thought it was a woman with a big skirt, I say. And when you told me that, I thought of the woman as Wee-ette, who squatted like a nesting bird, all hovering and vigilant. But you were afraid of her. You had bad dreams.

I did? Ruthie says.

My mother looks at me too, like the next thing I say might either condemn her or let her off the hook. But for what crime?

You were afraid that the house would stand up and walk away and leave us here.

I see it in my head the way she described it back then, two women and two little girls with nothing to protect us, the half circle of our pale backs turned to the cold.

That's childish, my mother says.

And I was just a child, Ruthie says.

I put both of my hands flat on the table. This is the middle of the story, I tell them. There's a new ending.

Ruthie looks at my mother. Tell Tilton the truth, she says.

What truth? my mother says.

Mrs. Devlin and her daughter.

What about them?

No one wants to get a TV repaired anymore. No one has record players and mixers rewired. Where do you get the stuff, anyway? Do you even give the poems to anyone to read?

I look at my mother and at Ruthie and then at my mother again, who can't even meet my eyes. I know that it's all been a lie. I know it the way I know a certain birdcall on a certain morning belongs to a certain bird before I even look out the window and see it on the limb, eyeing me with a wet dark eye.

My mother says, Hush, Ruthie. Why are you like this?

Honest? Ruthie says. Why am I honest?

I look at my mother and I ask the same question that Ruthie did. Where do you get the stuff, anyway?

My mother takes in a big breath and then lets it out. Goodwill, she says.

I say, Do you even give the poems to anyone to read?

Mrs. Gottleib, my mother says. She loves your poems. They sometimes make her cry.

Gottleib? I say.

She nods, chastened.

You've been lying to me, I say.

Things have to change, Ruthie says to my mother. It's already started. Do you hear me?

Oh, I'm well aware, my mother says. Very well aware.

If they keep talking, I don't know it because my whole body is pounding inside, like I have a million hearts and all of them are set to burst.

Chapter Eighteen

ANOTHER MIRACLE

Harriet

*E*xcept I was wrong. Eppitt had looked for me. Why had I never looked for him? Maybe I didn't want to find out he was dead or had gone mad from the war.

Sometimes I ate a late lunch after work down the street from the library in a dim restaurant. I ordered the same thing every time: pimento cheese sandwich and onion soup, always served too hot. I read while I waited for it to cool. But one gray spring day in 1935, it was simply too dark to read, and the lamps on the tables were gone.

"What happened to the oil lamps?" I asked the waiter.

"Not for the lunch crowd. Only for dinner now."

Since I couldn't read, I looked around. I wasn't used to looking around. A tall, angular man at the end of the bar, the only other customer, called to the waiter. "Hiram," he said, "can I have a saltshaker?"

This customer was leaning over a bowl of soup. I could make out only the back of his white shirt, thin and airy, see-through, really, revealing the outline of his undershirt. The shirt itself was pinned down between his shoulder blades by a pair of suspenders and puffed around his shoulders.

When Hiram gave him the saltshaker, the man looked at me, and I quickly fumbled for my book and pretended to read. I glanced *up to check if he was still looking at me, and he was, the saltshaker in his hand, frozen. I looked down again but heard his approaching footsteps and soon felt his presence, standing over me.*

"I don't need any salt," I said.

He hadn't realized he was still holding the shaker. He put it on my table and said, "No, no, it's not that. I know you."

"Yes, the library." *This happened sometimes. Libraries attract crazies—is it the books, the ideas within them, the airy space, the quiet, the free public space enabling one to get out of the weather? It wasn't unusual to find loons wandering the stacks, which was partly why it felt like home.*

"Harriet," *he said.*

"Miss Wolf," *I corrected, thinking he was being forward.*

He reached into his pocket and pulled out his wallet. I assumed he was trying to pay a library fine to me directly in the restaurant.

"No, sir," *I said.* "Only within the library during library hours. I can't handle fines anyway. That's Miss Price's job."

But then he held out his hand and there was a loosely wound circle of thread. It was taped at one spot and the tape had writing on it. "E. C. and H. W. 1913. Marriage."

"Miss Price?" *he said.* "No. I came over here because you're my wife."

THE WEDDING NIGHT

The deathy dream was over. I woke up. Let it be a lesson, my Wolf Women. Just because you're living in a deathy dream doesn't mean you can't wake up from it. Eppitt still existed in the world. He came back to me.

I stood up. The napkin in my lap dropped to my shoes. I stared at his face and then reached up and held it in my hands. I needed to feel him to know he was real. His eyes were beautiful—blue and sweet. His skin was soft, freshly shaven. His lips were puffed, his nose slightly crooked. Still thin, he'd grown into his overly dramatic face and his long limbs.

"Harriet," he said.

And that was the moment when I gasped, a delayed reaction. But it wasn't just a gasp: it was a wild ragged breath. My heart was stunned awake. "Eppitt. Eppitt. Eppitt."

He reached his hands around my waist and lifted me off the ground and held me aloft. He kissed me on the mouth, there in the middle of the restaurant. My mouth on his mouth. Tears slipped down my cheeks quickly, and he wiped them with his thumbs. "Harriet. Harriet. Harriet."

"I want my mother to see you, here at last."

"I'd like to meet her," he said.

Of course it was too late for that.

Hiram, who'd been watching behind the bar, called to the dishwasher, the cook. "You got to see this!"

They emerged from the back, drying their hands on their aprons.

"My wife!" Eppitt shouted to them.

"You just found your wife?" Hiram said.

"I lost her and now she's found!" Eppitt cried.

We sat at the bar and drank with the three men. We told them how, between two billowing sheets, we'd made a vow. We didn't mention that we were morons.

"How'd you get separated?" Hiram asked.

"The war?" asked the dishwasher, who was missing most of his hand.

Eppitt and I looked at each other and nodded. How else to explain what had happened? This felt close enough.

"War," I said. "Yes, we were separated by war."

Eppitt didn't take me to Mrs. Oblatt's boarding house, with its women, its shrill water pipes, and its pissy stink. We walked instead a few blocks through the cold to his apartment, our arms locked. His place was small, just a room with a kitchen attached, but it had its own bathroom, a luxury. The paint was old and peeling. There were no curtains, no soft touches. But I didn't care. I was his wife.

Eppitt lay me down on his bed. I was older now. A woman in her midthirties was ancient then. To everyone else, I was unmarriable. An old maid. I was a librarian who stalked the stacks. A biddy.

"Remember the Wolf Woman?" I said. "I clipped the story of her. She was alone and they shot her."

"I remember," he said.

"I've been alone for a long time."

"It's good that you didn't get shot."

We undressed slowly. We now had time. We weren't two children hiding behind sheets, exposed by a gust of wind, or kids hiding under porch boards.

Eppitt had a wide row of knuckles and long fingers. He unbuttoned my sweater and my blouse—a row of fake pearls. My own breasts surprised me, my fluted waist, my full hips. Where did this body come from? It had been hidden beneath slips and cotton and wool. It was like Eppitt had unearthed me. The mummy unwrapped, alive again.

And I'd never seen a man's brightly lit body before. Eppitt wasn't a boy who had to stay in the steam. With slatted ribs, his upper body broadened from his taut muscular stomach to thick shoulders. He had moles, here and there, which made his body seem like it had been partially thought out by a cartographer.

As kids we'd stayed fully dressed when pressed together, and I'd seen only anatomical drawings of male bodies in medical texts. I had just a vague image of what might be stiffened, but I'd imagined it incorrectly. I was surprised by its firm bounce, the rubber give of skin and toughness, and the perfect fit of it, shuttled in on his hips between my legs.

Our lovemaking was quiet and urgent. The women at Mrs. Oblatt's complained that men were grunting beasts, but Eppitt was beautiful and sweet and mine. My husband. At last.

After it was over, we lay there. I was ruptured. Again, there was blood. Eppitt remembered this about me too.

"The Bleeder of Stump Cottage," he said. He got towels and I bunched them between my legs and we lay down again.

"It's our wedding night," I whispered.

He nuzzled my neck. "Been a long time coming."

We could see the moon when we tilted our heads just so on the bed.

"What does my husband do for a living?" I asked.

"Your husband is a businessman who has a business partner. You'll have to meet your husband's business partner. He throws parties for all of his clients and constituents and allies."

"Is my husband a war hero?"

"Not really, not a hero. No." He turned to me. "And my wife..."

"Is a librarian." This wasn't exactly true. I was an assistant in the library, but it was close enough.

"My wife, the librarian—where has she been all these years?"

"Pining," I said. "Alone, lost, and pining."

"And now my wife is happy and found and not alone ever again."

"Do you still combine words?" I asked him.

"Sometimes," he said. And then he shouted, "Oh, how I love my wovely life!"

THE PROFESSIONAL HIDER

To get married officially seemed a betrayal, as if we would be saying that our marriage bound by string wasn't real. But still, the next morning, after I'd fried eggs and while we ate them in bed, Eppitt said, "Do you want to get the license?"

"No, I don't think I do."

"Somewhere down the line someone might ask for it."

"Do people really ask for marriage licenses?"

"I've never told someone I was married before so I've never had to prove it."

"What about your family? Would you want them to come to a wedding?"

"No," he said, his jaw stiffening as he chewed his eggs. "Some are alive. Some dead. I don't go back."

"What about your sister Meg?"

He shook his head. She was gone. "Would your family want a wedding?" he asked.

I wiped my mouth with a napkin. "My mother died," I said.

"I thought you said—"

"I do want her to see you," I said. "And she does, in her way. She's still with me."

His eyes turned moist. "I remember her grabbing you and hugging you on the lawn. I was as jealous as I've ever been."

"I'm sorry," I said, remembering the abruptness, the sudden abandonment.

"What? You couldn't stay on. You had to go and be happy."

"I loved my mother so much."

"What about your father?"

"I have no reason to talk to him. He sends some money to Mrs. Oblatt for rent. I wouldn't mind if he got a note one day from her

saying I was gone. I wouldn't mind if she never told him and kept the money for herself."

"I hated your father," Eppitt said.

"You knew him enough to hate him?"

He stood up and walked to a window. "I got out at fifteen, but it was hard for a while. Eventually, the new cotton mills needed workers and they weren't picky. Then I moved to the docks. I got up some money, enough so I felt proud of myself, like I could take care of us. I got on a bus and then hired a taxi to your parents' house. It wasn't too hard to track your father down. I stood outside and looked at the windows. Then your father walked out and was getting into his car, a Model T. I walked up to him and stated my intentions, that I was in love with you and wanted to marry you."

I try to imagine Eppitt at fifteen, my father by the old black town car. Somewhere behind one of the windows, I was probably dreaming of Eppitt. "What did my father say?"

"He asked me who I was and how I knew you, and I said, 'From school.' And he said, 'That place? It's hardly a school. Leave her alone. Her mother and I don't want any trouble. She's happy, for once. Let her be happy.'" Eppitt's back was to me, and I couldn't read his expression. "I followed you and your mother around—now and then. You were happy. I left you alone. It was the least I could do."

"You saw me with my mother?"

"On outings, on walks, going to the pictures. I saw the way you linked arms and talked like crazy."

"She was beautiful, wasn't she?"

"You were beautiful together," he said. "But it wasn't good for me to watch you like that. It was a sin, I think. But I couldn't stop until I met Isley Wesler, and my life changed. He got me better work. I had money and I knew you were getting older, marrying age. So

I came back to that house at seventeen. I gave a note to the house-keeper."

"My mother's nurse?"

"I don't know. I just handed it to her and said, 'Give this to Harriet, will you?' And she looked at me with her face blank and white. She said, "Oh, no. Harriet's gone, son." Eppitt started coughing and I worried again about his weak lungs, but then he started speaking again, his voice quiet and small. "The look in her eyes made me think that you were really gone. Dead. I looked up then and saw the notice on the door, the warning of Spanish flu, and I assumed that's how you'd fallen."

"It was my mother who died," I said. "I was hers for four years, but I couldn't stay after she died, so I made my own way," I said, avoiding any mention of my institutionalization. "All these years, you never got married?"

"I was already married to you."

"Even after you thought I was dead?"

"I never really could accept that. What about you? You never got married either."

"Me? No," I said. "So where have you been all these years?"

Eppitt said that when Isley found him he'd been carting bananas on the docks for Antonio Lanasa. I'd heard of Lanasa from my clippings. He shipped bananas in from Jamaica. There'd been an incident, a bombing of the house of a competitor, DiGiorgio, that was referenced in a lot of the articles. Two sticks of dynamite had gone off in an empty room—the DiGiorgios' three parrots flew off, untouched. Lanasa's partner, a Jamaican named Goffe, was put on trial but went free. Eppitt explained how the bananas came in on steamships, and then down a conveyor belt from the hulls. They put the stems on their backs and they hauled more than a hundred pounds of them at a time. And they fought on the docks too—ugly stuff: knives, cleavers. But he felt he was lucky to have the work. Then one payday he went to a pool hall. Isley was there, wearing a full-length coonskin coat. He weighed about 120 pounds, but had full cheeks and a buttery ring of fat around his middle, which Eppitt read as well fed and no heavy lifting. Isley asked him what he was hiding. Eppitt told him that he wasn't hiding anything. Isley said that that was the kind of thing someone who was hiding something might say.

"I kept a lot to myself," Eppitt told me. "But Isley said he had work for someone secretive and smart, so I became a professional hider."

I thought of the origami cranes I'd hidden under my mattress, flocks of them, all for Eppitt. I was a hider too, but I didn't know what a professional hider did.

"People want something hidden, something important," Eppitt explained. "They leave and I find a foolproof hiding place for it. When they come home, I give them an hour. If they can find it, I give them their money back. If they can't, I tell them the hiding place and they pay up."

"Do you make much money?"

"Enough. But I'm trustworthy, and now my head is worth a lot of money," he said. "I know where things are hidden all over this town. It's all up here." He tapped his temple. "Every last hiding place I ever made."

"Are you hiding anything from me?" I asked.

"No," he said. "I don't have to with you."

"That's what someone who's hiding something might say."

"I guess you're right."

TENDER AND TENDED

My mother once told me how Jesus mended the cut-off ear of a soldier. I saw the new ear in my mind, how it unfurled, pink and fleshy, not ornamentation, not an ear brooch, but a real ear, ringing again with sound. I was that ear. I was new and ringing.

A few days after Eppitt found me, I packed my things while he stood in Mrs. Oblatt's parlor, awkwardly ducking an unlit lamp hanging from the ceiling in the hallway. Mrs. Oblatt was doing needlework, silently. Her needlepoint no longer stayed within set patterns. While Eppitt waited, she sometimes glared at him as if he'd suddenly shown up, unannounced.

"What do you want? Who are you here to see?"

He'd explained many times that he was my husband. I could hear him because Mrs. Oblatt was nearly deaf by this point—perhaps as a means of self-preservation—and so he had to shout, which alerted the other women, who came down from their rooms, as I did, holding my small case.

They squinted at us, asking when the wedding was, where my ring was, why I hadn't ever said before that I was married.

"Excuse me now," I said. "We've got to go."

These women were my third set of outcasts: unwanted children, the unwanted insane, and now unwanted women. Would I ever be truly free of the company of the unwanted? I was sure that this was it. Eppitt wanted me.

Before I said my good-byes, I told Mrs. Oblatt that I would be switching my newspaper subscriptions, but it might take a while for them to follow me.

She simply said, "Good riddance!"

We went to the library, where I gave my notice, effective imme-

diately. Eppitt looked uncomfortable in the large airy openness. He shifted near the card catalogs, holding my bag.

"I'm a married woman now," I told those working the checkout desk.

The head librarian was out. "You'll have to wait and tell him in person," one of the women said as if she didn't think I had the courage.

"I'll jot a note."

I wrote, "I've found my husband, at long last, and am no longer in need of employment." I wondered if the last part was true. Did Eppitt earn enough money hiding things to make ends meet? I flushed suddenly, but it was too late. I slid the sheet across the desk and we left.

From then on, I was sure I would have someone to guide me. And I needed that guiding hand because I felt wild. I loved Eppitt wildly, the way a gibbon loves howling and swinging.

I decided that I had no more need for books. The truth that writers secretly harbor is that all books are failures. We try to do something that can't be done. Words. Is that all we rely on? Smudgy ink marks on a page? Pallid wisps and blotches? Text as scaffolding trying to hold up worlds?

Actually, no, it's not all we rely on. What's worse is our reliance on the reader. A writer is forever locked in an interdependent relationship. It's like building a bridge from opposite sides of a river—our flimsy words and their frail, overreaching imaginations. The bridge will never meet in the middle. It's not possible. Sometimes you haven't even decided on the same river. The Gateway Arch in Saint Louis missed in the middle by a matter of inches the first time around. They tried again and made it. Writers know we never will.

My clippings. I had no need for that either. I kept my books of

clippings with me, but clipping is what lonely people do—docu-
mentation of the living. I was no longer one of the lonely. I was one
of the living now.

Eppitt would go off to hide things for Isley Wesler's clients, and I
would stay in our small apartment, part of an old chopped-up house
now home to five families. Within days, I'd sewn new curtains for
its three windows. The Maryland School had taught me that much.
As soon as Eppitt arrived home, we made love. I was sore from so
much of it.

Sometimes he made small boxes of various sizes—thin plywood,
nails, epoxy. Some had little rings for handles. He made them from
dimensions scribbled on a notepad. I begged him to tell me where,
in an ordinary house, the little boxes might fit.

"Where you'd least expect to find them."

Sometimes he sawed and painted and made doors with fake
panels.

And sometimes we played cards—with me in my slip, him in
his drawers, and tried not to ravage each other. And then we'd rav-
age each other.

One day, he came home with a red envelope containing an invi-
tation to a party at Isley Wesler's house. The card was cream-colored.
The party was titled "In Celebration of Love and Freud."

"What does that mean?" I asked. I knew of Freud, of course.
There had been some Freudians at Sheppard Pratt, in fact.

"You never can tell with Isley Wesler," Eppitt said.

"Formal dress required," I read aloud. "The party's tonight. I
don't have a formal dress."

"It doesn't matter."

"But it says formal dress," I said.

"Wesler would be fine if you came nude."

I wore a blue dress with a wide belt and a collar that covered my collarbone. It was the dress of a librarian—my uniform. I wore my hair down in loosely puffed curls. I bought a tube of red lipstick and put some on while looking in the bathroom mirror, and then, feeling clownish, I wiped it off. "I can't wear lipstick," I called to Eppitt. "My face rejects it."

"Come out here," he said. He took the tube from me and said, "Make your lips taut." In a few deft movements—two for my upper lip, from the arches out, and one for the bottom lip—he drew an artful bow. "Rub your lips together."

And I did.

He held up a piece of tissue paper. "Blot."

I blotted. "How do you know how to do this?" I asked.

"I've watched." Eppitt had never married, but he knew women. He had a past. I decided not to ask about it. The main thing is that I remember this moment vividly because this is how we were together. We took care of each other in small, tender ways. We were never simply lovers. We filled all the roles for each other—mother, father, brother, sister, each the other's tender and tended.

ISLEY WESLER

Isley Wesler's parties were held in a house out on Joppa Road, where, years later, he would hang a homemade white clapboard sign: "Welcome to the Isley Wesler Museum of Antiquities. Free to the public."

But on that warm autumn evening in 1935, when Eppitt and I rode up to the entrance in a Buick, borrowed from one of his clients, there was nothing but a mailbox nailed to a tree wearing a pink ribbon sash. The ribbon was supposed to be cheery, maybe whimsical, but it had lost some of its tether points and now sagged.

"I'm nervous," I said. "Tell me what to expect."

"Impossible," Eppitt said.

We followed the long white fence to the circle driveway, jammed with cars. The adjacent field was packed too. The stone house was enormous. Summer had ended, and the air was chilled. I wore a blue wrap to match my dress. When Eppitt helped me out of the car, I could hear music, a number of different songs all at once.

He whispered, "This is really living, Harriet. It's how we can make up for lost time. We can be anyone here."

The last party I'd been to was the Armistice party, where we'd sung and danced on the Sheppard Pratt lawn. I hadn't told Eppitt that I'd been in a mental hospital, much less that I felt responsible for my mother's death. "We can be anyone," I repeated.

An animal barked nearby, but in a note higher than a dog's. The creature lifted heavily off the ground for a few feet before flopping down.

"Peacocks," Eppitt told me, squeezing my hand.

I searched out the birds' pinched faces and festooned heads, their bodies bobbing as they dragged their tails through dirt. I'd never seen one before. I thought of Ota Benga, mingling with peacocks in the Bronx Zoo. "Real peacocks!" I said.

"They're nesting in the chimney."

"They're beautiful!"

"And dirty."

"I think that makes them even more beautiful."

A drunken couple stumbled off the porch into the darkened yard and wove through the cars. The woman was glamorous, her dress elaborately beaded and her hair shining. She wiggled her fingers at me and said, "Toodles, Junie!" The seam of her dress was ripped up her thigh and the snaps of a garter glinted.

"Toodles!" I said back. We could be anyone.

The front door stood wide open. A man in a green evening dress *appeared and grabbed onto the frame as if he'd been thrown there. A wide hoop skirt belled around his ankles. "Eppitt Clapp! You are a darling boy!"*

"Isley!" Eppitt said, and the two hugged each other with loud claps on the back.

"This is my wife," Eppitt said.

But Isley wasn't listening. He was pale, his blue eyes oversized for his chubby face. The dress dipped into a hairless chest and his cleavage bulged, ridiculously overstuffed with tissues. His puffed belly pressured the seams of the narrow waistline. "I can't hear a damn thing. Five Philcos on five different stations in five different rooms!" He seemed enchanted by the idea of it. "I just set loose a dozen doves. You missed it! Let me introduce you around." He gave his breasts an excited squeeze, pulled a folded fan from his bosom, and charged into the smoky rooms.

I'd never seen anything like Isley Wesler. "That's him?" I said.

"In the flesh," Eppitt said.

The marbled hallway led to a large living room teeming with people. Blue and pink streamers flapped from the wire cages of blowing office fans. Still, the crowded bodies made the room humid. An enormous man sat at an upright playing a mournful version of "I've Got a Right to Sing the Blues." He reminded me of a plaintive wildebeest. A radio piped a jittery song. Its dial glowed like a moon. A small band of sweaty dancers bounced in a circle.

Isley was proud of the radios, and bragged about them excitedly: "They've all got four tuning bands, bass compensations, Super Class A audio systems, auditorium speakers, and illuminated station recording dials." He took my wrap and slipped it around his shoulders. A woman walked by with drinks on a mirrored tray. Isley grabbed two as she passed and handed them to Eppitt and me. I'd never taken a drink in my life.

Isley tapped Eppitt on the chest with the fan. "Didn't the invitation say formal dress required?"

"Was I supposed to wear a ball gown?"

"Doesn't anybody listen to me anymore?"

"What's on the piano in the large glass jar?" I asked.

"An eight-legged fetal calf," he said, pointing to the creature suspended in fluid. "Born dead. We had it preserved. One day I hope to have a display, 'Show of World Wonders.'" (Wonders—the word stuck in my mind.) He then introduced us to a blonde woman. "This is Beryl Wallace," he said. "I imported her all the way from New York City. She's been doing Carroll's Sketch Book.*" He tipped forward, acknowledging me for the first time. "It's a hurly-burly burlesque-y thing." He turned back to Eppitt. "But highbrow. Right, Beryl?"*

Beryl was bored. How could anyone be bored here? The music rang my ribs. The smoke filled my head. The liquor heated my chest. Beryl pointed her cigarette at Eppitt and me. "And who are they?" she asked Isley.

"These are ordinary folks." He stared at the two of us as if being ordinary alone made us part of his future Show of World Wonders. "Ordinary folks" was better than "moron," "lunatic," or "murderess." "True rarities, Beryl." He pointed at me. "And this one's name?" he asked Eppitt. "This one here?"

I sipped my drink nervously. It was strong, opening up my nose.

"My wife, Harriet."

"Your wife! My God! You're married? Are you sure?" Isley turned to Beryl. "Ordinary people are mad, Beryl, you see? Completely mad!" He said to Eppitt, "Don't bother Beryl, then, if you're married. Don't waste her time!"

He led us to a clot of somber people, hunched forward in high-back chairs. They pinched their cigarette tips tightly with index finger and thumb, even the woman among them. At first I didn't recognize her as a woman. "And, over here, some Commies," Isley told us. "They're a dark cloud. I wouldn't invite them if I didn't have to—you know, for appearances' sake." He hailed them. "Fellow citizens! These are ordinary folks. Eppitt Clapp, and who's this again?"

"Harriet!" I said.

"Harriet Clapp!" Eppitt said, and I must have stared at him, startled.

"What else would I call you?" he said.

"The venerable Mrs. Eppitt Clapp!" Isley said, sensing tension and joining in.

"Do you know Leon Trotsky?" I asked, having read a lot about him.

"Not personally," the woman answered flatly.

Isley's attention was drawn to the ceiling, as if wondering if it would hold or not. He grabbed Eppitt's arm and pointed up. "Can you hear her up there? You've got to tell me."

Eppitt looked at the ceiling too. "No. I can't hear her."

"Well, it took five Philcos! I hoped that would drown her out! I've got to go up. Hopefully no one's barged in! We've got a few in from Amsterdam. You can't trust them with intimate spaces normally reserved for sexual congress. I'm so partial to the untrustworthy. It's a true failing."

Isley walked off, stopping briefly in front of three midgets: two men and a woman. The men wore Stetsons, probably made for children, although I couldn't imagine who would buy a Stetson for a child. A black dog trotted by and licked the woman's face. She soured and slapped its nose.

Isley shouted across the room, "Come and get me if Moss Hart shows up. Or Fay Wray or the DeMarcos or the Brown Bomber. Show that girl the heart of the mongrel king, Eppitt!" Isley's dress was too short, exposing his ankles, clean and thin as a woman's. He was still holding my blue wrap over his shoulders.

I was thinking about Fay Wray, the DeMarcos. Would I meet Joe Louis, the Brown Bomber? "I like boxing," I said. "I'm a fan of organized brutality."

"Better than the unorganized kind," Eppitt said.

I followed Eppitt to the mantel and he pulled down a silver box. "Are any of those people really coming?" I asked.

"Huey Long could walk through the door in his pajamas."

"Huey Long is dead!"

"That's what I mean." Eppitt popped open the box's silver lid. Inside lay a small dark object, like a piece of desiccated fruit nestled in velvet.

"What is it?"

"A heart."

"Whose heart is that small?"

"I think it was once big. It's the heart of a mongrel king. A Wesler family heirloom."

"Why would anyone want someone's shrunken heart?"

"Maybe it's a spare." Eppitt shut the box and put it back on the mantel.

I heard the clattering from upstairs now. "Whose voice is he drowning out?"

"His mother is an invalid. She can't move a muscle except to write checks for him and bang on the floorboards with a broom handle."

"He's lucky to have a mother."

"I don't think he'd agree."

In the corner, a woman in a black shawl and plumed hat was taking photographs with a new Kodak. She winked at Eppitt. "Come on," she said. "Let's make a picture."

Eppitt asked me if I wanted to and I nodded. There was only one chair. He sat down in it.

"Get on his lap," the woman told me.

I did. "Our wedding portrait," I whispered to Eppitt.

Eppitt looked at me and smiled. "Gride and broom."

"Which one are you?" I asked.

"We're both both."

The photographer had a notepad. "What are your names?"

"Mr. and Mrs. Eppitt Clapp," I told her.

She disappeared suddenly behind the lens. "Look here!" She lifted her hand in the air. My eyes snapped to her hand. Eppitt patted my rump, the fleshy bit hanging off his lap. It shocked me, this little pat. My eyes opened wide. I wondered if Eppitt was drunk. His glass was already gone. The camera's flash went off. I looked around the room, and the flare pulsed each time I blinked. I was drunk now too. I felt hot and the room wavered.

We stood up, and Eppitt went to find the woman with the drinks. "Stay put," he said, but I wandered through the crowd. I was making up for lost time. I could be anyone.

I overheard a man say, "Did you see Baboona? Actual filming of baboons escaping from these wild cheetahs."

A woman with a tightly pursed mouth said, "No. But I saw Greer Garson in Accent on Youth onstage. Nicholas Hannen! Now there's a baboon!"

Near a punch bowl, another woman said, "Dear God! Can you imagine? Wax heads. Mussolini."

"Where's this?" I asked the woman. I could be someone who jumped into conversations.

"Madame Tussauds! I hear Mussolini looks quite handsome."

Dr. Wolff. For some reason, he appeared in my mind. Maybe because Mussolini's mug shot from 1903 had surfaced in newspapers—*his young arrest for vagrancy—and he looked a bit like Wolff: dark hair and eyes, tender in a way that you wouldn't expect. "I guess so," I said. Wolff, Wolff. Drunk, I felt a rush of love for him. He was dead and it felt almost new.*

Where was Eppitt? Had he left me? I decided that if he was gone, I'd stay. I'd stay here forever. I stood near one of the glowing Philcos like a lonesome moth and fluttered my hands, dancing a little. The asylum lawn was the only place I'd danced before.

A teenage girl with a ragged puff of hair held feebly by a ribbon tugged at my sleeve. "Do you have any Mistol Drops?" She rubbed her nose. "The fiends are in the yard. Kuda Bux is going to walk on hot coals. Do you have any Mistol Drops or don't you?"

"Hot coals?"

"Hot coals," the girl said. "So? Mistol Drops?"

"I don't," I said, "but I'd like some." I'd never heard of them before.

"Oh," the young woman said. "Get in line!"

I found double doors leading to a patio and a wide lawn. A crowd had formed around a path of lit coals—a garden of fiery blooms. "A fire in the flower bed!" I said aloud. Isley was back, wearing a gas mask, his voice so muffled one could barely hear him. He led a dark-skinned man to the coals—Kuda Bux, I guessed. Kuda was barefoot, wearing slacks and a pressed white shirt. As he walked the coals, the crowd clapped, louder and faster. He was serene. Once on the other side, he gave a small bow.

The fat pianist wanted to give it a go. He stepped on the heel of one shoe with the other, teetering, and then squatted to peel off a sock.

"Har-low! Har-low!" the crowd shouted.

Isley rushed at me, suddenly standing much too close and panting raggedly through the mask. He looked like an enlarged insect, his hair a wispy plume on his head. He was carrying an armful of gas masks. "They're all the rage in London!" He handed me one. "Try it!"

I strapped it on. It was too tight so I took it off.

"Do you like me?" Isley asked me through his mask.

"This is the most marvelous party I've ever been to!" I said.

"You know I saved Eppitt's life. He'd be dead in a trench, if not for me!"

"You were in the war together?"

"Of course not! I got him out of the war. I got him on with burlesque and provide his current employ. He's not bad with mobsters. When you grow up like him, without, you've got nothing to lose, right? He was a milksop before he met me."

"I don't know what you're talking about." Eppitt told me he wasn't a war hero, but had he not served at all? Burlesque? Mobsters? We could be anyone here. Eppitt was someone else. I said, "I've done some dancing myself, you know."

"The boards? You? Really?"

"Of course!"

"Maybe you could put on a little demonstration later."

I spotted Eppitt across the lawn, looking around, maybe for me. "Okay," I said, and I winked, puckered my lips, and unbuttoned the top button of my high-collared dress.

Eppitt bounded over.

Isley said, "I had no idea about her, kid! No idea."

"Where did you go?" Eppitt asked me, with jangled alarm. "I couldn't find you."

"Eppitt doesn't like people leaving him," Isley said. "Tell her you've forgiven me for all that old business. Tell me all's forgiven."

Eppitt reared a little. He put his hands in his pockets. "Well, sure!" he said. "Of course all's forgiven, Isley. What are you talking about? Our time in the war?"

"Oh, that!" Isley sighed wearily. "Are you still singing that old song, Clapp? She knows. I told her," he said. "Here, take a gas mask." He shoved it at Eppitt with such force that he had to take it. "You might need it. You never know!" He walked back to the crowd at the coals.

Eppitt was holding the gas mask gently with both hands like it was a kitten. I was dizzy. He was blurred.

"Tell me the truth," I whispered.

"What truth?"

"Pick one," I said.

"Will you love me no matter what?"

"Of course."

He looked over at Harlow, who was tripping over coals, and then veered quickly and landed on his rump in the grass. His face, a deep purple, pursed, and then broke into a howl.

"I wasn't in the war. Isley bribed someone to fail me on the physical. I might have failed anyway. He got me working burlesques. Security. One time he left me on a rum run and I got in trouble with the law. I did some jail time. He got me the hiding job afterward because I took the fall for him."

I understood jail, in my way. "Mobsters? Is that who needs things hidden?"

"Mobsters and some regular folks." He put his hands on my hips and then worked them up my waist. "But all that is okay here. We can live on the edges of things. No one cares what people on the edges do."

"I feel like a killer," I said.

He laughed. "Who'd you kill?"

"My mother."

He looked at me. "Tell me, Harriet, are you sure about that?"

"She was a shut-in and then I arrived and we went out. She died of contagion because of me. And then I was in the crazy house. Sheppard Pratt."

"You didn't kill your mother, Harriet. Not at all. You brought her to life. Don't you see that?"

I hadn't before.

He went on. "And around here, an asylum stint is something you could brag about. Jesus, did you know Zelda Fitzgerald has done time at Pratt? Isley had Scott and Zelda out for a lawn party. They fought over a game of croquet."

The edges. That's where we were. The girl looking for the Mistol Drops must have found the fiends. She was smoking something with them beyond the coals, along with the midget in the Stetson and one of the Communists. I could smell the sweet smoke.

"Let's dance," Eppitt said.

Inside the house, the dancers were frenetic. Beryl was swooped up by some man, and when she landed, one of her breasts popped up enough to show a nipple. She stuffed it back in, and left with a toady little man whose Adam's apple was more prominent than his chin. Eppitt and I tried a few steps but were unpracticed. Our hands slipped away from each other, and Eppitt was swarmed by a group of shimmy girls. When I spun and turned toward him again, his nose was crooked, his brow too dark. It wasn't Eppitt at all.

The stranger smiled at me. "Hello there," he said.

"Harriet!" Eppitt was calling me. I turned, but I couldn't find his voice. "Harriet! Here!"

Then I saw him behind the piano. I pushed through the dancers. When I reached him, I was breathless. "I have to go to the bathroom," I said, feeling sick.

"Upstairs!" he shouted.

I climbed the stairs to a dark landing with four closed doors. A light shone underneath one so I knocked.

"Taken!" a man shouted.

I knocked on the next door. "Isley! Isley Wesler!" It was an old woman's voice. "I hear you! I can hear everything!" I remembered my wrap. I'd last seen it on Isley's arm as he headed upstairs to talk to his mother.

"It isn't Isley," I said through the door.

"Come in! Come in!" the old woman shouted.

I closed my eyes. Walls spinning. I grabbed the knob, to steady myself, and then turned it and opened the door. The room was dimly lit, the bed high. There was the smell of old bed linens and something else familiar. The old woman lay in the bed. Her partially closed eyes were wet, the lids tight and small, as if it were the lids that kept her from being able to see. Her eyeballs shifted, exposing milky sky.

"My name is Harriet Clapp."

"Are you after my son?"

"No, I'm married."

"Keep your purse strings tight. Take care of your own. Or you'll end up destitute. Men die, Harriet Clapp. Men die. Men leave. Men are untrustworthy. But money. Money is tried-and-true. Do you have children?"

"No."

"Really?" Her eyes seemed to stare through me. The woman wasn't blind so much as I was invisible. "Pray for daughters, Harriet Clapp. Boys are worthless. My Isley is a menace. I'd strike him if I had a good chance." She clapped her hands violently and one of the walls fluttered. I could now see birdcages strung from the ceiling—Isley's doves. I smelled the bird shit, and again the familiar smell: newspapers. They lined the cages.

"I'm going to go," I said.

"Go, then. Leave!"

I backed out of the room and shut the door lightly. I went to the bathroom at the end of the hall. It was large, with a claw-foot tub. On the wall opposite the mirror, an enormous sword was mounted. Beneath it hung a photograph of a soldier—undoubtedly a Wesler, with his pale porky face and skinny legs—holding the decapitated head of a native by the hair, quite proudly. Sitting heavily on the seat, I peed. While washing my hands, I saw the sword and the framed photograph behind me in the warped mirror. I was too tired to go on. I sat in the tub, just to rest, and then lay down in it.

Eppitt found me asleep in the tub, picked me up, and carried me downstairs, where the dancers jerked wildly, like things made of wire. They bared their teeth and shook epileptically. I remembered the children at the Maryland School who were prone to fits.

"Our angels!" I said to Eppitt. "Look!"

"Hush now." He took me into the open air and sat in a wooden chair with me on his lap.

Isley sat down beside us on the ground like some fallen queen, his gown frumped around him. "Don't you want to stay all night?" he asked.

"It's almost morning," Eppitt said.

"I want to stay and stay," I said.

"Cole Porter didn't come! Neither did Luigi Pirandello. Aren't we three characters in search of an author? And Halliburton, that fellow crossing the Alps on an elephant like Hannibal. He didn't show. Perhaps he isn't back yet. I heard he had troubles with customs. And I didn't invite the Duke of Gloucester and his fiancée. There was a garden party at Bowhill, I hear. My invitation must have gotten lost in the mail!"

"It's a great party without them." Eppitt sighed.

"It's like our wedding party," I said. "We never had one."

"I don't even know your bride." Isley's lids were fat, his eyes bloodshot. "Are you from Sparrows Point like Eppitt? Before the industrial wreckage and poverty, it was a beautiful marshland. Named after those swarming sparrows. Beautiful! Imagine air muscled by thousands of beating wings!" He gazed at Eppitt. "Just when you've written me off completely, I go and say something worthwhile!"

"It was named after Thomas Sparrow," I said. I'd read too much. "Not birds."

Isley ignored me. "What I wouldn't give to be on the roof of the RCA building. They've got Japanese trees up there, a Tudor arch, a cobbled Spanish patio with a wellhead transported from Granada. And lemon trees, Eppitt!"

"It was a great party, Isley! Everyone will be talking about it."

"Really?" Isley asked, but then he quickly pouted. "Still, what I wouldn't give just to be in that horrible taxi dance hall on Fourteenth!"

"How could you leave your mother?" I said to Isley, thinking of my own. I stuffed my fingers through the opening between two buttons on Eppitt's shirt—like he was Napoleon and I was Napoleon's hand.

"Abercrombie & Fitch is selling riding breeches of cavalry twill!" Isley was wistful. "And all summer Tripler's had a hat of coconut fiber being worn by people throughout the Bahamas. And I'm only ever here."

"You could get a real job," Eppitt suggested.

Isley straightened and turned his head, as if smelling something sharp. "Work doesn't suit me. It's why I can never quite get on with the Communists."

Then the girl in search of the Mistol Drops appeared, cupping something in her hands. She'd lost the ribbon wound around her hair. She opened her hands. "It's dead!" she said, holding one of the doves.

"No, it isn't dead, dear!" Isley told her. "It's sleeping."

"It's dead," she insisted.

"If you go looking for tragedy, you'll find it! Clapp knows that. He's gotten married, for Christ's sake. Beyond all reason!"

Eppitt ignored him. He leaned toward the bird and then back toward me. "It's dead, Isley."

And it was, limp and lifeless.

"I'm sure it's barely dead," Isley said.

"It's dead dead," the girl said.

"Let's have a burial! We could have a ritual ceremony. Are you a virgin?" he asked the girl.

She looked up at him, wide-eyed.

"Don't worry. I don't believe in sacrificing virgins!" Isley comforted the girl. "No, no, dear. That's just a silly waste! You'll find I'm quite civilized."

He walked off with the girl, away from the house, the fiends, out toward a distant stand of trees, his green dress billowing in a puff of wind like a rising balloon. I thought of his mother in the upstairs bedroom, shifting with the caged doves. "Men die. Men leave. Men are untrustworthy." Doesn't everyone leave at some point—or we're the ones who get left behind? Isn't that what life had taught me? "Pray for daughters." It had never dawned on me to pray for anything, and I'd long since given up on the idea of having a child. But if I could be anyone, if this could be home, why not a family? Why not children?

I was drunk and everything was churning. My life was different now. This was a new world, and whether it needed me or not, here I was in it. I gripped Eppitt's shirt with my fists and held tight.

Chapter Nineteen

WOLPE'S METHOD OF SYSTEMATIC DESENSITIZATION

Ruth

I'm inside a Wawa waiting out a late-afternoon rain shower. Eleanor would call this dawdling. She'd have rushed out of the store by now, hunched over her purchases, and driven off in the driving rain. She pops into my mind constantly, forcing me to compare myself to her. It's like living my own life and my mother's at the same time.

It's been a few days since I promised Tilton I'd take her to George. She keeps asking if I've located him yet, whispering so that Eleanor can't hear. I'm worried about Tilton. She's agitated and restless but isn't leaving the house—out of deference to Eleanor?

Ron's called a few times, left messages that I haven't returned. He still wants to know if I'm coming to the wedding and the gala. He once said, "How about the rest of our lives? Are you in for that too?"

But I need him to look up George's whereabouts and I should touch base too. I can't keep avoiding him.

I call and he answers, "Yes?" He sounds harassed.

"Are you okay?"

"I thought it was Justin. I sent him for ice. Do hotels have ice machines anymore? Shit. He's probably lost out there." He shifts his tone quickly. "I'm glad you called back. It's good to hear your voice."

I say that it's good to hear his too, but I don't know how I feel. "Do you have Internet access?"

"You don't?"

"I'm living in 1974. I can't even hope for dial-up."

"I've got the laptop running. What do you need?"

"George Tarkington."

"Didn't you promise yourself that you'd never have anything to do with him?"

I walk past the antacids, tampon boxes. "Tilton needs this. And it will piss off my mother."

"Still devoted to pissing her off?"

"It's a lifelong vocation," I say.

It's quiet as he searches, and then he says, "I thought you might lighten up on her so close to the end."

"Oh, right," I say, remembering my lie. "I'm sorry about that. She isn't dying. I told you that so you wouldn't pop in."

"You lied to me?"

"We're all dying, technically."

"Damn it, Ruth! I told Susan Burchard." Susan Burchard is a cofounder of the Harriet Wolf Society. "She's been desperate to get in touch with you. Damn it!"

"My mother isn't dying. This is *good* news."

"I'm sorry. It's just...She was thinking that maybe before Eleanor dies, she'd give an indication. You know—"

"Eleanor isn't ever going to give an indication." Our mother made us promise to never talk about the book's demise, page by burnt page. Can I break a pact that was based on a possible lie? I scratch my forehead with the edge of the phone. The pact with Tilton is the one that matters. Wound string, labeled and kept all these years—it sits in the zippered pouch inside my pocket-book.

"You know what I think?" Ron says. "Tilton knows. She's a savant, isn't she?"

"Just look up George Tarkington. Oxford, Pennsylvania." I stare at the bank of fogged freezer doors and remember this winter party scene in one of Harriet's later books: the party has spilled onto the lawn because it's started to snow. Daisy watches from an upstairs window that's laced with ice. If only the Harriet Wolf Society would throw parties like the ones in my grandmother's books. Dance halls, boating parties, drunken picnics, gins in hand, Daisy weeping in a tub, Commies in the kitchen, men climbing trees in tuxedos—*that* would be worthwhile.

"Oh, look at him," Ron says of my father. "He's still in real estate and very toothy."

"Real estate agents are supposed to smile broadly. It's a pre-requisite." I dig a pencil from the linty innards of my purse. Ron tells me the address and phone number, and I write them on the back of my Wawa receipt. "Thanks."

"Wait," he says. "How are you really doing?"

"My mother keeps intruding on my thoughts."

"Trapped thinking," Ron says. "You've got to break it." And he reminds me about his first wife's struggle with OCD. "Have you ever heard her say 'Stop,' aloud, but kind of to herself?"

"No," I say.

"She used to all the time. Sometimes people around her would just stop, thinking she was talking to them. It's Wolpe's theory, fruit of the 1950s. I know what you're thinking—a real apex in psychological research, right?" This is not what I am thinking. "You say 'Stop,' take a deep breath, exhale, and divert your attention."

"Did it work?"

"She opted for high doses of medication."

"I'm thinking of Hailey too."

"Hailey," he says. "Well, Hailey." Ron has never tried to be Hailey's father, which is good. He's always known, too, in ways I couldn't even fully appreciate, that my relationship with Hailey would define me as a person, for better or for worse. He's been a parent longer and understands the depth of those waters. "Are you okay?"

"Just kind of out of my head, but fine."

"I was using Wolpe's theory a few days ago whenever I thought of you. But I don't want to stop."

Teenagers have bounded in from the rain, loud and wet. "Do you think we got married casually?" I ask. "Were we cavalier?"

"Cocky, yes."

"If we get divorced, will we have a casual divorce?"

"No such thing," he says. "I need to know what the rest of my life is going to look like. Don't you?"

"I need to help Tilton."

"Justin and I can still visit. We'd like to, but not if you're going to fake someone else's death."

"Don't."

I stare down at George's address and number. I won't call first. I'll pop in. Did he give us warning before he deserted our family?

I hear Ron's voice slightly distant from the phone. "The conquered hero returns! No ice?" I hear the thrum of Justin's voice in the background. "No ice," Ron says to me.

"No ice."

Chapter Twenty

THE HEART OF A MONGREL KING

Tilton

I have two hearts, Wee-ette, and you know why. Both of them are beating inside of me, still. One is the heart of a mongrel king that I ate from a museum display with you right beside me, and one is my own original heart. But now that they're both within me, there's no difference. I know what you're thinking: that heart I ate was a pruned and leathery thing that's long since moved through my digestive tract. But you're wrong. It's always been with me. It was supposed to make my father appear. It failed. Hearts always eventually fail us. (Take my mother's heart, for example—attacked. And yours, which stopped.) I wish I had more hearts—like one for my mother; one for my father; one heart just for you, Wee-ette; and another for Ruthie. And one for Benny Elderman? Maybe. And one for Hailey, even though I've never met her. My two hearts must do a lot of work: missing my father; missing you, Wee-ette. One wants to be with Ruthie out in the world and one wants to stay here and take care of my mother.

I need more hearts.

I'm in Ruthie's bedroom. I shouldn't be. She's out. But the doggies are with me, and it's their room too so I'm an invited guest. One of the dogs has very wet eyes, one of which is winky.

It has a shorter snout, legs, and tail, broader ribs. I call this one Pim. The other has a more fully fanned tail and head fur, more closely cropped ears. I call that one Pom. Both cock their heads when I make birdcalls. They understand that language better than English. It's clearer, more urgent, more honest.

I open one of the windows and look out, knowing that my mother would have a fit if she saw me at an open window. She was almost eaten by a window. But that's not true. That's just what it seemed like. It was her heart attack. If one of my hearts was attacked—or attacked itself, that is—I would have a spare. If they attacked each other, I would be a goner.

Am I at this open window because I want to get back at my mother because she's a liar?

This window is directly over the roof that protects people who knock on the front door in the rain. But no one knocks on our door in any weather except an occasional low-level political candidate or two girls from the local high school dressed in band uniforms, selling submarine sandwiches so they can go to Ontario for a competition.

I wonder what it would be like to go to Ontario in a band costume.

Ruthie climbed out of this window, onto that roof, and ran away in the night at sixteen. I could never do this. I'm sickly and weak, with lacy skin. I've had many illnesses: fevers, vomiting, coughing, sneezing. Sun can redden my skin. It can even blister and peel. I'm allergic to most greenery and animals, but not these doggies. I don't have enough body fat to float, much less swim. Milk gives me gas. I'm asthmatic; I get all breathy sometimes. Bee stings make the affected area swell. Mosquito bites too—my body overreacts and there's itching and puffiness.

I touch the tar shingles, warmed by the sun and wet from a fast rain. I lift each doggy so it can look out.

You know what's true? I ask the winky one.

She doesn't know.

Ruthie left us, I tell the dog. My mother didn't lie about that.

And here is the Eldermans' youngest son, Benny. I describe him this way: head of moderate size, oblong; neck long; arms and legs lanky; kneecaps bony, protruded; hair shaggy, dark, wavy; eyes blue with dark lashes; nose high at bridge, knotted; ears inconspicuous; lips nice. It's 3 p.m. He's stretching in the yard. He's one year older than I am, but he looks older. Maybe living in the world ages you—sun and weather—like a deck chair. He wears a visor—red, white, and blue, like a proud American.

As I lean out the window, I wonder if he'll notice me.

He does. He squints and puts his hand above his eyes, shading them. He then waves his hand, which seems loosely attached to his lanky arm.

I flip my hand up and back down and then dip back into the window and lean against the wall.

That was true. It just happened.

I'm thinking of my two hearts, beating wildly. The trip I took with you, Wee-ette, out to the museum was true too. My mother was agitated. You hadn't been out of the house in ages! Why now? Why this place? Why with Tilton? Tilton is only a seven-year-old! My mother had many whys—legitimate questions, she called them. But you didn't answer, Wee-ette. You used to say, It's my job to write the books, not to explain them. You got used to not explaining things, including yourself.

Since you couldn't drive and my mother wasn't invited, we took the bus. This was before I stopped doing things like public transportation. I was still in school. I was still almost normal.

The bus launched us through space into the country, which appeared, at first, like a filmstrip of fields and trees stuttering through the rows of windows. I felt loose in the bus's vinyl seat. It seemed possible to simply drift up, weightlessly gliding around in a test rocket. I offered to hold your pocketbook because I wanted the enormous weight to hold me to my seat. Sometimes I wondered if you carried a bowling ball around in your pocketbook. It was shiny and fat as a bee's rump. It seemed to be part of your body, with its straps clamped in the lock of your elbow. No matter how much lotion I rubbed into your elbows, they were calloused knobs, and one jutted out protectively, and the straps disappeared into that fine inner white skin of your arm, so delicate with its pucker of blue veins.

The bus's brakes barked lonesomely. We waddled down the rubber-matted aisle. You know this is why it's hard for me to go out, Wee-ette: everyone was waiting—their faces perched in our direction—and I took each face in, which is how I am. The faces were: shiny, dull, flushed, sad, hopeful, destitute. I held on to each for as long as possible. My mother doesn't understand. She knows only that it's too much for me. And it is!

Right this minute I am here in this room looking at the box marked Ruthie—Random, and I still remember one face on the bus, fatter than the rest, with a jubby chin that jiggled due to the bus's throbbing motor.

See how it is, Wee-ette? You know how it is. My mother says that my memory is one of my greatest burdens. But it's more than that too. Better and worse.

The bus doors opened, and we climbed down the big steps. The bus doors shut. And with a groaning cloud of dust the bus abandoned us at the end of a long road. It was late spring and everything smelled like honeysuckle—a version of sweetness I associated with my teacher Mrs. Blaskow, and her stiff hair and liver spots.

I'd never been in the country. Its wide-open spaces were unsettling. The grass rose up green and vicious everywhere. The buds of bristly, thick-necked roadside flowers gaped at me. My mother would tell me not to get close to greenery. It could be poison ivy. But there were birds. Warbling, fluttering.

We walked until there was a house. It wasn't a museum at all. Wild peacocks in the yard, their dusty feathers all knit together. Dogs howled near a statue of Saint Francis that was stained with brittle bird droppings.

A small white clapboard sign read, Welcome to the Isley Wesler Museum of Antiquities. Free to the public.

You knocked on the door, Wee-ette, while we blocked our crotches from the dusty dogs.

Isley Wesler was old and lispy. One arm clamped to his chest, he said the museum wasn't appropriate for a child my age. She won't understand, he said. His skull was dotted with liver spots.

She understands everything, you said back to him. Don't you, Tilton?

I do, I said.

Something was going on. The air had shifted. Wee-ette, I could tell you wanted something from Isley Wesler. We were there for a reason.

Isley Wesler took us around his house, half shuffly and half knee-buckly. He pointed out paintings of dead Weslers looking withdrawn. He pulled ancient curios from behind glass-front hutches, including a set of wooden teeth that his great-grandfather had worn. He was proud of a photograph of a Wesler wearing jodhpurs and a netted helmet like a beekeeper, holding someone's head—just the head. Above the photograph hung a sword that had supposedly done the job of removing the head. This Wesler wasn't bored. I figured that it took a lot to keep a Wesler's attention.

There was a small pantry-sized room filled with unopened letters.

Why don't you open them? I asked.

Oh, I've let it go. That's history.

Wee-ette, your eyes went wild over those stacks.

He hobbled upstairs. We followed him. Isley Wesler said, This is the bed in which my parents had relations and I took root in my mother, growing inside of her until I was a mere four pounds two. This is also the spot of my birth. I was pushed out of her and into the world. I was so small that they configured an incubator of sorts, surrounded by bricks that were alternately warmed in the oven and replaced. This is also where Weslers come to die.

I wanted to know if he was the last Wesler alive. Was the bed waiting for only one more? And what if he died while on the toilet or in the tub? I didn't ask. I'd said that I understood every-thing, so I kept my mouth shut.

The death room was small, with a double bed draped in mos-quito netting that was swooped up and tied to a ceiling hook. I imagined Isley Wesler dying there. I imagined myself dying there too.

He pointed out an eight-legged calf in a glass case perched in the corner. I imagined it staring at me while I died. But I was thinking of conception too, Wee-ette. And that's when I blurted, What does that mean, had relations?

The old man glared at you, Wee-ette, like he meant, I told you she wasn't old enough! And he rolled his eyes.

Then, Wee-ette, you turned to me and said, Oh, it's nothing,

Tilton. A man gets with a woman. He becomes herky-jerky like a mechanical pony in front of an old department store, grunts a bit, and a baby begins to grow.

Wee-ette, this is still just about all I know on the matter.

You make it sound so tempting, Isley Wesler said. His tone was filled with static electricity.

And you turned to him and you stared at him, leaning forward, nearly tipping over, and said, Eat your heart out, Mr. Wesler.

I don't know what you meant, except I knew it was part of the reason we were there. You'd known Isley Wesler before we'd arrived. This was part of your past. At that moment his eyes got overly large, and you looked at him like you knew that he knew exactly who you were. You and Isley Wesler were locked together and unable to come up for air.

I thought about all of this later, when I replayed it in my brain. Because in that moment I only existed below you two. I was thinking of eating a heart out. Was that where babies came from? Was that where I'd come from? Had my mother eaten a heart? Was my father, George Tarkington, now heartless?

Is that how it's done? I said. Is that how there's a mother and a father?

Your attention fell to me.

Yes, hush, you said, and you tightened your grip on my hand and hurried me out of the room and down the stairs.

Wait! Isley Wesler said. Don't go just yet!

And this is where it becomes strange and misty in my mind.

You paused, Wee-ette, at the foot of the stairs and turned, because you still wanted something from Isley Wesler.

And he said, One more thing: my heart!

I was thinking, *A heart?* It couldn't just be a coincidence, Isley Wesler pulling a heart out at this very moment.

He shuffled past us down the steps and into the parlor. Follow me! he said, and we did. He pulled out a silver box, gray from lack of polish, from a bottom dresser drawer.

Regardez! he said, which is French. Isley Wesler held the box out with his good hand because the other was wizened and tightly pinned, his curled fingers covering his frail chest protectively. He opened the box and whispered, The heart of a mongrel king!

The heart was a leathery prune sitting on velvet.

While tombs were ransacked, Mr. Wesler said, one of my ancestors absconded with the heart before it was lost in the tumult.

You started to back away, Wee-ette. This wasn't what you wanted, but I stood still. I didn't know what a mongrel was, but I wanted a father. I'd heard you tell the man to eat his heart out, and when I'd asked if that was how a mother and father came to be, you'd said yes.

And here was a heart.

I thought it would be better for my mother to eat the heart. But she wasn't here. It was up to me. Before anyone could stop me, I reached inside the box, popped the heart into my mouth, and hoped for a father.

The heart was nearly tasteless and very dusty, if you're wondering.

You gasped. Tilton, spit it up! Tilton! You slapped me on the back and rattled me by the arm. Tilton! Tilton!

But I gulped it as fast as I could—oh, the tight press as it made its way down my throat.

Mr. Wesler could barely breathe. Who, who would do such a thing? he shouted. How reckless!

But you pulled me to your bosom like a baby, although I was much too grown-up. How dare you offer such a thing to a child? You are a sick man! To offer a heart to a young child like it's a candy! You glared at Isley Wesler and said, *You* have been reckless, Mr. Wesler. *You* have been reckless with someone else's heart!

And that seemed like the reason we had come. You needed to say those words and here they were. You knew Isley Wesler because you had a whole big fat life. I don't know how I know this. I just do.

You didn't lie to me like my mother has, but you've withheld the truth. It's like a life is a pact that gets wound from the hands of one generation to the next, but if you don't tell your life, if you don't hand it over, you're cutting the string. Then the next generation has no tether. They float off like an astronaut, alone.

We have a pact. Only give them the book if there's an emergency. If all's going well, don't. But it's not going well. Maybe it never was.

This is what I remember: you marched me out of the museum, my head still clamped tightly to your chest. I could only see out of one wide terrified eye—the gaping flowers, the deathly honeysuckle, the greenery grasping at me, the dogs, the peacocks.

Isley Wesler appeared at the door, gasping, He's alive! Do you know that? He's still alive!

The mongrel king? I asked. His heart was beating inside of me—alive!

Eppitt! he shouted. Eppitt Clapp!

Is that the name of the mongrel king? I asked.

He still loves you! Isley Wesler said. It wasn't my fault! I saved his life!

The mongrel king loves you? I asked. I wondered how Isley Wesler had saved the mongrel king's life. By keeping his heart in a box all these years? Was I now the one to keep him alive—within me? Would he be coming for us to get his heart back, once and for all? Eppitt Clapp, I said to myself. Eppitt Clapp, the mongrel king.

You didn't say a word. Your breath was raspy. Your lips were crimped shut. I'd never heard the name Eppitt Clapp before, but I would hold on to it—my brain holds on to so much.

We walked down the driveway and waited for the bus, a half hour of silence. It appeared in a new whirling cloud of dust that I followed you into. And we returned. Right back here to this house.

I could follow my sister out onto the roof, jump to the grass, disappear down the street. Stranger things have happened. I'm not allergic to my sister's dogs. Benny Elderman waved to me and I waved back.

The book has stayed hidden, but it doesn't have to.

Chapter Twenty-one

A CONFESSIONAL IN WILDWOOD, NEW JERSEY

Eleanor

I sit in front of the television, the one that almost killed me. It's a big ugly box with a wide placid face that flickers at me, all bluish. With its rabbit ears perked and cockeyed, it talks and sings and praises itself, joyfully. This entertainment doesn't require an audience. But these past three days, it's not been bad company. I suppose *because* it doesn't need an audience. I can listen or doze. It needs no praise, no gentle reminding, no scolding glares. It doesn't have hair to brush, doesn't require feeding, doesn't look at me like I'm a disappointment—oh, the deflation in Ruthie every time she looks at me!—or like I'm a criminal, as Tilton does, like I'm suddenly untrustworthy, a suspect in an ongoing investigation.

On television, a woman judge who's very irritated with her work yells at people. Why does she work in petty disputes if she hates pettiness? What would the judge say about my lying to Tilton about broken toaster ovens and commissioned poems? Guilty as charged, heaven knows.

I lied to Tilton for her own good. It wasn't a crime until Ruthie deemed it so. Mrs. Devlin *could* have had a broken television. She *could* have wanted it fixed. Her daughter is already married, but she *could* have divorced and remarried. None of this was intentionally harmful.

Ruthie keeps inviting Tilton to join her on trips to the grocery store, the drugstore, the dog park. (I held my tongue, but Lordy! Dogs have their own parks now?) Tilton always says no, though I can tell by the way she looks at me that she's waiting for some encouraging nod, a blessing. If Ruthie knew what could happen, she'd stop pestering the girl! Still, Tilton proves her allegiance to me each time she declines. Tilton wants to be good. This desire doesn't seem to cross Ruthie's mind. Not now and not ever.

What's parenting really about, anyway, if they're born one way or another and stuck like that? I wish I'd been given a memo at the very beginning stating that all children are born more or less in a fixed condition. I wouldn't have tried so hard to mold Ruthie. I'd have left her alone, let her be more George-like. I would have cajoled less and shrugged more. My own mother didn't try to mold me. She shrugged plenty. I resented the lack of attention, but maybe my mother had received the parenting memo I missed.

Ruthie is out on one of her errands with the little dogs. Tilton is upstairs. Normally she would be doing things she loves, reading bird books, practicing birdcalls, drawing pictures, maybe even still writing poems or tinkering with appliances. These things contented Tilton before Ruthie came. But now Tilton takes long baths. She stares out the windows and taps the glass, like she's trying to get the attention of fish in an aquarium. She follows Ruthie around the kitchen, asking her strange questions. "Have you ever been in an earthquake?" "Do you believe in Mormons?" "Do you move around in your bed in summer to find cooler parts of your sheets?" Some of these questions embarrass me. I was responsible for Tilton's education. Surely I covered Mormons.

Tilton asks Ruthie about their shared childhood. Tilton's voice—the little bell of it—rings out in the kitchen. "Do you remember the worm hospital we made?" "Do you remember how our socks came wrapped in stickers and were hooked over little black plastic hangers?" "Do you remember lipstick samples in tiny white tubes?" They sing songs that aren't even vaguely familiar to me. It's as if Ruthie and Tilton had a different life together, one that didn't include me at all. Is this how sisterhood works? I wouldn't know.

The judge raps her hammer, rolls her eyes at the defendant, and tells some woman on the verge of tears how stupid she is. I say to the judge, "You exist in a big box, all furry with dust."

I close my eyes and from the nearby ball field come the sounds of batting practice. Years ago, the bats hit the balls with satisfying cracks. Now their pings are hollow. Aluminum bats. I know that much even though I know nothing about baseball, really. My mother had gaping blank spots in her understanding of simple things. It was like being raised by an immigrant. Her understanding of history was spotty. She was missing basic geography—Nebraska?—and yet could talk about extinct animals that had lived in African jungles. She didn't know any of the books I was taught in school, but she'd memorized entire poems by Yeats.

If I'd had a father during those years, I might not have noticed my mother's gappy grasp of the world. He could have filled in, provided a counterbalance. Maybe if I'd met my father, even briefly, everything would make sense. I was nothing like Harriet and so it stood to reason that I was *exactly* like my father. (A theory confirmed after I had Ruthie.) It was like growing up in a house without mirrors. Or no, not exactly. My mother provided a mirror of sorts, but when I looked into it, I never saw myself.

I pick up a plastic SMTWTFS pill container that Ruthie bought for me on one of her many trips to the drugstore. S, M, and T are closed but empty. And so I figure it's Wednesday. For some reason the row of hollow spaces reminds me of lined-up election booths, or no, something else: confessionals. How odd that election booths and confessionals are so similar.

Harriet told me her own mother had been Irish Catholic—an O'Keeffe from Dún Laoghaire, County Dublin. Harriet didn't miss going to church, but she said she missed the confessional, the way the close walls made her feel safe. And she liked telling the priest what she'd done wrong, although, she told me later, as a child, she lied about her sins. She never felt it was really any of the priest's business. "I believe in God," my mother told me. "The God in here." And she tapped her bony sternum.

We never belonged to a parish. But Harriet did take me to confession once while we were on vacation in Wildwood, New Jersey. It was strange to take a vacation in the first place, regardless of the confession. This was before my mother became a shut-in, but she had never liked going out anyway, much less so far away. A trip to Wildwood entailed hiring a car and taking a ferry.

It turned out to be a plodding, bitter, stormy weekend in October. My mother and I walked the beach, our chins stiffly tucked to our chests, braving a tenacious wind and pelting rain. I'd never seen the ocean. Like the sky, it was gray. My mother tried to explain what it was like in summer, with women in bathing costumes, men selling bags of peanuts, the warm sun pinking people's skin, the bright awnings of the boardwalk, the amusement rides, the hawkers in bow ties. I tried to imagine my mother having spent time there when she was younger. She claimed to have had happy family vacations, but she sounded more wounded than nostalgic. I liked the sand, the ocean, its unpredictability. It was angry about something, I was sure of it, and I appreciated its honesty.

We stayed in our rental a few blocks from the beach most of the time, and my mother cooked for us over a small gas burner. Oceanfront places were available too, but Harriet said that she didn't like the sound of the ocean—like it was clawing at her.

If she sounded wounded and it was cold and she didn't like the ocean, why had we come at all? My mother never said.

On our last day we walked past a bar, and my mother clutched my hand. "My God," she whispered. "Look."

In the window, there was the head of a lion. A real lion. Stuffed.

"Who would do such a thing?" my mother said.

"Hunters, I guess," I said.

My mother shuddered and then couldn't stop shaking. I felt the tremor in her grip. She walked quickly. I asked where we were going because it seemed we'd walked a long way. She didn't answer.

Eventually she stopped in front of a church. Inside, confession was under way. It was midweek, an afternoon, busy. There were maybe three confessionals—six little curtains, for priests and sinners alike. People were waiting their turn in the pews. Before Harriet stepped inside, she let me peer into the confessional—just a small dark closet with a seat and a screen, little holes of light.

She told me to sit in the nearby pews and pray. "I won't be long." After she walked in, she let me shut the curtain, a velvety thing that went *scritch*.

I fiddled with a songbook in one of the pews and popped the kneeler up and down for a few minutes and then my mother came out crying, her hand covering her mouth. "Come on," she said to me. "Let's go!"

I kicked the kneeler and shoved the songbook back into place, and each made a gonging sound that echoed. My shoes were too loud. Everyone was looking. My mother grabbed me by the elbow, and off we went out in the gray afternoon.

Years later I went back to Wildwood once, with George.

He was raised in New Jersey—Trenton, to be exact. When we were first dating, I told him I'd vacationed at the shore once, off-season. A few weekends later, he told me to pack a bag. It was summer. He was going to take me on an overnight. He drove us to Wildwood. We pulled up at a seaside hotel, ocean-front. He said, "A little better now, right?" I'd remembered the place as gray and battened down, rainy, bleak—filled with old people. But that weekend, I didn't relate the change to off-season versus summer. I related it to George. With my mother, the world had been gray and battened down, but with George all of that would change.

We got light sunburns, our skin pink and taut and salty, and we stayed in a single room with two beds. I turned on the faucet in the bathroom so he couldn't hear me pee. I didn't have sex with him, though he pressed. Falling in love at thirty, I was a late bloomer like my mother, who'd given birth to me in her late thirties. I was already an old maid who took care of my mother, as I had been doing since I was eleven, when my mother stopped going out. I was a housewife before I was even a teen.

George was my last chance, as I saw it. My mother had had one last chance, right? But that man hadn't stayed put. I didn't want to have this in common with my mother. I wanted a hus-band, a true escape. When I lay in the hotel bed that weekend, I watched George sleep.

Ping.

Ping.

The pinging of the aluminum bats has intruded again. I close my eyes once more and see the lion head in the barroom window. I remember—very clearly—that the lion was wearing a bow tie right above its severed neck, and a top hat pinned down its mane. But most shocking of all was its expression—not ferocious, not wild. It wore the wide-eyed and wistful gaze of the lovelorn.

Ping.

Chapter Twenty-two

KILLERS

Harriet

*F*or three years, Eppitt and I lived carnally. We were reduced to bodies. For me, it was a good thing to be a body, to be set free from the cage of my skull. When I think of this time, I remember my electric skin. I was always chilled or flushed or tingling—like a limb that falls asleep and returns with the uncomfortable needling rush of blood.

Food was saltier, sweeter, tangier.

This was still during the Great Depression, and so most wants were unattainable, but Eppitt and I were insulated from the Great Depression because of Isley Wesler and his invalid mother, because of mobsters and their need to hide things. Isley had us eating foie gras, partridge eggs, and perfumed puddings. With Prohibition over, we drank what we wanted and lots of it. Isley preferred home-made booze. We drove into western Maryland to buy liquor from homemade stills that had popped up during Prohibition, but now lingered based on reputation and to dodge taxes. "Hillbillies," Isley said, "with high-end hooch." He had a connection in Portugal too, and imported cases of Madeira, as well as plum wine from Asia, which he made us drink from eyedroppers. We tilted back our heads and opened our mouths.

There were more parties—loosed doves and dancing. Isley rode *through one naked on a white stallion. He married a sixteen-year-old named Mabel at one of the quickie chapels in Elkton, Maryland, the place where, one day, my Eleanor and George and the girls, still little, would see a plane hit by lightning, the accident that would pull that family apart. When I hear Eleanor tell that story to the girls all these years later, I think of wedding parties falling from the sky, all those brides and grooms that once packed Elkton's little chapels, an industry.*

Eppitt and I were Isley and Mabel's witnesses. While there, Eppitt asked me again if I wanted to make it official.

"It already is," I said, but my greater fear was that we were registered, in some way, as morons. Morons weren't supposed to marry and surely weren't supposed to marry other morons and procreate. I couldn't say this aloud, but maybe he shared my concerns or maybe he wanted to believe—as I did—that the pact we had made was pure and true. It was the best part of our childhoods. Getting married for real meant that the pact didn't matter, and perhaps that's what we didn't want to admit.

I should have claimed him. It could have made all the difference.

After we made love, I would lay my head on his stomach and Eppitt would pretend to be my phrenologist. He ran his fingers along my skull's ridges. "This is where you keep the girls' laundry, where we met." He'd rub the bump behind my ear and say, "This is where you've stored Mrs. Funk and Stump Cottage." He'd rub my temples and say, "This is your genius. Locked away. You should let it out."

"To do what?" What good had being a girl genius done me? I had nothing to apply it to.

"One day," he said. "One day."

"And where are my memories of my mother?" I asked once.

"Drilled into every bone," he said because he knew it was true.

"And where are you?"

He was always found in the nape of my neck, that wee dip where the finest hairs wisped and fanned. He would kiss that spot and we would start again.

I prayed for a daughter like Isley Wesler's mother had told me to—probably because I wasn't accustomed to maternal advice. I revered it without question. I prayed for a daughter so that I could have that mother-daughter relationship back again, here on earth. It was another part of our carnal life. I wanted to make a body with my own.

This praying went on all three years. I didn't tell Eppitt. I wondered if he knew that I'd been the one to save him from the operation, the snip-snip, performed on all of the other boys at the Maryland School. Did he know that I'd been spared the operations that the girls underwent? Or did he think I was sterile? I worried that Brumus had gotten him after all.

And then, as I'd almost given up, the prayers worked. My period—so punctual and heavy—was late. It was still a hunch, not a fact. I was going to see a doctor before telling Eppitt, just to make sure.

But then one summer night he came home from a hiding job with mud caking his thin-soled shoes and the hems of his pants. He poured himself a drink in the kitchen, slammed it down, and closed his eyes.

"Do you want to tell me what happened?" I asked.

His eyes were glazed. He rubbed dirt from his hands. "I know more than I should," he said. "My head's too full now. What I hid, where I hid it. Years of it."

"You need a hot bath," I said, even though it was a humid night. "Steam." It had been prescribed for his lungs as a child. Maybe it would do him good again.

I knew that he'd seen a dead body. I knew that he'd carried it through the woods somewhere. I knew this without his saying a word. I saw him in my mind's eye, struggling with arms and legs, dead weight.

I led him to the bathroom, started filling the tub. I took off his shoes, his shirt, and helped him with his pants. There was blood. Dried stiff, it had been hard to make out mixed with the dirt, but it had seeped through his pants and onto his skin, and once he was in the tub the water turned dark, tinged with red. Small churning rivulets twisted the way that blood does.

He said, "If I'm not here one day and you need money, it's there." He pointed to the top panels of the bathroom door.

"Stop talking like that," I said. "Close your eyes."

"When I close them, I don't like what's there."

I wiped his face and scrubbed his head, his arms and legs. I drained the tub and refilled it. I wrung a washcloth over his back, the way my mother had with me. I sat on the tub's edge and said, "We should have a baby."

"A baby?"

"To replace what you see when you close your eyes."

"A baby," he said. "That would be nice."

"But am I a little old to have a baby?" I asked, suddenly worried.

"My mother had me in her forties."

"Oh, Cat!" I said, calling on the pet name I'd used for him under the Duck Porch. "After all those other babies, she was used to it!" I wasn't ready to tell him that I thought I was pregnant—not till I was sure.

He looked up at me and said, "You really want to have a baby? With me? Is that what you're saying?"

I nodded.

He grabbed me around the waist and pulled me into the tub with him. The water sloshed up and over the lip. My clothes puffed and then clung to me. "A baby!" he said, and he kissed me. Then he laid his head back again. "A real live baby."

I put my head on his wet chest and wrapped the wet wing of my skirt over his legs. "Yes."

"I didn't do it," he whispered. "I was called in to hide it."

"I know," I said. "Hush."

"The man weighed over two hundred pounds. There was so much of him."

"A baby only weighs six or seven or so," I told him.

MOBSTERS

Eppitt arriving home covered in dirt and blood was a warning that we should have heeded. The next week, he didn't arrive home at all one night. I was at the window when one of Isley Wesler's cars pulled up. It was nearly midnight. A young redhead with bulky shoulders ran to the old house and eventually knocked on our door. I pulled it open.

"Where is he?" I asked. "What's gone wrong?"

"Mr. Isley Wesler's got a message." The kid rubbed his right hand with his left, like he'd recently punched something and was trying to work out the ache.

"Who are you? Where's Eppitt?"

"I'm Gerald."

"Okay, Gerald," I said. "Get on with it."

"He's in the hospital. Problems with some ribs and his jaw. He's looked better. Mr. Wesler says he can't stay in the hospital. He's going to get him out and send him away. For his protection and yours."

"What happened?"

"Mr. Wesler's waiting in the car. He says you need to pack up

everything. You got five minutes. I'll drive you out. Eppitt will show up when he can."

"Where are we going?"

"Mr. Wesler's setting you up. Don't worry. But once you're there, you can't try to reach him or Eppitt. It'd be too dangerous. For everybody."

"Five minutes?"

"Only four minutes now."

I looked around the apartment, panicked. *Eppitt's alive*, I reminded myself. *Jaw, some ribs—how bad could that be?*

"I'll meet you by the car," he said, and shut the door.

I grabbed my old suitcase. I lifted clumps of clothes, hangers and all, off the rods in the closet and folded them up. I packed the photograph of us taken the night that I attended my first Isley Wesler party.

Eppitt had held on to our marriage pact from 1913, but I wanted it now. I had tucked that pact and the one with my mother into the bed frame, as had been my habit in Norris Cottage. I got down on my knees and felt along the metal until I found one and then the other. I slipped both into the pocket of the suitcase's silky lining.

I ran to the bathroom and looked at the top of the door. The car horn sounded in the street.

"I'm coming," I muttered. *"I'm coming."*

I knocked on the two top panels. One gave a hollow *conk*, the other a heavy *thunk*. I pulled a chair to the bathroom door, ran my hand along its top, and felt a ridge. I pressed my hand along the ridge, and a ring for a handle popped up—the kind that Eppitt made for his homemade drawers. I hooked it with my finger and pulled out a box. I shoved it in the suitcase, which I buckled quickly and then hefted from the bed. I grabbed my pocketbook.

The horn blared again.

Isley was sitting in the backseat, drunk and propped up by his coat, which gaped around his collar. His tie was loose, shoved off to one side. Glassy-eyed, he stared straight ahead. I slid in beside him.

"Have you seen Eppitt?" I asked. "Is he okay?"

"It went wrong." He slapped his own cheek, hard, as if trying to sober up.

"Mr. Wesler," Gerald said from the driver's seat, "you want I should drop you off somewhere, or are you going all the way out?"

"Igor's," he grunted. Gerald started to drive.

I grabbed Isley's arm. "What's happening? Tell me."

Isley looked out the window. "Monies and whatnot went missing. These things belonged to people of influence. These people got very angry." He scratched his forehead; his nails were trimmed expertly. He started to cry, but then he coughed, gripping the legs of his pants. I thought he might get sick, but then he straightened. "They turned on Eppitt. He was the only one who knew the hiding place."

"Eppitt wouldn't steal from mobsters."

"Don't say that word." He glared at me. "Listen, they didn't think he stole it, just that maybe he sold the information to some other interested parties."

"He didn't sell the secret hiding place."

"Really? You know where he goes and what he does?"

"I know him, and he wouldn't," I said.

We drove in silence until Gerald said, "We're here, Mr. Wesler." He parked in front of a modest house in an elegant section of Baltimore.

Isley punched the seat. "This is no joke, Harriet. They could have killed all of us. You hear me? If we make the wrong move, they still might." He grabbed my face so hard that the insides of my cheeks rubbed against my molars. His breath stank of alcohol. His eyes were red-rimmed. "Get it through your fucking head," he whispered. "You don't look for Eppitt or me. You do what Gerald tells you. Understand?"

I nodded, his hand still gripping me tightly.

He pushed my head back and let go. I'd never seen Isley this way. "Gerald," he said. "Show her we mean business." And he shoved his way out of the car, slammed the door, and lurched up the front stoop. He kept his hat low over his eyes, and glanced around before knocking.

MARGARET SHIPLEY

It was three o'clock in the morning when Gerald pulled up to a cedar-shingled clapboard cottage three blocks from the beach in Wildwood, New Jersey. The only thing I knew about Wildwood, really, was that it had marathon dances. In 1931, the winning couple danced from June 25 to September 14. I imagined that one held the other up so he or she could sleep. And there'd been a story about a man who'd been dancing for eight weeks straight when, from the pier, he spotted a boy drowning. He jumped into the Atlantic Ocean in his dress shirt and slacks to save him. The boy lived. The man didn't.

Is that what I was in for? Delirious drowning?

Gerald unlocked the door. The place was nearly empty, just a few pieces of furniture. My heels clattered and echoed. I'd spent the three-and-a-half-hour drive imagining Eppitt's ribs and jaw. I wanted to put my hands on his skin, as if I were a healer. When he got here, I would set him up in the bed with pillows behind his back and make broths so he wouldn't have to chew. I couldn't look for him, but he would find me. We'd found each other once before. We would again.

I let Gerald bring in my suitcase. I was a pregnant woman now, most likely. (I'd have to wait a cycle or two more to be absolutely sure. I'd learned from the women who lived at Mrs. Oblatt's house that this was what doctors would tell a woman.) I shouldn't lift things. That's how a good mother-to-be would behave, right?

"It might take a while for Clapp to show up," Gerald said, "but we'll let you know if he doesn't pull through."

"You said it was only his ribs and his jaw."

"If he takes a turn," Gerald said.

"Someone will come and get me, right?"

"Right."

"Tell Isley Wesler not to forget about me here."

"Shipley," Gerald said. "I forgot that part almost. You got to go by Margaret Shipley."

"Who's that?" I asked.

"You," he said, and he looked around the little living room. He flipped the lacy curtains up. "You're a cat, though. You land on your feet. You want to tip me?"

"Tip you?"

"You know." He swiped his hat off his head, his hair bristling orange. "I drove out all this way."

"I don't have any money."

"That's not what I meant."

"I don't want to tip you."

He walked up close. I stepped back, my heel against a wall. He reached up and touched my face with three fingers. "Mr. Wesler told me to make it clear we mean business."

"That's been made clear."

"Mr. Wesler wants me to make it crystal clear." He reached around my back and pressed himself against me. His chest was tough with muscle.

When he touched my face again, I growled and bit his fingers as hard as I could while pinching and twisting skin through his thin shirt—the savage defenses I'd learned as Hairy Wolf at the Maryland School for Feeble Minded Children. He screamed and tried to pull back. I kneed him in the crotch. He doubled over. I ran to the bathroom and locked the door.

"Get out!" I shouted. "Get out!" I whipped back the shower curtain. There was a small high window.

"You bitch! You're crazy!"

"Yes!" I shouted, climbing into the tub and working the window's latch. "I'm insane! I'm a killer! A moron! A savage! A Wolf Woman!"

He crashed around the house, but just as I'd loosened the latch on the window, I heard his feet clomp out and the door slam shut. I slid down the wall and sat in the tub, the taste of blood in my mouth. Eppitt had once found me in the tub at Isley Wesler's house. He wasn't coming for me now. I realized that I needed Gerald. How else would I get word about Eppitt?

"Margaret Shipley." I'd been so many people. What was one more? I pushed myself up and out of the tub and walked to the front door. I locked it.

I turned my suitcase to its side and unbuckled it. There, on top, sat Eppitt's homemade hiding box. I fit my finger into the ring and pulled. Tightly rolled dollars fell out—mostly fives and tens. Lots of them. Had he sold a secret hiding place? Was he a real criminal who lived among criminals?

Last of all there was a piece of wound string—brown, as if it had been soaked in blood. At first I thought that Eppitt had another marriage pact, another woman somewhere out there. But the tape read "E. C. and I. W., blood brothers, 1922." Isley Wesler, of course. The string was brittle. I was Margaret Shipley. But who was Eppitt Clapp?

A WIDE OCEAN

I stayed in bed until it seemed my legs had been sewn into the sheets. I was love-blanched and listless except when my heart hammered: Is he dead? Is he dead? Is he dead? I remembered the water nozzles of Sheppard Pratt, the cold sheets, the lumbar puncture. I was light-headed. Feverishly, I imagined old-world cures for my old-world lovesickness—leechcraft, the tight suction of leeches on skin. I thought of the word "kleptomaniac." There'd been one at Sheppard Pratt. Indiscriminate, he stole tea towels, flowerpot labels, and a few cards from each deck. I was being stolen from, again.

Klept, klept.

Heartklept, loveklept, breathklept.

My platelet disorder caused the place where Isley had gripped my cheeks to bloom into splotched bruises. Could I die like this—scrawny, abed, alone? No, I couldn't. I was a mother now. My blood was not my own. My body seemed to know this.

The curtains gusted full sail. It was summer at the beach. People out roving.

I dressed and walked to a small corner grocery store run by Poles, who reminded me of Mrs. Funk. She had seen God in me. Little Girl Jesus of the Dreaming Wounds. Where was Mrs. Funk now? For that matter, where was Little Girl Jesus? I ate lemon Popsicles and salty chips—for some reason the only things I could keep down. I walked to the beach, long and broad and cluttered with people. Short-skirted bathing suits boxed women's thighs. Some of the men's suits were belted high at their waists. Family members poked one another's scalded skin and shouted over the roaring ocean.

Isley had taken us to the bay a few times. We didn't have swimsuits so I'd taken off my stockings and waded in fully dressed. Isley and Eppitt had worn their drawers. And then, at night, after we'd eaten from a picnic basket, we took off our clothes and slid naked beneath the glassy moonlit surface. Neither Eppitt nor I could swim. We kept our toes in the muddy silt and bobbed. Isley spouted water from a thin gap in his front teeth, and then sang, operatically. This wasn't the same person who'd grabbed my face.

The beach turned into a misty haze in either direction and the ocean went on forever. I watched the families pack up shovels, sandwich tins, books, and chairs.

I couldn't shake what Gerald had said about Eppitt taking a turn. Maybe if he knew that I was pregnant, he'd fight harder to live, instinctively. I felt hollow even though I was far from hollow.

When the beach cleared out and it was nearly dark, I took off my shoes, lifted my skirt, and walked toward the waves, which washed up over my stockinged knees.

Eppitt Clapp belonged to Isley Wesler, not me. I was no one's wife. I was Margaret Shipley, and maybe Margaret Shipley was owned by Isley Wesler too.

I remembered the Lings' niece drowning in the fishpond, and the marathon dancer, arms whirling, legs scissoring, but not enough to keep him afloat. I imagined one of his shoes slowly drifting to the ocean floor. What would it be like to let the ocean hold me, suspended, like the eight-legged calf that Isley kept on display on top of his upright piano? To be preserved in sea salt?

I imagined the baby inside me, tumbling in my waters, swimming madly. Every time I jumped to keep my head above a wave, I felt it tug me back to shore.

I pinched my nose and dipped under. The water was cold and dark. There was another tug.

I lifted my wet head, turned, and looked back at the boardwalk's lights, those frail gimmicks of human invention. I thought of Dr. Wolff. The world doesn't need me, but I need it. That was no longer

*enough—but you, Eleanor, you were the reason. I wasn't alone. I
had a baby inside of me. I had to live for you. And in this way, you
saved my life—as well as your own.*

I couldn't save my mother, Eleanor. But you saved yours.

*The ocean shoved me in the back and then drained away from
my legs. I felt heavy and unsteady, like a newborn colt. I tottered,
and then I staggered to shore and looked for my shoes.*

They were gone.

EPPITT

*A few nights later, while I was asleep, I felt a hand on my shoulder.
I looked up and saw Eppitt, but his face was monstrous—his jaw
wired shut, nose broken, eyelids puffed so tight they were nearly
sealed, shining in the dim light. The bruises on his face were black.
He was listing to one side; his left set of ribs contracted.*

"Lie down," I said. "Here."

*And he sat on the bed. I got up and untied his shoes, took off his
socks. One foot was purple. He winced.*

"My God," I said.

He said nothing.

*"Lay back," I said. I unbuttoned his shirt. I unhooked his pants.
I undressed him until there was his body before me—raw, blood-
ied, a pulp of a thing, broken inside. What had they used to do this
damage? I was thinking of bats and chains. "Eppitt, what did they
do to you?"*

*His throat strained. The cords of his neck flexed. He was speak-
ing. I put my ear to his lips. "Remember..." He pointed to his chest
and then mine. "Feeble-minded," he whispered. "Crazy."*

"At school, yes. When we were kids," I said.

"Love," he muttered through his clenched jaw, "is how we're bloomed."

I leaned in close to his face. "Bloomed?" I said.

He shook his head. No, he'd collapsed words. That's not what he had meant. "Doomed," he whispered, "and blessed." He wanted to say more. I put my ear to his lips. "I love you," he said.

Stay. This was what I wanted to tell him. Stay. I had to ask if he was going to. If he said yes, I would tell him I was pregnant. And if he said no, I wouldn't. "Are you going to stay?"

But as soon as I said the words, I knew the answer. He couldn't. Either it was still too dangerous or someone owned him now. It was the middle of the night. Somehow he'd stolen away, and this would be fleeting. I put my fingers to his mouth. "I like 'bloomed' better than 'doomed' and 'blessed.'"

He raised his hands. He fit one inside the other and then pushed that hand up and spread his fingers like a flower, blooming.

I washed him with a soft rag from a kitchen bowl of soapy water. I rinsed him clean. There were so many questions I wanted to ask: How did he get here? Where would he go? But I didn't want to force him to talk. I kissed his body and said, "One more pact."

I got up and pulled a thin red ribbon from the belt of a dress. I pressed my hand to Eppitt's, which was scabbed, the knuckles blue and raised. He'd fought for his life. I wound and wound until there was no more ribbon, and then whispered in his ear, "Sterbe nicht."

He looked at me, uncomprehending.

"Don't die," I said. "Promise me that. I wouldn't survive it."

"Sterbe nicht," he said, the two words thick in his throat, on his tongue.

I fell asleep, and in the morning he was gone.

THE MOTORDROME

A few days later, a man knocked on the door. I felt immediately sick. Someone was coming with news. I opened the door a crack and blinked into the bright sun.

"You Margaret Shipley?"

"Yes, I am," I said. "Please just say it. Say it fast." If Eppitt was dead, would I become the girl on the sunporch after her mother died? Who would take me away this time? Where would I be strapped down?

"What?" the man said, perplexed. He was squat and balding. He rubbed his nose in a small angry circle. "I'm Dobish. Mr. Dobish. Is that what you want me to say fast? I run the Motordrome."

"Do you have news for me?"

"I've got a job for you. We have a friend in common who said to give you a job. My wife, she gets sick sometimes. Sick and tired. Our mutual friend owed me a favor so he said you can be a substitute. You can come on Saturday? At noon? Unless—" He cocked his head. "Unless you don't need the money."

Was he told to ask this? Was he hinting that any money I had was money that wasn't rightfully mine? "I need the money," I said. "Who doesn't?"

"Not that it pays a lot. But you can stay here, in addition."

I didn't want to stay, but this place was now the tie between Eppitt and me. If he was going to come for me, he'd come here. "Where can I meet you on Saturday?" I asked.

"Like I said. The Motordrome. You know how to drive a motorcycle?"

"No."

"You only got to ride it in circles, though. It's not so hard. You afraid of animals?"

"Not really," I said. "Like pets? A dog or something?"

"A dog!" He laughed. "You think people on vacation from Philly would pay to see you ride with a dog in the sidecar? Philly people—I tell you, they want bang for their buck. You coming on Saturday or what?"

"I'll come," I said. "Is our mutual friend..." I didn't say Isley Wesler's name, though I was sure it was him. I wasn't supposed to look for him. "Did our friend have a message for me? Something personal?"

"No," he said, "no news. Sorry." I couldn't tell if he knew more than he was saying. "Saturday noon. The Motordrome. The Wall of Death. Wear some makeup. Doll up a little. You know, for the crowd." He turned and walked down the front steps.

I called out, "If it's not a dog, then what is it?"

He turned around and looked up at me. "Well, a lion, a course. Nothing else would be worth the price of admission."

A lion.

This is what I mean. The world is astonishing, mainly because of its persistence. It keeps going on, but sometimes we need lions to keep us transfixed, to remind us that we're human.

Chapter Twenty-three

CHAUNCEY

Ruth

It's called trespassing, technically speaking. But I'm banking on George Tarkington not calling the cops on his own daughter. And if he does see someone skulking through his wilting rhododendron and he calls the cops, I'll say I wasn't really trespassing. I was merely pausing at the waist-high chain-link fence visible in his side yard while on my way to the front door.

I should knock on the front door, but for the moment I have a clear view to the backyard, where my father is in his natural habitat—skimming the pool with a long-handled skimmer, wearing a Speedo and an unbuttoned shirt and loafers, no socks. When the wind kicks open the shirt, it exposes his belly, a pinkish-tan stripe down the center where the shirt parts, fading to pale skin on both rounded sides, which means this must be familiar attire for him, at least in the yard. He's got a Scotch in his other hand, half resting on his belly. As far as bellies go, the word "cauldron" comes to mind. The firmness almost makes it seem like something he's worked for, a protective fatted armor, like he belongs to an era in which people drank mead and complimented the cook with flatulence. I imagine telling this story to Ron. "I could describe my father better if I'd actually taken Marcus's course in Old English," I might say.

George walks across the lawn to a shed and pulls open the door. The grating of metal on metal alerts a collie that bounds over, albeit arthritically. George takes out a bucket of old tennis balls and sets it on the patio. He talks to the dog, ruffles its ears, riling the old boy up. Is he calling him Chauncey? He throws a ball across the yard, out of my line of sight. The collie runs off, fur rippling. George waits, one hand on his hip, in an almost matronly way.

The house looks like it was built in the 1980s—dark brick, pitched roof, winding footpath through a wooded front yard. It sits on more than an acre. The shed is likely home to a riding mower.

I imagine my father riding the mower in his short-sleeve button-down, his Speedo and loafers, drink in hand. How could I have feared being rejected by him? That man, right there, stirring his Scotch with his finger? Banana-hammock George?

I stand up tall and lean over the metal gate as if I'm one of those neighbors who stops by with news about some other neighbor's nesting termites. "George!" I call. "George Tarkington!"

He turns his head and waves without knowing it's me. Likely he has glasses he doesn't wear, and after refusing them for so long, he's become used to waving at blurred faces. "Hey there!" he calls back. "What can I do you for?" This practiced folksiness reminds me that my father sells houses for a living.

"I'm Ruth," I call, as if this is casual.

He takes a few steps forward and it washes over him. My face must be coming into focus. Ruth. Maybe he's doing calculations to try to gauge how old I would be now. Sixteen plus how many years has it been? "Ruth?"

"Yes," I say. "Ruth, your daughter."

He stops. The collie rushes up and shoves the ball at his slack hand. "Stop it, Chauncey. Not now."

"Chauncey, huh?" I put my hand up to the chain link for Chauncey to sniff. "A collie."

"Ruth. Jesus. Do you want to come in? I could get dressed, for shit's sake." His pink thighs are nearly hairless.

"I wouldn't want to barge in on your family situation. Isn't it *delicate?*" I ask. "You know, on the home front."

"It's just me," he says. "Edie died three years ago. Pancreatic cancer."

"Edie," I say. "I'm so sorry." And then, just to underline the fact that George hasn't been in my life for many years, I add, "That was your wife, I take it? Edie?"

"Yes, yes," he says. "Do you want a drink? Celery with cream cheese?"

"Um, no thanks." I'm angry now. Had I expected him to be more contrite? What happened to Marie Cultry? "Tilton wants to see you," I say, hoping it will sting a little. "I mean, I have vague memories and saw you briefly that one time. But Tilton, well, for her you don't really exist. And Eleanor has had some recent health problems."

"Is she okay?"

"She's fine," I say. "She's, you know, Eleanor."

"That's what I always liked about her." He smiles warmly.

"Are you drunk? If you're drunk, I can come back later."

"No, no. Sober as a church mouse, more or less."

"How would you feel about coming to the house?" I ask bluntly.

"With Eleanor there? She'd hate the idea. I thought you'd *all* hate the idea. Persona non grata!" Chauncey runs to the other side of the yard, barking at a squirrel. "Chauncey!" George yells. The dog doesn't listen.

"Tilton doesn't leave the house much, but I can probably get her out, for this kind of thing."

"Doesn't leave the house much? You mean, like Harriet was?"

I shrug. "I guess. Can we not go to a Steak 'n Shake this time?"

"Of course not. Jesus!"

Chauncey's still barking. George yells the name again. His loafers are worn at the top, over the big toes, which protrude from his shoes ever so slightly, perhaps because no one has loved him enough since Edie died to help him keep his toenails clipped. Is this my future if I leave Ron? Long toenails?

"Your mother," George says. "She has a presence in the world! I've always known that I'd be able to feel it when she died. Not a blackout—just a dimming of the lights."

He swirls his Scotch, takes a sip, winces. "I wanted to stay in it, you know, but she wouldn't have it. I might have been able to get partial. Weekends or some shit. But that would have killed me, seeing you being torn apart again. I was forced to become otherwise engaged."

He'd wanted to stay in it? "What about after I turned sixteen? You knew I wasn't under her thumb anymore."

He stretches out his hands, mea culpa. "What could I do?"

"Edie," I say. "I get it. It was delicate. And it's been delicate with her dead too? Three years now? Do you know how I found you? A Google search. A couple of seconds. Why haven't you tried to get in touch?"

"What would we have to talk about?"

"We're talking now," I say. But then the conversation stops. I look around his yard, the leaves in the pool, the tall brick house.

"You never had any intention of trying to make this right. Did you?"

George squeezes his forehead with one hand. "I can wear a suit and tie. We can do dinner. I clean up nice."

"Well, it's got to happen quickly," I tell him. "I'm leaving town soon. I've got a life to return to, I think. Either that or I have to make one up, which will be time-consuming. This is how we would have talked, I guess, if we'd worked this out sooner."

"I don't really know what you're saying, what you mean."

"And you're problematic for me on many levels," I say.

But then, almost as if he's actually responding to a fatherly instinct, he reaches over the chain-link fence and puts his hand on my shoulder. I didn't know he was capable of it. "Your mother is going to pull through," he says. "She isn't going to die. It's not her style."

"We're all going to die one day," I say flatly.

And he pulls his hand back and holds his glass with his fingers knit. He looks at the deep end of the pool, at Chauncey nosing the nearby shrubs, and then back at me, as if I've hurt his feelings. "Don't tell the collie," he says. "They're a sensitive breed."

Chapter Twenty-four

TUFFY

Harriet

I never met Mrs. Dobish. Mr. Dobish said, "She's not right, not right in the head, and it's not her fault. Not a bit." The subtext was that she'd driven herself mad—in circles—in the Motordrome with a lion in the sidecar. Not a problem. I was already not right in the head.

The lion should have alarmed me, but I was past alarm. Born dead, brought back to life, deadened, brought back again... I couldn't fear injury or death, teeth or claws. I'd been blindsided by Eppitt's disappearance. Any notion that this job was a strange turn for my life to take went unnoticed by me. I had no eye to recognize it; in this way, I saw no better than the milky, half-lidded eyes of Isley Wesler's invalid mother.

The lion was named Tuffy. He had an incomprehensible girth, massive paws, and a thick rope of tail. More than three hundred pounds of him, and yet he seemed to barely touch the earth. His mane was coarse but the thick wrinkled fur covering his knotted backbone was soft. He'd been born and raised in captivity and treated so roughly growing up that by the time Dobish got him, Tuffy was submissive and, as Dobish put it, easy to boss around with the promise of some meat. Tuffy and Dobish worked together with the same resignation.

Dobish taught me how to ride a motorcycle out in a field, then on the streets of Wildwood, and finally in the circular hold of the Motordrome. One day I showed up, and Tuffy was already locked in the sidecar.

Dobish gave me an old apron, told me to raise it up behind my head and stand tall. "Look him in the eye," he whispered. "And talk to him."

"What does he want to talk about?"

"You can tell him anything you want. He's better than a priest like that. Just use a firm voice. Say it all with conviction."

Dobish was right. I rode in circles, confessing with great conviction to a lion. No one could hear over the roar of the engine what I was saying, and so I was honest. You know what I said by now—all I was holding on to. Guilt and more guilt. I loved that lion because he took it all in, and when he roared—so loudly I felt it in my own ribs—it wasn't an admonishment, but a recognition of my suffering. He understood suffering. Wearing a strap-on bowler and bow tie and sitting in a sidecar, the lion was forced to deny his true self, as it goes.

The Motordrome was a wooden, circular pit. We drove in circles, nowhere else to go. I wore lipstick and Mrs. Dobish's tight pants and a jacket with lots of hooks and eyes. (How long would it fit? At some point I was bound to start showing.) I also pulled on a pair of high shiny boots each day and carried a riding crop. I was part doll and part lion tamer.

When Tuffy roared, the crowd screamed—even the men. They taunted him too. But their faces were blurs, a pattern of quick pulsing color over our heads.

Often dizzy, light-headed, I vomited a few times.

Sometimes, in my dreams, I was the one with the giant girth, the one who wore the strap-on bowler and didn't seem to touch the earth.

On breaks, I made the rounds through the boardwalk. Families were gliding down the giant slides and zipping around in Custer cars. Fake guns popped round after round in a shooting gallery. I loved to idle near the Live Bunny and Bird Village, where children pawed at the mesh cage. The brightly colored birds paced the little walkways and picket fences, squawking loudly while the bunnies pressed their ears flat to their heads and hid beneath the bridges.

The African curios exhibit had no Ota Benga; he was dead. Instead there were shrunken heads, spears, and monkey skulls.

I would take my time at the live monkeys. Unlike Tuffy, they drove their own cars on the Monkey Speedway. The summer before, thirty-five of them had escaped, and it was said that the town called in Boy Scouts to gather them.

I passed the tunnel of love, called Ye Olde Mill, and the Ferris wheel that, like every Ferris wheel I've ever seen, desired only to pull up its stakes and roll out to sea. Fishing boats that doubled at night as moonlight cruisers glided on the horizon, like distant bulbs. Glenn Miller's band played at the Ocean Pier. I walked past, heard the bass, the horns, the shivering cymbals, the drums.

Major C. Nowak, the thirty-five-inch-tall policeman, greeted people in his small cop uniform, while Mario Lanza was discovered on the electric trolley cars. Still just a kid named Cocozza at the time, Lanza would sing the upcoming stop in a sweet tenor. I heard him once. If you hear something like that, you never forget it.

The girly shows, the ruckus, the beer gardens, the fortune-tellers. Freaks, in one way or another. And I was on display amid all of them. Margaret Shipley. Unlike the marathon dancers, I was alone in my exhaustion, no one to hold me up.

Time marched on. Summer wore down. A chill popped into the night. The town atrophied. Shops closed up, and the beach emptied out. *The trolley switched to an abbreviated schedule. Meanwhile, I started to feel bloated. Mrs. Dobish's outfit was getting taut.*

And then one day I noticed a man following me. He was over-dressed for the boardwalk. He sipped colas and kept his eye on me. I thought it was my imagination, as if I wanted Eppitt so badly that a man had appeared. The wrong man. But there he was. I also feared he wanted to kill me because of something Eppitt had done. I thought of the Black Hand, the mafia, the war over bananas, docks, laborers with cleavers. Was someone going to light two sticks of dynamite under my cottage—which wasn't even mine—and blow it up? Did he want the money in the hidden box? I would have given it to him, but I didn't want him to know that I'd noticed him at all.

I'd still know him, if I saw him today. Wiry, small. A chin that nearly curled upward. Sunken cheeks. He'd eat from folded napkins while he followed me. He ate so quickly and angrily—his cheeks puffed like gladiolus bulbs—followed by large gulping swallows, that I feared he'd swallow his own tongue. I hoped for it too.

PEGGY PEG-PEG

One night that fall, after the last show of the season, I was in the dressing room. I was still barely showing—it wasn't something someone else would notice—but it was getting clearer to me. I'd heard that first pregnancies in particular could remain hidden for months, but still the costume made me claustrophobic. The changing room was a little closet with a mop, a bucket, and bleach. I stripped quickly and threw on my dress.

Mr. Dobish knocked. "Man here to see you."

I'd given up on Eppitt appearing again. I was sure I would be

Margaret Shipley for the rest of my life. As for the man who'd been following me, he didn't seem the type to come calling.

I opened the door, and there stood Isley Wesler, dressed the same way that Eppitt had said he'd dressed in the pool hall the day they'd first met—in a full-length coonskin coat—though it was too early in the season. I hated Isley Wesler, and hadn't realized how much until this moment. But he was the one who might bring Eppitt back to me, so I also felt like throwing my arms around him. Dobish was standing there too, wringing his apron, darkened by dried blood. He'd fed Tuffy recently.

"Sweetheart!" Isley said, all smiles. "Look at that hair!"

I was sure he was here to tell me that Eppitt was dead.

"We were just talking about a friend Mr. Wesler and I have in common," Dobish said. "An important friend who made your job here possible."

I was surprised to learn that Isley Wesler himself wasn't the mutual friend I had with Dobish. "Who's that?" I asked.

"Ramagosa," Dobish said. "The king. Who else?" Ramagosa was the king of the boardwalk. He owned everything.

"A friend of Ramagosa," Isley said, clapping Dobish's shoulder. "That's a friend of mine. You too, right, Peg-Peg?"

"I'm thankful for the job," I said, though the mention of Ramagosa had made me nervous. I wanted news of Eppitt, but not in front of Dobish, of course.

"So! Show me this lion," Isley said. "I've been to Africa. Big game."

I doubted this. Dobish led us to the back lot, past large bins, oil drums, a row of mini cars under a tarp. Tuffy's cage had thick iron bars and just enough room for him to pace. He was lying down, his haunches worn, his fur patchy.

"That's a real beast," Isley said.

"A real beaut," Dobish said. "But sweet as sweet can be."

I bent down and looked into Tuffy's eyes—wet, goopy, maybe a little infected. Tuffy looked at us as he always did—a gaze filled with both love and sorrow. He had no other expression. Tuffy understood loss. All he had was loss.

"He gives me the shivers!" Isley said.

"Really?" I said. "After all the big-game hunting?"

Isley gave an insulted sniff.

"He ought to give you the shivers," Dobish said. "He could gut you with one claw."

"I've got a car," Isley said, looking around, his coonskin coat flapping at his boots. "You want me to give you a lift home, Peg-Peg?"

"I can take you home, Margaret," Dobish said. Clearly, he didn't trust Isley.

"It's okay," I said. "I'll take the ride."

Isley's car came with a driver, but not Gerald, thankfully. We sat in the backseat. I ran my hand over the leather. "Where's Eppitt?" I asked.

"He's on the mend."

"Why isn't he here?"

"Part of the deal. I worked it as best as I could. He's alive, Harriet. That's the good news."

The driver kept tabs on all of the car's mirrors, nervously.

Isley tapped a cigarette on the window. We were passing stately old Victorians now. "It's a good thing you two never made it official!"

"Made what official?" I said.

"The marriage," he said.

"How do you know that?"

"Your pact at the feeble-minded school?" he said. "C'mon, Peggy, Peggy, Peg-Peg! Eppitt told me everything."

The driver stopped for a passing trolley car. Dark profiles glided past.

"Just tell me what you came to say, Isley."

"Someone within the circle of influential people to whom Eppitt is now indebted—as they kindly didn't kill him outright—had an indiscreet relationship with a woman. She got in a family way. The actual father of said child is already married. So Eppitt? Let's just say he could do this favor, and it would make everything right again."

I turned from Isley and leaned my head against the window. We bumped along past a row of small houses. Someone was walking a pony down the street. I thought of my mother's hand against mine just before she died. I thought of myself on the porch—wild with grief. "Does he love her?"

"You can't ever see him again."

"Does he love her?"

"He has to."

"What about me?"

"Well, you had a nice run here. But now Eppitt and his wife are getting set up in town. They're very family-oriented, these people. Don't make a mess, you know? Don't cause any trouble."

I clamped my hands over my ears. "Shut up, Isley! Shut up!"

"I don't care to be spoken to in that manner!"

"I didn't like you telling Gerald to rape me."

"That was a misunderstanding. I didn't tell him to go after you like that. I wanted him just to scare you—for your own good, so you'd know how serious it was. Did you bite him? Is that true?"

I closed my eyes and spoke in a low voice. "I won't believe anything unless I hear it from Eppitt."

Isley grabbed my wrist. "Don't fuck with this, Harriet. They'll cut you up and feed the pieces to that lion. This marriage has to be pristine! Completely clean."

I ripped my wrist from his hand and rubbed it. The car stopped in front of the cottage, all its windows dark.

"I have some things for you," I said. "Inside."

"Go ahead and get them."

I walked quickly to the house, to the bedroom, got down on my knees beside the bed and felt for the strings, my hands shaking. When I stepped out of the house, there was Isley's pale, chubby face in the rolled-down window. While walking slowly to his car, I again saw that wiry man, lit by someone else's headlights.

"Why's he following me?" I said to Isley. "He's been following me for a week."

Isley glanced in the man's direction. "Never seen him before."

"Does the driver know him?"

"Nah," the driver said.

I assumed they were lying. I handed Isley the blood brothers pact. "Here."

"Jesus. We were kids once."

I also had a pact with Eppitt, the one marked "E. C. and H. W. 1913. Marriage." I unwound the thread—old and worn from decades in Eppitt's wallet—and pulled until it broke in half. One half I gave to Isley, and the other, the one with the tape, I kept for myself.

"Give it to him," I said. "I'm only asking this one thing."

Isley took the string and shoved it into his breast pocket. I wondered where Eppitt, the great illustrious hider, had tucked away his thin red ribbon. Sterbe nicht.

"I want to report that you're going to be a good girl," Isley said. "That you're not going to try to contact him. That you're cooperating."

"Or what?"

"Or they'll send you an unpleasant message."

I leaned down and clamped both of my hands on the car door. "I could do anything! Tell them whatever you have to."

Isley stared at me a moment, coolly. "Your choice." He shouted at the driver, "Let's go!"

The driver put the car into gear and drove off.

I looked down the street at the man who'd been following me. Hands in his pockets, he was slouching, his eyes hidden by the brim of his hat. My heart was pounding in my throat and ears. "Hey you!" I shouted.

He looked up.

I ran toward him. Was I allowed to run? A mother-to-be? "What do you want?" I shouted.

Flustered, he reached into his jacket. I expected a gun. Shoot me, I thought. I stopped right in front of him and opened my arms.

He pulled out an envelope. "Are you Harriet Wolf?"

"Who wants to know?"

"If you're Harriet Wolf, your father is dead. He has a will. You have some things coming to you."

"My father's dead?"

"Are you Harriet Wolf?"

"My father's dead."

Chapter Twenty-five

GREAT EXPECTATIONS OF GEORGE TARKINGTON

Ruth

Two nights after I trespassed on my father's lawn and talked to him over a chain-link fence, I'm in the kitchen with Tilton, the two of us getting ready to meet George at the Howard House, a restaurant in downtown Elkton, Maryland.

Eleanor insisted on doing the dishes. She's sudsing the swirled glass knob of an orange juice squeezer. "I hope you don't intend to drive with that convertible top down," she says. "A lidless sardine can. It's a good way to get decapitated."

"I'm really not expecting decapitation," I say.

"What are you expecting?" Tilton asks. She's patting the dogs, who lie on the linoleum with their hind legs kicked out, trying to stay cool. Tilton looks elegant. She's wearing a vintage dress from the 1920s or '30s, fitted and blue, modest with a high collar and a shawl. She found it in Wee-ette's closet. Tilton shares Wee-ette's narrow waist, boxy hips, dainty ta tas, and reedy arms and legs. I wanted dainty ta tas. Even as thin as I am now, my breasts seem weighty, keeping me down, gravitationally speaking.

"I wouldn't expect much from George Tarkington," Eleanor says. "He got out while the getting was good."

This isn't true, as I now know. He didn't want to "get out."

Yes, he gave up too soon and too completely. But that's something I understand. Someone tells you what's best and you believe them. I think of the strawberry-scented letter from Hailey in my wallet. Perhaps it was really an invitation to fight for her and I misunderstood. I let my mother's comment slide. "Okay, get your pocketbook, Tilton. We're ready."

"I don't have one," she says.

Eleanor wipes her hands on a towel draped over the handle of the oven door and pulls a canvas bag off the back of a kitchen chair. "Here," she says, and hands it to me. When I peek inside I see that it's filled with medications, an EpiPen, an inhaler, and ointments. "There's a set of instructions too," Eleanor says, "explaining how to use everything."

"She doesn't need any of this," I say.

"Indulge me," Eleanor says, stiffening her arm and rattling the bag.

Tilton grabs it, rolls it up as tightly as possible, and shoves it under her arm. "I'm ready."

"You look beautiful," I say.

"Very nice," Eleanor says, grudgingly.

"You know that Mrs. Gottleib can stay with you," I say to my mother. "She volunteered."

"Please God, no."

"Okay," Tilton says, agitated. "Let's go."

Eleanor reaches out and touches a wisp of Tilton's hair, tucking it behind her ear. "Just don't get your hopes up. Your father will never love you like I do. He doesn't have it in him."

"Can we not sour the whole thing before she even leaves the house?" I say.

"Just stating a fact," Eleanor says.

"In the past three minutes alone, you've told her she might

be decapitated, suggested that if she somehow survives she'll probably die anyway, facedown in the restaurant due to imaginary allergies, and if by some miracle she survives that, her father will break her heart."

"You of all people should know by now that motherhood isn't all gin and roses!" Eleanor says. But she must read something awful and raw in my expression because she stops and turns away.

"You're upsetting Pim and Pom," Tilton says quietly. She closes her eyes, covers her ears, and starts whistling—not a tune, but strange little birdcalls.

"You've completely derailed her life," I say. "For some reason, you can't let her go. Me? Oh, I was fine. You let me live under the dining room table for weeks! You didn't once even try to talk me out of it! You left plates of food on the floor, but never came to drag me out! To you, I was gone! So be it."

"This is about you, then. Not Tilton at all. Right? Selfish. Always were. Just like your father!"

I clasp Tilton's wrists and pull them a few inches from her ears. "It's time to go."

"She's in no condition!" Eleanor shrieks. "She's reverted to bird language!" Then she slams her fist on the table so lustfully that, for the first time in my life, I think, *My God, my mother's had sex.* "Just go!" she shouts.

I stiffen. Eleanor is terrifying. One of the reasons I ran away was because my mother scared me.

But I usher Tilton to the kitchen door and out we go, into the humid evening air, as Tilton flutters her arms and says, "Flight!"

Chapter Twenty-six

LOOSE

Harriet

*M*y father's death meant that I could go home. I was the only surviving child. The house was mine.

I walked into the Wildwood cottage and lay down in my bed with the large envelope on my chest, and I stared at the ceiling. But I didn't want to go home. I was waiting for Eppitt to tell me the truth. I would swell, and he would see me on the street, and he would know the baby was his and we would run away together.

I saw my father in my mind's eye—walking into the administration building, his mustache, his useless cane an affectation. Father of a girl genius—but that had meant nothing to him.

The next evening, at around six thirty, there was a knock at the door. It was a breathless teenager, skinny and tan, his jawline dotted with pimples. "Dobish sent me," he said. "I'm his nephew. He wanted you to know that Tuffy escaped. He got loose!" The boy looked over his shoulder quickly. "Can I come in?"

I opened the door. He took two quick strides inside, and I locked the door behind him. "Start at the beginning."

He told me that Dobish was going to feed Tuffy, as always, at 6 p.m. sharp. But the lion was gone. Some thug was there instead. "He was shaken up, said somebody wanted to scare some sense into somebody. My uncle asked who. And he said some name he never heard of. And my uncle said, 'Who's that?' And the guy said the girl who rides the motorcycle."

And then I knew that word had gotten back that I wasn't going to cooperate, that I was demanding to see Eppitt. Had Isley told Ramagosa's men that I needed to have some sense scared into me? I imagined someone suggesting that they cut me up and feed me to the lion. Maybe just using Tuffy to scare me was considered a compromise. "Where's the lion?"

"He killed a hawker and dragged the body under the boardwalk. The fella was getting into a car, foot on the running board, and Tuffy came up and dragged him off by the neck. There was a kid in the car with him, just some ten-year-old—his father owns the auction house. The kid saw it all. He got out and sat on top of the car, crying. Then they shot Tuffy. He's dead."

I must have staggered a little because the boy reached out and grabbed my shoulder.

"You all right?"

I imagined Tuffy's mane, his ribs and backbone, the softness of that coat. His teeth and claws. Majestic. The way he looked at me. Those eyes were now glassy with death. The hawker, dead. I thought of the boy frozen on the hood of the car.

"My uncle thinks maybe somebody was going to put Tuffy in your house, loose him in your yard or worse. Sorry I have to say all this, but Dobish told me to."

"It's okay," I said.

"He's all broken up about it. But my uncle told me you should go. He hopes you've got people somewhere. He said you never talked about family, but he's hoping you've got somewhere to go to, Miss Shipley. You got people?"

Chapter Twenty-seven

VULTURES

Eleanor

I sit at the table a moment. My daughters are gone and the house is quiet, but my heart is loud and, for the first time since the heart attack, it feels bullish. Ruthie. I remember her under the dining room table, of course. She was only eight years old. She'd stolen a couch cushion, taken the pillow and sheet from her bed, and set up house, hidden by the white tablecloth with its yellow flowers. She had a flashlight, a few books, a small stack of Wee-ette's plain white paper, and pencils wrapped in a rubber band. This was shortly after we'd come to live at Wee-ette's, after I'd given up on George's return. My mother had warned me not to trust George, but I was pretty sure she didn't trust any men. My missing father was clearly untrustworthy. And Harriet had never said a kind word about her own father—not an unkind word either, mind you. The only information I had to go on was from Weldon and Daisy's lives of eternal melancholy and miracles. My mother needed me, and I think, early on, George had needed me. Maybe I confused neediness with love. A heady young man, George once said, "You mellow me, Eleanor. You make me feel like I've got my feet on solid ground." In retrospect, what we had wasn't love at all. It only sometimes mimicked it. Plane crash or not, we were doomed. I think I knew early on, but couldn't confess it to myself.

When I called my mother to tell her I was coming home, that George was gone and had been for some time, my mother whispered something I barely heard and never really understood. "It got you too." Did she mean love had gotten me? The best of me?

My mother fired the help she'd set up after my wedding and we settled into a routine—Harriet helped a little with Tilton and Ruthie, and I did all of the interacting with the outside world, including the literary world, once again. Although I was heartbroken, the arrangement was working fairly well.

And then Ruthie decided to live under the dining room table. Kids do things like this. It's normal. Ruthie wanted to run away and this was as far as she could go. The problem was that it lasted a full day, and then two. My mother told me to go under the table and drag her out, but I refused to. George had left me. I couldn't grovel for my daughter. Emotionally, I let Ruthie go, and I know it seems impossible, but she knew it and she never forgot it. I let her live under the table for two straight weeks. Part of me knew that all she wanted was for me to fight for her. I was just too stubborn. Tilton became my only hope for the love I craved.

I stand and walk to the stairs. I take them slowly, using the handrail like a rope to pull myself up. Midway, I stop to catch my breath. My heart—the ramming bull. I soldier on. At the landing, I walk into Ruthie's old room and to the box marked "Ruthie—Random." I set it on the bed, pop the cardboard flaps. I find the folded fabric quickly and pull out the white tablecloth, its small yellow flowers having faded some.

I hold it to my chest and walk out of the room, down the

stairs again—taking them slow and easy. I rest at the foot of the stairs, where I'm met by the little puffy white dogs. How small their brains must be.

I stride to the dining room, feeling sturdy, and lay my hand on the rich dark wood of the mahogany table. In the shine of the varnish, I see the faint reflection of my own face—the pouches at either side of my mouth, the drooped skin of my neck. I wonder about my granddaughter, this Hailey. Does she look like us? Is she troubled? Has she already broken my daughter's heart? I open the cloth and spread it over the table, inching it—all slippery—one way and then another to get the hems even on both sides.

Ruthie.

I never should have let her go. My eyes sting. The tears surprise me. They slip down my nose and dot the cloth. I'm not a crier. My mother wasn't either. In fact, I saw my mother cry only one time—during a signing for her second book, the last signing she ever did. They'd already become circus events. Once, a man had stolen her sweater, cut it up with scissors, and sold the pieces. This time policemen stood on either side of her to keep order. But in the middle of the signing, she got up, grabbed her coat, and walked out. This was in New York City. I went with her everywhere; she had never left me behind like that. I ran after her into the street, clumped with gray snow. My mother was leaning against the pole of a street sign, crying breathlessly.

"What happened?" I asked.

She wouldn't tell me. She just shook her head. "Ghosts," she whispered.

This was when I started to hate my mother's readers and her books too. If my mother went crazy—her eyes skittering off into the sky like Daisy's eyes—and she never looked at me the same again, the readers and the books would be to blame.

Now I feel unsteady. I pull out a chair and sit. I remember Ruthie on the night of the plane crash in her helmet with her sweaty bangs, how she arched and slammed against the seat.

I grip the cloth and then release it, edging off the chair to my knees and crawling underneath the table to sit with my back against one of its legs. It reminds me of a white tent. From the kitchen door comes a knock. Gottleib? Vultures? For the first time in my life, I don't care. Let them come and peck away. I lie down, kicking my legs out from under the table, the cloth, and stare up into the table's underside—its paler wood beams. The knocking comes again, and this time the dogs start yapping. This is what I should have done back then—not try to drag Ruthie out, but join her.

Chapter Twenty-eight

HOME

Harriet

I took a bus, and then a taxi. The rain came and went. When I finally arrived, my old house looked small, hunkered against the gray sky.

I walked up to the front door, covered by the small jutted dormer. I put my hand on the door. I turned the knob. The door was unlocked. Inside, the air was stale and cold and smelled vaguely medicinal. I didn't know how my father had died or how long he'd been dead, but now I thought it might have been a lengthy illness.

Room upon room seemed filled with bulky ghosts—white sheets covering armchairs, couches. I ripped them off and left them in a pile in the kitchen, which was bare. I thought of Brumus where I'd last seen him while I was ironing a ding made by my father's ring on the lowboy. Maybe Brumus was dead now too.

I moved to the stairs, expecting to see bodies moving—the nurse, at least, tidying. I saw new water stains on the ceiling as I climbed upstairs to my old bedroom. It was stripped of everything but a bed, nightstand, chest of drawers, oval standing mirror. For a long time, I stood there with my eyes closed, smelling the slight tang of glue.

Looking in my full-length mirror, I turned to my side and pressed my skirt to my pelvis. There it was. A belly. A baby. Undeniably true. I was going to be a mother. When my mother was dying, she mistook me for her own mother. Mother and daughter—did the difference really matter?

Down the hall, I opened the door to my mother's room and stepped inside. That tall bed—where she had birthed her dead babies, where she had birthed me, dead too, or so the story went, and where she herself had died. I climbed onto it and curled up. I had once lived as an orphan, but now I suddenly was one, truly.

This is my room now. My bed. It's where I, too, will die one day. I knew it in that moment. When I die, will I mistake one of you for my mother—Eleanor, Ruthie, Tilton?

This bed is mine—my first bloody sheets and my last. Home.

Chapter Twenty-nine

THE MONGREL KING WHO CAME BACK FOR HIS HEART

Tilton

Ruthie drives to the restaurant with the top down. The music is very loud. A woman is singing about broken hearts, which reminds me of my two hearts and how two is not enough. I put my hand on the rolled-down window and smile at myself in the small mirror. I barely recognize my own face with my hair whipping around it.

Ruthie shouts above the radio and the wind, There's something I want to ask you!

I shout, What?

And she shouts, Why did you cut my hair when you were little, that time I was sleeping? I looked like an idiot!

I was trying to grow a tree, I say, using your hair as seeds in the backyard!

She looks at me.

I shout, I have the desire to put my hands straight up in the air.

Do it! she shouts.

And I think about it and then I do it. I curve my hands down and they pop back up. Ruthie takes one hand off the wheel and throws it toward the sky. She sings loudly along with the music. I don't know the words but I don't have to. It's not that kind of song. I sing too. When the song ends, I pull my hands in. People do get decapitated in convertibles. I remember the decapitation photograph at Isley Wesler's and then the mongrel king's heart. Isley Wesler said the mongrel king was going to come for us, and I held on to the name Eppitt Clapp forever.

I say to Ruthie, You know how I ate the heart of a mongrel king?

I do remember that weirdness, she says.

He came to the house one day, I say.

The mongrel king? she says.

He knocked on the door, and Eleanor opened it, and I was there behind her like usual and you'd already run away. Wee-ette was in her room, sick by now. In fact, she died pretty soon after this. He said he was there to see Harriet Wolf.

I close my eyes with the wind churning up my hair and picture him in my head. He was old, wiry, and kind of nervous, like people who came to the door asking for Wee-ette always were. He had a hat in his hands.

He didn't look like a mongrel king, I tell Ruthie. And he lied about it too. When Eleanor asked him if he was a Wolf scholar, he said he was. But he wasn't anything like the Wolf scholars who came with notebooks and copies to get signed and mini cassette players. When Eleanor told him to shove off, he said, Just tell Harriet that Eppitt Clapp is here. Just tell her that. The name sprang up from my mind like a jack-in-the-box.

Eppitt Clapp? Ruthie says.

That's the name of the mongrel king, I explain. Eleanor left the room pretending to go tell Wee-ette. Of course, she just dawdled a minute in the living room. She didn't even go upstairs. But while she was gone, I said to the mongrel king, I have your heart. He looked at me very surprised. He said, You do?

And I said, And I can't give it back. How did you get it? he asked. And I told him that I got it at the Isley Wesler Museum of Antiquities. He said, Wesler's passed on now. I said, That's sad. He said, Is she going to let me see her? I said, Nope. Wee-ette doesn't see people anymore. He said, Tell her Eppitt Clapp—. And I said, I know. I know. Eleanor came back and said, I'm sorry, sir. She's not up to it. He stood there and he looked at me and I gave him a nod. He nodded back and then he wandered into the driveway. His car was parked on the street, but he stood there awhile, looking at the house like he'd been through all of this before and he was dazed by a memory.

Ruthie says, Eppitt Clapp, huh? Did you ever tell Wee-ette?

I told her the mongrel king had come for his heart, but she didn't understand because she was dreaming toward the other side by then. But when she died, Eleanor and I were there, and she said his name. She called for him. She said, Eppitt, over and over. And she stared out the window. The heavy curtains were drawn back. I remember that a rosebud had sprung loose from the trellis and it was tapping the window. The window-panes were all bright and she said, I do, Eppitt, I do. She looked at me and Eleanor and she said, My angels are looking on.

And? Ruthie says.

I told her that Eppitt had come for her. I said it again and again. She only said one word.

What was that? Ruthie asks.

Bloomed, I say. And then she died.

Ruthie's eyes are watering, but I don't know if it's because she's sad or if it's the windy car. Bloomed, she says. Doomed and blessed. And then Ruthie coughs and sits up straighter. She says, I never heard that story before.

You weren't here, I say.

Soon after that, we pull into a parking space not far from the restaurant. I can see its sign. She turns off the car and opens her pocketbook. I'm ready to get out of the car but she says, Wait. She opens her wallet and pulls out a small piece of pink paper. She unfolds it and hands it to me. It's a letter addressed to Mom and signed Love, Hailey.

Are you sure I should read this? I ask, and she nods.

In the letter, Hailey tells Ruthie that she wants to live with her father because he knows who she is and she's way more comfortable at his house. It's one of the saddest things I've ever read.

It's strawberry-scented, Ruthie says. Smell it.

I tell her that I'm allergic to strawberries. But as soon as I say it, I'm not sure it's true, and even if I am, these aren't real strawberries. So I lift the pink paper to my nose and sniff it. The strawberry smell has faded, but I say, It's still there. Just the littlest bit.

A FATHER

This is what restaurants are like: loud, busy, talking faces in chairs, small dining room table after small dining room table, booths too, all shoved up against the walls, windows that show you a porch, waiters, waitresses, circular trays, beaded water glasses.

We walk up to a podium like we might be asked to give a speech, but someone gets behind the podium and says, How many?

Ruthie tells her we're meeting someone.

Our father, I say, like it's the beginning of the prayer. I clarify. Not the prayer. The person. The man.

Oh, the woman says. I think he's already here.

She walks us through a room with framed newspaper clippings on the walls. Wee-ette would like a restaurant with clippings all over the place. But one, I swear, one says, Dead Fell from Sky, in big huge print.

And I say to Ruthie, Dead Fell from Sky!

Don't start, Tilton, she says. Not now.

I wonder if I am crazy. Even if a restaurant puts up famous clippings, especially of the local area, why would they put up *that* one? Who wants to eat while reading about dead people falling from the sky?

We follow the woman, who has two menus under her arm. She stops in front of a table. A man's sitting there. But he's not George Tarkington. This man is old and fat. His nose is no longer sharp and decurved. It's rounded, as if he's gotten fat on the tip of it, in addition to everywhere else, and there is a divot between his eyebrows like he has worried all his life or maybe just squinted a lot because he's confused.

But this man stands up and he says, Ruth! And he hugs her.

Thanks for making this work, she says.

And then Ruthie grabs my hand and pulls me forward. Tilton, this is George.

I have no reaction.

So she says, Dad.

At this, the woman with the menus says, I'll put these here. She lays them on the table and adds, Your waitress will be with you shortly, and then scurries away, duckfooted, flap, flap, flap.

But I thought she was our waitress, and this makes me wonder if we weren't good enough somehow. Why is she leaving us? I say.

She's not leaving us, Ruthie says. She has other customers.

George says, It's really nice to see you, Tilton. I'd have recognized you anywhere! You were a beautiful baby, and look at you now.

I can't look at me now, I say. There are no reflective surfaces.

We sit down in our booth seats, me next to Ruthie, scoot, scoot. George has a golden-brown drink that sits on the table, sweating. He's sweating too. I am too. The sweat is pooling in my armpit trenches. I'll soak Wee-ette's dress. I know it. No one's saying anything. They pick up their menus and so do I, but I can't focus on any of the words, which are jumping around.

George puts his menu down. Do you all want to split some crabs? he asks. That's what's good here, you know.

That sounds great, Ruthie says. Some Old Bay Seasoning to make our lips burn a little. She looks at me.

I nod and smile, but I don't want burning lips.

So, don't you have some questions? George says.

Don't you? Ruthie says.

Should we replay our lives up until this moment? George asks.

I could, I say. But it would take too long.

Exactly, George says. So what's the highlight reel?

Jesus, Ruthie says.

Lordy! I say. Lordy, Lordy.

George says he likes golf. He's been to four European countries. He once fell off a ski lift, a very bad incident, and he's never forgiven the guy he was with, though he probably should before he dies.

The waitress, a completely different woman from the one who met us at the podium, tells us she's going to be taking care of us. Her name is Janie. George explains our crab order. She leaves, and George resumes his highlight reel. He likes sushi and saw the Rolling Stones live a few times. He misses Edie.

Who's that? I ask.

His second wife, Ruthie says.

And George says, No, my third.

So you did marry Marie Cultry? Ruthie asks.

Yes. Yes, I did, he says. But she left me, went home, and married a high-school sweetheart. Someone she'd dated right before she met her first husband, the one who died in the plane crash.

Did you love her? Ruthie asks, which seems very personal.

I loved your mother more, he says, but sometimes you make a rash decision and you're forced to live by it.

And that makes no sense at all except I shot my hands up in the convertible and what if they'd been cut off and I had to live with it. I feel a little sickish, like I might make a decision right now and have to live with it forever. Janie the waitress brings us water glasses, and I'm glad she's taking care of us, because I need to press the cold water glass to my wrists. She also puts down newspaper—more stories, more print, more ink. I think of Wee-ette. Ruthie is talking about academe like she loves to hate it.

The crabs come in a big stack. Their bodies lie on top of each other—bright pink and red—their beautiful serrated pincers, their antenna eyes. They're hot. We're given mallets and picks.

Dig in, Janie says.

And it begins. George and Ruthie rip off claws and bite chunks of white meat. Ruthie says Hailey likes soccer and camps. She talks about her first and second husbands. The crabs have pale undersides tinted slightly bluish. George pulls the softer exoskeleton like a tab on a soda. The hard shell unfastens, exposing puffy lung membranes, fine squiggly entrails, a paste of mustard-colored innards. George and Ruthie take turns dipping white meat in melted butter cups.

Lordy, I whisper, still holding my dead crab.

Are you going to eat? George says.

I sip my water but my hand is shaking and water spills on Wee-ette's dress.

Tilton? George says. Tilton, you okay? I thought this was going pretty well. Am I wrong?

No, Ruthie says. It's going fine.

But then I start talking aloud. I say, I once ate the heart of a mongrel king. Wee-ette said, My angels are looking on, and died, and after she was dead, Eleanor rubbed her body, trying to keep her warm and alive with us on this earth. And then my mother bought birds and tried to release them. But the birds just pecked around in the yard.

Book five, *Home for the Weary*, Ruthie whispers. After Daisy's mother died, they released birds.

I'm afraid of many things, I say, but not birds. Birds breathe in their own bones. And the house tried to eat my mother. Albert Gottleib is dead. I can fix a lot of mechanical things. Coach Flynn did or did not defile children, but he did try to shoot me. I miss Wee-ette. This is her dress. I know more than you think I do. Benny Elderman used to wear fedoras but now he's out of work and jogs at 3 p.m. I'm a widgeon. And I'm not convinced that you are my father.

That is when I start shaking, my whole body. The crab in my hand rattles the newsprint.

Ruthie takes the crab from my hand and puts it on the table. She says, Okay, Tilton. She pushes me from the booth, scoot, scoot. She takes one elbow and George takes the other.

My body is vibrating from the inside out. George gives a wad of bills to the woman behind the podium.

Why did you leave us? I shout at her.

But George answers, I didn't want to. You have to believe me. I didn't want to.

I'm shaking so badly that Ruthie hands her keys to George. He'll drive and she'll hold me tight in the backseat. Holding, holding, holding. The way my mother held me when I got like this as a kid.

Ruthie's phone rings. She says, Hello? Ron?...What? Why would you go peeking in windows?...I told you not to come!...I can't hear you! Is that Justin?...Why does he think that? Her voice goes hushed and rough. Go to the next-door neighbor's house, she says. Get a key. We're on our way. And then Ruthie shouts at George, Slow down! Jesus! You'll get us all killed!

I think of the bedtime story, of George driving in the pouring rain. The sky is overcast. Clouds are moving in. We pass a great field, dotted with grackles. It was in a field like that, I say.

Hush, Ruthie says. Hush now.

It was in a field like that, I say again, where the dead fell from the sky. We are coming to the new ending.

Chapter Thirty

A GOOSE IN FLIGHT

Harriet

*I*n this house, I started to write. I bought a small desk, a type-writer, a stack of plain white paper. Just like the book my father had once given me, I would fill these pages. My old books of clip-pings from my four years with my mother were here, boxed in my old bedroom closet. I took them out into the backyard, put them in a metal bin, and burned them. I decided to reconstruct my life. I would turn one thing into another. I would tell a different kind of truth, a truthful kind of lie.

Or maybe it's as simple as this: the past spoke to me and I was an untrustworthy translator. The people of my life moved quickly and then slowly through time. They skipped forward. They reverted to infancy. They were born again and again. No one stayed dead. That's realism, isn't it? Has anyone I've ever known stayed dead? Tuffy prowls the house, a lion in a bowler. The hawker hawks in his bow tie, "Lookee here! Lookee here!" Wolff paces the hall. My mother, she tells me tales of Killiney Hill. My father whispers that my genius was wasted—a girl, a girl, a girl.

And so I wrote girly, except that means I wrote of sex and death. Look at my work and you'll see my life disguised. It's all there, though, legs as bloody wings, a forest of moaning hoot owls, steam that's good for one's lungs rising up from a dark lake, fatherish mad-

men, parties, doves, captivity, gunshot wounds, blind mothers, wild animals dressed in suits and ties, roads that wound only in circles. Eppitt and I shifted and soon Weldon was kissing the nape of Daisy's neck, the stem of her brain. Her lover, her phrenologist.

Dear Lord, did I write.

Eleanor was twisting within me. I knew, medically and rationally, that I was creating a human being, but I had no real concept of it. The idea is too absurd. How could I really believe that I was making boned hinges, muscles and ligaments of webbed pulleys attached to a system of varied weights, the marble work of skin, doughy thighs, the piping trim of dainty veins, rubbery joints, electric wiring, enamel—each tooth a white machine that would one day know how to muscle up like a razor clam. My God, these are the most ordinary miracles of them all.

In the hospital I told them my husband was dead. I suffered alone like an animal that wants to crawl out of its skin—to birth or be birthed. Then there she was—anxious with her dark brow. She cried because she existed. It was an existential crisis, for both of us. This existence, it's worth crying about.

Did I love her enough? I don't think I was capable early on. I'd lost all the ones I loved. I was afraid of loving her because I was afraid of more loss. Still, I was amazed by her. When I wasn't writing, I was gazing at her puckering face, her hands—gripping and ungripping. I began to know that her eyelids went pink just before a cough. When she was hungry, she nursed furiously. Frothy and pink, like a rabid piglet, she was a mauler, a lunatic with a madness for flesh. She squeezed my skin until it was blotched and nicked. Her fingernails were jagged. Pinprick scabs jeweled my breasts. Her tongue was her wisest muscle, the wet engine of her discontent. It fastened itself by a purse bead of spit while her hands, elegant, conducted around her cheeks and some-

times primed the pump. But I felt she absorbed my sadness. Once she wrenched herself loose from suckling, she ate sorrow as one flexed hand always twisted to her open mouth so she could gnaw her own fist. She slept with her ear pressed to my freckled chest, cupped to my heart. And when she was awake, she stared back. She was a loud presence in the world. Born with a foothold, she squalled to keep it. Red-faced, she bawled her dissent. Sometimes I squalled with her.

Still, I wrote. I would wrap Eleanor in my robe, curl my arms around her, and bang on the typewriter.

Before she was old enough to have memories, I took a taxi out to the grounds of the Maryland School for Feeble Minded Children. I thought about telling them I was a writer, but I'd published nothing. So instead I told them that I was looking for my lost twin, a lost half of myself. It wasn't untrue. They let me wander with a guard. There were children still, lots of them. Had anything changed? A little. There wasn't hard labor. This was quieter work, mostly busy-work. But aside from that, no, nothing had changed. Not at all. The world still put children away somewhere when it didn't know what else to do with them.

I saw Eppitt then, in the six-paned flowery glass at the top of King's Cottage. So long ago, but not over. I was a writer now.

In one of the basements on the grounds, Eleanor and I were left alone. I pawed through photographs until I found the one I would steal. At first, I thought it was just geese on a lawn, the way our white shirts caught the sun. But when I got it home, I put it under one of my father's high-powered magnifying glasses until one of the faces, the one who'd broken loose and was running downhill, arms flung open toward the camera and the photographer, bloomed wide.

It was my own face. Me, as a little girl. The only photograph of me from that time that exists. A goose trying to take flight. I *burned it a few days later, obliterating this scrap of the truth of my past.*

Time passed, and Eleanor grew to be the age I was in that photograph. I couldn't tell her the truth. I didn't have words for it. I couldn't process my own life. I was trying to—by constructing an alternative. But she sensed a falsehood. I know she did. She resented me for it, and to be honest, I was jealous of her. She had a mother. It was all I'd ever wanted. How dare she want a father too?

And yet she did. One afternoon when she was seven years old, I was overworking a sordid rendition of "Danny Boy." I dropped flats and sharps consistently. A gummy broth was boiling on the stove. A pot lid jiggled, a soft distant cymbal.

Eleanor—already an excellent young pupil with a good bit of muscular energy—stood and said, "I don't have a father. But I know I did."

I took up the charge with gynecological sterility—a formality I'd learned from institutions and libraries. "A woman has a vagina," I started. "And a man has a penis. And...and then..." It had been so long that I worried I might get this wrong. Was I going to start talking about the Owl and the Good Wheel and Brumus? I stammered a bit, and then gathered myself and continued. "And then the man inserts his penis into the woman's vagina, and the sperm—"

"What I want to know," Eleanor said, "is, where's that penis now?"

"You mean—"

"My father's penis. That's what I mean." She didn't even know how she sounded, and later in life, when she did understand her own tone, her frankness, it would be too late to change. Or perhaps she was too stubborn.

I said flatly, "You are a bastard, Eleanor. And there's nothing wrong with that."

This was a surrender, but I made the best of it. "In fact," I went on, "this is a good thing. Fathers can do a good deal of damage. I once knew a psychologist and he told me that people will often say they were never sure if they were loved by their fathers." I was talking about Wolff, of course. "Grown-ups go into psychologists' offices and cry like babies. You don't have to worry about anything like that. Your father never knew you existed. How could he have scarred you by not loving you? You'll see that you have an advantage." Funk had seen advantages to our childhoods at the Maryland School for Feeble Minded Children. Surely this would be an easy sell to someone more privileged, like Eleanor?

"What about your *father?" she asked.*

"He gave us all of this. The house, some funds. You can't fault a man for providing!"

It was a lie. And Eleanor knew it. But what made her angry, I think, looking back, wasn't that lie or even the fact that her father, wherever he was and for whatever reason, was gone. She was hurt that I was trying to put a positive spin on it. Insulted. She marched off to her bedroom, which is now her bedroom once more.

I wasn't a good mother, Eleanor. But you are making up for my lack. I see you being pulled by the tide of these children, and you don't complain about raising them alone, but I know your struggle. These children, beautiful girls, have gulls in their throats. They caw for you. There is the bludgeoning sun of summer followed by the chill rattle of winter and a cold bed. You press on, exhaustion sewn into your skin. You scrub floors on your knees. You shovel the walk alone in the snow and salt the driveway. You take care of these children as you've always taken care of me. Did you ever have a childhood? Perhaps I mistook a daughter for a mother just as my own mother had on her deathbed. Is this my greatest sin?

I did look for your father once after you asked all those questions.

I felt guilty and knew I had to try—for your sake, not my own. We went to Wildwood in winter. It was wet and gray. We cowered under the low sky. Not wanting you to know the purpose of the trip, I handed shopkeepers small notes that inquired after Eppitt, rather than talking about him aloud. But after looking at the notes, they all shook their heads.

I found instead the lion's head. Tuffy, stuffed and on display, behind a plate glass storefront window. Dead because some mobster had decided to use him to shake me up. I'd come here out of guilt, and guilt sought me out. I found a church, sat Eleanor down in one of the pews, and went to confession.

"I wasn't really married," I said to the priest, "but I thought I was."

"Were you married in the eyes of God, in the church?" he asked.

I thought of the twin sunlit sheets, a steeple, and the angels on the porches watching on. "Yes," I said.

I walked out, holding tight to your arm, Eleanor. A gift from God.

Hold tight, I thought, *hold tight.*

I feel death inside of me now. It's not far off. But sometimes death feels like the wings of a goose—sturdy, broad, a sloping lawn before me, the possibility of flight.

Chapter Thirty-one

LITTLE KNOT

Tilton

The car stops. I open the door and fling myself onto the lawn, and then I'm up, running as fast as I can.

In the house there's a man and a grown boy. Mrs. Gottleib is there and shouts, Tilton! Don't worry! Your mother is fine! She was just under the dining room table for some godforsaken reason!

My mother is sitting at the dining room table. I see the shape of her backbone, a knotted column that runs down her back—the shoulder blades where wings would grow if she were winged. Instead they poke out beneath her dress, stunted, skeletal. Our bones don't breathe, like bird bones do. We're forever tied to the ground.

Ruthie is here now with George behind her. He's breathing heavy.

Jesus! Ruthie says. What the hell, Ron? What are you doing here?

I scream, and everyone turns.

But my mother isn't shocked. There are my girls, she says.

I sprint out of the room and up the stairs, and she says, Let her go. Let her get it all out.

Soon I am in Wee-ette's room. She told me to release the

seventh book only if the family needed it, only in case of emergency. This is an emergency! The new ending is hurtling toward us all! Wee-ette! I call out. Wee-ette! It's time! Now!

I run to the windows, grab hold of the curtains, and pull with all of my weight until the rods break from their wall hooks like hollow bird bones. This is what Wee-ette taught me when she read the bird books to me—that every space has a space within it.

I pull the rods apart. The curtains huff and fall. I pick up a rod and shake it. The pages, rolled up tight, slip from the rod, loose, and shiver to the floor.

I shake the other rod. Pages, all clumped, hit the carpet. I pick up the bundle and throw it into the air—flight, flight as it unfurls.

I don't know what to do next. But there is only one thing, really.

Leave.

It's my turn.

I rush into Ruthie's bedroom. I open the window. I climb out onto that small roof. It's raining now. Cool drops touch my skin. I get right to the edge. If I leave, my mother and Ruthie will be drawn together, knotted. My mother's need will roam to Ruthie, and Ruthie will be tended to, at long last.

A light shines in Benny Elderman's bedroom. His body holds a space, a cavity, that he carries around with him—maybe for his soul. I imagine being with Benny in his room, two side-by-side soul cases wearing fedoras. That's possible because the book is loose—the seventh book.

I kick off one shoe. It falls. I kick off the other, and it falls too.

Bodies fell from the sky.

I take a deep breath, spread my arms wide—and I jump.

A human. A girl, but not a girl. A woman. A woman in a blue dress. Not a bird. Then the earth is there.

The wind is knocked clean from my lungs. I lie there.

Wee-ette, your words are all free now. And the story can go wherever it needs to go. Like a string was broken but now it's mended. I'm the little knot. There will be a pact to make all of this new. I gasp as my lungs fill up. I stand on my own two feet and run.

Chapter Thirty-two

ACTS OF LOVE

Ruth

I almost saved your mother's life!" Ron says. His eyes are roving madly; he's in the home of Harriet Wolf, after all these years. He crosses his arms on his chest as if trying to contain his heart, or perhaps to restrain himself from reaching to touch things that Harriet Wolf may have once touched. Pim and Pom claw at his pant legs. "You should have seen her!"

"It was bad," Justin says, wearing a ball cap twisted to one side. "Her legs were just poking out, all pale and deadly."

"I was fine!" Eleanor says. "Hell's bells! I can lie down wherever I want to. It's my own goddamn house."

"I'm going to wait in the car," Justin says. He's not used to being spoken to sharply. Ron gives him a nod of approval, and Justin is gone.

Behind me, George is half hidden by the kitchen door. "Eleanor," he says, but no one really seems to have heard him.

Overhead, Tilton has quieted down. Is she in bed? Crying? I pushed her too hard. In some sense Eleanor was right to be worried. Tilton is delicate, after all.

I glance at my father. What does he think of this place, its stagnation, its utter frozenness? Does he grasp that the house's inability to move forward in time has something to do with him?

Eleanor sits at the dining room table, her back to the kitchen, head bowed, but with one fist clenching and unclenching the tablecloth.

The tablecloth—white with pale yellow embroidered flowers. My mother found it and spread it over the table. And according to Ron, she was found prostrate underneath it, the same place where I once made my home as a little girl. Was this an act of love?

Gottleib says, "The whole thing almost gave me a heart attack! I'm next, you know! It's just a matter of time!"

I walk to my mother and stand beside her. When she looks up, I see the slightest palsy of her head. It's just a matter of time. "George is here," I say.

"And?" Eleanor says, possibly without registering the information.

I sweep my hand across the embroidered flowers of the tablecloth, as lightly as if I'm reading Braille. My desires, I realize, are as childish as Tilton's. I want my family back together again. I am about to say "Nothing," because I can't put words to these desires, but then my mother reaches across the table and grabs my hand, squeezing my knuckles. This is supposed to mean everything. It can't, of course. But in this moment, Eleanor and I both want it to mean everything. That alone—the two of us wanting the same thing—strikes me as miraculous.

George walks into the dining room. "Shouldn't we check on Tilton?" he says. "It's very quiet up there." And that quickly, the mood is dashed.

Eleanor stands, her knuckles pressed into the table, and then wheels around, gripping the back of the chair. She glares at George. "How dare you."

He rubs his hands together as if they're cold and then looks at the floor. "I think someone should check on her."

"Something's wrong," I say, and my heart flutters.

Eleanor heads for the stairs. "Tilton!" she screams.

There's no answer.

"Is everything okay?" Ron says.

I run up the stairs and down the hall, heavy footfalls behind me.

The door to Wee-ette's bedroom is wide open. Paper lies scattered everywhere—curled individual sheets and clumps like scrolls. The heavy-duty curtain rods have been ripped from their hooks and stripped of the curtains.

George comes into the room and says, "What is this?"

"Wee-ette's book," I whisper. Tilton knew where it was all along. I rush from the room and call, "Tilton! Tilton!" But I know already that I won't get an answer. She's gone.

I throw open Tilton's bedroom door. The magazine cutouts of various bird species shudder on the walls. The room is empty. Hearing more voices on the stairs as I go, I walk quickly to my own bedroom.

George is there already, leaning out the window. "It was open when I came in," he says. "It's raining like mad!" He pulls his upper body back in through the window, clipping the top of his head. He rubs the spot. "Do you think she jumped?"

"She jumped," I say. "She's gone."

The others have found Wee-ette's manuscript. I can hear them all chattering. Ron's voice rises up, admonishing everyone, "Don't touch it! Don't touch it!"

I walk into the hall and find my husband. His hair is wild. He puts one hand on his forehead, the other on his waist. "Ruth, you won't believe it."

I know I'll leave him. It's over. I'm not going to a wedding or a Harriet Wolf Society gala. I'll be on a plane to see Hailey within days. I want to fight for her, and the best way to do that is to go to where she is and hover. Hover with love. Hover *madly*. Perhaps we're all doomed to fail as mothers, but if so, it's better to err on the side of showing too much love, not too little.

I need to be with Hailey. Soon enough, Ron will just be someone I once knew very well.

"We found it," he says, his voice a holy whisper. "And it's in first person. You have to see this. It's *historic,* Ruth. Historic!" He steps back into the room, gets down on all fours, and starts reading a page on the floor at a breathless pace, but he stops and looks up. "Eppitt? Who's Eppitt?" he says with a quick exhale, and then he answers his own question: "He's an entirely new character! This is a whole new novel!" Eleanor is turning a slow circle in her mother's bedroom, taking in the damage.

"Easy now, Eleanor," Mrs. Gottleib says, her hands outstretched as if she's ready to catch her. "Easy now."

But after all the years of hating vultures, Eleanor doesn't even notice Ron or the villain in the only fairy tale that she ever told me: George. For this singular moment she doesn't even seem to register that the child she's dedicated her life to protecting is gone. She grabs a bedpost and drops to one knee. She picks up a few pieces of paper—not to read them, no. She presses them to her cheek. "My mother," she says. "She's been here all this time." She holds the pages to her chest like they're part of a hand-knit blanket. She looks at me, her face streaked with tears.

On one of the sheets on the floor, I spot that name again, the one that Tilton used for the mongrel king: Eppitt Clapp. "She's written a love story," I say. "A true one."

"Let's not rush the interpretations," Ron says dubiously.

I kneel next to my mother and put my hand on her back. "Tilton's gone," I say, "but I'm here." My mother lets the pages fall to the floor and she hugs me, both of us still on our knees, and though it felt as if I weren't ever really here, I am now. "Let's go find Tilton," I tell my mother.

Chapter Thirty-three

BLOOMED

Harriet

I only saw Eppitt Clapp one more time in my life.

I was at a book signing in New York City. It would be my last. Because of him? Yes, but I was tired too—of being handled, of strangers thinking they knew me, intimately, of being a woman writer in a man's world.

Two boys came up in the signing line. One was eleven or so, about Eleanor's age at the time, the other a bit younger, a tagalong. The older boy had already bought his copy and it was well-worn—the kind of thing the bookstore hated to see when there was a stack of new books beside me, for sale. But I had a policy of signing any of my books that made their way to me—new or old. Nervous, the older boy tried to get the book opened to the right page to have it signed.

"Here you go," I said. "I'll do it." The line behind him was long. "Whom do I make it out to? You?" I was curled over the book, poised to write.

"No," the boy said. "Make it to my father."

"What's your father's name?"

"Eppitt," the boy said.

I froze a moment, my pen bleeding on the page. "Eppitt what?" I asked, unmoving.

"Clapp."

I lifted my chin then, and I looked up at the two of them. The older boy had shiny dark eyes and gave a wide smile, but the younger one, the tagalong, had Eppitt's buckled nose, his quick eyes, a familiar swirled cowlick. I craned my neck, looking for Eleanor. She often stacked books so they were already opened to the signature page. I spotted her about twenty feet away, opening a new box with a salesgirl. Eleanor loved this work, the efficacy, the adulthood.

"Okay, then!" I said. "With a C or a K?"

"What?"

"Never mind," I said.

I wrote, "Eppitt Clapp, Happy reading! Sincerely, Harriet Wolf." I stared at the page. People shifted in line behind the boys. I added under my name, "Aka W. W." Wolf Woman. Would he remember? "Is your father here?" I asked.

"He doesn't like crowds," the older boy said. "He's waiting outside."

"Just as well," I said, but I didn't hand the book back to him.

"He wanted me to tell you he didn't die."

Sterbe nicht. *He'd kept his promise. "Tell him that I didn't die either," I said.*

"And he said he had something for you on page thirteen."

My hands were fluttering. I turned the pages. There on page thirteen, nestled in close to the binding, was his half of the piece of string, looped a few times. I placed my finger on it and drew it down the page. I cupped it in my palm. "Thank you. Tell him thank you."

"Okay," the boy said.

I shut the book, touching its cover for a moment, and then slid it to him. The boy smiled and almost bowed. He grabbed his little brother's hand and they ran off toward the door.

The next person in line was a blonde woman. She wanted to

know when the next book was coming out and what was going to happen to Daisy. "I don't know," I whispered.

"Excuse me?"

I stood up, pulled my coat out from under the skirted table, and put it on.

"Aren't you going to sign my book?"

"I'll be back," I told her. "I just have to…" And I turned and ran through the stacks, past the cashier, out the door. It had been snowing, but there wasn't much left, and what was still there was coated in car exhaust. I looked in one direction and then the other.

I saw Eppitt then, from the back. He was holding the boys' hands. They were crossing the street. Eppitt held the book under his arm. So he had two sons, one of whom was clearly his own, biologically. He had a wife, a house.

But I remembered him under the Duck Porch, giving me a tour of our make-believe kitchen, our dining room, our imaginary plates with blue flowers ringing their edges.

Now he'd made a real home—without me.

I wanted to shout his name but I couldn't. What would come of it?

As if he sensed me standing there, he looked back over his shoulder. When he saw me, he stopped and turned. His mouth opened. A white cloud of breath. He fitted the book in the pocket of his overcoat. He raised his hands to his chest and, fitting one hand under and then through the other, he opened his hand wide.

Bloomed.

Love isn't how we're doomed and blessed. It's how we are bloomed. He remembered that, which meant he remembered all of it.

The boys stopped and looked back too, trying to discern what had gotten their father's attention, and from this distance, the little one looked just like Eppitt trapped behind the glass window at the top of King's Cottage. Before the boys had a chance to spot me—and what must I have looked like, alone and breathless?—Eppitt tugged them forward. They walked on.

Soon Eleanor was there, panicked. "Why did you run away? Why are you out here? It's freezing cold!"

I don't know what I said.

But eventually I put my hands on the top of her head, and then down along her soft hair, cupping her face. "I'm right here," I said. "Right here."

And I still am.

One day I will die, and though my Eleanor saved me and kept me alive, and though Tilton is burned into my mind, into my heart, into my eyes when I close them, and Ruthie is a magnificent force like a silent whirlwind stuffed into a small body—a jar of lightning—I know what I will whisper when I die.

My own mother whispered for her mother in the end. People do. They revert to the first love they had on this earth. But my mother was my second love.

I will whisper the name of my first. I will call out for Eppitt Clapp.

Chapter Thirty-four

THE NEW ENDING

Eleanor

Ruthie is at the wheel. I sit beside her. George is in the back-seat. She says that, on the way home from the restaurant, Tilton pointed out this field not far from the house. Tilton said it was a field like the one where the dead fell from the sky.

For reasons I can't explain, I feel like something inside of me has been ripped open. I sit in the car like I am gliding toward an oncoming calamity. But Ruthie wears no helmet this time. There's no foil-wrapped leftover in my lap. No cigar. No radio.

No lightning, no thunder.

But there is rain. A heavy dousing. The windshield wipers pound and pound.

I'm breathless. I can't even look at George. I fold my hands in my lap, and I know I'm going to pray, but not to God. I grip my hands tightly and think of my mother. The smell of burning paper at the end of each day, for years—years! The piles of ash in the small metal trash can by her desk. That faker. The thought makes me smile.

I wonder what the pages on the floor of my mother's bed-room will offer—some small bit of the truth for once? Will there be some hint of my father? One final shred she volunteered before she died?

This is praying, I tell myself.

I'm suddenly glad that George is alive—especially for my daughters.

Ruthie passes a car, to get in the far lane. I love her conviction. She comes from me, after all.

"Would it have been better?" I say to George.

"What?" George says.

"If we'd stayed together," I say softly. "Confirm or deny."

"What's that, Eleanor?" George says. "Do you see something? Do you see her?"

"There!" Ruthie shouts.

Tilton is a dark silhouette with bare legs in Harriet's blue dress. She could be my mother, young and alive. It occurs to me that maybe no one ever really dies until everyone who remembers you has died too. It feels as if the heart attack has electrified and recircuited the wires in my brain. For the moment, there's such a blur of love that death doesn't matter. Harriet before me and Tilton and Ruthie after me. I'm a joint, an axis, a hinge—with love on either side.

The field is beyond the divided highway. Ruth puts on her blinker and, barely slowing, she U-turns. Up ahead, caught in the glare of headlights, there's a dog—or is it a fox? Ruthie hits the brakes. The tires catch the scrim of water, and the car starts to spin.

Everything slows, even my own heartbeat—I'm sure of it. The headlights tour the divider, the long highway, the field stitched together by a weave of roots and individual blades of grass. Again and again—until one of the tires bumps into the field itself, and the tread catches the mud.

The car stops abruptly. Ruthie's air bag pops into her face—a gust—but mine doesn't. Then the car is silent.

The headlights point into the field at the distant trees, the air between trees. The car fills with our breaths—George, Ruth, me.

Where is Tilton? Where is she?

And then there's a tap, tap, tap on a back window. A door pops open and Tilton slides in the backseat. She shuts the door.

My bedtime story has always ended the same way: "The family was torn apart and it couldn't be put back together again. The end."

And yet here we are.

Tilton says, "I'm the little knot." She says, "This is the new beginning."

My heart twinges—its threaded capillaries, blushing veins, and shushing valves. It's an old, familiar ache, a pain that reaches back to my adoration of Tilton and Ruthie, to my first rush of love for George, that needles all the way back to my mother and my anchorless love for my lost father. I was so sure everything was over, sewn up, ended, but the rain thrums and beads on the windows.

Begin.

ACKNOWLEDGMENTS

I've worked on this novel for approximately eighteen years. The research slowed me down, yes, but I've never written a novel that has gone through so many profoundly different drafts. The first piece of this novel was published more than ten years ago at failbetter.com, and about five years later, two more pieces were published, one in the anthology *Behind the Short Story: From First to Final Draft,* and another in the *Chattahoochee Review.* The anthologized story became a thirty-page section of the novel that has now been whittled to one paragraph, as it goes. Aside from these early publications, I've kept these characters close. I've grown to love them, deeply. I admit that there were times when I walked away from the book—working on it was like wrestling bears—but the characters always called me back. This novel represents a large swath of my creative life, and it feels foreign to hand over these lives to the world, but I'm honored to.

I'm thankful for a historical book that documents Sheppard Pratt called *Gatehouse: The Evolution of the Sheppard and Enoch Pratt Hospital, 1853–1986* by Bliss and Byron Forbush and for the small footnote within it that mentions the Maryland School for Feeble Minded Children. That footnote sparked this novel, in many ways. More than a decade ago, the good people who work at what was once the Maryland School for Feeble Minded

Children allowed me to walk the grounds and look at the old records, which I photocopied and held on to. These were incredibly precious documents to me. I don't know if those beautiful, old, asbestos-ridden buildings still exist. I've lived far from them for a long time. I'll tell you this: if you saw them, they would break your heart.

I'm thankful to the University of Delaware Library, where, during my early career as a writer, I was allowed to roam the stacks with a card that cost twenty dollars a year. In those stacks, I randomly came across a book called *Man Bites Man: The Scrapbook of an Edwardian Eccentric;* his name was George Ives. It was a discovery of pure joy. I'm also thankful for the library's deep collection of old magazines.

A special thank-you to my father, as ever. He has always been my greatest researcher. When I was a child, he let me sit in the booth at the Howard House in Elkton, Maryland, with the framed clipping that read "Dead Fell from Sky," and he didn't hide it from me. Instead, he told me his recollection of the tragedy. I'm thankful for friends of the family Jack and Abbie Fassnacht, who were witnesses and kind enough to recount the tragedy for me over eighteen years ago. My father also tracked down the wonderful people at the Wildwood Historical Society; they were incredibly generous with their time. I appreciate David W. Francis's historical book *Wildwood by the Sea.* I'm also thankful to Peter McCall and Bill Perkins for discussing the inner workings of the heart with me.

I'm thankful to my fantastic agent, Nat Sobel, who is always there for me, as well as the brilliant Judith Weber and all those who've worked at the agency: Kirsten Carleton, Julie Stevenson, and Adia Wright. I'm thankful for Justin Manask, manager extraordinaire. You all allow me to follow my whims, and I love you for it. Special thanks, also, to the brilliant and wonderful Caitlin Alexander and Kara Cesare. And, of course, thank you to Ben George for tackling this novel with me.

And I'm forever thankful to my mother, my father, and my husband, who have loved this book for years, have guarded it protectively, and have pushed me to live up to the promise it holds, a promise of the imagination — my imagination and now yours, dear reader.

I'm thankful for you, as ever.